LATE SEASON

Christobel Kent

sphere

SPHERE

First published by the Penguin Group in 2004
This reissue published by Sphere in 2018

A CIP catalogue record for this book
is available from the British Library.

ISBN 978-0-7515-7115-8

Typeset in Bembo by M Rules
Printed and bound in Great Britain by
Clays Ltd, St Ives plc

Papers used by Sphere are from well-managed forests
and other responsible sources.

MIX
Paper from
responsible sources
FSC® C104740

Sphere
An imprint of
Little, Brown Book Group
Carmelite House
50 Victoria Embankment
London EC4Y 0DZ

An Hachette UK Company
www.hachette.co.uk

www.littlebrown.co.uk

For Louis, Kitty, Hamish,
Molly and Beatrice

Acknowledgements

With thanks to Bernard Keeling, for his insights into Roman foundling hospitals, among other things, and to Bruce Johnston for his hospitality in Rome.

Chapter One

Anna saw the cars arrive from her terrace in the dusk, and watched as they disappeared down the lane and into the trees, where it was already quite dark. There were two estate cars with English plates and a little airport hire car trying to keep up with Montale's pick-up as it careered ahead of them on the dirt road, kicking up clouds of white dust and scattering the loose stone of the road surface beneath its fat tyres. As she watched them disappear Anna wondered whether they knew what they were in for.

The dust hung in the darkening air for a while before settling, the roar of the cars receded down the valley into the woods, and Anna sat down again on the terrace to catch the last of the evening sun. The vine that hung in tendrils from her pergola was turning red and the few sharp black grapes it produced were almost ready for picking; summer was over and the sharp breath of winter not far away. At this time of year the temperature dropped fast as evening fell and it seemed to

Anna more important than ever to catch the lingering warmth of the sun slanting low through the leaves. Montale's pick-up came back up the lane alone just as Anna stood to go inside, glass in hand, her old red cushion and her book under her arm, and he raised a hand in greeting, squinting at her in the fading light. Anna nodded, smiling faintly at the red-haired farmer she had known since he was a boy, and turned to go inside.

Anna Viola's small farmhouse stood just on the edge of the natural reserve of the Alto Merse, a series of densely wooded valleys in southern Tuscany through which the dark, peaty waters of the river Merse wound. The outside was built partly of stone, partly of the crumbling red brick common in and around Siena, although now only the vestiges of faded pink stucco still clung on here and there to the friable surface. The farmhouse was set into the lip of the hill, which sloped up a few hundred yards behind; an area overgrown now with brambles, birch and wild plum, dark and cool even in the summer. But at the front the stone façade faced southwest, and in the evenings the little terrace, which was set off to one side, would flood with the pale yellow light of the sun as it dipped. It was not always sunny, naturally, and in the winter, still a month or so off, the sun would have set by four, slipping down behind the range of black hills to the west. Then the house would turn cold very quickly, and it would seem a lonely place, perched as it was above hundreds of hectares of dark and almost uninhabited forest, on the edge of the wilderness.

In the next valley, down six miles or so of *strada sterrata*, or unmade road, it appeared that the foreigners Anna had glimpsed from her terrace had arrived at their destination. A modest stone farmstead in a clearing of scrubby pasture on the valley floor, Il Vignacce had, until a year or two earlier when Piero Montale had inherited it from his aunt, been nothing more than a ruin, commented on once or twice a year by passing walkers as picturesque in a desolate sort of way. The walls had been built of limestone and tufa, the pitted volcanic rock of the region, and had been a foot or more thick, but the window openings had stood empty for decades and the chimney stacks, one at either end, had long since collapsed.

But Piero Montale was a tirelessly industrious man, always out on his tractor, hauling water, ploughing, sowing, working away at every corner of his land. Hating the idea that such a resource as Il Vignacce might moulder away unused, he had determined that the ruin would make him some money and doggedly he had set about investigating what grants might be available for the restoration of the property. There were funds to be had for the reinvigoration of the countryside, after all, the most commonly sought after funds were those available for the development of *agriturismo*: the combining of agriculture with holiday letting.

An *agriturismo* might be a palatial hotel complex in the corn-fields of Lazio, or it might be the humble conversion of a pretty stone pigsty in the Po valley (the pigs long since relocated to modern barns which, although airy and hygienic, did not have quite the same charm) into holiday apartments. Some continuing agricultural component was stipulated in order for the owner to qualify for a grant, which was why the owner of the pigsty might plant a hectare or two of Lambrusco vines to substitute for the pigs. So Montale kept a small herd of long-horned Maremman cattle down in the valley, where, winter and summer, they would wander through the trees behind Il Vignacce, their bells clanging mournfully as they went.

Montale had obtained his grants for the restoration of the old farm, and despite murmurings from the locals as to the wisdom or desirability of the conversion of so lonely and isolated a ruin, and a place, into the bargain, around which any number of rumours circulated, he had proceeded with his plans. The contractors had grumbled as their trucks skidded and plunged through the forest loaded with wood and cement, tanks for water and drainage, and pallets of new red cotto tiles. But with the blessing of five straight months of fine weather Il Vignacce was rebuilt. Even the old wood-fired oven on the north elevation, originally quite essential to the farm's self-sufficency, was reconstructed, and the exterior stone staircase that mounted the front wall diagonally, no longer necessary for a farmer to live above his animals but attractive and above all, authentic, was lovingly filled and re-pointed. To furnish the place Montale weeded out the pieces of furniture from his own home that his wife had long wanted to replace – an old oak armoire with the wormholes filled, an old-fashioned marble-topped sideboard, a mirror or two. He sorted a couple of elderly fridges, missing a few attachments but sound enough, from among the junk that sat in his outbuildings, and only then did he take the pick-up to a newly opened Swedish discount furniture warehouse just outside Florence to fill in the gaps with cheap pine beds and cheerful linen.

The track to Il Vignacce from the main road was a project that Montale had left for another day, or perhaps another century, there being no public funds available for its restoration. The track was ten, maybe twelve kilometres or so of variable road surface (to put it charitably), not finished enough even to appear on the few maps available for the region. The thought that not all his foreign visitors might take it in their stride as easily as he did, bumping down it in the truck or a tractor, a couple of times a day, was one that he pushed to the back of his mind. So far, after all, none of his guests had actually got stuck down there, as Montale himself had once a year or so back, caught in a downpour that had washed away a whole section of the road. He had been forced to sleep in the cowshed adjoining Il Vignacce for a night while the rain pattered relentlessly on the tiles over his head, and his wife bawled him out on his mobile until the signal went. It had not been a night he would have wished to repeat, even in more comfortable conditions; perhaps it had been to do with the depth of darkness surrounding him, but the place had made him uneasy, and Piero Montale was not a superstitious man. He'd got back up in the end, cursing and skidding around each sodden bend, and as a result he'd taken a few basic measures on some of the more precarious stretches.

And now, at after eight on a late September evening, the broad pasture Il Vignacce surveyed was swallowed in darkness and the only vestige of the day was a faint lemon glow diluting the navy blue of the sky over to the west. The old farmhouse, long and low, all but one of its heavy iron shutters closed against the night, sat in a small pool of yellow light cast by the exterior lamp over its massive front door. For the last tenants to be staying at Il Vignacce this year, the holiday had begun.

The three cars in which Anna Viola had seen the English visitors pass her house were parked to one side on a skirt of close-cropped grass beneath the trees, ticking and sighing as their engines cooled in the night air. In the dark the trees seemed to come very close to the house on all sides but the front, where the light shone on open ground; they stood tall

5

and still in the night air as though playing grandmother's footsteps and just waiting for a moment of inattention by the inhabitants of Il Vignacce to creep ever closer. The house was divided in two, the larger half being on the south side, and here the iron shutters to the windows had been thrown open carelessly. A square of brilliant light shone on to the grass below the window, and inside, standing around the long wooden dining table, long enough to seat ten comfortably, stood the new arrivals.

'Jesus Christ!' exclaimed Lucien cheerfully. 'What a road! Did they say anything about that on the website?' He stared around goggle-eyed in a pantomime of amazement and, despite herself, Justine laughed. She shook his arm in mock reproof.

'It won't seem so bad once we've done it a few times,' she said, but, looking round at their faces, tired and grey after the day's travelling, still taut with anxiety over passports and tickets and timing, she wasn't so sure.

And the journey, or at least the final stretch of it, had come as quite a shock. The farmer had turned abruptly off the main highway and the pretty terrace of a little farmhouse had come into view; for a brief moment Justine had thought they had arrived but the dusty pick-up had bounced past on the uneven road surface. They'd followed him down a steep slope into dense woodland, the trees absorbing what remained of the day's light and plunging them into deep gloom.

Justine tried to remember whether there had been anything about the miles of dirt track in the description of the house; perhaps there had been a warning that the access road wasn't suitable for all types of vehicle? Whatever there was had not conveyed the reality of five or more miles of lurching through dense forest on loose stones as darkness fell, descending hundreds of metres to the valley floor, climbing to cross a ridge only to start back down again. And all the time they had been obliged to keep up with the dusty pick-up rattling remorselessly on ahead.

On one ridge they had glimpsed a muddy-looking reservoir carved out of the red earth and beyond it the lights of a distant village. They passed through a bleak clearing where a logging lorry stood while a gang of ragged, dark-skinned labourers loaded it silently in the twilight, turning their heads to watch the cars as they bumped past, but offering no greeting.

Their little convoy had paused to open a gate about halfway down, giving rise to a weary cheer from Louisa and Tom's car, but with a wave onwards the sandy-haired farmer climbed back up into the cab of his truck and set off again at speed. The sharp bends and precipitous dips had gone on for another ten minutes before they finally arrived, in pitch darkness, at the house. Il Vignacce. And even now Justine felt herself quail a little as the memory of the journey returned, and with it the sensation of having arrived at the most obscure and isolated place she had ever seen. She looked around the room to see how the others were reacting to the day's journey.

Lucien looked the most buoyant of them, every detail of his appearance shrugging off the journey, but then he usually managed that kind of insouciance. Lucien's dark hair was springy, and his smooth brown face, faded cotton shirt and worn corduroy trousers gave the impression that he belonged in such a rustic setting; this was his stock in trade. His photograph had always looked so perfect beside his short-lived gardening column that Justine sometimes wondered whether his face, and his gamekeeper's shirts, had got him the job, rather than any expertise in the subject.

Lucien smiled as he looked around the room, giving off his habitual cheerful optimism. It was hard to believe, to look at him now, thought Justine, that Lucien had been reluctant to come on this trip; he looked as though he was ready for anything.

For the others the burden of expectation that accompanied every painstakingly planned holiday, that crucial time away from the office or the school run, was all too visible on their strained faces, along with the awful possibility of disappointment as they looked around the house, checking for ugly furniture, cramped accommodation, inauthentic fittings, a blighted view. Not much chance of the last, thought Justine, as they seemed to be miles from anywhere, not a light nor a sound. Although in the inky darkness that enveloped the house it was impossible to be sure. Looking around the room, Justine thought it didn't look too bad at all; the floors were terracotta, the steel shutters painted a muted brown; old country furniture was set about with a few functional modern additions.

Justine looked at her husband again. Perhaps it was because Lucien didn't work, at least not in any conventional sense, that he wasn't really looking at the trip as a holiday and therefore wasn't expecting perfect relaxation; for him it was a challenge. And of course whereas the others had been driving across Europe for almost three days, Lucien and Justine, unencumbered by children and all their paraphernalia, had only had to travel from the airport.

'Good job we stopped at that supermarket,' said Lucien. 'God knows when we'll feel up to getting out of here again. Shall I start cooking?' And he pushed up his sleeves and pulled open a kitchen cupboard at random.

'Saucepans look all right,' he said, holding one up for

inspection. 'Nice and heavy.' He began to sort through the carrier bags piled at his feet.

Louisa and Tom were sitting at the table, a couple of chairs apart, and they made no move to help Lucien, although Louisa smiled approvingly when he suggested lemon risotto. Two pendant lampshades hung low over the table, casting a warm light on the couple's faces and from over their heads came the sound of children's feet running, and the squeak of bedsprings. The lampshades trembled slightly with the vibrations transmitted through the terracotta by some vigorous bouncing.

'He is marvellous,' Louisa said, turning to Justine. 'You're so lucky. What I wouldn't do for a man who can cook.' She looked pointedly at her husband, who smiled in a benignly unfocused way, and ignored her inference with what seemed like equanimity.

'I mean,' Louisa continued, 'you would have thought that a restaurant critic might have some interest in cooking his own food, wouldn't you?'

Tom nodded and smiled. 'Too many cooks, though, darling,' he said, mildly. 'We can't all be multi-talented, can we? Clattering away together in the kitchen.'

Poor Tom, thought Justine. Not because Louisa was getting at him, again, but because whereas Louisa looked no older than she had when they first married, her short hair still a bright untarnished blonde, her skin smooth and golden against the clean pink cotton of her shirt, Tom looked old, suddenly – not just middle-aged but almost decrepit. His blue eyes were faded, and his fair skin had reddened, become as coarse as if he worked outside. Or lived rough, she thought. Although, obviously, given the perfect comfort of Tom and Louisa's Regency house in Hammersmith, with its cream sofas, polished wood and silver-framed family photographs, that was not a possibility. Perhaps it's just age, Justine thought. We're all getting older.

Behind Tom and Louisa in the warm kitchen, where the light faded into the shadows at the far end of the long table, stood Martin, his serious, saturnine face shadowed with a day's growth. Justine wondered where they'd stopped on the way down. Some motel in the Rhone valley, Martin had said, where perhaps he had not thought to shave. Perhaps he's letting things slip just now, thought Justine; something about that wasn't right. Martin had always been a very clean man, his clothes crisp from the iron, a smell of soap – even in the middle of all the turmoil. She thought of Martin's modest North London house with Evie in it, the door opening on to a place that was always warm and bright, everything it contained somehow organized, speaking of a purpose and a proper place. Martin's shirts on the ironing board, Dido's sports kit bagged and labelled, the boots ranked in the hall. For the first time it occurred to Justine, who had only herself to organize, that Evie might have found it a burden, keeping all that order in others' lives. Not any more.

By Martin's side stood Dido, drooping a little, swaying almost imperceptibly with tiredness, her smooth dark head resting against her father's shoulder and her face blank with the need to sleep. Almost as tall as me now, thought Justine. And suddenly she remembered her visit to that London maternity ward fourteen years earlier: the dusty, unwashed windows, the black eyes in the sallow, exquisite newborn's face. Dido staring up at her from out of a cotton hospital blanket, cradled in her mother's lap and, shining like a lighthouse above Dido, her mother's face, beatific with happiness. Evie's face.

'You've got to do it, Just,' she had said, glowing with life and with the urgency of her message, happy like Justine had never seen her. 'It's the best thing.'

Oh, Evie, thought Justine. Where are you now?

Behind her a cork popped as Lucien opened one of the dozens of bottles they'd bought at the supermarket on a dismal trading estate outside Florence. Their trolley, comically overloaded with alcohol, had seemed to Justine to mark them out as foreigners, or more precisely as British, as the sprinkling of Dutch, German and French shoppers also cruising the aisles didn't seem to have the same priorities; the proportion of groceries to wine in their baskets seemed something like three to one. Their own was roughly the inverse. Justine was not, however, embarrassed enough to suggest that any of it should be put back; she thought they would probably need the lot, and more.

At the sound of the cork popping Justine saw Tom's head jerk up from his examination of the table, his eyes coming into focus. Louisa's lips were compressed with the beginnings of disapproval, and behind her Martin, his arm around his daughter, seemed to relax at last although his expression was, to Justine, as opaque as ever. Justine had never known Martin very well; her connection with him had always been through Evie, really. And, after all, she thought, looking around, how long is it since any of us were really friends? Fifteen years? And for a moment her heart dipped. What are we all doing here? she wondered.

11

Chapter Two

It was late by the time he phoned but, as he had almost certainly known, Anna was not in bed yet. The older she got the harder she found it to settle, to decide to go to bed. Although, if she was honest, it had been like this since she had been alone again.

Anna ate modestly and early these days: a salad with chicory from the garden, perhaps a little piece of meat if she was feeling the need, or some peperonata with a slice or two of hard Tuscan bread. And always a glass of wine on the terrace, just one, to iron out any lingering anxieties the day might have brought her, to allow her to daydream, to permit her to count her blessings. Anna liked food well enough; loved cooking, when there was someone to cook for, but she couldn't rid herself of the idea that eating alone was a waste of a meal. So she got it out of the way by seven, then she would light a fire, and curl up on the old divan in her little drawing room to do a bit of sewing, embroidery, knitting – something to calm her and give her a sense of purpose. She liked embroidery, particularly, because napkins, pillowcases, with an initial or a posy of flowers in the corner, were always useful and could be given away at random for weddings, christenings or birthdays. Knitting was not so neutral; it had a physical body in mind, and always reminded her that her son was too old to want her loopy sweaters any more, and there was no grandchild.

By eleven Anna's eyes would be too tired to go on with close work. So she would leave the fire to die down and wander through the few but comfortable rooms of her house, straightening and patting and putting things away: a velvet cushion, her solitary knife and fork and plate by now quite dry on the draining board, a rug askew on the sofa. The house had two good-sized rooms downstairs, with a broad stone staircase leading upstairs between them, and the kitchen, which led out on to the terrace. The old kitchen door, with its thick distorting glass, now stood closed against the night. There were two bedrooms above, one of which was Anna's, with a small stone balcony where she could step out and feel the cool morning air on her soft ageing skin. Both rooms were square and solid with chestnut beams overhead and undulating cotto floors thick with the red lead of centuries. Both looked out across the valley to the west, to the grey hills that rose and fell, one behind the other in darkening shades as they receded.

Sometimes Anna asked herself why she had come back here after all those years in the city. Her friends in Rome thought she was mad, certainly, to give up the city's comfort and friendly chaos and her little flat nestled between the roofs in Trastevere, with her view of a belltower and a green sliver of the Tiber, and a glimpse across the rooftops to the Villa

Borghese from the bathroom window. Anna knew why, of course. Not that she was sure she would know how to explain it to them, and after all she had not burnt her boats completely. The terms of her lease on the flat permitted her to transfer it to her son, and now Paolo lived there. Although it saddened her to think how little her flat – hard-won and precious as a jewel to her once – resembled a home these days.

When the phone had rung, at just before midnight, Anna was on her balcony in her nightdress and woollen shawl, standing under a sky speckled with stars and looking down in the direction of Il Vignacce. She was wondering about the English, who had arrived in their dusty cars when she had thought the season was over – the pale, serious faces she had glimpsed through the hedgerow. There had been children, she was sure. Perhaps September is not so late for them, she thought: they're from the north, after all, and, besides, the sun this year had continued to shine throughout the harvest, making the faint, misty chill that had begun to creep in morning and evening seem benign, clearing the air and sharpening the colours of the leaves as they began to turn.

Anna pulled her shawl more tightly around her shoulders all the same, as she thought of Il Vignacce beside the dark, silent river so far below her in the woods, hidden by the deep folds in the mountain, the slabs of limestone pushed up millions of years ago, and the miles of undulating birch and ash and oak. She had heard the ring of the telephone downstairs, and hurried inside, grateful for the warmth that greeted her.

'Mamma.' Anna's heart lifted and she smiled at the sound of her son's voice, forgave him the almost imperceptible impatience perhaps only she would have heard in his voice, forgave him the lateness of his call and the gruffness that could not entirely disguise his affection.

'*Caro*,' she said. She could hear the unmistakable background noises of the hospital, an urgent, distant siren, the squeak of a trolley, and a conversation, the raised voice of a parent in distress and a surgeon's soothing reply. She could picture Paolo exactly, standing in the cold concrete lobby where the lifts arrived, between his ward and the operating theatre. Orthopaedics. Broken bones. Trauma. He was smoking a cigarette, she could tell from the sound of his breathing, and using his mobile, standing beneath the sign that prohibited both activities. She could tell, too, that he was frowning, his high forehead almost permanently furrowed these days, since Olivia left him, or he left her, whatever the truth of it was.

'Don't smoke, *caro*. It's not good for you.' She heard him sigh. 'So what about tomorrow? Are you just beginning your shift, or are you going home now?'

'Just beginning. Well, an hour or so ago. I just did a broken elbow, a little English boy on holiday fell in the street, but that went well, he did just what I told him, tough little kid. He liked watching me put the bones together on the screen. Looks like it might be a quiet night, fingers crossed. I might even get some sleep.'

Anna found herself nodding, feeling a flush of pride as she thought of her son patiently mending the broken bone, maybe talking haltingly in his broken English to reassure the child. Her pride mixed with anxiety as she registered the weariness in his voice.

'Don't come if you haven't slept, darling,' she said, with a sigh. 'It won't be safe. And the roads are terrible back into Rome on a Sunday evening. But—' she stopped.

'Look, Mamma,' Paolo said gently, I'll come if I feel rested enough. Like I said, it looks like it might be a quiet night. And I've got a few days off, so I won't have to rush back. Now I've got to go. A kiss for you, OK? Maybe see you tomorrow.'

Softly Anna put the phone down and climbed back up the stairs to her room, where she closed the long window on to her balcony, climbed gratefully into her soft old bed and fell asleep, at last, to dream of things that happened long ago, things that, waking, she would no longer remember.

Justine lay in the dark, Lucien beside her breathing evenly. It had been one of the things that Justine had first found irresistible about Lucien six, seven years ago: his knack of instant, tranquil sleep, his breath as regular as a metronome, his certainty. She had felt safe, sleeping alongside such a healthy, untroubled physicality, like a child's body next to hers.

Justine had opened the window and pushed back the metal shutters to let in some air and the deep black of the clear night sky. Why did the shutters have to be so heavy, she wondered? They seemed to be made of solid steel. Perhaps because the place was shut up all winter, and, after all, you wouldn't want to be making that trip down to check on things too often. A sensible precaution, then.

It was the children who voiced the feelings the adults had not expressed upon their arrival at Il Vignacce. Not Dido, who had remained silent throughout the meal, and who perhaps no longer counted as a child, all things considered, but Louisa's two boys: Sam, the eleven year old, a large, fair, open-faced boy with Tom's amiable smile, and his smaller, fiercer, darker brother Angus. They had taken the opportunity while Lucien made his risotto to investigate the house, flinging open cupboard doors and wrestling on the beds; they even appropriated the key to the smaller half of the farmhouse where Justine and Lucien and Martin and Dido would be staying, and rushed out into the darkness whooping and squealing to see whether it contained any more useful surprises than their own accommodation. Hoping for a television.

'It's a bit spooky, isn't it, Mummy?' Sam said, uncertainly, his exuberance distinctly muted as he came in out of the darkness. 'I mean, it took ages to get here from the road, and there aren't any lights or anything. It's like – you know, a story or something. Like – Hansel and Gretel, that kind of story. And it's very quiet. You can hear stuff in the woods, noises and stuff.' He looked at them earnestly.

The adults sitting around the table all smiled at him, at least partly in recognition of the fact that, to all of them, the lonely house in the dark woods recalled the same stories. But by now they were in a mood to be indulgent about superstitious associations; the table had been laid and a second bottle of wine had been opened. Each adult face seemed softened, the lines expressing weariness and tension and anxiety ironed out by alcohol. Even Louisa looked a little flushed in the kitchen's warmth, and kinder; beside her Tom sat with his arm around her shoulders and looked up with fondness at his son.

Martin and Dido were at the table, at least showing some willingness to be included in the party. Dido had been given her own glass of wine, and she sat with her hand cupped around it as though it was warming her. Justine had watched the girl as she looked around the table, the simulacrum of a feast, the illusion of a happy extended family united, and saw loneliness in the girl's dark eyes.

Then Lucien had brought the risotto to the table, pale

17

yellow and scented, and a salad full of the different coloured leaves he had rhapsodized over in the supermarket when he'd seen them stacked in bunches in their wooden trays, some shavings of parmesan, some grilled aubergines. A creamy, custard-yellow tart dusted with pine nuts and icing sugar sat on the side in its plastic box, testimony to the fact that Lucien always thought of everything.

Martin gave a little sigh, although Justine couldn't have said whether of satisfaction or resignation; Tom and Louisa murmured something complimentary, backing each other up with enthusiasm. Sam and Angus, however, wrinkled their noses at the approach of the plate of pale, steaming rice and hunched their shoulders in silent refusal. Louisa sighed, stood up and went to the elderly fridge, which shuddered as she opened it, and brought them back bread and *salami* and triangles of processed cheese. This started Lucien off on one of his riffs about modern eating habits and the state of the nation and Justine could have kicked him this time as she watched Louisa struggle to justify her capitulation without starting an argument. Tom sighed and buried his nose in his wine glass.

'Come on, Lucien.' Everyone looked at Martin, who had barely spoken until now, his voice a little hoarse, as though rusty with underuse, but mild. 'Wait till you've got children of your own. It's not that easy.'

Lucien opened his mouth, but perhaps he realized for himself that the first night of their stay was not the right time to get started on the junk-food conversation, because he just shrugged and smiled.

'Yeah, right. So, who wants risotto, who wants Dairylea triangles?'

Suddenly everyone seemed to be united in hunger. The

long plate of risotto was handed up and down the long table and the boys busied themselves stacking up meat and cheese into toppling sandwiches they could hardly get into their mouths. The air drifting through the window was still warm and smelled sweet and foreign, the smell of acres and acres of uninhabited forest, some rich melange of wildflowers, decaying leaves, ripening fruit and river water. In the trees all around them the insects sang while they ate, steadily and happily. At the table Lucien put his arm around Justine and she leaned in against him gratefully.

'How's that?' he said, kissing her lightly on the cheek. 'Better?'

Justine nodded, and looked up at him, feeling herself soften and relax, tucked in beneath his arm. Across the table Louisa smiled fondly at them and although the smile creased and wrinkled the skin, just growing papery now, around her eyes she looked younger to Justine, more vulnerable. Perhaps it was the food, or the wine, but it felt as though this was really a holiday after all.

'Good risotto, Lucien,' said Tom. 'Very good.' He stuck his thumb up cheerfully and planted a kiss on Louisa's cheek. She blushed and smiled. 'What's for pudding?' Everyone laughed, and Justine experienced such sudden affection for all of them, from the squabbling boys with their cheeks shiny with grease, to Martin who had been unable to stop himself smiling at Tom's indefatigable good nature, that she could feel it welling up behind her eyes.

On that point, somehow, the evening turned; it was as though, under the influence of wine and food and even perhaps an awareness that they were so far from anywhere, they had decided the holiday was going to work after all. Lucien, who had spotted the pizza oven on one side of the farmhouse and registered the ample supply of firewood littering the forest floor, began talking about self-sufficiency with an enthusiasm that seemed to communicate itself to the others.

It grew late, past eleven, and the boys were sent to bed, to dream of fishing in the river and lighting fires in the woods. Justine washed up in the big stone sink; Dido offered to dry but Martin shook his head at her as she yawned.

'Go to bed, sweetie,' he said gently, and took her next door to the smaller half of the farmhouse which they were to share with Justine and Lucien. They had hardly looked inside when they arrived, Justine thought, just dumped their bags and gravitated here for a drink and some food. Justine felt reluctant to move out of the warm bright kitchen to go next door; it seemed extraordinarily dark outside now, an inky, velvety black beyond the small circle of light cast through the open door. When he came back Martin took her place beside Justine, silently and carefully drying and sorting and putting away.

'How was your flight?' he asked, for something to say perhaps, but his tone was friendly.

'Oh,' said Justine, surprised, 'all right. You know.' Lucien hated flying, hated everything about it: the stewards, the food, the other people. It brought out his most fastidious side, and made him irritable. She said nothing more, and for a moment or two they continued in silence, the shrilling of the insects saturating the darkness beyond the window.

This can't go on though, thought Justine, with determination. We're all going to have to talk, sometime.

She glanced over her shoulder into the room at the others, smiling and chatting in the glow around the table. She took a breath.

'How is Dido, Martin?' she asked, tentatively. 'She seems so – grown up. And worn out.'

Martin looked down at the tea towel in his hands. 'I don't know,' he said briefly, and fell silent. Mechanically Justine continued to hand him the dripping crockery. Then he spoke again, and this time he looked at her.

'I've never been – very good at talking about things,' he said. 'I didn't need to, with Evie. I thought I didn't. I never expected—' He broke off, looking down again.

'No,' said Justine, as gently as she could. 'None of us did. It's not your fault.'

Although of course she didn't know if it was Martin's fault, or not; although they'd known each other for fifteen years, spotted each other at parties, had dinner at each other's houses. Martin had always remained on the edge of things, uncommunicative, mysterious, reliant on Evie, as he said, to do his talking for him. None of them had ever got to know much more about him other than the fact that he was very good at making money, and that once, at a party early on in their relationship, he had broken a drunken guest's nose when he'd said something that upset Evie. That had left him with something of a reputation, but it hadn't encouraged intimacy.

'I miss her,' she said, without thinking, and saw Martin's head dip as she said it, eyes closed. She heard him exhale, a hopeless sound.

Justine thought of the last time she'd seen them together, Evie and Martin, a supper at their pine table piled at one end with the accumulated debris of their daily lives: school reports, circulars, telephone directories, a grey school skirt with a rip waiting to be mended. She and Evie had sat across the table from each other under the low pendent Tiffany lamp that

21

glowed multi-coloured in the warm kitchen. It had been – when? Late spring last year, warm enough to drink a glass of wine in the garden first, warm enough for Evie to be wearing a dark sleeveless dress; as she reached for her glass her long arm was pale and slender. Upstairs music had been pounding in Dido's room, reverberating in the dark hall and down through the kitchen ceiling, and they'd both smiled over it, the thought of Dido's mysterious existence shut up in her dark, noisy cavern of a room.

'They're hard to understand, girls,' Evie had said. 'I think boys are different. Louisa says so. I don't know what goes on in Dido's head.' She had looked sad; even, very briefly, lost. Perhaps that was it, thought Justine, that was the moment I should have asked her what was wrong.

'Adolescence,' was all Justine remembered saying, shaking her head, thinking of the terrible business of growing up. Thinking of herself, probably. She passed a secondary school every day on the way to work, and they seemed like aliens to her, fourteen year olds, suddenly spotty, their noses and ears and chins all too big as though their features grew faster than the rest of them. Some girls with greasy centre partings and flat shoes, eyes cast down and hands jammed in their pockets, while others wore full make-up, the right shoes, and had a boy's elbow to cling to through the school gates. Not a level playing field, growing up. Looking at Evie in the lamp's soft glow, it had seemed clear that she must have been one of the lucky ones, with a clear skin and an easy smile. Dido too, probably, although perhaps it was too early to tell. But, looking back, Justine thought maybe she had been wrong about Evie, maybe at school she hadn't been the girl everyone wanted to take out. Maybe it had been a cover-up.

Martin had been there, not at the table, but standing leaning against the counter, out of the light, watching them, looking at Evie in that way he had, as though she was not his partner but literally his other half, an extension of his own self. Justine had always thought that romantic: Martin's certainty, right from the start, that he and Evie belonged together. But she remembered seeing suddenly that evening when, having watched them until he was satisfied, Martin had slipped out of the room, softly closing the kitchen door behind him, that there might be something claustrophobic about it. To be looked at like that, watched hungrily; such passionate intensity seemed out of place in a long-married couple. But Evie had shown no sign of finding it oppressive; it was as though she no longer even noticed, going on with their conversation, about children.

Darting a sideways glance at Martin now, Justine wondered suddenly how he could possibly have survived it: the loss of Evie. But as they went on with the washing-up, and it seemed to Justine that at least Martin was happy to be with her in the shadow by the sink, to leave the others at the table in the light. They were talking animatedly at first about trips to Siena and Florence, maybe a visit to some unspoilt hill-town Lucien had heard of down towards the Argentario coast. Tom mentioned a restaurant he wanted to visit, maybe write a piece about, somewhere in the hills. Slowly the conversation wound down under the effects of the alcohol until, more or less as Martin dried the last plate and Justine put it away, they all came to sleepy silence. Tom made a half-hearted attempt to persuade someone to join him in a glass of grappa, but found no takers and finally they dispersed, each making their separate ways to bed and the delicious, virgin promise of someone else's clean linen.

Lying now in the soft, foreign bed, Justine listened to the new sounds of an unfamiliar house and its systems restoring themselves to equilibrium, the pipes ticking and gurgling, the creak of beams and stairs as the building settled back down after the day's invasion. Someone turning in bed in the next room: Dido or Martin. As her eyes adjusted to the light Justine could see a square of stars outlined by the frame of the window, and a distant ridge of trees silhouetted by the faint, ghostly luminescence they shed. She heard the hollow call of an owl from across the valley, unmistakable despite the fact that it was a sound that Justine, a city girl born and bred, had never heard in nature before. Suddenly she felt the thrill of being in so foreign a place, far more foreign than she had expected; a place where anything might happen.

Chapter Three

Justine and Louisa, and Evie too, despite her absence, were the reason for this holiday: they were the connection. The men had come later.

The three of them, not in the least like each other, had been friends almost from the beginning, or at least the beginning of their adulthood. They'd met on their first day at university when they'd been allocated the same landing in a huge, dreary Victorian hall of residence in West London; there'd been others on the landing, of course, but they came and went, drifting in and out and making little impression. Justine, Evie and Louisa stuck, for one reason or another.

Justine, the first of them to take up residence, had met Louisa's mother Julia before she met Louisa herself. She thought afterwards that if it had been the other way around she might never have taken to neat, repressed, circumspect Louisa. Her mother was a tiny, fragile-looking, lovely woman, elegant as a miniature Cecil Beaton model, with a nineteen-inch waist, lemon blonde hair that curled around her high cheek-bones and huge, luminous grey eyes. She was a monster, too. Clever but thwarted, ambitious and snobbish, she had suffered the ignominy of a husband who had promised well but turned out to be a manic depressive, forcing her to settle her consid-erable expectations on her only child.

None of this Justine knew on first sight, of course, but as Julia stalked up the grimy stairwell of the mansion block commenting in her languid voice on the ghastly colour the stairwell had been painted, the picture was already beginning to form. And when Louisa appeared behind her mother, the image of a dutiful daughter but with the glint of rebellion in her blue eyes, Justine found herself smiling at her.

It became obvious that from early childhood Louisa had been the vehicle for her mother's ambition; Justine, who came from a very different background, quailed even now at the thought of being the focus of such attention, but Louisa had her own way of dealing with it. From the moment Louisa left home for university she began to make her own deci-sions about what she wore, who she saw, and what she read, making sure in each respect her choices differed from those her mother would have made, and politely she kept her mother at arm's length. In this light her pink lipstick (denounced by her mother as unflattering), her Laura Ashley dresses (badly made, fancy dress), her neat, short hair (dull), looked like dangerous subversion.

As they grew older, and saw less of each other, Justine real-ized that in fact Louisa resembled her mother very closely in some aspects of her character, not least her determination. But to Justine then Louisa's attention to the detail of her own life, her dedication to quietly resisting her mother's intellectual snobbery and ceaseless attempts to decide her future, seemed heroic. And then Louisa had married big, untidy Tom Fane, and her mother had given up.

No one had ever taken the slightest interest in Justine's future, it sometimes seemed to her; perhaps, she thought on meeting Julia, she should be grateful. The fourth of seven children, Justine had grown up in an unruly, bohemian household in a cramped terrace in Muswell Hill almost unnoticed. Justine's mother, Sonia, was an art teacher, a romantic, dishevelled woman addicted to the production of children whom she then largely ignored, sometimes looking at them as if she couldn't quite place them. Her husband Victor, a copy-editor at a large academic publishers, had been more committed in theory to his children as individuals, but distracted from the practical application of his love for them by the effort of earning enough money to keep the household running. Justine had been named for a character in a book, as had her two brothers and four sisters, and at moments of dipping self-confidence she sometimes wondered whether her parents were able to distinguish their offspring either from each other or from their literary namesakes.

Sonia became a widow at fifty when her husband died suddenly at his little grey desk in Victoria, of a heart attack. Justine, who had been sixteen, had been more grief-stricken than she would have thought possible at the lack of a man whom, for most of her childhood, she had hardly seen – granted only her small share of the hour every evening that separated his return home from work and the children's bedtime. Secretly, her own overlooked among the grief of so many others, Justine had avidly stored away the few memories she had of her father. The occasional bedtime story read with sound effects and funny voices or her turn on the sofa beside him in front of the television. A day spent in his office once when she had been ill, sharpening pencils with a machine he kept on his desk while he worked beside her; lunch at the Golden Egg and a paperback from Smith's for a treat.

The suddenness of her father's disappearance from her life, having left for work one morning never to return, had left Justine with an abiding sense of how quickly things she had thought immutable could change. It had made her a melancholy schoolgirl, escaping into the rambling, introspective essays she would write for her English teacher and shying away from the risks involved in developing a social life. And then, quite suddenly, she had begun to notice something that was happening to her body: a failure of pigmentation, quite unobtrusive at first, just the odd pale patch with an irregular outline like a white island against her golden skin. The condition was diagnosed as vitiligo. It commonly began around puberty, she later learned, but Justine always connected it, however illogically, with her father's death.

Once it had been diagnosed as progressive but not dangerous, Sonia had little time for her daughter's condition in the aftermath of her husband's death. Although at the time she seemed more annoyed than bereft by his loss. She was busy enough worrying about being left alone with the children and no money, although most of them, by then, were supporting themselves. And so Justine had taken herself to the doctor, to find out that there was nothing that could be done about the faint markings on her skin, the scattering of white hairs that sprang up one night at the left temple. She learned to ignore it, at least that was how it appeared to her friends, and in fact it was hardly visible as long as she was clothed. Justine applied sunblock carefully and without complaint, wore long sleeves in the summer, kept her clothes on. She kept her head down, and worked.

Now Sonia lived in a small, dark cottage in Essex which smelled of cats and paraffin, its damp back garden overgrown with brambles and mildewed roses that had begun to obscure the little sunlight available. She still taught art, part-time, at an adult education facility, and often complained to her neighbours that her children never came to see her (as they would inform Justine on her twice-annual visits), and what was the point of having children, after all? The truth was that Justine's sisters, Juliet, Rowena, Isabel and Tess, with two, two, one and three children respectively, could not stand their mother now that they had children of their own and realized to what extent they themselves had grown up neglected.

Oscar, Justine's lazy younger brother and closest sibling, lived on benefits in a Colchester bedsit, endlessly studying, or so he said, for an open university degree in philosophy, and never washing his clothes. Occasionally he went home to his mother to borrow some money; he was introverted, and rarely spoke. Dan, the oldest of them, had died of a drug overdose while at art school aged twenty-one; Justine, eight years his junior, could barely remember him any more. She remembered the shock of being told that he was dead, the disbelief at how easily it could happen, just one mistake and everything stopped. Time up. She had lain in her room and thought of all the things that Dan would never do, now. And every year more of Dan slipped away from her until he was nothing more than a tangle of blond hair and a bedroom full of blue smoke and psychedelic posters. He would have been forty-three if he had lived.

As is sometimes said to be characteristic of middle children, and perhaps more so if the middle child in question feels herself to have some flaw for which compensation is required, Justine had been – and was still – industrious and determined. She had worked hard at school, often staying behind in the silent, ill-lit school library to do her homework, always scrupulously organized and punctual; when she got home, she would change into jeans and go to the pub, where she had since the age of fourteen had a part-time job collecting glasses. This had allowed her to escape from her family – from her sisters in particular, with whom she fought almost in rotation – and to earn money. When her efforts were rewarded and she arrived at university with three hundred pounds saved to take up residence across that draughty landing from Evie and Louisa, Justine was as happy as she had ever been in her life. The dusty jewel colours of the stained glass on the stairs, the long, unkempt grass of the communal garden, even the roar of traffic on the Fulham Road, everything about her new circumstances seemed wonderful to Justine, and she was ready to make her neighbours her new family even before she had seen them.

Evie had turned up fashionably late that September, days after Justine and Louisa had bought mugs and instant coffee, arranged their books on their shelves and put up their posters. She had stepped off the bus from King's Cross, a year older than them, her skin nut-brown and peeling, she said from six months' travelling across Europe and North Africa. She was carrying a bulging leather suitcase with a broken hinge, and it had burst on the checkerboard tiles of the mansion block's doorstep.

Justine thought perhaps some people might have said she wasn't beautiful at all. You could have said, Justine supposed,

30

that her shoulders were too broad, for example, or her nose a little too long, her hands too big. But there was something she gave out that meant not exactly that you didn't see those things, but that made them delightful; a kind of ineffable sweetness, a glow of health and heedless happiness. She was always smiling, it seemed, even when she was commiserating, as she often did, or relating a misfortune, which was rare; she radiated a constant human warmth. It came off her even then, at that first meeting, as she stuffed knickers and scarves and shorts back into her case, laughing up at them as she apologized.

Evie had said, as they sat over coffee in Louisa's room, the contents of the suitcase between them in a dustbin bag (Louisa, being organized, already had a stock of them) that she had come from her grandmother's house in Chalk Farm. An only child, she had been living with her parents in a dilapidated farmhouse in Spain since the early seventies, but the previous year they had died in a car crash on a notorious stretch of road between Malaga and Granada, on their way back from a party. The police had told her, Evie said; it had taken them a while to find her, and she had waited for three days, wondering whether her parents might have just headed off to another party without telling her. They had gazed at her, Louisa and Justine, round-eyed at the tragedy of it. She had smiled at them then, kindly, and talked about something else.

Louisa and Justine never met Evie's grandmother, and Evie reached an arrangement with the university accommodation board to be allowed to stay on in the halls of residence when term finished. She would spend the time sunbathing in the communal gardens and prompting calls of complaint from the few remaining non-university tenants of the mansion block,

31

who looked forward to a summer without students and held a particular grudge against golden, voluptuous girls like Evie, stretched straight out like a Bonnard beside the dahlias and not visibly applying herself to academic study.

Although when Evie had first told them about her parents' death, Justine had been aghast at the horror of it; once Evie was no longer there to confirm or deny the story Justine sometimes found herself wondering whether it had all been true. The exotic, tragic childhood, so poignant, so perfect a setting for a jewel like Evie, so fully realized in every detail. It might have been something she had dreamed, or perhaps Evie had made it all up and, like the sacred myths of childhood – that one's mother was beautiful, one's father powerful – it would dissolve like smoke if subjected to adult scrutiny. Is this what happens when you die? Justine wondered; your garden turns to weeds, your possessions lose their meaning all heaped together on a jumble-sale table, and all your carefully constructed life falls into pieces when you are no longer there to say, this is who I am.

Certainly Evie arrived in Evelyn Gardens alone; she did not, however, fit their image of an orphan. She was not small and wan but big and beautiful; she glowed with robust health, long shiny brown hair as straight as glass and dark-blue eyes, Evie already knew a great deal more about sex than Justine or Louisa, and was as generous in passing on her knowledge as she was with her spectacular wardrobe, which was stuffed with old satin ballgowns and ragged black mantillas she said she'd bought at Spanish markets. Evie didn't care what anyone thought of her, or so it seemed then; whatever her background it seemed to have taught her that life was too short to sit and wait for something to come along. There were always plenty of boyfriends, and although none of them, until Martin, was allowed the chance to settle in, Evie was always kind to them, even when she was telling them that she thought perhaps things weren't working out. To Justine and Louisa she was the model of an adventurer, and they watched, rapt, to see what might happen to her.

Friends at eighteen, though, are different kinds of friends by the time they are twenty-five. Within five years of the three first meeting Louisa had married Tom in a church off Fleet Street wearing a satin gown with a thirty-foot train of Russian lace her mother, with even more spite than usual, denounced as vulgarly ostentatious. They bought their house in Hammersmith, practically the suburbs; it was a shabby, peeling Regency villa that had only recently been vacated by squatters, and it had been all they could afford at the time. From that point on Louisa divided her time between work, to which she applied herself with fierce single-mindedness, and the restoration of their house, from plaster cornices to wrought-iron railings. Needless to say, she had succeeded in every detail and the house had proven to be an extraordinarily good investment, but there was little time left over for social-izing. There was the odd wine-bar sandwich snatched in a half-hour lunch break, and a phone call, now and then, just to keep up, but it wasn't the same.

Evie had met Martin when she was out with Justine one evening, drinking in a student bar in Bloomsbury. Louisa had stopped living like a student as soon as she was able, what with married life and a smart job as a PR in Belgravia, but Justine and Evie didn't shrug it off quite so quickly. This bar, which offered cheap alcohol and a cheerful, noisy crowd in the basement of a decaying student building just off the roar of the

Euston Road, was the kind of place they often visited in the early days of their working lives. At that time Evie had been learning to restore stained glass in a workshop in Fulham; she was good at it, and hardworking, although dismissive about her talent. It was the first of a series of artistic skills she managed to acquire over the subsequent fifteen years, although she never made money at any of them, and sometimes it seemed she did that deliberately, shy of making too much of any talent she had. Meanwhile Justine was laboriously trying to become a copy-editor like her father in her cramped cubicle on the third floor of an office block.

They were both impoverished and on the ungroomed side of pretty, although, where Evie exuded physical confidence, Justine had a tendency to hunch and to pull her sleeves down. She always found, though, that after an hour or so with Evie she would be standing up straighter and laughing louder. Evie was a crash barrier and a safety net, encouraging, putting her arm around Justine, laughing helplessly at her stories of office life. That evening there had been a live band crashing away in one corner of the basement room and a few people were lurching drunkenly to the music, then Martin had appeared beside their table and asked Evie to dance. He was abrupt and his expression was serious, but Justine had known Evie wouldn't say no; she never did.

Justine had watched them together across the room; Martin had barely moved, Evie in front of him had begun to dance exuberantly as usual but had slowed down, they moved closer to each other and Justine could see that they were talking although she couldn't hear what they were saying. She could remember quite clearly that even across the crowded bar Martin was different; unlike any of their other contemporaries he didn't seem like a boy at all, but full-grown. Even at twenty-one he exuded a kind of strength, an intensity that Evie responded to without being able to help herself, as though she was physically being pulled in by him. She was tall but he was taller; from that distance he made her look delicate, vulnerable, in need of his shelter, her face tilted up towards his, fascinated. Perhaps, looking back, Justine thought what she had been too naïve to think then, that it had been a sexual thing. And certainly that had been a part of it. But there had been something else, too; a fierce, unsentimental quality to Martin's intelligence that had mesmerized her, demanded her attention and her dependence. Later, Justine had wondered if those things had somehow ceased to be enough for Evie.

It was clear that something had happened when Evie got back to Justine that evening: her eyes were bright and although Martin remained on the other side of the room, leaning against the wall with a glass of beer in his hand, she told Justine that she was going to see him again the following evening.

At first, of course, Justine and Louisa had assumed that Martin would last no longer than Evie's other boyfriends, but soon enough it became obvious that she couldn't let him go. He took Evie away from them in a way no other relationship had; they met alone in new places, rarely going out with others. But Evie was in love with him, that was clear; whenever Justine saw them together it was obvious that they would rather be alone, they didn't want things diluted in some noisy communal space where they couldn't hear what each other was saying. They went away that summer to Morocco for three long months, both on unauthorized absence from their courses, and when they came back, dark and exotic from travelling, there was no coming between them.

And they did look right together, somehow: Evie so vivid and Martin sombre; she seemed to need him as much as he needed her, which was not how it usually worked with Evie. And it turned out, soon after their return from Africa, that Evie was pregnant with Dido. She didn't need to announce it, she just grew, insouciantly, under their noses, and then, with three days' notice, invited them all to her registry office marriage to Martin the month before Dido's birth.

They had all stood there on the steps of Marylebone Registry office throwing confetti over Evie and Martin, Evie defiantly huge in scarlet satin, her belly standing in for a bouquet, while the traffic roared past on the Euston Road. Like a bright caravanserai they had all paraded across six lanes of traffic in their finery to the reception, which was a picnic in the rose garden of Regent's Park with champagne drunk from the bottle and chocolate cake. Looking back, Justine thought that Evie had showed no sign of having been forced into it, either by Martin or by social pressure. As some of their friends had suggested at the time; she had seemed extravagantly happy.

Justine, however, remained single, and she didn't mind at all, or thought she didn't. Living in a bedsit in a blackened, crumbling Georgian terrace on a main road in south London, she relished the order and tranquillity of a solitary existence. She was working as a junior editor in the fiction department of a large publishing house, had her own small office, neat piles of tagged and annotated manuscripts bending the cheap shelving and filling her with pride. Barely paid enough to cover her modest rent, Justine looked forward to her work, and rode the bus up to Bedford Square every morning full of eager anticipation; she had a few friends to lunch with, her own space and peace. That seemed to be enough, for the time being, although she certainly assumed that this was not always how it would be. It seemed a long time ago, now, to Justine; a time when she had thought it was just a beginning, all that patient, close work on manuscripts that would, one day, lead to something greater.

Then Dido arrived. When Justine came into hospital to see her Evie had seemed so happy it seemed as though she needed a curtain pulled around the bed to disguise it, for decency. But she was changed, too, somehow. Somewhere she kept quite secret. Justine had seen it, almost by chance, when she had decided to drop in one evening to see Evie about a month after Dido had been born. Instead of the radiant mother she'd seen in the hospital, Justine found Evie pale, red-eyed and thinner; her strong shoulders fragile, her jawline sharpened. Alone with Dido in her arms in a cold, untidy kitchen she had actually looked afraid. Justine had never seen her look afraid of anything before.

'Is she breathing?' Evie had asked, straight away. 'I don't know – sometimes she seems to be hardly breathing.' She had held Dido out to Justine. The baby looked, to Justine's inexpert eye, perfectly healthy, golden and round-cheeked, and most certainly breathing. Bemused, Justine had shaken her head a little.

'Of course she's breathing,' she said. 'What's the matter, Evie?'

Evie pushed a sweaty tendril of hair out of her face. 'She had a cough, that wouldn't go away. Wheezing. Nothing serious, the doctor said, but I lie there listening to her breathe at night, and I don't know—' She broke off, breathed a deep painful sigh.

'You just haven't had enough sleep, Evie,' Justine guessed.

'Look at you. Sit down, I'll make a cup of tea.' She turned to put the kettle on but Evie didn't move, stood there swaying in the middle of the floor.

'I sometimes wake up,' said Evie, almost talking to herself, 'at two, or three, before it's light and I think, what if I couldn't move? What if the baby was crying and I couldn't get out of bed to go to her? It's not just me, you see, not just me now. If I've fallen asleep on my arm and it's gone dead, I just panic. I—'

Then she had stopped, abruptly. Justine had made her a cup of tea, they'd sat at the table and talked about something – clothes, work, breastfeeding. Evie hadn't said any more then, nor ever again, not explicitly, and when next Justine had come round, making sure to ring first this time and let her know, the kitchen had been warm, and ordered, and Evie's hair clean. It seemed as though she was entirely her old self, smiling again, encouraging, holding out Dido for Justine to hold. Justine was surprised by how relieved she felt.

The three of them maintained contact – Justine, Evie and Louisa – although they probably saw a little less of each other as every year passed. At first it was dinner most weeks in one household or another, but gradually this dwindled to a drink now and then. This was natural; it happened among other groups of friends, they observed, as responsibilities other than those belonging to friendship intervened in their lives. And Evie in particular, Justine felt, was always close; even if they hadn't seen each other for six months, they would pick up again as before. She would admit things to Justine perhaps she didn't tell anyone else; when Dido had a tooth extracted under anaesthetic only Justine ever knew how terrified Evie had been, and when Martin went through a difficult patch with the business and was hardly there.

Louisa and Tom would always invite Justine to their sought-after parties, though – a summer one in the garden, with tubs of clipped box and strawberries in the punch, and another at Christmas, with branches of yew and trailing ivy, in their huge drawing room. Sometimes Evie was there, dressed in something bold and impractical, a red velvet coat with bare legs and scuffed stilettos, Dido toddling at her feet, sometimes with Martin, too, gazing at her. Sometimes they didn't come.

Justine always went, at the beginning, then she began to feel ill-at-ease, not quite groomed enough in the glamorous company Tom and Louisa had begun to keep. Tom was an influential journalist by then; he wrote about the food industry, breaking stories about inhumane conditions and adulterated foodstuffs that won him awards. As a result their parties were full of booming news editors and women in cocktail dresses and high heels looking sharply around, gauging the calibre of the company with a professional eye. Justine had missed three or four of the Fanes' parties in a row when she told herself one Christmas that she was being a coward and a disloyal friend, plucked up her courage, and got on the tube to Hammersmith. She had splashed out on a new dress, black and close-fitting with long tight sleeves, and found herself knocking on their dark-green front door on a frosty evening.

It was Lucien who had opened the door for her, Tom and Louisa having been detained elsewhere; he had been invited because he and Tom worked for the same newspaper. He'd looked her up and down approvingly on the doorstep, until she'd blushed and tried to push past him.

And that had been that. He had kept her next to him for two hours, holding her forearm as they talked in a quiet corner of the breakfast room, the overflow from a particularly well-attended evening. Afterwards they had gone home together to his house in Notting Hill which at that time had been full of junk sculpture and Edwardian display cabinets they had tripped over in the dark. Justine had often thought of that night since as she lay next to Lucien while he slept, wondering whether these were the kind of memories that kept marriages together.

Even in the dark Justine had removed her clothes with caution, but the next morning when Lucien drew back the curtains and let in the wintry morning light she had not had time to draw the sheet up and her body had lain there, exposed. He had said nothing; Lucien had never said anything and so she felt he must not mind it, the marks and configurations of brown and white on the concealed parts of her body, the pools of bleached skin that over her adolescence she had watched expand overnight like an oildrop on water; to Justine then the relief had been so powerful as to feel more like a victory. Later, of course, she had not been so sure.

For a year or two Justine, and Lucien, became regular visitors again to the parties in Hammersmith. But then Lucien had given up the gardening column when he'd felt it cramping his style, and they hadn't been back since to Tom and Louisa's.

Justine had gone on seeing Evie, of course; Lucien did not entirely approve, for some reason, of the idea of a girls' night out. He implied he thought it tacky; disapproving largely on grounds of taste, it seemed. Evie would escape from domesticity for a snatched drink in a pub near Bedford Square now and then, but more often Justine found herself turning up for supper at their little house, where Dido would be put on her knee to bat the table with her small hands and shriek. Once Dido had started at school she would shyly bring out her pictures for Justine, big splashy poppies or detailed drawings of her home with furniture and stick people in the rooms. Evie didn't go on about Justine having children of her own, but Justine would sometimes catch her looking at them together, Dido on her knee playing peek a boo behind her hands, and she knew what Evie was thinking.

Evie's outward life didn't change, not much; she did some freelance restoration work, learned how to proofread for a pittance, the odd review for an old boyfriend, and her bedroom was still a heap of tangled silver sandals and Victorian piano shawls, beads hanging from an etched glass mirror on the dressing table. It wouldn't have occurred to her to learn to drive, or wear something sensible, like jeans, just because the other mothers at Dido's school did.

Once or twice Justine did find herself wondering where it had all gone, the time, the potential, all the things they had thought Evie would do. And occasionally she looked tired, and right at the end Justine remembered noticing that she looked her age, suddenly; grown up; thirty-five. Beautiful, still, and perhaps more beautiful; her waist a little thicker, little lines around her eyes, her cheekbones sharpened, but not a girl any more. That was how she'd looked under the Tiffany lamp that last evening, talking about adolescence, questioning Justine about her marriage, was she happy. Had something been bothering her? She hadn't talked about herself, or Martin. She never talked about him, in fact.

Martin was a biochemist by training, had started up a small business involved in the manipulation of genetic material which turned out to be very profitable; he never discussed his work with Justine or any of them, so she knew little more than that. He worked to a very strict schedule, but he was not like other businessmen of Justine's acquaintance, the few men at the publishers' she worked at, for instance; he never seemed to be late home because he had gone out for a drink with colleagues, and he always turned down invitations to conferences in exotic locations, Venice or San Francisco or Berlin. His first thought on finishing work always seemed to be to get home to Evie and Dido; they were his passion, a physical addiction. Martin had no time for trivial activities, golf or socializing.

And although Justine had wondered when they had no more children, the three of them did seem to her to be perfectly, economically happy, wound tight around each other in their little warm house. There had been many times over the past year that Justine had found herself wondering whether she had missed something, whether going over there with her own problems, she hadn't paid any attention to something Evie had wanted to tell her. And the uncomfortable conclusion she arrived at each time was that it was entirely possible; she could easily have failed Evie.

The trip to Il Vignacce had been Louisa's idea; almost a year to the day after Evie had died, she'd found somewhere really cheap on the internet, and it would be good, she said, for Martin and Dido, or for Dido at least.

'The poor girl,' she'd said, phoning Justine at work and taking her by surprise. 'Don't you think it would be nice for her, more of a family to be with, not just the two of them?' When she had made stalling noises, thinking of Lucien, Louisa had insisted, 'Come on, it'll be fun. None of us have had a decent holiday in years, and it's pretty cheap, isn't it? Of course it'll cut into term time a bit, that's why it's not so expensive. But it'll just be a week, ten days at most – I've booked two weeks, but really it's so cheap we can leave when we want – and I can sort that out with school, and I'm sure Martin can too.'

'Well,' Justine said, unsure still, 'I'll talk to Lucien.'

'Do, darling,' said Louisa, 'because it won't be the same without you. And I'll need someone to talk to, won't I?' So Justine agreed, just a little bit flattered that Louisa wanted her to come so badly, and considering, on reflection, that a holiday with someone other than just the two of them might not be a bad idea.

And Lucien had grumbled, first at the expense because he hated spending any money at all, perhaps because he didn't earn any. Then there was the thought of spending more than an evening with Tom, with whom he did not get on. And other people's children. But Justine had persisted, and it was her money, after all, although she didn't say that.

So Louisa had booked Il Vignacce. In fact it was Martin's response Louisa had worried about, not Justine's, or Lucien's; although she wasn't one to shirk a difficult conversation she had found herself feeling uncharacteristically nervous, waiting for him to pick up the phone so that she could invite him and Dido on the holiday. But he had agreed straight away; it had almost been as though the whole thing was already on his agenda.

Chapter Four

Il Vignacce faced south, and in the morning the sun rose over the ridge to its left, the shadow cast by the tall trees receding only slowly from the broad pasture that stretched out in front of the old stone building. The river was on that side, too, although they couldn't see it, meandering silently along the eastern side of the clearing at the foot of a steep, wooded bank that concealed it from the house.

The wooded spurs and valleys that made up the hundreds of hectares of the reserve of the Alto Merse where the farmhouse lay hidden were interlocked like fingers, the river zig-zagging between them. There were side valleys too, where tiny tributaries would come down from the hills to the north or east to join the river and the walkers who occasionally visited the area could easily, unless they were very experienced or in possession of a carefully annotated map, lose their way entirely. Following the river did not always work in establishing the walker's bearings, as where it met a tributary it might appear to fork; sometimes it seemed to dry up entirely up a blind valley, or end in a boggy, flooded field with no clear outflow. Signs would appear on gates: Bestiame in Brado, or Toro Pericoloso, Attenzione, that might throw the nervous walker entirely and send him back to retrace his steps rather than confront a snorting bull in so enclosed a space.

Although the animals themselves were more often heard than seen, on the valley floor there was plenty of physical evidence of Piero Montale's livestock. Their hoofprints marked the soft black mud of the valley path where the river overflowed in spring, and everywhere horseflies hovered and buzzed, glittering like jewels over the animals' splattered dung. The dangerous bull the sign referred to, however, was in fact more of a red herring. He was a docile creature and the only male among thirty or forty heifers, all of them considerably more confident than he, and with bigger horns. Just like me, Piero Montale would say, gesturing at his wife as he sat with his cronies in the village bar. Outnumbered. Outgunned.

Sometimes the little herd would appear without warning from the woods above Il Vignacce and thunder down through the corral Montale had fixed up, designed to separate them from the visitors and lead them to the small barn that stood some distance from the farmstead. Sometimes they would come up from the river, galloping and clambering up the small steep path through the trees that hid the water from view, to the pasture where they would spread and out and stop, quite suddenly, cropping grass peaceably as though they'd been there for hours. They seemed to look on the occasional human visitors to the valley with absolute indifference, as though secure in the knowledge that these were only temporary invaders and soon enough they would have the place to themselves again.

There were two calves this summer, both born in the heat of August and only just over a month old. They would buck and jump once they were in the open, mounting each other and tossing their curly heads, but the heifers only occasionally raised their huge eyes from the ground to look at them in mild reproof.

A French family had complained earlier in the season that the herd attracted flies to the holiday cottage, but Montale had just shrugged at them sleepily. If they wanted to be free of flies, they could go to the city, he thought, where they would find mosquitoes instead. The truth was, Paolo Montale didn't really understand the concept of the holiday, where one travels far from home and yet everything must be perfect; surely these two, he believed in common with many of his generation, were incompatible. Home was where comfort lay, and as for adventure, well, adventure was quite over-rated.

This morning, the first morning of what would probably be the last rental of the season, the sky was perfectly blue and clear. The pasture was sparse and dry, dotted with clumps of thistle, and the woods around the clearing in which Il Vignacce stood looked almost black, darkened by months of uninterrupted summer sun. Beyond the reserve and out of sight over the horizon towards Siena, the smooth round hills were glittering with stubble and the end of summer, but in the woods change came more gradually. It was early yet for the colour of the trees to turn, but in any case there was a good proportion of evergreen among them, mostly holm oak, fir trees and a few umbrella pines higher up, and the forest canopy would remain more or less intact throughout the year, concealing the life carried on below.

At the outer boundary of Montale's land some sweet

chestnut trees grew, which he harvested; chestnuts could be candied for marrons glacés and a good profit, puréed and canned, or dried and ground for chestnut flour. These trees, along with the dainty birches, were the first to colour, making a rusty yellow flare across the hillside when the first frosts arrived in October, but now their leaves were only just beginning to brown at the edges.

Higher still, on the ridge where the new arrivals had passed the logging crew the night before, there were pine trees growing more sparsely, their numbers thinned regularly for firewood and fencing. The loggers this year, as they had been for several years, were immigrants from eastern Europe. No one was ever entirely sure where they came from, or indeed where they went at night; it was rumoured that they lived rough in makeshift camps buried deep somewhere in the hundreds of acres of forest, and the lumber yard who paid them well below the minimum wage turned a blind eye. The woods, however, had for centuries harboured all sorts of exiles from society; hermits, runaways, deserters and dropouts could all be accommodated easily in its fifty hectares of secluded terrain.

The ridge was the highest point for many miles and on a day like this it offered a view across the whole reserve, but there was hardly a habitation to be seen: only a chain of electricity pylons swooping between the valleys and a single, incongruous stack of radio antennae and dishes at the top of a distant hill bore witness to the advance of civilization. Hidden among the trees and brambles were the remains of the odd shepherd's hut, the wall of an old stone barn here and there or an overgrown chapel, but for the most part these were ruins that had decayed beyond the point at which they were distinguishable from their

47

surroundings; they had been already absorbed back into the land. Even Anna Viola's house was too far away and too small to appear as more than a terracotta smudge on the black hills.

When Justine had first opened her eyes the sky through the open window had been silver grey at the approach of dawn, the air in the room was cool, and Lucien was asleep beside her. At home Justine often woke even earlier than this, unable to go back to sleep and unaccountably anxious – what about? Her doctor suggested she was under stress at work but Justine just laughed at her. 'They're just books,' she said, but her heart sank a little as she thought of them in their raw form, piles and piles of paper bending her shelves, her head full of other people's words. 'I'm not a captain of industry. Plus I've got a full-time househusband to look after me, and no kids.' The doctor, who had three children and for whom flexi-time was not working particularly well, had nodded, and Justine could see that she agreed. She had nothing to worry about.

But this morning just before dawn Justine opened her eyes, looked around, and went straight back to sleep; when she woke again the sky was a brilliant, incandescent blue and beside her in the bed was only a tangle of sheets where Lucien had been. Luxuriously Justine stretched; her body felt changed, transformed by a few hours' extra sleep and the sun slanting across her bed.

Cleaning her teeth at the window in the bathroom (which was nicely plain, Justine noted with satisfaction: white porcelain, terracotta floor and a worn marble shelf), she found herself looking out into the woods that, on this side of the house, came very close. The trees were pale, tall and spindly, their trunks splotched and blistered with lichen, and they stretched back as far as she could see down a slight incline behind the house. The sun didn't seem to reach down this far, and only a greenish light filtered down through the leaves to the dusty forest floor. Next to the house stood two bent old plum trees, their blue-black fruit littering the short grass behind the house in various stages of decay, and a nylon washing line strung between them that would be quite useless in the gloom.

Having grown up in the cramped terraces of north London, Justine didn't have much of a feel for the countryside; she thought of it, if she thought at all, as dark, damp, and faintly threatening. The nearest part of countryside to Muswell Hill, after all, was Epping Forest, a place of shallow graves and bodies discovered by early morning dog-walkers, and to Justine a beauty 'spot' had always meant a lonely place where young mothers were battered to death while their toddlers watched. At eight or nine years old she and her nearest sister, Rowena, would spin off down to Wormwood Scrubs on their bicycles to wheel them along the canal bank, where brambles grew in the shadow of the vast, rusting gas tanks that rose and fell mysteriously, and pages from dirty magazines were scattered among the reeds. It was as wild a place as anywhere she'd seen since, and the presence of vegetable growth – the coarse grass with its pornographic secrets, and weed like drowned hair just below the oily surface of the canal – had never seemed to Justine a sign of life, but of corruption.

Even as an adult, Justine didn't volunteer to leave the city; the walks she endured with her mother on visits to Essex were either through a dismal wood beyond the village, slimy underfoot with rotting vegetation, or along a river path where they had to pick their way in chilly, damp air through dog-turds in various states of decay. Here, though, it was different; perhaps it was the emptiness, or the foreignness of it: the warmth of the air, the quality of the light or the sweet smell of dry leaf mould that hung in the dusty air, but Justine found it exhilarating. There was almost no sign that anyone had been before them, or at least no sign that Justine could read, and it stood silent and untouched, like a prehistoric forest.

Between the trees out at the back of the house she saw a fire-circle, ringed with logs, and thought how much Lucien was going to enjoy himself. Lucien liked the countryside, although he had never lived there; he was always wheedling to buy a wreck a long way from London, somewhere unspoilt like Dorset or Shropshire, and plant a vegetable garden.

The house they lived in now was Lucien's, the same Notting Hill house where they had stumbled over his experiments in art on their first night together. Lucien had bought it when he had left university with a matured trust fund, and it was worth a bomb nowadays, or so everyone was always saying when they knew what it had cost him. It was a small Victorian terraced house with an old plum tree in the front garden, a pale blue-grey stucco façade and floor-length windows beneath a delicate verandah. The dainty glazing bars on the long windows were fragile with age but they were original, as were the pre-Raphaelite stained glass panels in the porch; it was shabby but beautiful, and in a part of London Justine could never have otherwise hoped to live. She loved it so much that she sometimes found herself surprised by a twinge of envy that Lucien should have come by it so easily; she wished it was hers, really hers.

Justine had never earned enough to buy a place of her own, and with prices these days it was quite out of the question. It worked well: a fair division. Lucien did the housekeeping, cooked, cleaned (after a fashion) and provided them with a roof over their heads; Justine earned the modest cashflow. They had a nice circle of friends and they lived in an interesting part of London, thanks to Lucien; they could go to parties two or three times a week if they wanted and Notting Hill was full of bars and clubs. Sometimes, to satisfy Lucien's longing for a rural existence, they went away for weekends, staying in a borrowed cottage in Norfolk (Lucien was good at that, calling in favours and offering house exchanges) or Dorset. Lucien would cook up something rich and foreign, a carbonnade or a daube, and they would go on frosty walks. And in the week, coming home from work after half an hour strap-hanging on the tube to find the house warm and full of the smell of new bread, or herbs and wine, Justine felt pampered, and loved. Justine's workmates thought it was the perfect arrangement; it was funky, and modern, it was empowering to be the breadwinner and it'll be great, they said, when you have kids.

It wasn't that Lucien couldn't get a job; he was, everyone always said, one of the most competent people you could imagine, say, in a desert island sort of situation. He gardened, an interest that he had developed from very little knowledge when an old school friend had offered him a couple of weeks covering a gardening column for someone on sick leave on Tom's paper. He made it work, though, keeping their small household supplied with ruby chard and cavolo nero out of the tiny back garden throughout the winter, making jam from the damsons on the tree at the front. Justine remembered suddenly that Lucien had once become quite annoyed with Tom for suggesting that his damson jam might have quite a high lead content, given the proximity of the North Circular to their front garden, and wondered whether that was the cause, or just a symptom, of their mutual dislike.

Although Lucien had never completed his engineering degree – he had been sidetracked by a newly discovered passion for wood and had broken off to do an equally short-lived apprenticeship for a cabinet-maker – he would probably be able to construct a decent shelter. He was not like most men, that was the impression Justine had first formed of him when she had met him at the Fanes' house and that was what had seduced her, that and his blue-green eyes. He didn't talk about his job, or his car, or television, he talked about growing things, making things with his own hands. The feeling that she had Lucien's undivided, passionate attention was quite new to Justine, who had spent her school life feeling as though she was being jeered at for her studiousness, her eccentric siblings or her mother's artistic dress sense. Although there had, as her sisters knew but hadn't told her, been boys who had fallen in love with her, none of them had been brave enough to say anything, so she never found out. So when Justine had suddenly felt Lucien looking at her the effect was as though she had drunk something strong and sweet that had gone straight to her head. He was so warm, so exuberant, so heedless. He was irresistible.

Justine sometimes tried to imagine Lucien working in an ordinary way, with all the compromise and wasted time that involved, pretending to agree with a boss he would inevitably despise; Lucien wanted time to spend getting things perfect. And if that was a luxury not many people could afford, it was still a principle that was difficult to fault, or so she persuaded herself.

*

52

The house was empty; downstairs in the kitchen just the memory of coffee lingered in the air and a cup of dregs stood on the table. Justine walked out into the sun, still in her cotton dressing gown. This was a holiday, after all. Angus and Sam were hanging upside down from the fence, over by the barn, and they waved at her, without righting themselves. It was hot already, and she wondered what the time was. Lucien walked out of the wide front door of Tom and Louisa's half of the cottage, and smiled at her indulgently.

'Hello, darling. Sleep well?' He looked her up and down, still in her dressing gown.

'Yes, lovely,' Justine answered. 'Where is everyone? How long have you been up?' She looked around.

'Oh, you know. A couple of hours.' He spoke lightly, but she knew it was important to him, that she should have been asleep while he got on with things. Although she couldn't imagine what things, exactly. He went on, 'Tom and Louisa are inside, I think, sorting out some stuff for a picnic. Dido and Martin have gone for a walk, looking for the river. They went a while ago now'

Justine looked across the open pasture, to a distant fold in the trees to the south, a darker place that might or might not have been a path leading between them.

'He sort of pointed down there, last night.' She nodded across the field.

Justine was the only one of the group with more than a word or two of Italian; Lucien spoke impeccable French, prided himself on it, but was clumsy in Italian and so refused to try. He disliked being less than perfect at anything. So when they had called at the owner's house to be taken down to Il Vignacce and it had become apparent that neither Montale nor his wife spoke any English, Justine had been hastily chosen as their spokesman.

The farmer had been friendly enough, though he had gazed at Justine's chest for long enough to make her regret the low-cut sundress, and had asked them to follow him down to Il Vignacce. 'Strada sterrata,' he had said, peering into Justine's face to make sure she understood that this was not to be a smooth ride. His wife, fortyish perhaps, and not Justine's picturebook idea of a farmer's wife, was a small, hard-bitten blonde in designer sunglasses. Hauling on the collar of their huge dog, some kind of bloodhound the size of a large calf, she had looked narrowly at Justine, then at Louisa, who was sitting nervously upright beside Tom in the car. The dog had jumped and bellowed at the car ceaselessly before, with a final yank on its chain Signora Montale had turned on her heel and back into the great baronial hall of their farmhouse. It had been an unsettling beginning.

On their arrival at Il Vignacce the previous evening Montale had first instructed Justine to keep the rough wooden gates in the fencing closed against the grazing animals, shown her the gas tank, the electricity meter and two metal cages for rubbish, tucked away behind the house. Then as an afterthought he had mentioned the river, and pointed out across the field in the darkness to show her where they could swim. That much she could remember, but she had not asked for detail, assuming that in daylight it would be easy enough to see where the river was. However it was by no means clear now; a path led across the front of the house and then forked; one way led immediately into the woods, the other went off at right angles, skirting the trees along the pasture.

Lucien made a rueful face. 'Well, they went that way,' and he

pointed the other way, where the path led downhill and immediately into the woods around the house. Justine shrugged.

'Well, I don't suppose you can get lost as easily as all that.
Not if there's a path to follow'

'I found a map, too,' said Lucien. 'On the wall inside.' He
turned towards the door and Justine followed him inside.

The room was cool, the windows at the back open to the
woods and letting the green light in. The big steel-shuttered
front door opened directly into the kitchen, which was all
Justine had seen of the house the night before; she wandered
on, through the sitting room in search of Louisa, while Lucien
began to manoeuvre the framed map down from the sitting-
room wall.

There was a bathroom, then a big bedroom off the sitting
room, and there Justine found Louisa bent over the bed sorting piles of clothes and putting them away. The room was
pretty; painted a vivid china blue, the ceiling was striped with
beams of some dark wood and rough, pale terracotta tiles
resting between them. It was not bright, but flooded with
a grassy light reflected through the window from the broad
pasture outside. Through the same window Justine could see
Angus and Sam sitting on the fence and jousting now with
sticks. Louisa squinted in the dim light as Justine came in,
then smiled.

'Did you sleep well?' Justine asked, looking around the
room. 'Everyone's been up for hours, while I was asleep.
Where's Tom?' She saw the smudged dark circle of a wine
stain on the marble-topped bedside table.

'Oh, somewhere,' said Louisa, carelessly, but her eyes were
averted. 'Supposed to be helping me sort stuff out for a picnic.
He has a habit of wandering off.'

Justine nodded absently. 'How are the others? Martin and Dido?'

Louisa frowned slightly. 'It's hard to tell,' she said, with a sigh. 'I didn't want, you know, to launch right in. Talk to them about Evie straight away. I mean, maybe they don't want to, I'm sure I wouldn't.' She sniffed. 'Anyway,' she went on, 'Martin just had a cup of coffee with us and he was straight off with Dido, he didn't seem very keen on hanging around to chat. But there's plenty of time.'

'Mmm.' Justine felt a pang of disquiet at the thought of Martin's predicament – and Dido's, come to that, although she might feel differently – stuck out here in the middle of nowhere, the focus of all their sympathy and curiosity for the duration. She might have said something, but then Lucien called her from the next room.

'Come on,' he was saying, with satisfaction, 'here we are. I've found us.'

Chapter Five

The hospital where Paolo Viola worked stood on a gently sloping hillside on the northern edge of Rome, and was one of a
handful of hospitals serving the historic centre and the towns
in the city's northern orbit. A long building of some eight
storeys high, the hospital had first been built in the nineteen
thirties, when the deep balconies along its eastern face had
surveyed terraced gardens with a distant view of Rome, but
now suburban development had eaten away at the land, and a
four-lane arterial highway hummed beneath the walls.

Higher up the hillside, though, a handsome, decaying
villa was still visible through its overgrown garden, once
the summer house of some extinct ducal family, and this
was the view from the staff room on Doctor Viola's ward.
As he collected his jacket and battered leather briefcase from
a metal locker Paolo looked up through the grimy window
at the fading red plaster of the old building's façade, almost
obscured by a great fig tree still heavy with unpicked fruit that

was now turning black and withered. A balustraded balcony missing a pillar or two overlooked the rear of the hospital, but in eight years Paolo had never seen anyone appear on it, unless you counted the wild cats that roamed the grounds. He thought of his mother and her own little terrace on the edge of the wilderness and sighed, another furrow appearing on his already rumpled forehead. He felt chilled, bone-weary, and decided he needed a coffee before he set off. But the aluminium pot on the staff room's electric ring was cold, and he pulled on his coat, picked up his bag and took the lift down to the hospital bar.

Tucked away on the first floor in a windowless corner of the hospital the bar was run by two women, Katia and Nicoletta, one pretty, one not, but both sharp-tongued and sardonic, always raising their eyebrows at each other as they shared some secret joke that Paolo generally interpreted as being at his expense. There was also a henpecked barman who did not speak unless spoken to and kept his eyes on his Gaggia. One of Paolo's patients, a mechanic from the city who'd broken both legs and his collar bone when a car fell on him, sat in a wheelchair by the door, unshaven, his neck in a brace and smoking meditatively. Paolo nodded to him and the man raised a hand.

Katia, the pretty one, was working the till; she was a dyed blonde, with sparkling blue eyes and frosted pink lips, wearing a white shirt with a bow tie. She pouted at Paolo as he asked for his espresso, calling him Dottore with exaggerated deference and winking at Nicoletta, who stood behind the pastry counter which, at this time of day, contained nothing more appetizing than a sticky, flaking croissant.

Refilling the cabinet with sandwiches for the lunchtime rush, Nicoletta was barely tall enough to see over the counter but she was straight-backed and strong as a horse, if her short forearms, ropy with muscle, were anything to go by. Her hair was spiky and dyed aubergine, with pale, heavy skin and capped teeth, and she bantered with Katia in an odd, high-pitched voice, breathy as a cartoon character's. No, wonder the barman keeps his head down, Paolo thought, not for the first time, as he took the thick china cup from the bar. How old am I, he thought, still seventeen, to be scared of these girls? After all, he could only go on blaming Livia for so long. And he winked at Nicoletta, who shot a glance at Katia, and giggled.

Paolo took his coffee to a zinc shelf against the far wall, where he was hidden by the heavy fluorescent coats of a group of ambulance drivers. They were winding down after a long night, drinking grappa. Paolo took out his mobile.

Paolo could hear that his mother was in the big kitchen by the echo on the line, and he knew that as soon as he rang off she would get out the eggs and the flour and start on the *agnolotti* and one of his favourite *secondi*, maybe a nice slow-cooked *stufata*. Sad, he knew, but after a couple of weeks making himself packet risotto at the end of a working day, or guiltily eating a sandwich standing up under the mocking eyes of Katia and Nicoletta, the thought of a day or two with his mother was infinitely comforting. Even if she would feel the need to interrogate him, again, about Livia's departure.

When he had said goodbye Paolo tucked the little silver phone into one of his pockets, took the cup back to the barman, who received it without meeting his eye, and nodded a gracious goodbye to the two women. As he walked out of the warm, smoky bar and set off downstairs Paolo could hear their laughter ringing behind him in the cold concrete stairwell.

*

In her kitchen a little more than a hundred miles to the north Anna was standing at the big kitchen table where her mother had made pasta for special occasions just like this one; birthdays, Christmas, feast days. The return of the prodigal son, not that Paolo had ever been a prodigal, not really. The table was topped with smooth, cold marble and had a groove in the wood along one end to hold the long rolling pin, also of marble, that was necessary to roll the pasta dough to the proper elastic fineness. The table top was floured and covered with fat crescent-shaped *agnolotti*, stuffed with veal and ham minced very fine; Anna had made too many, of course, but Paolo could always take some back with him to Rome, with a jar or two of sauce. People were always saying you could freeze fresh pasta, a notion she regarded with some suspicion, but the thought of Paolo returning home with food she had made comforted her in ways she could not fully articulate to herself.

Certainly these days, she decided, one never knew what an unscrupulous supermarket might put into their ravioli, and she suspected Paolo didn't pay too much attention nowadays to what he was eating. He wouldn't seek out a proper *pastificio artigianale* in the backstreets of Trastevere, where the pasta was rolled by hand and the stuffing made only from fresh ricotta or good cuts of meat. If such a thing still existed, Anna reflected sadly, thinking of the city she had once known. She wiped down her rolling pin, and weighed it in her hand considering, not for the first time, what an excellent weapon it would make if, as she was always being warned, a gang of *Albanesi* were to come calling in the middle of the night.

Anna set the *agnolotti* on a tray, cleaned the floury table and got started on the *stufata* that was one of Paolo's favourite dishes. She had a nice piece of shin of beef that she had bought the day before in Montequercio on a gamble that Paolo would be able to come, taken off the bone and cut into pieces. She chopped some shallots, a piece of pancetta very fine and a stick of celery, and set them on the stove to brown in a big enamel dish that had been her mother's, like most of the contents of the kitchen.

The house, too, had belonged to Anna's parents; it was where she had lived as a child with her parents and paternal grandparents on the edge of the forest. The family had for generations farmed a small piece of land between the house and Montequercio, to the northwest; perhaps two hectares of arable fields and a little bit of grazing that supported four or five dairy cows. Anna's grandfather had planted a few vines at the back of the house, where the soil was pale and chalky, not red with metalliferous minerals like the earth in the forest below them. Her father always said their vineyard was a little patch of soil that must have been cast up millions of years ago from the Val d'Orcia thirty miles to the east, where the best wine came from. It was God throwing them a little something over his shoulder, a handful of wine-making soil so that Montalcino shouldn't have all the best grapes. Their secret, the Violas' and God's. Montale worked the land now, a state of affairs that would have mortified Anna's grandfather.

In the front garden, overlooked by Anna's terrace, there were five little olive trees, silvery even in winter. Their fruit went to the co-operative oil press with everyone else's every December. A few buckets of olives went in, and a demi-john or two of oil came back, eventually. The same went for the grapes; it was subsistence farming more or less, but, with the vegetable garden supplemented by mushrooms and chestnuts from the woods below, they had managed between them.

61

The war barely affected them to start with, but after a year things changed, and the war was no longer something that was happening a long way away. The Germans arrived, and Anna's grandmother took to burying flasks of oil and wine to hide them.

Then one day in the late summer a young man had arrived at the house while Anna was in the vegetable garden picking beans before supper. His Italian was jumbled and he spoke with a peculiar accent, stuttering and over-enunciating his vowels and dressed in an odd mixture of clothes – green serge trousers, a worn striped shirt, a peasant's cap – none of them clean. Anna could still remember him as clearly as though it had only been yesterday that he'd walked out of the forest, a pleading look in his pale blue eyes. He had had untidy fair hair, thinning back from a high forehead although he was still young, only a few years older than Anna, she thought. His skin was a golden brown, not olive like an Italian's; he had spent the last six weeks, most of July and all through August, walking north and the back of his neck and the tops of his ears were burnt and peeling.

He had come from near Naples, he said, standing in the kitchen as the five of them stood around him. The Germans had a camp for prisoners of war there. He had escaped with three other prisoners one night, just by running the wire when they calculated that the guard was looking elsewhere. Two of the others had been shot before they got over the fence, and he hadn't seen the third since Rome, where they'd decided to separate, for safety's sake. He'd tried to take a train just north of the city, but had panicked when he saw the grey of soldiers' uniforms on the platform. He was without papers, naturally, and could not risk any confrontation with the

Italian authorities or the German troops, so he began to walk. Anna had thought of him walking all that way, and she could not imagine it. She looked at his feet, in heavy boots white with dust, and considered how long it took her to walk into Montequercio, no more than seven or eight kilometres from her home. She thought of having to do almost a hundred times that distance in a country far from her home, and she felt sorry for the prisoner as he stood between them and pleaded.

Anna's parents and grandparents had gone off together into the front room, looking serious. They left her in the kitchen with the young man, where she could hear them whispering fiercely next door. Sitting on the rush-seated chair that still stood beside the back door, he had tried to smile at her, but there had been something so desperate in his look that she just stared down at her hands. They had come back in and taken him outside to the granary at the back of the house, and she hadn't seen him again. She had heard the noise, though, shouting and banging when the Germans came a few days later to see how much grain the Violas had harvested and found something else besides.

You had to keep something hidden – oil, wine, chestnut flour – her mother told her, just in case they turned up looking. Perhaps in the panic of the moment of the escapee's arrival it hadn't occurred to her parents that the soldiers might come looking in the granary at this time of year, or perhaps they thought the young Englishman would be gone in a day or two and the risk was a calculated one. In the granary, at least, they could say he'd found his own way in there, they hadn't helped him. But, as it turned out, the enamel plate with olive stones and a crust of her grandmother's bread on it, that the soldiers tripped over in the dark when they opened the big wooden door, gave the game away as certainly as if they'd found the escaped prisoner drinking coffee in their kitchen.

And that was how Anna's childhood came to an end. On a September morning much like this, with the trees still dark around the house, grapes on the vine and the last of summer in the mild air, she had watched from an upstairs window as the soldiers led her father and the young Englishman away, not towards Montequercio but down the dirt road into the woods, towards Il Vignacce and the river. She could see her grandfather hold tight to her mother's arm to prevent her from running after them, and her grandmother's face stony with grief as she watched them go. When the soldiers came back they were alone, and since that day Anna had not been down that road, not all the way to its end.

The house was cold and silent in the days following her father's disappearance, and Anna's grandparents and her mother talked in whispers. Anna wanted to go into the woods and look for him, but she was not allowed to leave the house and at night she heard her mother weeping in the bed beside her. Her grandfather went out, though, two nights after her father had been taken, and had come back at dawn with dirt under his nails, his eyes red-rimmed with lack of sleep, or something else. Three days later a German convoy was ambushed on the main road nearby with a homemade mine. Rumours ran around Montequercio about who might have been responsible, and suddenly more soldiers arrived. A platoon commandeered the presbytery as a military post and groups of them were to be seen in the bar, challenging anyone they didn't like the look of. They didn't come back out to the Violas' farm, though: perhaps they were biding their time, or perhaps they thought they'd flushed out the subversive element there.

On the Sunday two weeks after Anna's father had been taken, a handsome woman in city clothes appeared at the house. Her name was Eleonora Vannucci, a cousin from Rome, and Anna's mother had been expecting her. They drank small cups of coffee at the kitchen table and ate a cake Anna's mother had made for the occasion, talking in hushed voices that sporadically were raised with emotion. Anna's mother and grandmother appeared to be in disagreement over whatever was under discussion, while their guest acted as mediator; Anna could hear her speaking in a soothing, reasonable voice to Anna's mother when she seemed on the point of tears, although she could not make out the words.

Anna's grandfather stayed outside, smoking; she could see him from her window, pacing between the olive trees. Then they called Anna into the kitchen. The war, it seemed, changed everything. Montequercio had become a dangerous place for their family, who had lived there for generations, and Anna was to go back to the city with Signora Vannucci. She was to be apprenticed at sixteen years old, as a seamstress to an atelier in the city.

Signora Vannucci had offered to accommodate Anna among her own family, to feed her and act as her guardian for as long as she was away from home. The family apartment, though, was at odds with her cousin's smart clothes. On the ground floor of a crumbling tenement below the walls that ran along the Tiber at the heart of the city, it was dark and damp and it smelt of drains all year round. The stove was dirty and there always seemed to be a crusted pot sitting on it, a reproach, reminding Anna of her mother's scrubbed and spotless kitchen and making her feel queasy. In the summer the air was thick with mosquitoes. Anna's bed was a small cot behind a curtain

65

in the kitchen, but she worked too hard to spend much time there.

The city was full of Germans, but Anna spent her days up high above them in an attic in Trastevere that contained four trestle tables, two highly polished sewing machines and a wall stacked with rolls of cloth and trimmings. The seamstress under whom Anna was to learn the trade was more of a businesswoman than a worker herself, these days, a well-built woman with heavy red gold in her ears and five girls doing the sewing for her. Two of these were more accurately described as mature women than girls, and were motherly towards Anna, for which she was grateful; the atmosphere was not unlike school, in fact, strict silence with occasional outbursts of gossip and laughter, and Anna found it easier to settle to the work than she had expected. She stayed in the attic workroom nine hours a day, embroidering flowers, sewing invisible boning into bodices and beading on to silk crepe for wedding dresses and evening gowns. Somebody somewhere obviously still had the money to buy these things, and occasion to wear them; Anna never asked where they were to go.

She had found it hard to get used to the noise, at first; not just the cars and motorbikes, their spluttering engines amplified by the tall buildings and narrow streets, but the hard sound of foreign voices below the window, and steel-capped boots ringing on the cobbles when everyone else was inside under curfew. In the evenings as she walked home through the grimy, narrow streets Anna found herself longing for the soft outlines of trees and hedgerows and the long meadow grass around her, imagining them silver in the dusk and breathing out the scent of river-mist and dead leaves. And at night she dreamed of the silent forest, her mind played out scenes in which she ran from the invaders and hid among the bracken on the ridge and the hazel along the riverbank. Over and over again she escaped, she saved her father, her mother, her grandmother and hundreds of faceless prisoners and she ran and jumped from rock to rock and ran on again through the bent, twisted red trunks of the cork trees, looking for her home. She had always planned to come straight back, as soon as she could, but things changed.

Time passed and Anna couldn't leave, not just yet; she had no money saved, and her apprenticeship was barely begun. Her mother came down to the city on the bus once, but she looked so sad and small in her worn coat and darned stockings, bewildered by the traffic, the raucous city voices and the towering buildings, that Anna didn't ask her to come again. Anna's grandfather died, less than a year after Anna left, and her grandmother – his wife – found him among his vines, a pruning knife in his hand, dead as he reached up to rub the bloom off a heavy bunch of grapes. Anna went home for the funeral and if her mother and grandmother had said any word to her that they needed her she would have refused to return to the city. But they said nothing, only looking at her sadly, as though she had become a stranger and they weren't sure how to talk to her. The Germans were still in Montequercio, settling in as if they owned the place now; Anna felt as though she was slipping away.

After her grandfather's death Anna would return home for snatched days here and there, going back to Rome each time with cardboard suitcases filled with any eggs and ham and cheese that her mother had saved for her, because rationing meant that these things were almost impossible to find in the city. Anna suspected that the Vannuccis might have had this in mind when offering their hospitality to a country cousin, and certainly they all ate very well in the month or two following one of Anna's visits to Montequercio. But the time between trips home was long, and to begin with she felt her separation from the country very keenly.

On Sundays sometimes Anna would go for a walk in the Borghese Gardens, but although she liked to look out over the city she found it a sad, dusty place, every stone bench occupied by a courting couple and not much in the way of greenery. You could walk beside the Tiber in places, but that too was just an alien, polluted reminder of the rivers at home: the Ombrone and the Merse, so dark and cool and smelling of the forest. So Anna preferred, in the end, to wander in the market at Porta Portese on her day off, jostled by the crowds and pickpockets. The air was heavy with the rich smell of tripe cooking in onions and tomatoes, and a sour whiff came off the cheeses piled for sale at every corner. The din of hawkers and bartering customers deafened her, too, but at least it was a place that could never remind Anna of home.

As the war changed, the city became a terrible place. The English began to land in Sicily and then closer, at Anzio, and it seemed that the Germans would not, as they had boasted in the streets of Rome, simply throw them back into the sea. There was no food; people were starving in the streets, eating boiled shoe-leather and setting traps to catch larks and swallows in the parks. No one could say whether it was better to stay put or leave the city; there were dire warnings against returning to the countryside, where there were pockets of intense fighting and the Americans flew low over the hills, bombing the refugees as they fled the city. While she was unable to return home Anna was determined to save; that was her only goal, but gradually it became clear to her that her money was worth less every day. Finally there was nothing left to buy, for love or money. However hard Anna tried, after she had given the Vannuccis something for her keep (the few beans and rice and dried figs that constituted their diet now that she could no longer go home), there was nothing left.

Then, at last, after months of skirmishes and the daily drone of bombers over their heads, in a vast final conflagration, the war burned itself out. The retreating soldiers bombed some parts of Rome into ruins, but once they had gone and the smoke had cleared, although the streets were now filled with someone else's army, what remained was once again recognizable as their own city. A farmer who had come to town with black-market eggs brought Anna word that her mother and grandmother were safe, and, for the first time in months, she cried. Sometimes, later, Anna thought she should have gone back home then, but she had nothing to offer them; she had saved nothing. She gave the farmer a bolt of cloth that she had been given in lieu of wages to take back to her mother and asked him to tell them that she was safe, too, and would visit as soon as she could. He didn't seem surprised that she was staying, but just nodded.

'Best to stay for a bit, eh? There's nothing out there in the country at the moment, the Germans took everything they could lay their hands on, hard enough feeding themselves just now I should think.' And Anna, biting back a retort that the city wasn't exactly paradise, either, had agreed.

Things did look up, though, and it didn't take long. Once the war was over, everyone who had a penny put by seemed to want a new dress, one with a tiny waist and a big skirt, just like they were wearing in Paris, so it was said. They wanted little jackets with hidden padding in the shoulders, beading on the lapels and embroidery on the pockets, pearl-buttoned chiffon blouses and figured silk cocktail frocks with sweetheart necklines, and trade became brisker than ever. The mistress of the atelier praised Anna's work, looking at her sharply for any sign that her best worker was homesick and exclaiming over the neatness of her stitching.

The truth was that Anna had begun to enjoy her work; she realized that she did, indeed, have a talent, and that afforded her some satisfaction. And after the war years when nothing but cheap stuff was delivered to the atelier and they had to make do with that and whatever they had put by the materials improved, too. For years the woollen cloth they could get hold of had been handwoven on wooden looms in the mountains, the weave coarse and uneven and it didn't wear well at all, but even that had been in erratic supply. But then things began to change; it didn't happen overnight, but surprisingly soon after the English and American soldiers had swept through the country and the ships and trains began to run through Europe again, rolls of machine-made cloth began to turn up, and of a quality Anna had never seen before.

The room in which Anna worked was suddenly flooded with brilliant colour and seductive texture. Satin-backed crepe, heavy and slippery as water; alpaca and merino from Milan; French silk velvet and Swiss lawn so fine it was almost transparent, the rolls of cloth all stood in ranks almost covering the walls of the workshop. Boxes filled with tiny bugle beads, silvered glass baubles from Murano and buttons of jet and cut crystal appeared. Reels of coloured thread and skeins of embroidery silk, and the travelling salesmen who brought them had the spring back in their step even as they hauled their cardboard suitcases up the stairs to the fourth floor. So Anna, who in her heart of hearts knew that there would be no market in little Montequercio for the skills she had acquired so painstakingly, had stayed put. Soon the sense of having betrayed someone – her mother, or herself, or perhaps even the forests and fields of her childhood – faded, although it never quite disappeared. And when the attic flat next door to the atelier came up at a good rent, she moved out of the Vannuccis' kitchen and into her own place.

The apartment was small, of course, no more than two rooms with a door between them, but it was a palace compared with the Vannuccis' place, and actually quite sizeable by the standards of the time. Anna would never have got the chance to rent it if her employer, suspecting Anna's dissatisfaction with her living conditions and fearing that she might run away home, had not put a word in with the landlord, and quite likely paid him a little something up front too. The floors were dark cotto, red, thick with wax and undulating where they had been worn down or the old building had moved. But Anna could still remember to this day the joy of closing her own front door behind her, watching the dust motes dance in the sun that poured through the windows, breathing in the clean, dry smell of her own home.

She had scrubbed the place until every surface gleamed; she polished the windows with a rag and a drop of vinegar in the water, scrubbed the floors and the cracked white tiling in the corner that served as a kitchen until her hands were red and blistered. She had washed the window-frames and the shutters, cleaned out the gutter outside her window, pulled down the cobwebs from the rafters, and even climbed a ladder to clean the beams overhead. She had no furniture of course, to begin

71

with, although there was a little terracotta stove for cooking and warming the place, and the *padrone* had left her an old iron bedframe. It squeaked and had no springs, only a kind of arrangement of interlocking wire hooks, but had been much improved by the purchase of a new mattress. Eventually she had picked up a chair or two, and a table, from the market at Porta Portese, and she liked the way the two rooms began to look. Everything was simple, and clean, and each modest item of furniture, a rush-seated wooden chair, a painted bedhead, a linen cloth on the table, represented a choice she had made.

Best of all, the apartment was at the top of the building; its small whitewashed rooms were full of light, and Anna was far from the mosquitoes, the smell of drains and the intrusion of footsteps always overhead or in the street. Each room had a window looking out over the rooftops to the south, the curved backs of the terracotta tiles slanting this way and that as far as the eye could see, a palace or a church here and there pushing its profile above the houses of ordinary people. Anna would stand there in the early morning, watching the sun rise over the Villa Borghese, the slice of river gleaming silver off to the right and far below.

Naturally no one had approved, particularly not Anna's mother and grandmother, who considered it extraordinary, if not immoral, that she should want to live alone, but there wasn't much they could do to stop her. Anna had a mind of her own, and always had, they agreed. For their own part the two older women had stayed on in more or less peaceable companionship at the farm together. They still tended the vegetable garden and harvested the olives themselves, although they had given over the farming of the land and the care of the vines to Piero Montale's father in return for an annual rent.

By now Anna knew what she wanted, and she knew she would be able to pacify her mother, in the end; she was almost thirty and she had had enough of living in the Vannuccis' kitchen. Cousin Eleonora and her husband had always been kind to her, in a perfunctory sort of way, and she knew they had once needed the money she brought in, but they needed it no longer. She had seen off the advances of the oldest of her cousin's sons, Giannino; her second cousin once removed, he obviously considered the family connection to be distant enough for intimacy to be acceptable, even if Anna didn't. And if Anna couldn't have the freedom the hills and fields around Montequercio would allow her, at least she could have her own place in the city.

In a way, of course, Anna's mother had been right about the hazards of a woman living alone. If Anna had not had her own place, she wouldn't have ended up with Paolo, either. But then there were so many pieces to that particular puzzle. If the Germans hadn't killed her father and the war hadn't changed things, if she hadn't been a good seamstress, if Cinecitta had never been built and the film stars had not come to Rome, if she had been blonde not dark, rich not poor, then Anna would never have met Paolo's father. The same variables as applied to every union, in fact. Where Anna considered herself fortunate was that, with her own place, she had managed to keep Paolo, whereas a more dependent woman, a woman more closely observed, might have lost him.

Standing in the old kitchen over her mother's pan and stirring, Anna shook her head fiercely at the memory. She had never wanted a husband and she certainly hadn't wanted a baby, not at thirty-eight. But of course when he had arrived she wanted him right enough.

The onions were beginning to brown on the stove and Anna put in the pieces of beef, half a jar of her own tomatoes, marjoram and a glass of wine. She put on the pan's heavy lid and turned the heat down low, wiping her eyes with a corner of her apron, and tutting. Onions. The *stufatina* needed two hours or so, which was just enough time for Paolo to get from Rome to Montequercio. Anna took off her apron, picked up her cushion and went outside to the terrace, where the sun would dry her eyes for her, while she waited.

Chapter Six

By the time Martin and Dido arrived back from their search for the river, Louisa, Tom and the boys had left for their picnic in the opposite direction, up into the woods in search of adventure and a ridge with a view. Lucien was looking for firewood among the trees above the house; Justine could see his dark shape moving against the pale trunks from where she sat, a book unopened in her lap. She had found some deckchairs stacked below the stone stairs, their striped canvas bleached almost white by many seasons' exposure to the elements. Her sleeves pulled down, her face shaded by a wide brim, Justine sat in the delicious, illicit warmth of the sun with her eyes closed and let her mind go as blank as the golden glare through her eyelids.

What would Evie be doing if she was here? She would be lying beside Justine in another deckchair, with Dido – too big for it but that wouldn't have bothered Evie – on her lap, arms around her neck. She would have been planning a shopping trip for them, subverting Louisa's cultural agenda, Tom's restaurant visit. Girls all together off to Rome or Florence in the car, Evie describing the perfect pair of shoes, shoes she knew she'd find in some back alley if she looked hard enough. Declaring how wonderful Italy was, the blueness of the sky, the sweetness of the peaches, how lovely it was to be all together. Feeling a prickle at the back of her eyes, Justine squeezed them together then opened them again in the glare. No one there.

Louisa had packed up some of yesterday's bread, tomatoes and supermarket ham and called the boys down from the fence, but Tom was still nowhere to be seen, so Justine had left Lucien still poring over the map and gone to look for him. She had found Tom sitting at the foot of a tree, hand curled around a beer bottle, looking up at the canopy of leaves glowing over their heads in the midday sun. He sighed when Justine sat down beside him, and looked up at her.

'Are they all ready?' he asked. The sound of the boys' excited voices, arguing over what they were to carry, was audible on the far side of the house.

Justine nodded. She thought of Tom's sons, who were so intent on the present, so uninterested in the adults. It had struck her when she saw them, as it often did with children – perhaps because she had none of her own – how remarkable a thing family resemblance was. How odd it must be, she thought, to be reminded of yourself whenever you look at your child. Like going back into the past; the temptation, as in science fiction, to change the future, to start all over again.

'They're lovely boys,' she said. 'Sam's very sweet to his brother, isn't he? And he looks just like you.'

Tom brightened. 'Yes,' he said, 'and Angus is just like

Louisa. Always rushing about, furious about something.' He fell silent again for a moment, and Justine wondered whether he hadn't understood they were all waiting for him, and she was going to have to pull him up bodily. But then he went on.

'How could it have happened, Just? She should be here too.'

Justine knew he was talking about Evie, and she shrugged helplessly. 'I know,' she said with resignation, relinquishing once and for all the hope that the holiday might have been a chance for all of them to move on. She sighed. 'I can't help thinking I should have listened a bit more carefully, she might have wanted to give us a clue she was unhappy. But it never occurred to me. Evie was never unhappy.' Justine frowned. 'Or that's what I thought.' She looked back towards the house, no longer sure.

Tom put the beer bottle to his lips and upended it. When he put it down again he was frowning. 'Well—' There was something in his voice, a note of hesitation, demurral, that made Justine lean forward, wanting to know what he was about to say. There was something confused in the look he gave her and for a moment Justine thought he was about to confess something to her. But then they heard Louisa calling from above them, a distinct edge in her voice now, and Tom shook his head.

'Time to go,' he said, and with a groan he stood up and walked towards the sound of his wife's voice.

Now they were gone, Tom and Louisa carrying their insulated bags and a rug up the dusty path while the boys scrambled behind them, and in her deckchair in the shade of the plum tree while Lucien went on with his wood-gathering Justine was thinking about Tom's state of mind.

Justine had known Tom well for almost fifteen years, on and off, and over that time she had learned to take his ebullient good temper for granted, and to grow very fond of him. She was on his rota of lunch companions, all of whom had to be willing to submit to minute interrogation on subtleties of flavour, restaurant decor and table service in return for a free meal – if not always a good one – in his cheerful company once or twice a year. Now she thought about it, the most recent of these lunches, perhaps five months earlier, had been less comfortable than usual.

The restaurant was brand new, open for less than a week but already trailed in advance by almost every column except Tom's. He had arrived late, and she'd had to wait outside for him, not knowing what name he'd used to book. Not for more than ten minutes but, still, Tom was never late. Once inside, against the bleached wood and sleek leather banquettes he suddenly looked old and uneasy, out of place in a way he'd never been before however modern the decor. The impression had been confirmed during the meal; Tom had been distracted, hardly paying attention to any of the details he was supposed to register. For once Justine had had to prompt him, offering her opinion on the menu, the atmosphere, the waiting staff, before it was asked for. The lunch had troubled Justine for some time afterwards, although she persuaded herself he must still have been recovering from a bout of flu Louisa said he'd succumbed to the previous month, just after Christmas.

Now, sitting in the warm shade, in a place where they should all have been at their most relaxed, Justine found herself wondering whether even that flu had been a disguise for something else. Since their arrival in Italy there seemed to have been a melancholy subtext to everything Tom had undertaken, even his efforts at bonhomie the previous evening. It occurred to Justine that she hadn't seen Tom and Louisa together for some time, and with a lurch she wondered whether their marriage was going wrong. She found the thought upsetting, and to her surprise she realized that she had always considered them a model of the attraction of opposites, or of the marriage that can survive the test of time and imperfection, even more than Martin and Evie's more mysterious, passionate union.

Justine liked to think that underneath Tom and Louisa's quarrelling, and their always obvious differences, there existed a mysterious elastic strength that held them together; love, or something. She was half aware that this was wish fulfilment; compensation for the fact that she knew no such thing bound her and Lucien, and that where she had always thought marriage indissolubly perfect, such as between Martin and Evie, it had turned out quite the opposite. Evie had disappeared from her perfect union of thirteen years; she had walked out one wet morning in late summer and had not come back.

Justine heard footsteps some way off in the wood, and opened her eyes. She saw Martin and Dido appear up the stony path below the house and shielded her eyes from the glare with her hand; when they came into view she jumped up, and her book fell to the ground. It was clear straight away that there was something wrong.

Martin was walking beside his daughter, and as they approached it became apparent that he was almost holding her up. Her head was leaning over towards him, and she was very pale, one side of her face drooping as though paralysed and her eyes half closed as if she was drugged.

Martin tried to smile. 'Migraine,' he said. 'At least I think so. It's happened before.'

Across the grass, up under the trees Justine saw Lucien straighten and look over at them.

Justine came around to Dido's other side and supported her; she felt clammy and cold to the touch. Surprisingly light, too, despite her height, as though Justine could have carried her single-handed, and she realized that Dido had hardly spoken a word since their arrival. She felt a surge of pity for the girl, her loneliness.

'Let's get her upstairs,' she said to Martin. 'Does it help if she lies down in the dark?'

Martin shook his head, helplessly, and there was something desperate in the look he gave her. She saw Lucien approaching across the grass.

'Come on then,' she said, and between them she and Martin carried Dido up the broad stone staircase. At the back of the house, their room smelled warm and aromatic, of old wood and sunlight. The shutters were pulled to but not closed tight, allowing a little dim light into the room. A bright blade of sun shone through the door as they entered and Justine quickly closed it behind them, as Martin laid Dido on the bed.

In the half-light Justine took in the fact that the room was tidy, the beds made and suitcases stacked in a corner. Not like a teenager's room. She knelt and carefully took off Dido's dusty sandals. The girl lay on her side, a hand across her eyes, and when her shoes were taken off she drew her knees up and made a small sound, as of pain imperfectly repressed. Downstairs Justine could hear Lucien moving about, but she didn't call out to him; she didn't even want to move suddenly.

'I'll get a bucket,' she whispered to Martin, 'In case she's sick.'

He nodded, but he didn't take his eyes off Dido's curled shape on the bed, and Justine tiptoed out of the room.

Lucien was standing at the foot of the stairs.

'What's going on?' he said, and Justine couldn't quite make out his tone; irritation, perhaps, or impatience. Distracted, she dodged past him in search of a bucket and over her shoulder she told him.

'It's Dido, she's got a migraine, or something. Whatever it is, it's knocked her out, poor girl. And I thought, maybe she'd need a bucket in case she throws up.'

Justine straightened from her position below the kitchen sink and held the fruits of her search out to Lucien: a plastic bowl.

Lucien took it from her with what looked like reluctance. 'I didn't know children got migraines,' he said, looking down at the bowl.

Justine shrugged. 'Don't ask me,' she said. 'But she's almost not a child any more, is she?'

Lucien nodded thoughtfully, turned with the bowl and headed upstairs.

From outside Justine could hear the sound of the Fanes' return; the boys' shouting, breathless as they ran downhill with their sandals skidding on the stones, and Tom and Louisa laughing, further away.

Tom was flushed with the walk, but looked cheerful, and Louisa was smiling. The boys were white with dust.

'We saw a wild boar, Justine,' blurted Sam, Angus pushing at him.

'I wanted to tell her,' Angus roared, pulling Sam over by

the hem of his sweatshirt. They rolled on the grass, Angus pummelling Sam, who laughed helplessly.

'Stop it,' said Tom, without turning to look at the boys, looking at Justine. 'What's up? Where are the others?'

'Upstairs,' she said. 'Dido's not well. Martin says he thinks it's a migraine. It came on while they were out walking.'

Justine saw a look pass briefly between Louisa and Tom.

'Come on,' she said. 'What?'

'Nothing,' said Louisa quickly. 'Just, poor girl, you know.' She turned to grab at Sam and Angus. 'Shut up, you two, Dido's ill. Go and look for wood, or something.' The boys fell silent, and Angus stopped punching his brother and rolled off on to the grass.

'We'd better go in,' Louisa said.

That first afternoon passed slowly. While Dido lay upstairs in the dark, silent house, as if by mutual agreement the others gravitated outside, and although nobody said anything it seemed to Justine they felt a communal reluctance to wander off too far. Perhaps it was the thought of leaving Dido alone, up there in the dim room, but certainly they were also subliminally aware of the days stretching out ahead of them, and the need to ration activities and excursions for the holiday to come. From below them in the trees, down where they imagined the river to be, the hollow, doleful clang of cowbells sounded intermittently. Tom, who was already flushed from the sun, sat beneath the pergola with his eyes closed and a beer bottle in his dangling hand. Martin sat at some distance from the others, on a stone ledge against the house, leaning against the wall and reading with silent concentration. Perhaps it was just her imagination, thought Justine as she looked at him, but

82

she felt a kind of negative energy coming off him, a resistance to their advice, their questions, their curiosity.

Justine and Louisa lay in the sun, side by side on the dry, scratchy grass in front of the house, leaning up on their elbows as they watched the boys playing a war game with Lucien. The boys were armed with water guns so disproportionately large that they ran at a tilt, the weight pulling them down to one side, and Lucien was chasing them. The three of them dodged silently around the house, the boys occasionally yelping as they slipped on the fallen fruit from the plum trees that littered the ground. Lucien wore a pair of old army shorts; all his clothes were already old when he bought them. Justine thought he liked to take on someone's else's life, somehow, by buying clothes with evidence of years of work, a life spent building bridges in Malaysia, perhaps, or running a tobacco farm in Africa. His smooth, bare chest gleamed with water as he ran past them, a muscular blur in the mist sprayed by the boys' oversized water pistols.

Lucien was strong; he never seemed to sit still at home, always moving things around, furniture, wood for his carpentry, digging in the garden; and as a result he had textbook muscular definition. Broad shoulders, curved biceps, flat stomach; you could see that Lucien liked the way his body worked, like a perfectly engineered and serviced machine. Justine watched him chase Sam and Angus, fast and intent like a hunting animal, and despite the smile he flashed when he saw them watching she could tell that to him this was not a game. Justine looked at Louisa, who was watching the three of them too, and smiling, and Justine knew what she was thinking. What a wonderful father he'd make. She sighed involuntarily and turned over.

Since their marriage Lucien and Justine had had the conversation – the one about having children – fifty times or more, in different guises, each one in a heavier disguise than the last. At first it was all very relaxed, or had seemed so at the time; looking back Justine wasn't so sure. Naturally enough she had assumed that they would have children; it was one of the few reasons people bothered to get married these days, even if Lucien hadn't mentioned them specifically when he proposed. Under the circumstances, which were idyllic – sitting side by side on a velvet cushion in their Venetian *trifora* window in the Danieli on a weekend away Lucien had spent months planning – it might have seemed unromantic if he had come up with so practical a reason for their marrying. Perhaps that was what she thought at the time, anyway. Perhaps that was why it didn't occur to her to make sure. For Lucien their marriage was about love, commitment to each other, celebrating their happiness, creating a perfect home together. Not about anything so mundane as reproduction.

It was perhaps a year after their marriage that Justine had made an idle comment one evening as they sat watching television together, her head on Lucien's shoulder. There'd been something on the screen about genetics, and she'd speculated about whether a child of theirs would inherit his green eyes or her brown. After a moment's silence – with hindsight of course that moment was freighted with significance, but even at the time she had noticed it, the heartbeat too long before he responded – Lucien had murmured something vague about double recessive genes, then changed the subject. Now, of course, she couldn't believe that they hadn't talked about it before, because it changed everything.

84

The realization that Lucien did not want children had crept up on her gradually, given Lucien's disinclination for direct confrontation, his desire to be the good guy. At first he had agreed that, yes, they would have children, of course, almost certainly, just not straight away. The house wasn't suitable for children, it had to be sorted out. A pretty little Victorian cottage, Lucien's house was full of junk with a half-built extension when Justine had moved in, a state of affairs that, over the years had changed but not significantly. She had felt a twinge of sadness when she left her Georgian bedsit to move in with Lucien, she had loved its high ceilings, crumbling plasterwork scrolls and acanthus leaves ornamenting the cornices, its single long window, although perhaps not the frowsty shared bathroom. It had been hers; she had thought that, in time, Lucien's place would become hers too, but as she looked back now, from this distance, it never had felt the same.

Justine had packed her few junkshop things in a box and taken them with her: a gold sunburst mirror, some chipped turquoise-rimmed plates decorated with rosebuds, an old flowered eiderdown; to date they had not been unpacked. But Justine had not moved, after all, because she wanted a new home, to arrange all her things about her and choose tiles. She had wanted to be with Lucien; she didn't think she could live without him.

Gradually, however, as she grew used to cohabitation, Justine became aware that this continued to be Lucien's space, not a shared one; his junk sculptures were usurped by half-built escritoires and experiments with marquetry, and the extension was built but remained unplastered. It still did not seem a place for a family; everything was his; he built it, at his own pace, he offered it to her, the kitchen with its smoothly sliding drawers and hidden cupboards, clever little niches and rails, hanging Venetian glass baubles and perilously lopsided chandeliers. All she could offer back were her wages, and she felt he was the benefactor, she the beneficiary, for a long time.

Although it was still not finished, the house was not squalid or uninhabitable; Lucien had a gift for arranging things so that they looked interesting: a work in progress, a collection of shells, or tools, a talent that was referred to as styling on home makeover shows, although it was not a word Lucien would have used. The garden was pretty, as Lucien had put a lot of work into it when he had his gardening column. It still looked very charming, although now all but the vegetable patch had become rather wild and rambling.

When they entertained, as they often did because Lucien liked to show off his cooking, he would put all his creative energies into the task: planning menus, laying the table, finding old linen napkins and bits of family silver, and their guests would marvel at the whole deal, the perfectly presented food and all the beautiful objects on display. Justine was proud of Lucien, and he would look at her with triumph after a particularly successful dinner as she cleared away, the guests gone home, as if to say, what a perfect life we have. But after a while, and when feeling low, Justine couldn't help thinking that the sorrel soup and homemade bread, the Indian wooden eggs, the rusty Victorian utensils and the smooth pebbles arranged on the floor were standing between her and a child.

Justine didn't want to replicate her own crowded family. The shrieks and feuds and grudges, the lack of privacy, and the necessity that she find her own way out of it all and into the light, like a plant in an essentially hostile environment, were all too fresh in her mind. Nor had she ever been aware of any physical instinct, the kind generally referred to as maternal, no yearning when she saw others' babies. It seemed to be something more primitive still than that, embedded in some inaccessible lobe or cortex, something connected with basic survival. When, as now, she was with her friends and their children, some of them like Dido, approaching adulthood, she felt herself slipping between generations, aware that she was neither old nor young, neither a daughter any more nor yet a mother, and soon she wouldn't be a grandmother, either. And despite herself, knowing as she did that to define herself or her friends by their biological function was demeaning and narrow-minded, she would be overwhelmed suddenly by a sense of her own pointlessness.

Justine didn't know, and still didn't know, why Lucien didn't want children; he had never admitted outright that he didn't and had therefore been able to avoid giving any explanation. Perhaps it was his own family background; most things, after all, came down to that; but examine it as she might – or what she knew of it, which was little – she could find no clue there. An only child of wealthy parents, he had had a privileged upbringing in an opulent Edwardian house on Barnes Common. His father was a stiff, dull, distant man, a partner in a big City firm of solicitors; he had shaken Justine's hand and asked what her father did. Lucien's mother was an heiress who, it seemed to Justine, suspected her husband of having married her for her money and who drank too much, and, on the only occasion Justine had met them, she had found her chilly. There was no leavening of humour in her, a tall woman swathed in bohemian splendour who lavished a great deal of querulous attention on Lucien, her only child, but addressed not a single question to Justine.

It wasn't that Justine envied Evie (or Louisa, or any of her other parent-friends) the sleepless nights, the mooning about Mothercare, or even the tiny, blinking, grimacing babies they held so tenderly, their opaque little eyes and soft mouths opening and closing like primitive sea creatures. What she wanted was their certainty, the look in Louisa's eyes, even at her most infuriatingly efficient, as she narrowed them to scrutinize Sam and Angus; the look she'd seen in Evie's as she looked down at Dido in the maternity ward. What they saw – or what she thought they saw, which was perhaps not quite the same thing – was incontrovertible proof of their survival: a baby. Justine was dimly aware that this desire for security might not be considered a good enough reason to become a parent; that the more loftily self-satisfied among her acquaintance might consider it an indication that there was something else wrong in her life that she should fix first. Which was the reason Justine never articulated it to anyone; that and an obscure sense of shame that she should want a child and should be unable to persuade Lucien that they should have one.

It was hot on the grass outside Il Vignacce, and Justine could feel the sun on her back through her T-shirt. Reluctantly she pulled her sleeves right down to her wrists; she knew she should go into the shade, but sometimes she so missed the sun. She felt as though she was being purified, burned clean in the dry heat. The only sound was the scratching of the cicadas in the trees, pulsing in time with the heat haze that shimmered over the pasture; the birds had all fallen silent in the half-light of the forest, and Justine imagined the cows, which they had not yet seen, must be asleep in the shade. The pace of the water fight around the house was slowing, and, as Justine and Louisa watched, Lucien slipped into the house while the boys were around the back. They went on running all the same, around and around, pelting each other with plums for variety, and when Lucien did not reappear they seemed to run out of energy quite suddenly and collapsed in the shade of a tree, lying across each other like dogs.

Justine turned over and saw Louisa looking at her.

'So how are things? With you and Lucien?' Louisa asked. Her tone was light, but Justine could tell there was more to it than a polite enquiry. Louisa had known Lucien longer than she had, after all, and Justine had always thought she had a soft spot for him. He had that effect on women. Some women.

'Oh, you know,' Justine said reluctantly, trying to deflect Louisa's probing but unable to bring herself to utter a blatant lie.

'Mmm?' said Louisa, raising her eyebrows.

'Fine,' said Justine wearily. 'He's getting into this cabinet-making now, you know. He likes to have something on the go.'

Louisa nodded absent-mindedly. 'He is so clever at that kind of thing, isn't he? Easily the most creative man I know. It's . . . odd that he doesn't ever . . . want to go and make money doing it, don't you think? I mean, he could get a job tomorrow, couldn't he?'

Justine knew what she was getting at and decided not to give her any ammunition, not just yet. 'I think he will, with the cabinet-making, once it's up and running. It's a question of the word getting round, building up a client list . . .' She trailed off as she heard the lameness of her reply.

Louisa nodded. 'And I think it's such a good idea to put

off having children until you're sure. They are a total commitment, you know' She pulled a face. 'All that struggle to get your figure back, putting their names down for the right schools. And you've got a wonderful job, it's not as though you're unfulfilled, is it? You've got your lives so well sorted out, you and Lucien.'

Justine opened her mouth but said nothing, unable to decide which assertion to respond to first, and Louisa smiled at her from behind her dark glasses. And then Lucien came out of the dark interior of the house wearing a T-shirt. He looked over at the boys dozing in the shade and walked across to the two women, lowering himself down beside them on the grass.

'All right for some,' he said, and Louisa pretended outrage. 'We are on holiday, Lucien,' she pouted.

Lucien, leaning on his elbow, looked down at Justine with a half-smile. He smelled of grass and sweat and his blue-green eyes were almost luminous against the dark skin of his face.

'I thought I'd go off for a walk. I'm sure I saw some wild fennel growing higher up, when we arrived. This place is full of great stuff.' He looked at Justine for a half-second, but when she said nothing he directed his gaze back at Louisa.

'How lovely,' said Louisa. 'You mustn't do all the cooking, though, Lucien. I'll do it tonight, how about that? Or we could have a barbecue.'

Lucien shrugged. 'Fine. Whatever.' And he jumped up and with a wave headed off towards the wooden gate in the stock fencing, and the dirt road that led out of the valley, back towards civilization. Tom was still motionless, slumped in his deckchair beneath the pergola, but Martin raised his head briefly from his book and looked at Lucien as he vaulted the gate. Above him the shutters to the house were all closed against the heat and Justine wondered how Dido was doing.

The two women watched until Lucien disappeared from view, then Justine laid her head down on the grass, and with the warm sun on her cheek she pretended to sleep.

Chapter Seven

Anna had kept the shutters closed all day against the heat, and the dim room was deliciously cool. Paolo set the dishes from lunch down on the table and as his eyes adjusted to the light he looked around the room that he still thought of as his grandmother's kitchen.

The aluminium canisters of sugar and coffee and flour, the stone sink and the chipped green enamel gas cooker were all exactly the same as they had been in his childhood; his mother saw no need to change anything, to put in a washing machine, a dishwasher (just for my one plate and one glass? she would ask him when he made the suggestion) or a heating system. Montale would bring her logs for the stove in the back of his pick-up, and she would split them herself on a chopping block behind the house, unless Paolo was here to do it for her. He resolved to cut a pile that would last her, if not until his next visit, then at least for a week or so.

Paolo loved his mother without reservation. As a child he

had only slowly become aware that she was unlike other children's mothers in many ways, the least of which was that she had no husband. Even that wasn't so uncommon; there were plenty of young widows about in those days, but soon enough he had learned from his classmates, from the fact that some of the mothers were not so keen for him to associate with their sons, that there was something less acceptable about his own mother's single status.

Throughout his childhood Anna had treated him with careful seriousness; gentle and softly spoken, she never raised her voice against him except once – when he had stepped off the pavement in front of a car – and even then he had heard the anguish in her voice as she reprimanded him, and then burst into tears. Anna had always seemed interested in his thoughts and opinions, giving them serious consideration in any discussion, whether it was the reason for the sky's being blue, or the injustice of his not being allowed sweets, or to go to buy firecrackers with a school friend of whom she disapproved.

Anna had taken him with her to work, too, if he was ever off school with a bad chest, as happened some damp winters. He would sit quietly with his school books on a little stepladder that turned into a stool in a corner of the wardrobe lot in Cinecitta where she worked then, and he would watch out for film stars. Although mostly all he saw were extras coming in for repairs.

Their costumes, Roman tunics or peasant outfits that might be used a hundred times in different films, were rarely washed, presumably because the cinema audience couldn't smell them, and they had a peculiar odour, multi-layered, sweetish and musty, that made Paolo cough for all its exoticism.

Cinecitta wasn't what it had once been, even at seven or eight years old Paolo could see that, and the seamstresses spent a lot of time grumbling about its decline. There was little money for new costumes, and by then much of their labour consisted of unpicking and re-making old things, making do. The productions were vulgar, and close-up the props were chipped and peeling, their gold and red, their painted brick and clapboard fading in the sunshine, and the plaster on most of the great hangar-like buildings that accommodated the film sets was coming off in slabs. The studios seemed to the small boy like a great surreal necropolis, a graveyard full of the carcasses of old films, the bones of ancient Rome shoved up against the remains of a wild West saloon.

In the late forties, the years of *neorealismo*, Cinecitta had been a place of great Italian artists, passion and high principles. Then, after that, the money had come in from the Americans in the years after the war, when they weren't allowed to export currency from Italy and had to put it somewhere, and the studios became a boom town. He had heard the story from his mother, in fragments here and there; the Americans had come looking for good seamstresses in Rome and had found Anna, who had been finishing a spring suit for an American producer's wife at the time; a suit of violet shantung silk with amethyst buttons. She had been seconded from the workshop in Trastevere to make costumes at Cinecitta and had become one of hundreds of artisans and craftspeople – carpenters, plasterers, jewellers, watergilders, architects, painters, all drawn by American optimism and American money, but united by a kind of passion too.

'It was really like a city, full of life. Beautiful,' she would say, with a little smile.

She must have met his father there too, Paolo reasoned, and on his visits to Cinecittà as a boy he had looked out for him, surreptitiously. He knew Anna would have put a stop to such nonsense if she'd known exactly why he found the place so fascinating; the topic of his father was the one thing she sidestepped.

'You don't need to know, Paolino,' she would say, her face stubbornly opaque, looking down at her work. 'It won't do you any good.' Then she would look up, take in his expression of frustrated longing, and shake her head. 'You would only be disappointed, and it's not as if you could go and see him.'

His father was dead, that was what she always said, and sometimes he believed her. But the film studios were such a place of surreal invitation as to encourage his fantasies. Walking back to the station in the evenings they would pass actors heavy with make-up, cigarettes dangling from their fingers as they gossiped in costume, Egyptian slave girls or can-can dancers, the men lounging in groups in their spurs and stetsons or eating plates of pasta while they waited for their call to the set. It was a world in which the usual rules did not apply. Some would nod to Anna, or wave to Paolo as they passed, and he would feel the glow of their attention all the way home.

When he wasn't looking out for his father Paolo had liked to watch his mother sewing, a furrow of concentration between her eyebrows, her fingertips rough with pricking, a callous on her right ring-finger where her brass thimble rubbed the knuckle. She must have been in her late forties even then, but he had thought her very beautiful, with her fine arched eyebrows and serious expression, her small waist and rounded white forearms. And clever too, able to gauge the width of a seam by eye when obliged to disguise an actress's pregnancy, or to let out an evening gown for another who had put on weight. He sometimes wondered whether his mother wouldn't have made a fine surgeon, given the right education.

Through the door that led outside Paolo could see Anna's shadow moving to and fro, clearing away the remains of their lunch. His mother was slower in her movements these days. He registered this fact on each visit, although the pile of exquisitely embroidered napkins – for whom? he wondered – on the polished side table in her sitting room bore witness to her industry. Not that she had any choice out here, with wood to chop for the stove and snow to clear from the path; even the knowledge that chestnuts and mushrooms were now ready to be gathered in the next valley, Anna saw as an imperative, summoning her on a walk of four kilometres or more.

Although professionally Paolo was well aware of the benefits of exercise for someone of his mother's age he couldn't help but feel impatient with her boldness. He knew what might happen to her, so far from anywhere, if for example she were to slip while shovelling snow; he could visualize her bones as clearly as if he saw them on an X-ray screen, hollow and brittle as a bird's. Anna appeared in the doorway, silhouetted against the warm golden light, the vine leaves glowing as the sun shone through them above her head.

'Well,' she said, 'there's some English down at Il Vignacce, and so late in the season too. Shall we have a fire tonight?'

Paolo frowned at the apparent non sequitur. 'Mamma, are you quite well?' he asked. 'Are you cold?' The room was cooler than it was outside, but still, it had been like high summer as they ate their lunch on the terrace in the sun.

'No, no.' Anna sounded mildly exasperated. 'I was just thinking, it is September, they will be cold down at Il Vignacce, the sun goes so early. And even up here it's cool in the evening, and a fire is so nice, isn't it? That's all I was thinking, I'm not losing my marbles, not quite yet.'

Paolo's brow cleared, and he put an arm around his mother's shoulders, that had once seemed broad and strong to him, and now were as insubstantial as a child's in his embrace. 'You're right,' he said. 'I'll split some wood for you.' He paused, considering Il Vignacce, which he still thought of only as a heap of stones down by the river where Montale had some pasture, the cows cropping the tough grass that grew among the ruins.

'English down there? Well, they're supposed to be hardy types. And it's fine just now, eh? As long as it lasts.'

It was late, and down in the valley the black trees that towered over the old farmhouse were silhouetted against a sky darkening every moment, from cobalt blue to navy; Il Vignacce was in darkness except for the single light over the front door. The windows were dark, although not all of the shutters were closed; they had been opened for some air in the boys' bedroom where they lay asleep uncovered on their beds, their quilts tumbled together on the floor. They were open too at the back of the house where Dido was sleeping, soundly now, on her front with one hand beneath her body and the other hanging limply down to the clean basin that had been left on the floor by her bed. Her pale face, turned sideways on the pillow and facing the window, was smooth and peaceful; it had lost the odd, lopsided look Justine had seen earlier. The windows of Dido's room opened inwards and on their glass the reflection of a flame leapt and flickered in the dark.

The fire was burning strongly in the woods behind the house, casting the flickering shadows of the five adults around it against the slender trunks of the few trees illuminated by the flames. Four large slabs of wood, massive as railway sleepers, had been set perhaps by Montale around the fire, and on these Lucien, Justine, Louisa and Tom had arranged themselves. Martin was standing, leaning against a tree and looking into the flames.

Beyond them the forest seemed very dark, but not entirely still; the night was full of small sounds. Justine was lying on her back on the wood, feeling the warmth along the side of her body and looking up through the dark filigree of leaves to the blue-black sky beyond them. As she looked, one hand shielding her face from the fire's glare, she began to see the stars, more than she ever remembered seeing before. The air, still warm to Justine's northern skin, was electric with the trilling of insects and suddenly she felt outnumbered; how few the five of them seemed, huddled around their fire while out in the forest the dry leaves rustled with the tiny footsteps of a hundred different species and over their heads the sky pulsed with thousands of silent, winking stars.

Tom sighed contentedly, and Justine looked over at him. The children were asleep, they had all eaten a campfire supper of fat, spicy Italian sausages fried over a makeshift griddle, tomatoes and the remains of yesterday's bread, and a bottle or two of red wine from their dwindling store had been drunk. Everyone seemed tired, even after a day spent doing very little, and no one spoke. Perhaps it was down to the previous day's hard travelling, but Justine thought it was more likely to be due to the strain of co-existence, the small stresses attached to accommodating another set of adults and more; maybe this was why so much tranquillizing alcohol was necessary on holiday. And there was the worry over Dido, although she had seemed better on her brief reappearance among them. In her pyjamas, a boy's striped pair, she had seemed pale and very young as she came down for a glass of water, her footsteps soft and light on the wooden stairs. Dido had seemed a little shaky, but at least she no longer looked as though she was suffering.

Justine and Lucien had never really been away with other couples, bar the odd night spent under a friend's roof; Lucien liked intimacy, and he disliked crowds, and other people's children. (Justine always found herself justifying his inability to tolerate children in this way, as though he would like his own, although, she admitted in her gloomier moments, she had no proof that he would.) But before she had met him Justine, as a single woman without responsibilities, had often served as a useful last-minute substitute on various villa holidays with assortments of friends, at least once before with Tom and Louisa. In Justine's experience without benefit of wine on shared holidays a fight would break out within twenty-four hours, and as it was, most reached a low point after three or four days. It was around this time that the holiday accommodation suddenly turned from a perfect sanctuary into a grubby, untidy house just like the one they had left behind, and resentments – over cooking, over restaurant bills, over where to go in the morning – would have had time to reach the boil.

All the same, Tom's sigh seemed happy enough, so far. Leaning up on his elbow on his wooden bench he looked across at Louisa, her fair, skin glowing pink with the reflection of the flames.

'Where shall we go in the morning, then?' he asked.

'Well,' Louisa and Lucien both spoke at once. Louisa went first.

'We need to buy food,' she said. 'And wine. There's a super-market in the village, what's it called?'

'The village? Montequercio,' said Tom. 'It doesn't seem to be in the guide books, but it looked OK. From what I saw on Saturday, anyway. Didn't you think?'

'We don't want to do that drive too often, though, do we?' said Lucien. 'We should be able to stock up for several days at least, if we're careful.' He sounded enthusiastic. 'Get flour and yeast, I could get that wood oven going, make bread. Tins, pasta, that kind of thing.' Lucien leaned forward, elbows on his knees, and looked into the fire. Justine saw the reflection of the flames in his eyes, and she knew he was relishing the prospect of their – his – survival techniques being tested.

'Mmm,' said Louisa, doubtfully. 'What about fresh milk, though, we won't be able to get more than a day or two's supply of that?' Justine smiled with relief; like her, Louisa obviously didn't see subsistence rations as part of the perfect holiday. 'And fruit and salad, fresh things – the fridges are awful. They dribble.'

Tom snorted. 'And besides, we don't want to go stir crazy, do we? Or spend two weeks eating pasta and tomato sauce.'

Justine saw Lucien curl his lip. 'Come on, Tom,' he said, mockingly. 'Where's your sense of adventure?'

'Oh, adventure,' said Tom. 'The thrill of the foreign supermarket? Tempting, but no, thanks. I'm just a humble wage slave, we don't like adventure much. Not on hol-iday, anyway.' And he smiled, but Justine could see that both men were squaring up for a row. Already, she thought with exasperation, and caught Louisa looking at her. They exchanged weary glances.

'All right, all right,' said Justine. 'Tomorrow, anyway, we've got to go and get stuff.

'We – some of us, anyway – we can see what there is in the village. There might be a market; do you think Dido would be up to that?' She looked up at Martin, who had until then neither moved from his position nor spoken.

He nodded. 'Maybe,' he said. They looked at him. He sighed and went on. 'I think she needs some peace and quiet, for a while. If we ever find the river, just walks and a bit of swimming.'

'What happened, then?' asked Lucien curiously. 'This afternoon. You didn't find the river at all?'

Martin shrugged. 'Well, we found a trickle; we should have followed it, I imagine it would have led down to something more like a river. But there was a sign about a bull, and Dido seemed – anxious, so we cut across country for a bit. Then we took a while finding our way back to the path; it can be quite tricky, and I think she got a bit panicked. We had been walking for a long time, and I think she could tell I didn't know where we were. That's when she began to get the flashing lights in front of her eyes.' He stopped abruptly, as though aware of having fulfilled his obligation to deliver the information requested.

'OK,' said Tom kindly. 'We can take it easy for a bit. Justine seems to think the river was the other way, anyway. We'll find it tomorrow.'

Martin nodded, and pushed himself away from the tree. He stood over them for a moment. 'I think I'll go up,' he said. 'I don't want to leave her alone for too long. And I'm tired, too.'

At once they all agreed with him, nodding and wishing him a good night, and together they watched him go into the house.

For some moments no one spoke.

'Are you going to review any restaurants while you're out here?' Lucien asked Tom casually, as though to fill a gap. 'Tuscany must be stuffed with them. Get us all a nice blow-out on expenses?'

'Well, it's not quite that easy,' Tom said, amiably. 'But I'd be happy to treat you. There's a little trattoria in Florence I want to have a look at. There are some pretty good places in Siena, and I think Grosseto has one or two, as well. That might be an idea, it's a bit more unusual, Grosseto, off the tourist trail. Unspoilt, so I hear.' He pondered. 'That might make a nice trip. It's by the sea, too, so we could take the boys for a swim.'

'Nice work if you can get it,' said Lucien, and Justine thought she saw Tom look at him sharply. After all, Lucien was not on safe ground in that particular argument; she had no idea what he managed to do with himself all day, she realized, nice enough work, too. She wondered what was the matter with him, needling Tom like that. She said nothing.

Tom rested his head back on the wood and looked up at the stars. 'Someone's got to do it,' he said mildly. 'You'd be surprised how little fun it can be, sometimes.' Turning, he raised his glass to his lips.

'Do you think Dido's really all right?' said Louisa, out of the silence that followed.

'She did look awful, didn't she?' Justine said. 'I don't know anything about migraines.'

'My mother gets them,' Louisa said, shortly. 'Psychosomatic, if you ask me, in her case anyway. Certainly Mama's seem to occur at awfully convenient moments.'

'Yes,' said Lucien, thoughtfully. 'They can be a sign of underlying problems. I'm sure I've read that somewhere. Allergies, trauma, abuse. That kind of thing.'

'Abuse?' said Louisa.

Justine looked at Lucien disbelievingly. 'Lucien,' she said, a warning note in her voice.

'I didn't mean—' Lucien looked around, avoiding Justine's eye. 'But you have to say, she's not in an ideal situation. Their relationship is – well, intense, to say the least. And let's face it, if it had been the perfect family Evie would still be here, wouldn't she?'

'Bloody hell, Lucien,' said Justine. 'Shut up. Dido's lost her mother. Martin – can you imagine what that feels like? Migraines would be the least of it. The way Evie died too. Dido must feel absolutely abandoned. What's Martin supposed to do, send her to boarding school?'

She could have gone on, but saw them all looking at her, and closed her mouth with a snap. Feeling a stinging behind her eyes, Justine lay back down and stared up through the trees.

'She's right,' said Tom, after a moment. 'Let's give them a break, shall we?' And Justine heard something in his voice, something more than friendly counsel.

'OK, OK,' said Lucien. He didn't sound repentant, just placatory. 'Sure. Maybe he'll warm up a bit, give us a chance to help.'

For a long moment or two they all fell silent, the only sounds the hiss of the fire, not much more than embers now, and the singing of the insects over their heads. Justine swung her legs down and got to her feet.

'I'm going to bed,' she said, Lucien nodded with a half-smile but he didn't follow her.

And as Justine walked past the silent house she looked up and saw that the window of the room where Martin and Dido slept stood open. Inside all was dark.

Chapter Eight

'I'm going into town, *caro*,' Anna called up the stairs in the bright morning light. 'Just to catch the market. Anything you want?'

'No thanks, Mamma.' He sounded awake, but tired.

'Go back to sleep, darling,' she said. 'I've filled the coffee pot, you just turn it on.' And she closed the door softly behind her as she left the house.

Anna Viola had postponed learning to drive, like a few of life's other milestones, until it was almost too late. When her mother had died, eighteen years after her grandmother, Anna had been sixty-two, and she had known that either she would have to sell the house in the country or move back there, and if she moved back, she would have to learn to drive. It didn't occur to her that anyone would think that her age would disqualify her for the task and if it had, it would not have bothered her. As it turned out Anna had got her *patente* without fuss, and bought herself a tiny car, a red Fiat 500 that still served her very well for trips to the market or the shops once or twice a week and the occasional long haul back to Rome, although she had not done that for a while. This morning the car had warmed up nicely in the sun and started first time, and Anna bounced and jolted down the lane towards the main road and Montequercio.

Having passed her test, all that time ago, Anna had told Paolo that she was going to leave Rome. He was still at home, anyway, sleeping on the same hard single bed in the little bedroom under the eaves where he'd slept since he was six months old and Anna had reluctantly moved him from her side. Anna had the impression, although he'd said nothing to her for fear of hurting her feelings, that Paolo had been thinking about looking for a place of his own for a little while – since girls had entered the equation, in fact. He had just got his first job as a junior casualty doctor in a city hospital, and almost straight away he'd begun to go out with Olivia, who worked as a technician in the pathology labs in the hospital. He'd met her in the hospital bar, where she'd asked him to light her cigarette; it had been obvious even to Anna that she'd picked him up, though Paolo didn't seem aware of it at the time.

All the same, Anna had been gratified to see Paolo look a little lost when she announced her decision and the realization that he was on his own at last began to dawn. She was pleasantly surprised, naturally, that his first thought had not been of the freedom her decision would afford him. But he had got used to the idea of his mother's departure quickly enough, and when the time came he had helped her to load the few possessions she wanted to take – not much really, to show for all those years of work; her clothes, of course, all handmade, a few rugs, a lamp or two – into the little red car. And Anna had come back home at last, to the empty house on the edge of the forest, after forty-five years away.

It was odd, really, that it still felt like home, Anna thought now as she drove through the trees towards the main road. The golden light slanted down on to the road ahead of her, shifting like water as the leaves moved in the breeze. But then sometimes Anna still felt like a sixteen year old herself, as though the years between had left no trace, except Paolo. She had spent almost twice as long in the city but its comfort and its charm had slid off her like water. All she had ever wanted was to be back here.

Set on a rounded hill top on the edge of the densely wooded region of Tuscany south of Siena known as the Alta Maremma, Montequercio was ten minutes from Anna Viola's house by the fast main road, but closer to twenty-five from Il Vignacce. More like a large village than a town, the population of Montequercio was a mere fifteen hundred souls, which was not much more than it had been when Anna had been a child. The village was picturesque enough, but too remote, down poorly maintained country roads that wound in and out of valleys and spurs, to have ever found an established place on the tourist map.

The Maremma, a place of marshland criss-crossed by Roman drainage channels, wild dark valleys and inaccessible charms, did not figure large on the tourist map. It could not compete with the smooth chalk-grey hills of the Val d'Orcia, each one, it seemed, topped picturesquely by a country chapel and a couple of cypresses, with the pretty villages tumbling down the hills around the Val di Chiana nor with the vineyards and castles of Chianti, but it did have its own select band of admirers. In recent years the inhabitants of Montequercio had been taken by surprise by a small but regular and increasing number of visitors, perhaps because unadulterated nature was gaining in popularity, or because they were simply running out of room elsewhere. Local opinion was ambivalent as to the usefulness of tourism to the region, their quiet, secluded, pristine forest. Some were genuinely hospitable, others supposed it was as good a way as any to make money, but there were those, too, used to the peaceful monotony of country life, who found the incomers arrogant, inconsiderate and intrusive.

At any rate, Montequercio presented an unusual aspect to visitors; the tall brick houses that ringed the hill's summit formed an unbroken wall and they all faced inwards, presenting only their blank rear walls to the outside world, so that the village seemed to turn its back on strangers. From the road that passed beneath them the faded red walls, marked only here and there by a shuttered window to show that they were not ramparts but houses, looked distinctly unfriendly. On closer inspection, however, the fortifications could be entered easily enough through one of three gates, and once inside the village revealed itself. Anna indicated to turn inside.

Just within the walls there was a large oval piazza containing a monument to the fallen dead of two world wars and another, stuck with faded portraits, to the partisans, some car parking spaces and two bars, facing each other on opposite sides of the market place. The old red brick houses that ringed the piazza were in varying states of disrepair; some had the remains of painted render crumbling away from their façades while others had none left at all and only a few had been the subject of any restoration. Here and there a house had been done up with new green metal shutters and window boxes bright with geraniums, but mostly they were warped and faded wooden ones, and the overall impression was of a sleepy town, unused to offering itself up for inspection.

After a leisurely drink and a wander around the piazza the small number of visitors to Montequercio, which did not figure in many guidebooks, would walk on in search of what else the village might have to offer, but they found only quiet, shuttered alleys, and few signs of life. There were a couple of *cantinas* offering cases of wine, Chianti Classico or Brunello di Montalcino in wooden display boxes, a little pyramid of miniature *salami* made from wild boar, some cheeses, but they kept erratic hours, the supply of customers being irregular at best.

A narrow brick path, tucked down a side alley and easily missed altogether, did lead steeply uphill to another, smaller piazza, in its centre a stooping elderly holm oak that was the last representative of the trees for which the village was named. This tiny piazza sat on the top of the village and above most of the houses, and on one side, facing east, offered a near-panoramic view of the surrounding countryside. On a clear day in spring an undulating patchwork of fields, grey just tinged with new green, could be seen stretching in one direction, up towards Siena; just now, at the end of summer, some were golden with stubble and others had already been ploughed. The other way lay the forest, silver in the morning but black at dusk, like a great soft dark eiderdown draped over the hills.

Often in the summer a couple of minivans would turn up in the piazza and one or other of the scout troops of the region, overgrown children in shorts and neckerchiefs, would be disgorged with their bedding rolls and rucksacks, ready for a week's camping in the woods. It was a popular destination among scout leaders, offering a taste of the wilderness, rocks and rivers and well-trodden paths, some interesting flora, fauna and geology all in one package. These days there were rumours about the *Albanesi* living rough in the woods and there were some dissenting voices among the parents, but these simply kept their children at home. After all, before the *Albanesi* there had been other, different rumours, about deserters lost since the war, wild men, predators of one kind or another for whom the empty hills were useful cover.

Anna parked her car just inside the village walls, where the car park was busy with traffic to and from the market inside. She felt the need of a nice cappuccino on a bright morning like this, and once inside the gates she walked across the piazza towards Il Cinghiale. There was not exactly rivalry between the two bars in the village, as they attracted quite distinct groups and were not therefore in competition, but neither was there any love lost between their proprietors. Il Cinghiale was the smaller bar; run by Piero Montale's cousin Giovannino, it sat at the top of the sloping piazza. It had a clientele composed almost entirely of local people; visitors seemed to realize this very soon after their arrival in the village because, despite its pretty appearance, they did not gravitate towards it.

Il Cinghiale was situated on the ground floor of a small, red-fronted building beside the post office; only two storeys high, it had a little ornate iron balcony on the first floor, and a wisteria wound up the front, golden-leaved in summer and adding to a very charming impression. There were a few tables outside, for the warmer months, but it was very difficult to find a seat there as an outsider, as each of the bar's regulars had his or her favoured position for a certain part of the day and was reluctant to budge once settled in. Inside there was always a whole *porchetta*, or roast suckling pig, to be found lying in splendour on the wooden slab above Giovannino's glass-fronted cool cabinet, golden and fragrant, its tender meat studded with garlic and stuffed with fennel. In the cabinet below were black-skinned pecorino cheeses and a few other, less significant meats; sausage, the salted, air-cured Tuscan hams and *sbricciolona*, a huge pink *salame* spiked with fennel seed, but the *porchetta* was the main attraction.

Today three local men, drinking small glasses of some dark, viscous *aperitivo* and dressed for winter in padded jackets despite the sun outside, stood elbow to elbow at the counter and watched as Anna crossed the piazza towards them. Beside them the beer delivery man, whose truck was blocking off three parking spaces outside, was talking to Giovannino, but even he turned to see what the others were looking at.

Anna did not look like the average countrywoman; even now, at seventy-five or so, she stood out among them. She was still handsome, Giovannino acknowledged to himself, watching her approach as he polished a glass, but it was more than that. She stood upright, her hair was still dark, and she always pinned it up neatly, revealing a firm jaw and a full mouth. She wore her old clothes well, handmade stuff she had brought back with her from Rome all those years ago, and she had the walk of a much younger woman, quick and careful as she crossed the cobblestones of the piazza.

Giovannino still remembered her arrival back in Montequercio; to him, of course, just a boy, she had been a stranger, although his parents had known who she was. They had grumbled over her city clothes and the unfriendly way she had with her, no doubt also acquired in Rome; by this, he knew even then, they meant that they would have liked her

111

to come over and inform them of every detail of her life since she had left the village, down to her employer's maiden name. When she did not oblige they called her changed, corrupted, untrustworthy. To Giovannino as a boy she had seemed mysterious and – although he would not have admitted it, then or now – beautiful, soft and sweet-smelling, with a small waist and a rounded bosom. Quite unlike the mothers of his other friends. And the fact that she had a past had been a part of the attraction. Anna, framed by the glass door now, pushed it inwards, and the little bell rang. The three men at the counter turned back to their wine.

Anna smiled a crooked smile at the men's hastily turned backs and took a sugar-dusted pastry from the cabinet and the cappuccino Giovannino pushed over to her. He nodded to Anna with the ghost of a smile, which she returned. Sometimes Anna felt like laughing out loud at the faint look of suspicion Giovannino was never able entirely to disguise when he served her; instead she took a little bite from her cake, and the icing sugar dusted her lip. She turned to look out through the doors into the sun, and wondered whether the English from Il Vignacce would be up here today, buying provisions.

The first place to look for the foreign visitors to the village, who were still enough of a novelty for the Montequerciani to be curious about them, would be in the second of its bars, the Bellavista. It had never been the locals' favourite, perhaps because its owner, Carlo, was a northerner by birth and had only married into the village. Set in one of the tall houses that formed the wall that ringed the village, the Bellavista had been expanded some twenty years earlier to accommodate a large, gloomy pool hall with a juke box and slot machines.

Carlo did make money in the summer; his big front terrace,

despite having a less favourable aspect than that of Il Cinghiale, was packed with French and German tourists from April until October, paying top prices for weak caffe latte and Carlo's very inferior mass-produced ice cream. There were plenty of Germans: tall, friendly, brown-skinned people with stubble-headed children whom Anna found very difficult to connect with the grimy, hard-faced invaders of her childhood. There were not so many English visitors; perhaps they were less adventurous, less interested in the countryside, speculated the locals, or maybe they just had different guide books.

Perhaps because it had been expanded, the interior of the Bellavista always seemed empty, summer and winter. A few bored children sent in by their parents might be found wandering desultorily through the dim, cavernous interior in search of modern attractions, prodding the buttons on the jukebox or smearing the sweet cabinet with their sticky fingers while Carlo restrained himself from rapping their knuckles. And despite its name and its position in the city walls, the bar didn't have much of a view. In recent years great trees had sprung up on the steep slope around the village like weeds in the void, blocking out the sun and replacing it with a dim greenish undersea light. Standing at the back of the pool hall beside the picture windows was like being in the jungle, looking out from a tree house suspended over a ravine.

Apart from the two bars, set a little way back and up some broad stone steps the piazza contained a squat marble church undistinguished by architectural ornament except one stained-glass rose window looking on to the square. Visitors, having drunk their caffe latte at the Bellavista and for want of anything else to do, would regularly wander inside when they found it open, but they generally emerged looking bemused

113

and a little disappointed; it contained one or two undistinguished eighteenth-century oils and a plaster madonna but no frescoes, by Piero della Francesco or anyone else.

Anna did not go to church; chief among the advantages of having left the small community for so long, she found, was the opportunity to discard certain kinds of conventional behaviour, such as churchgoing, without attracting too much in the way of hostility. After forty years in Rome Anna felt she had gained the dubious status almost of a stranger in the village; she thought they had washed their hands of her. In practice this meant that, although she was from time to time issued with dire warnings about the dangers of the *Albanesi* at large in the forest, she could live there alone without interference, she could dress as she pleased, and, most importantly, she had been able to return to her village with a grown son and without a husband, and no one could say a thing, at least not to her face.

This morning there was a market and the oval piazza was bustling with activity; Carlo's outside tables were all occupied. From her vantage point Anna could see at least two families, parents and children alike dressed in the tourist uniform of shorts and T-shirts and all eating big confections of Carlo's pastel ice cream, great mounds of the stuff stuck with wafers, *cigarettes russes* and tissue paper parasols.

Perhaps the English were here at the market; wandering among the stalls. Anna tried to remember what they had looked like in the half-light of Saturday evening as their dusty cars had bumped past her house, and failed. Children, yes, and one dark woman and one fair, but that was all. Anna looked about; the English were not easy to spot by their clothes, but their colour usually gave them away; particularly after a day in Italian sun, their thin, pale northern skin would flush, turning an unmistakable pink, like a salmon or a sunset. Anna paid Giovannino, picked up her basket, dusted a mote or two of sugar from her coat, and walked out into the sunshine.

The market came to Montequercio twice a week: Monday and Thursday, and it was popular with the foreign visitors. There was a hardware stall selling cheap pans, coffee pots and chopping boards, another hung about with flowered pinafores and aprons, a vegetable stall and a man from Pienza who set out pungent roundels of *pecorino*, black and yellow and burnt orange, on a trestle.

Sometimes in high season a woman from Siena came down with rails full of old white cotton petticoats and nightgowns, embroidered, lace-trimmed and pintucked, or just plain shifts with a stitched initial to distinguish them. The visitors bought armfuls of them to take back to England or Germany or Holland, but Anna found it poignant to see them heaped up, the very same garments her mother and grandmother would have worn, sometimes still with nametags sewn in for the owner's last visit to the hospital. They were hand-stitched and rough with years of bleaching and although the lace was mostly just machine-made she could still remember her mother coming home from the market with a couple of metres of the same lace for trimmings and exclaiming over it.

These days there was competition for the market in Montequercio; there was a supermarket in the village now; not quite within the walls themselves but just outside, handily situated on the main road where it caught much of the passing trade. The local people, by and large, seemed to like its brightly lit shelves and more generous selection of produce than the dark, poky little shop in the village had ever offered, and they were as happy to stand and gossip there, blocking the aisles, as in the piazza.

But although it was clean and smart and new, with automatic doors and ranks of shining trolleys, many of the foreigners would not have considered it much of a supermarket. It closed for almost four hours for lunch, for one thing, and in the scalding afternoon heat disconsolate backpackers could regularly be seen sitting on their rucksacks waiting by the supermarket's doors, which would remain firmly closed until a quarter to five, while inside the supermarket's workers were to be heard, tantalizingly, enjoying their leisurely lunch break. It ran out of fresh milk and bread in the morning and its wine shelves, vegetable stands and delicatessen counters contained largely only local produce.

In fact Anna didn't mind the supermarket at all; it seemed really just like a larger, better-lit version of Signora Montale's old place. And it was an excellent opportunity to observe the goings on of the incomers as they stumbled over their shopping lists at the bread counter and stacked their trolleys with items the regulars would have considered quite unnecessary. Today, though, it was Piero Montale she bumped into outside the supermarket, looking a little sheepish as he tried to conceal some shop-bought ravioli from her.

'Signora Viola,' he said, smiling his benevolence. Anna. How's it going?' He clasped her hand between his and pressed it in a warm, vigorous handshake.

Anna extracted her hand carefully, but smiled at him all the same. 'Good, Piero, thank you. My son's staying with me, he's getting some things done at the house, you know.'

'Now you know you can ask me, don't you?' the farmer said, opening his arms in an expansive gesture. Anything you want done?'

Anna looked at him shrewdly; she was fond of Piero Montale, but she knew these farmers, nothing was for free. She nodded, all the same.

'Thank you,' she said. 'You've got some English visitors down there by the river, then? I hope it stays nice for them.'

Montale shrugged. 'Yes, of course. It'll be fine; summer's not quite over yet, is it? And for them, you know, they're used to nothing but rain over where they come from, isn't that right? Who am I to argue?'

Anna nodded absent-mindedly, watching as two cars with English plates rounded the bend. They had come from her direction, from the woods, and they looked very much like the cars that had passed her house on Saturday evening; she saw confirmation in Montale's eyes as he followed her gaze, and raised his hand in a salute to the cars' occupants. They swung in across the road from the supermarket and parked.

Chapter Nine

Paolo had chopped half a winter's worth of logs, most of them pine and ash, each split neatly in four and now stacked beneath the overhanging roof of the lean-to at the back of the house. Now, showered and dressed in a fresh shirt, he stood on his mother's terrace and looked out over the hills. There was something about the soft September light, the mild blue air, the damp sweet scent of autumn just beginning to creep in below the summer overtones of dry grass and stubble, that inspired in him an involuntary sigh of deep satisfaction. Paolo drank his coffee, black and sticky with sugar, down in one, the little cup almost hidden in his large hand; on a day like this he could see why his mother lived here.

Paolo was not a country child, as his mother had been; he had not been out of Rome until he was seven or eight, when his great-grandmother had died. Until then his territory had been the hard cobbled streets of the city, thronging with people at every hour of the day and night, the black flocks of

118

priests on every corner, shopkeepers in their doorways, and the noise of their traffic never ceased. On his battered bicycle Paolo would rattle through the steep, narrow alleys of Trastevere on his way to school or dodge between café tables on an errand for his mother, recognized everywhere by barmen and grocers and flower sellers. He didn't even notice the noise; to him that, had always been simply how life was led, every moment filled with sound, every street with people.

The countryside had been a revelation to Paolo, as a boy; its vast emptiness, and its silence. Nor was it just the absence of traffic, the whine of *motorini* echoing against the solid stone of the narrow city streets, the insistent puttering of little delivery vans, horns sounding; even the voices of the country people were quiet by comparison with those of the city dwellers, as though they had forgotten how to speak. They would chew every utterance over like a ruminating animal for long moments of silence before delivering it, and when they did open their mouths they seemed determined to cut their words as short as they could.

As for the landscape, Paolo had seen grass before, and trees, naturally, growing between the stones of the Colosseum, out among the catacombs, in the park of the Villa Borghese and the private gardens to be glimpsed through Roman archways and behind the studded doors of great houses. But this had been different – wilderness stretching as far as the eye could see, not ornamental, not enclosed, not safe.

Paolo looked out over the undulating black hills and wondered whether it was true, what they said about the *Albanesi*. Perhaps the valleys and forests of Albania were much like this, perhaps they were mostly country people for whom the prospect of living rough in caves and derelict cowsheds held

119

no fears. Certainly the immigrants from Eastern Europe to be seen around Rome seemed to be afraid of nothing, rattling through the streets in their beaten-up old cars that practically scraped the cobbles, always smoking, dark-skinned, unsmiling and ruthless. His grandmother's house was not well enough secured to withstand a determined burglar; although the doors and shutters were stoutly made and kept in good repair there were no steel reinforced triple-barred security locks, such as the foreigners seemed to require. But Paolo was fond of the old house, and reluctant to persuade his mother to blight its pretty façade with heavy security, even had he thought such persuasion would succeed.

It had taken Paolo some time to understand on his first visit as a boy that this was the house in which his mother had grown up and that the tiny, silent old lady to whom she introduced him, dressed in faded black and wringing her hands, was his grandmother. Her face was dark and deeply lined; she had small, rough, very clean hands that she had placed on either side of his chin, soft and cool as little paws against his skin, holding him still and looking into his face. It seemed to him that she was looking for something. As Pablo grew older, as his visits to Montequercio became regular and he came to know his grandmother, he did sometimes wonder why Anna had not brought him sooner. Eventually, of course, he understood, just as he came to understand what his grandmother was looking for in his face.

A mild breeze stirred the birches below the house and as he watched the leaves flutter Paolo suddenly felt glad to be out of the city. The sky was a bright clear blue, incandescent in the morning sun, the day was already beginning to feel warm, and he decided to go for a walk.

*

Two cars were gone from Il Vignacce, but the little Italian hire car remained below the trees, irrepressibly shiny and cheerful in the gloom. Justine walked to the bright opening of the door from the kitchen, holding her coffee, which was black because the milk, like most of their other provisions, had already run out. She leaned against the warm stone of the door surround and looked out across the pasture. For the first time since they had arrived Justine was alone, and as she looked at the empty expanse of trees and listened to what seemed at first like silence but turned out to be composed of many small sounds she felt a delicious, guilty sensation of relief and exhilaration mingled.

She had been surprised that Lucien had gone back to civilization so eagerly, after all his eulogizing the simple life, but then, of course, he could never resist a foreign market, the possibility of picking up some obscure condiment or cooking tool for a couple of pence. And the food, too; Lucien would not have trusted Louisa and Tom to come back with the proper provisions and she could imagine them squabbling in the supermarket over what kind of pasta to buy, how many tins of this and that. How much wine.

Tom had been drinking a lot, Justine thought absently, much more than she remembered; perhaps that was why he was looking old. Lucien wasn't much of a drinker, really, he never had been; he liked to remain in control. His abstemiousness had always marked him out from the men she'd known as a student, it had made him seem mature. Now, Justine sometimes thought she wouldn't mind if he got drunk, once in a while, if he just let go. The thought drifted into her head that she might find something out if he did, and as she looked out over the field at the grazing animals that were now scattered across it, she let the thought settle. She decided that she would

121

find the river; that would be her task, and when the others returned she would have something to show for her day of leisure. At the moment, however, the cows lay between her and the path Montale had indicated the other night in the dark, and she wondered whether, despite Martin and Dido's failure, there might be another way.

The cows had appeared that morning, as they were all getting ready to go. Much earlier, just after dawn Justine, lying in bed, had heard the chunter of an invisible tractor somewhere across the pasture, a strange, faintly sinister mechanical sound after two days in which their senses had become accustomed only to the soft organic noises of the forest, the sounds, at first almost inaudible, of birds and insects, and leaves falling. The perpetual clang of the cowbells, somewhere just out of sight. As Justine lay there listening the noise had changed to something in a different register, like a water pump. Lucien, who was awake for once, had decided that the farmer was filling a tank with water from the river, perhaps for the cattle. The pump had stopped after a time, the tractor engine started again and eventually puttered away into silence. But Justine wondered whether the sound might not have registered with the herd as some kind of signal, because they appeared as abruptly as though they had been summoned.

The shadows cast by the trees had begun to shorten as the sun rose higher in the sky, when a bellowing had started up in the trees behind the house. Extraordinarily loud against a background of only birdsong and insects and almost shocking in so apparently empty a landscape, the lowing had echoed around the hills, the same call repeated again and again. Then a great dun-coloured cow, as beautiful as a painting, had galloped up out of the trees and stopped in front of them as they loaded the cars. The first cow was swiftly followed by others and they thundered on the dry pounded earth through the corral that led them to the pasture; the children ran to climb on the fence and look at them, even Dido. They seemed obscurely delighted by the animals' appearance, as though they were longed-for guests, and they whooped and shouted as if they were at a rodeo.

Justine had been surprised to see that only two or three of the cows wore bells, despite the din they had made, and those the large, sleek ones; the Alpha females, she christened them. All the fully grown animals had long curved horns and were a pale creamy colour; there only seemed to be one bull among them; a modestly sized, docile-looking creature, he had smaller horns than the rest. There were two calves; darker and redder than the adults, but with large white-lashed eyes, their uninhibited jumping and kicking mirrored the activities of the younger humans squealing at them from the fence. Justine had watched Dido perched above the boys and happy at last, her wide, radiant smile startlingly like Evie's and unfamiliar at the same time.

Justine didn't think Martin and Dido would stick with the others in Montequercio, or at least not for long; there was some ruined abbey or other he'd said he might take her to. She couldn't help but feel sorry for Martin, particularly after last night; he wasn't the kind of man to let anyone know what he was thinking, which was why they speculated so hard about him. A witch-hunt. Perhaps it was because Justine had loved her own father so much that she felt protective of Martin and Dido's relationship; she was biased. But then again, it seemed as though he needed someone on his side.

Reluctantly, Justine found herself thinking about Evie.

Before the holiday, she had begun to forget her, she realized. She had resigned herself to the fact that Evie no longer existed, she hadn't just gone off on holiday, on another adventure. She had – she thought they all had, she, Tom, Louisa, Lucien – somehow accepted the disturbing circumstances of her death as a kind of abstract problem that could never be solved. Perhaps that was how life worked, she'd thought; however terrible something seemed when it happened, in the end you forgot. But the moment she had seen Martin and Dido again she had realized that she was just deceiving herself. It wasn't finished, not forgotten, not yet, not for him.

Reluctantly, Justine allowed the awful bare facts of Evie's disappearance to reassert themselves; she had forgotten nothing, it seemed, after all. On that last morning Evie had taken Dido to school, which in itself was unusual; when Evie did not come back and that night Martin phoned Justine to ask if she knew anything, it was one of the only clues, and he seemed to fix on it. Dido went to a school in West London, not far, in fact, from Tom and Louisa's house in Hammersmith and a forty-minute tube ride from the Laws' home in Crouch End. Since the age of eleven Dido had been trusted to make the journey on her own; there was no sense in going by car in the rush hour, and even if the time and money needed for one of her parents to accompany her had been immaterial, she wouldn't have wanted them there.

On that particular day Evie had taken the tube with her, though, all the way to school and perhaps Dido had been pleased at the novelty, just for once; the thought brought tears to Justine's eyes. She wondered how many times Martin must have asked Dido what Evie had said when she said goodbye, and with what anxiety and grief Dido must have tried to recall the last words her mother said to her. Justine found herself shaking her head involuntarily in an attempt to rid herself of the image. She sat down on the stone steps that led across the front of the house, looked out across the field and sighed.

In the pasture the cows were almost motionless, their heads all lowered to the short, dry grass. Occasionally one would turn and seem to look across at the house without curiosity. The silence and the space, all to herself, suddenly seemed immensely luxurious to Justine, like a great private garden. It was such a relief to be alone. A guilty pleasure.

The sun's heat prickled the back of Justine's neck and the sound of the insects in the trees seemed to intensify. She walked around to the back of the house, to see where the herd had come from. Behind the house the shade of the trees, where the cattle had spent the last two days wandering in the cool green light, seemed very inviting, and Justine could see that a shallow, rocky, gorge led down through the trees, mossy and leaf-filled, like a dry, overgrown river-bed. Perhaps in the winter it channelled the rainwater down to the river; Justine knew from the map she and Lucien had pored over yesterday that the river, in fact, wound around the house, that it lay just out of sight down the hill.

On impulse, Justine went closer, then opened the small gate behind the house that led into the trees. She began to climb down the rocks, moss-green and velvety with lichen beneath her feet. All around her the trees stood in ranks like silent, motionless figures, and Justine felt the first prickle of apprehension as though she was being observed, as awkwardly she made her way down the steep incline. She could see no sign of the river, although some way off sunlight seemed to penetrate the forest to a greater depth, as if perhaps there was a clearing further ahead. But the air seemed hazed by something, cobweb or a mist of tiny insects, and Justine could not see clearly. She turned to look back up at the house, but she had descended further than she thought and it was no longer visible; it might have been miles away and she alone in the woods. Then she felt something on her face, the touch of something light and clinging, and that was enough. Her heart thudding painfully in her throat, Justine ran back up the hill, two or three leaping steps and the house came back into view, but she did not slow down until she was back inside the gate, the cropped grass surrounding the house beneath her feet.

In the sunlit pasture nothing had changed, the animals with their heads down as still as a photograph and overexposed, the colour bleached out of the whole vista to Justine's eyes, which were still adjusting to the light. Leaning against the house, she took some deep breaths, and tried to laugh. No more off-road, she decided; better to follow Montale's path, cows or no cows. And despite their impressive horns the cattle suddenly seemed friendly to her now; after the spectral gloom of the empty forest, they looked familiar, companionable and tranquil, and if she followed the fence around the edge of the pasture she would be safe enough even from a charging bull. She sat quiet for a few moments, then decided to go, now, before she changed her mind, like falling off a horse. She felt invigorated suddenly, to be doing even this small thing on her own, without Lucien to lead the way, to advise and warn and take charge.

If she was going to be methodical about her expedition, Justine decided, she should shut up the house even if she only planned to be out of sight for half an hour or so; Tom and Louisa had already secured their portion, so there wasn't much to do after all. As she drew in the shutters in the kitchen, at the back of the house the trees seemed very close in the half-light, and she heard the soft thud of a plum as it fell on the meagre, dusty grass. She went upstairs.

Justine had closed their shutters earlier to keep out the heat of the sun as it fell full on the front of the house; on the threshold of Martin and Dido's room she paused. Beside Dido's bed the basin lay still, clean and empty, and both beds were neat, their blue and white checked quilts smooth and straight. Two of Martin's shirts hung on a rail, but she could see nothing of Dido's. Justine wondered who bought Dido's clothes for her now, who took her shopping? Maybe Martin just gave her money; the thought made her unaccountably sad, of the lonely girl wandering about the shops and trying to remember what her mother would have wanted her to buy. A scuffed sports backpack leaned against the foot of the girl's bed. Justine gazed at the little nylon bag, the last repository of Dido's privacy; she thought of the child's pale, tortured face as they had lain her on the bed in the dark. She tried not to think of Lucien's insinuations, but suddenly she felt a kind of creeping dread, that none of them were taking responsibility for Dido. What if, like Evie, she had secrets she needed to tell them, but didn't dare? And before she could think about what she was doing Justine knelt down and pulled the zip open.

Inside there were two rolled T-shirts, a pair of jeans, shorts and a tangle of underwear and beneath them a couple of paperbacks. At the bottom of the pack was a photograph in a small leather frame. Justine recognized it immediately; it was a picture she had taken of Evie several years before on a picnic, head on one side, Dido's small arms around her neck. She was smiling a little, and it seemed to Justine now as though there was something wary in the look she gave the camera, something in her eyes that didn't match the smile. Slowly Justine pulled it out, remembering the day, remembering Lucien standing behind her and telling her about the light meter, how to set the shutter speed. There seemed such a distance between that bright spring afternoon and the day they found Evie's body, so much road to be travelled to get her to that point, to despair.

Justine turned the frame over in her hands; a grimy piece of folded paper had been pushed in behind the photograph and without thinking she began to pull it out. At the top she could just see something in Evie's handwriting: 'Dearest'. Suddenly Justine pushed the paper back in and thrust the frame back into the backpack, the paperbacks on top of it and the clothes, and zipped it shut. She felt a wave of cold shame at her curiosity, at how easily she had justified her invasion of Dido's hiding place. *If she wanted to say something to us, surely she could? She's known us all her life.* Quickly Justine closed the shutters, the darkness blotting out the backpack, the clothes, the sad, neat beds. She took the stairs back down three at a time.

The cows barely registered Justine's passing as she skirted the trees, although an angry horsefly circled her as she walked bare-headed under the midday sun. Batting at it, even that small effort bringing her out in a sweat, she looked back at the house, fortified now against intruders, every shutter closed. As she approached the trees at the far end of the pasture an opening appeared that had not been visible from the house, a broad path thick with weeds leading steeply downhill, the path still hugging the fencing to her left, and a clearing below. The herd obviously grazed down here too, to judge from the pats of cow dung worked over by parasites, and Justine was glad that she hadn't met the big animals lumbering up that narrow path, where there would not have been room for her too. This was much more their territory than hers, after all, and for a moment Justine felt a flicker of curiosity about the forest's native inhabitants. Not just the animals but the people too, the farmer, the villagers tending the olives higher up; they might be in there now, for all she knew, walking or foraging, invisible beneath the miles and miles of forest. After all someone had even lived here in this deserted place before it had been turned into a holiday home.

In the shade the horseflies disappeared, the terrain flattened and suddenly Justine could hear water, trickling and gurgling somewhere to her left. Behind the fence now was a hazel coppice, great thick clumps of slender wands that arched towards each other gracefully and joined overhead like the vaulted ceiling of a cathedral or something less lofty, like a crypt. The clumps enclosed a dark, musty space, and the ground, beneath them was thickly carpeted with dead leaves. The sound of the water, it seemed to Justine, came from beyond the hazel screen and she could smell the river now; cold, mysterious and seductive.

The path ended in a small turnstile surmounted with a sign warning of grazing animals, and carefully Justine fastened it behind her. She walked through a stand of some giant umbelliferous plant, dusty with seed and swaying in the light, she felt the sun on her face and suddenly she was there at the river. Straight ahead of her it flowed in a wide bend around the semi-circle of loose gravel and weeds where she found herself standing, and the far bank was a great cliff of rock, sandstone stippled with lichen and moss and more than forty feet high.

Upriver the water's course flowed down towards her, straight and shallow as far as the eye could see, its banks crowded in with vegetation. To Justine's left, downriver and back towards Il Vignacce it narrowed substantially, pouring through some large boulders that almost blocked the river's flow and acted as a dam, creating the deep pool she could see in front of her. Apart from the ceaseless, slippery gurgle of the water, the little beach where she stood was cool and very quiet, and with the trees enclosing her from behind and the massive, sombre cliff-face ahead, it could not have been more secluded. Justine felt as though she had walked through a door into another world.

In the summers he had stayed here as a boy Paolo had spent many days wandering in the valley below his grandmother's house, and although he could no longer be sure of all the pathways that criss-crossed the nature reserve, some having been erased by new growth and new ones worn by the forest animals, many were still the same.

These days Montequercio, it seemed to him as he trudged down through the trees, was full of old people. He wondered where all the other children had gone, the ragged companions of his boyhood summers, and where their descendants were? A new generation. Some of his generation, of course, were still around although they were no longer young; Montale's baby brother Giovannino, who ran the bar now, had been one. Paolo wasn't young either, but the life of the *contadino*, always out in the elements tending to olives and vines, had turned those of his contemporaries still in the village into little old men. Some of his generation, he supposed, had left the village to work in the city – in Siena, or Grosseto, or even Rome – and those who had remained had generated few or no children to run about in the piazza as they themselves had done, or to play war games in the woods.

Anna's was the only remaining *podere*, or farmhouse, for quite some distance now. When it had been his grandmother's house, they had had two or three neighbours, not close, but near enough, a little two room shack between them and the main road, and a small stone house with a tin roof higher up the hill, but the new generation preferred to work in computers than to tend the land and these little farmsteads had fallen into ruins. Sometimes the old people, the parents who now lived in flats in a block on the edge of town, would come out to potter about the overgrown olive groves. Creakily spreading out the nets to catch the fruit in the winter, cutting back the weeds, gathering a few wild plums or mushrooms, they were to be seen everywhere in the countryside these days, scratching their heads and spreading their sinewy old arms in despair at the way nature had got the better of them, and time, and something called progress that took their children away from the land.

As a town boy and the son of Anna Viola, Paolo had been treated with suspicion at first, but as his ancestral family was at least local, he had eventually been allowed to join in. And in the summer holidays a different set of rules seemed to apply among the children. Outside the schoolyard and out of reach of their parents for most of the day, they formed their own alliances. Paolo and a loose group of five or six others, a subset of which would meet up most days in July and August, had built a tree house together in the oak across the road from Anna's house one year, and a few of its nails and planks were still visible now.

As they grew older and bolder they had dared to venture further in from the inhabited edge of the forest, to stray from the paths where their parents had led them in search of mushrooms or chestnuts. There were some marked *sentieri*, ramblers' paths, through the woods, which were signed with splashes of red paint on the trees, although they were not always reliable. The local boys knew their way around, however, and soon enough Paolo learned to as well, recognizing this tree stump or that odd-shaped growth of ivy, a rock or a stream or a clump of hazel. The route he had taken today, down to a waterfall they had often visited as children, Paolo had chosen because it was the most familiar; he didn't want to get lost.

Only once had the young Paolo come close to losing his way in the forest below his grandmother's house, and that was because he had set out too late. His mother had always told him not to go off after three or so in the afternoon because once darkness fell, it would be too late; he would never find his way out and would starve there. And although she didn't name it, he knew she didn't like the thought of him going right down to Il Vignacce; if he wanted to swim, she would say, why not go to a bathing place higher up, in the light? But there had been three of them, Giovannino, Paolo and another boy whose name he could no longer remember, he'd been dead so long, hit his head and drowned in the same river at the age of seventeen. They had egged each other on, off on a hunt for a mythical cave where there might be treasure, or dead men's bones.

They had been still at least a kilometre from home when twilight had come quite suddenly, with a mist that seemed to rise up from the uneven leafy ground and a dimming of the outlines of things. Overhead the boys had been able to see that the sky still held some brightness but was beginning to take on the electric blue of dusk, the shreds of cloud turning pink

132

high above them in the setting sun. And down among the trees the green and brown, the patches of sun that filtered through the leaves all suddenly turned grey and indistinct, darkening away by the minute.

The baker's son had whimpered about ghosts, and Paolo had thought of his grandfather, buried somewhere out here in a shallow grave with an English soldier, and others, no doubt: Italians, Germans, gypsies. Giovannino's olive-skinned face had suddenly seemed very white in front of him, a bleached moon shape looking back in alarm, but by some miracle, by some trick of character, some combination of determination and an instinctive, tenacious understanding of the landscape, it had been Giovannino who had pulled them round. Like a whirlwind he had suddenly set off uphill at speed, dragging the other two in his wake, and he had not stopped until they reached the brow of the hill one along from the *podere*, Paolo's grandmother's light visible from where they stood, and the road.

It was odd, thought Paolo, that Giovannino and he did no more than nod at each other now across the zinc of his bar, but, then, life was like that. Giovannino had been married, so he'd heard, but had not had children and was divorced now, and somehow Paolo could not bear to hear about all that. Perhaps that's how it will all end for all of us, he thought, despondently, trying to put the image of Livia and his own barren, failed marriage out of his mind. Livia had wanted no more than one child, she had told him firmly early on in their relationship. But then, of course, she had seemed to change her mind about even that.

As his promotion at the hospital proved slow in coming she had begun to look at him with a kind of lingering, doubtful consideration, weighing up the pros and cons of their union quite openly and without including him in the debate. The subject of children had become – critical, and suddenly it had opened between them, wide and dangerous as a crevasse. Paolo closed his eyes involuntarily at the thought, stopped in the silence, and breathed deeply the clean scent of vegetable decay. Now she was kept in a grand apartment out in Monteverde by her new lover, a wealthy man in late middle age who had already had a family. For all he knew she sat there looking out over the city from leafy suburban isolation and had given up work altogether, because she had left the hospital. It was no longer any business of his, but still he couldn't quite erase the memory of her, of what she and he had done together; he couldn't pretend it had all been meaningless.

Firmly Paolo closed off that train of thought and surprised himself by successfully stopping the unravelling of guilt and humiliation that usually followed when he began to think about Livia. Perhaps it was doing him good, being away from the city; it wasn't just for his mother's sake, after all, that he came. And besides, he could smell the river now; the air grew fresh and cool, he always thought, near the water, and the sound of it slipping over the rocks was infinitely seductive. He quickened his pace.

The waterfall that gushed out between the two great square slabs of sandstone wasn't much more than a trickle now; in the spring the river above it would be at least a metre deeper with the accumulation of the winter's rains, and the evidence of the April floods was visible even now. The grey stalks of the vegetation beside the river still held the clogged remains of last year's leaves, and dried-out weed was caught, tangled like hair, high in the bushes along the bank. Paolo climbed the few steps up on to the rocks and looked down at the deep black pool below the waterfall. In the air before his eyes an iridescent blue dragonfly appeared, hovered briefly on black wings then dropped to the water's surface, a swallow on its tail. Paolo remembered coming here to fish, or play at fishing, mostly just sitting on the warm stones in the sun and dive-bombing into the pool below. The turquoise of a kingfisher flashed across the dark water, then from behind him, quite distinct from the soft liquid rush of the river over the atones, Paolo heard a sigh.

Upstream as she lay back and floated in the cold, dark water Justine looked up at the leaves moving gently over-head against the pale sky. She could feel the warmer water that lay on the surface of the river and beneath it the cool of the constant moving current slipping onwards, moving like something living around and below her. Justine sighed invol-untarily in response to the sensation, and closed her eyes. She hadn't brought a swimming costume; she hadn't thought of swimming, just of finding the river, but had suddenly found herself seized by the luxury of her own private river, where no costume was needed. She had thought it would be just a muddy stream but when, in the heat, she had seen the deep pool beside the cliff of rock and had felt the cool breath of the river air her only thought had been to get in.

It had seemed such a wonderful piece of luck, suddenly, that she should be here alone, and the day so warm; Justine knew that she wouldn't get another chance like this. She spent so much time confined in her clothing, long sleeves, thick sun-screen, that sometimes she found herself wondering whether her body was suffocating. But here, dappled in the green shade, supported by the cool brown water, she looked down at its undulating outline below the surface and it looked as though that was how it was meant to be, the configurations of pigmented and unpigmented skin like those on a leaf changing colour, or moss on a stone.

Justine stood up, the bottom of the river soft and sandy beneath her feet, and the water came as high as her hip. She looked up at the blank roughness of the cliff face, the water sliding off her back into the river, and wondered what was on the other side.

Paolo heard another sound from upriver, a tiny disruption in the smooth, regular gurgle of the water and, curious, he began to make his way in that direction, jumping carefully from stone to stone and trying instinctively not to make a noise himself. He didn't know what he expected to see, exactly; an animal perhaps, an otter or a deer splashing in the water, but whatever it was he didn't want to disturb it. At the bend, where the river curved back and opened out beneath a cliff he saw something white flicker and raise itself on the other side of a willow clump, and he looked.

He had seen a woman's body before, of course, seen Livia's countless times. More recently, though, his patients' were the only bodies he examined, and the effect, naturally enough, was not like this. It seemed a long time since he had seen a body that was whole and private, not suffering, not offered to him for his professional opinion. And with Livia it was the other extreme; there had been no vulnerability in her nakedness, no part of it that was revealed heedlessly, without careful calculation of its effect, all flaws carefully concealed.

She was standing oblique to him; through the insubstantial screen of the willow Paolo could see her back, the flare of a hip, the hollow curve from the hipbone into her belly and the outline of one sloping breast. Her head was tipped back and her hair hung in a single dark hank between her shoulder blades as she looked up at the cliff. Her skin was very pale, and her whole white voluptuous outline was reflected back at him again in the motionless silvered surface of the pool. He could not tell in the flickering shade cast by the moving trees above them but he thought he saw something on her white skin, something like a tracing, faded lines drawn on her body; a map. Then, before he could think what to do next, she turned and walked out of the water, and the effect of the full length of her walking carelessly out of the water brought him down to his knees.

She picked up something that was in a heap at the edge of the water, with a quick movement and pulled it over her head, something light and thin that stuck to her wet skin; hidden from her at least for the second or two in which her head was shrouded by her dress, Paolo ducked his head down. He sat back on the small stones beside the water, his head in his hands, finding intolerable the possibility that she should find him watching her. He sat there for some minutes without moving, and when he raised his head again, she had gone.

Chapter Ten

The afternoon was advanced and the light was beginning to leave the pasture when at last Justine heard the crunch of the car's tyres on the gravel road above the house, high up and far away at first, ominous in the silence as they approached, very slowly. As she watched the car's shape moving slowly down to her through the screen of trees, it seemed to Justine a long time since Saturday night and that first, endless, drive down through the forest in the dusk. She felt a strange reluctance when she thought of taking that road again, out of the woods, as though she was growing to love her captor.

There was only one car, with Martin and Dido in the front and Lucien lounging on the back seat. He waved up at her, grinning, as she swung open the gate and closed it behind them.

'How have you been? Any sign of life down here?'

Extracting himself from the car Lucien came over to her and stroked her back reflexively, low down at the base of her spine.

Over his shoulder Justine could see Martin looking across at them, and she felt uncomfortable. She couldn't imagine what kind of a ride home they must have had, Martin and Lucien; they seemed quite determined not to communicate in anything more than the most perfunctory way. Suddenly she felt quite impatient with them. Registering Lucien's question, she stepped back from him to answer, and let his hand fall away.

'No ... No. No one. How was the village?'

'Nice. I mean, nothing special, but there was a market and a good restaurant. Surprisingly good. We had lunch; I mean, we thought once we'd done that road, God, it took for ever, we might as well stay out for a while, don't you think? The others went to Siena, and these two' – he gestured with his head back at Martin and Dido, now unloading plastic bags from the car's boot – 'they went to some monastery or other, or an abbey, the one we saw in the guide book, with the relics. A bit of the true cross, or something; a Cistercian abbey, ruined. They picked me up on the way back.'

'Mmm.' Then, realizing something more was expected of her, 'Sounds good.' Justine didn't quite feel like telling Lucien about her day somehow.

'Oh,' Lucien said, as an afterthought, 'and we met our neighbour. Our landlord introduced us, the farmer, what's his name. Montale. He was at the supermarket.'

'Neighbour?' Justine frowned, and looked around at the empty hills.

'Up at the top. You know, just where the off-road bit starts, the beginning of the reserve.'

'Oh,' Justine said, remembering the pretty old house she'd thought might have been theirs before Montale had roared on past it. 'What are they like?'

'An old lady, Anna something,' said Lucien. 'Friendly. I think she was, anyway, neither of them speaks English, not really, not her or the farmer. Dido worked some of it out, didn't you?' He turned and Dido, who was just emerging from the house, looked at him enquiringly.

The old lady?' Dido brightened. 'She was nice, wasn't she? She seemed to like us, I mean the boys and me, the children.' She coloured a little, bobbing her head down. 'She said we should go and see her and she'd give us some of her olives.'

'Did she really?' said Lucien. 'I didn't know you spoke Italian, Dido.' He sounded curious.

Dido shrugged and turned away. 'I've been doing it a year,' she said.

When she didn't say anything more Lucien turned back to Justine. 'Aren't they wonderful, the Italians,' he said, full of enthusiasm. 'So hospitable.'

Justine nodded, but her heart sank at the thought of Lucien working his charm on the locals. Then she thought of something. 'Dido,' she said, 'I found the river. Do you want to come for a swim?'

'Oh, yes!'

Justine was taken aback by the enthusiasm of her response.

'Brilliant. Dad!' She turned to Martin, who was already looking at her. 'Can I go?'

'Of course you can go,' he said, a quizzical expression on his face that warmed Justine to him a little, a look of fondness, and Dido ran past him into the house, leaving a little hum of happiness in her wake: On impulse Justine turned to Lucien.

'I think maybe,' she said, uncertain of how to phrase it, 'it would be nice if it was just me and Dido, for a bit? You and

Martin can sort the supper out, can't you, put stuff away or something? Come down later.'

She thought for a moment that Lucien was going to resist, as something like annoyance flickered briefly in his eyes, but then he shrugged.

'Okay,' he said. 'It'll be getting dark soon, anyway.'

Dido appeared in the doorway, a rolled towel under one arm.

'I'll get mine,'said Justine.'Just a sec.'

'Wow,' said Dido, 'oh, wow.' She turned in a circle, looking up at the cliff. Already it was cooler down here; the sun had almost left the little clearing, and the river was even darker in the deep shadow below the cliff. The effect was to make the little clearing mysterious.

They ran into the water together, and Justine was surprised by how cold it was. She turned, waist high in the centre of the stream, and faced Dido. There was something about the girl's shape that recalled Evie, strong, rounded and golden with health. Her temperament, however, and her body language, seemed quite different. Where Evie had been expansive and uninhibited, Dido seemed turned inward, her shoulders drawn together, elbows tight against her ribcage.

Perhaps it was Dido's age that made her shy – although Evie had not been much older when she and Justine had first met – or just the physical shock of the cold water. Justine didn't want to think about Evie, not standing here in the water. She didn't want to remember the way she had been told Evie was found, floating face down in a muddy estuary, her body bloated by a month's immersion, her hair caught in the samphire and pale marsh flowers. She found herself wondering whether Dido had seen her mother's body; had she asked to see it? Did she dream of Evie coming back, walking out of the water, as Justine sometimes did?

Dido smiled at her, a tentative smile, then turned to look up at the cliff. Justine caught a glimpse of something, a flash of colour low on her back, hip height. It was a tattoo, a tiny scroll inked in red; it said, Love. And suddenly Justine realized that Dido might have quite another life than the one she had imagined for her, not the life of the serious child she had known always sheltered by her mother's bountiful, vivid presence, the girl who was now bereft. She was a girl who'd gone along to a tattoo parlour, who maybe had a gang of friends, who thought about clothes, and boys.

'Is that real? When did you have that done?' asked Justine. 'You're brave, aren't you?'

Dido turned, blushing, her hand on her hip covering the word. 'Dad was furious,' she said. 'Went on about hepatitis, but I was careful about where I went. It was registered and everything.'

'Did – when—' Justine didn't know how to ask, but Dido seemed to guess what she wanted to know, and shook her head.

'It was a couple of months ago. After Mum – but she wouldn't have minded, you know, she would have stuck up for me. And it took my mind off it. Everything. I just wanted to do it.' Dido stuck out her lower lip defiantly.

'OK, OK, it's – pretty, anyway. Nice.'

Justine ducked down in the cold water, laughing at the shock of immersion, and swam off down to the rock face. Dido followed her, and they sat together on a small ledge that protruded from the base of the cliff. The rough stone felt warm still against their backs, but around the small clearing the colours of the trees were growing dark as the light faded overhead, where birds had begun to wheel and scream in the dusk. Autumn was coming, Justine thought, as she saw them massing high in the sky in great swarms, tiny and black as insects.

They sat there watchfully for a moment or two, both aware of the darkness falling and the trilling evening song of the cicadas as it started up among the leaves all around them, but both of them, Justine thought, reluctant to go back quite yet.

'When did your migraines start?' Justine asked, wondering aloud. Dido looked down at her hands, which were white against the dark water.

'A couple of years ago. The doctor said that's common, they often come on with puberty. They got worse when – since Mum died.'

The word rang cold in the air, and Dido looked at Justine with her chin up, as if to say, there, I've said it. Justine returned her gaze, and nodded. She looked down at her thighs, the paler patches flowering over her knees, and absent-mindedly placed a hand on one to cover the white.

'I expect that's normal too,' she said. 'Have you been – all right, without your mum? I mean I know you can't have been, really, but—' She felt herself floundering.

'Dad's managing OK,' said Dido quickly. 'He's good, actually. A good dad, you know' *Good*, thought Justine. *Bloody Lucien; why did he have to say that about Martin?*

Dido went on. 'I just – sometimes it's horrible. Not knowing, why she did it.' She turned to Justine. 'Do you know? Why she did it?'

Justine stared at her, taken aback. Something in Dido's voice and the directness of her gaze gave Justine the impression that she wasn't asking her out of desperation, not casting about for

143

help from any source; it was as though she thought Justine might actually have the answer. She felt overwhelmed with pity for the girl, caught between childhood and maturity, not knowing what the adults knew, afraid of the secrets they might be keeping from her.

'No,' she said. 'If I knew I would have told you and your dad a long time ago. I think, if it wasn't an accident – which it might have been – then she must have been very unhappy'

'Yes,' said Dido, but she was frowning. For a moment Justine thought Dido was going to say something else, but if she was she changed her mind, because suddenly she pushed herself away from the rock and in a few strokes swam across the dark water. She turned back smiling towards Justine as if, despite herself, the water had released her. She's longing to be set free of all this, thought Justine.

Looking at the wake that flared behind Dido in the black water, suddenly Justine became aware that the light was almost gone from the sky it reflected, and that the path back to the house led through the dark trees. She shivered. 'Time to go,' she said, wading past Dido and out of the river. Together, shivering and laughing in a panic that was only half-feigned, they tugged their T-shirts on over their damp bodies and made for the little lych-gate in the trees while it was still just visible.

Up on the brow of the hill Anna's house was closed up against the night, only a crack of light visible here and there from the outside where the shutters didn't fit tight. On her terrace an iron chair was tipped forward against the table, in case it rained, although the inky sky was still as clear as it had been in the day. The air was cool, though, cooler than it had been the night before, and if Anna and Paolo had still been on the terrace looking down across the valley they would have seen the beginnings of a mist lying feather-soft among the trees far below. Along the course of the river and out of sight of Anna's terrace it was drifting and settling, between the clumps of thorn and thistle in the empty pasture and through the hazel and bog-oak where the black water rippled and slid over the stones in the shallows.

Inside the house was warm and bright, and a sweet blue hint of woodsmoke from the stove hung in the air. Anna stood in the doorway between the kitchen and the little sitting room with a cup of coffee for her son and found him standing over the stove, looking down and frowning. He had been quiet all day.

'What's wrong, *caro*?' she asked. He cleared his throat and looked up; he didn't look unhappy, just a little dazed, unfocused.

'Is it Livia?' And suddenly his face cracked open and he smiled, the wide easy smile that she hardly remembered having seen since his childhood, when he would run towards her with something to show her. It had not occurred to her before that it was his father's smile, but now she saw it.

He's Luca's age now, she thought, well, the age he was, when I fell in love with him. Can so many years have passed? And to her astonishment, because it was so utterly unfamiliar a sensation, she felt like crying. Suddenly the sense of having been cheated, or having cheated herself, was overwhelming, the thought that not only her life but her son's too, had been all eaten up by hard work and stubbornness, her determination only to look ahead, never back.

But Paolo was shaking his head, still smiling at her. 'Not

Livia,' he said. 'Mama, you know it's all over between Livia and me, don't you? It's all right, I don't care too much about it any more. And you can admit it now, you never really liked her, did you?'

Anna shrugged, pretending indifference, but she was smiling too. 'She might have grown on me,' she said, but Paolo was laughing now. He put his arm around her, and gently took the cup from her hand. 'Never,' he said. 'Now, let's have some of that grappa you made, with the plums.'

By midnight the last light was off at Il Vignacce, and all three cars were back in their place below the trees, two of them streaked with dust from the day's expedition. The farmhouse, which by day sat solid and respectable in its clearly circumscribed plot, surveying its pasture and dominating the landscape, was now invisible, swallowed up in darkness. Around it the night sounds of the forest seemed to have taken charge, quick scuttlings and rustlings on the leafy floor, the ebbing sound of the insects, gradually silenced by the cool night and an owl far away somewhere. Overhead the great starry expanse of sky hummed with light, as billions of miles away the gases of tiny nameless constellations flared and burned and shooting stars arced silently down to the horizon.

Justine and Lucien lay side by side in the moonlight, and, for once, Justine was not the only one awake.

Lucien turned on his side to face her. 'Is something wrong?' he asked. Justine frowned, looking straight ahead through the open window for a moment before reluctantly meeting his eye.

'Why?' she asked, half evasive, half genuinely curious to know Lucien's reason for asking.

'Well,' he hesitated, and Justine knew he was trying to find

146

a way of phrasing it that didn't make him sound plaintive, but that made him sound innocent. He didn't want to have a conversation about babies, and suddenly Justine realized that she didn't want to either. She waited.

'You've been very quiet,' he said. 'And I haven't seen much of you.' He put a hand out sideways across her body beneath the quilt and stroked her stomach through the thin fabric of her T-shirt. Justine turned away very slightly, and his hand stopped.

'I know,' she said, 'I think it's seeing Martin and Dido, you know. It brings everything back.' She was aware that this was only half the truth, but that was something at least.

Lucien let out a faintly contemptuous sound; he tried to turn it into a pensive sigh, but did not succeed entirely. 'Look, I know you sympathize with him, obviously, but – don't you think he's – odd? He's hardly said a word since we arrived. Do you remember how many times the police interviewed him when Evie disappeared? They must have thought—'

Justine interrupted him, knowing that if he went on she would not be able to sleep, she would be so angry 'Yes, Lucien, I know you don't like him, but not everyone's like you. Give him a chance. He must feel pretty uncomfortable—' but Lucien, musing, or thinking aloud, interrupted her this time.

'Yes,' he said, 'there is that I mean, all of us always wondered what on earth Evie was doing married to him, he must have known that's what we were thinking. Christ, it makes you wonder what Louisa was thinking of, getting us all out here. Particularly—' He stopped.

'Particularly what?' asked Justine.

'Nothing,' said Lucien. 'Just, well, we weren't ever that

147

close. Not with him. Not a recipe for a relaxing holiday' He sounded uneasy.

'That's not what you meant, is it?' said Justine. There was a silence, then Lucien sighed heavily.

'Well, you know Tom was always – mooning about over Evie. In love with her.' He pronounced the word with impatience. 'It was a standing joke, you must have noticed. At his parties?'

'No,' said Justine, 'I don't believe you, that's just Tom, being sweet.'

Lucien snorted.

'And Evie had that effect on all sorts of people, anyway. And what about Louisa? Tom loves Louisa.'

'All right,' said Lucien, impatiently 'Whatever you say.' He took his hand away. 'Let's leave it, then, shall we?' And he closed his eyes.

As she lay beside him in the darkness Justine thought of how physically irresistible Evie had been; there had been a time when she had longed, hopelessly, to have Evie's sweet-smelling hair, the curve of her waist, her wide dark-blue eyes, her radiant smile. It hadn't saved her, though; who knows, it might even have killed her. She thought of Evie, hollow-eyed and pale as she had stood in her kitchen, Dido in her arms. There were things she had been afraid of. They had never asked. Justine sighed and turned over in the darkness, waiting for sleep to come. Not everyone was in bed; the children were, Dido with a hand flung up over her head on to her pillow and Martin lying straight beneath his single quilt like a knight on a tomb, hands folded on his chest. But behind the house Tom was sitting beside the dead embers of the previous night's fire, leaning forward in the darkness, with his elbows on his knees and an almost empty wine bottle by his side. He seemed to be looking down the hill towards the sound of the river, through the motionless columns of the trees, to where the mist came creeping silently up from the valley floor, and he was crying.

Chapter Eleven

Evie had taken her passport with her, Martin said, and that was what had given them hope; not that it had occurred to them that she might, as was later suggested in the inquest, have been suicidal. What Justine and Louisa were afraid of was that harm might have been done to her. The papers at the time were full of murder, or at least that was how it felt to Justine in the newsagents every morning, where the tabloid headlines seemed to shriek violent death at her: a child abducted, a young mother bludgeoned to death in her bathroom, a whole family immolated by an estranged father.

Justine had been alone in the house that whole week, at the chilly end of a long, empty summer. Lucien had been away on one of his courses, and she had felt panic creeping towards her every night as she lay awake listening to the slurred voices raised in the street outside and the crash of broken glass on the corner as the pub closed. Lucien had phoned eventually. He had a Luddite streak, or something, and had scorned mobile phones then; Justine had to wait for him to call her from a phone booth in a crowded bar somewhere. When he heard what had happened Lucien had asked her if she wanted him to come back, but Justine had said no, wanting to appear more self-sufficient than she felt. Now, though, she wondered if she shouldn't have allowed Lucien to see how she was really feeling; after all, what harm would it have done? She was beginning to feel weary of her role, so proudly vaunted by Lucien, as a tower of strength.

Martin had said the passport was gone, there was no mistaking it. They kept all the family documents together, driving licences, passports, Dido's birth certificate, and Evie's had gone. The police did try to hint that it wasn't definitive, that it might have been taken to disguise Evie's intentions and that her failure to withdraw any money from their joint account was, after a month, a more ominous sign. The passport was on her when she was found; Martin said they'd discovered it tucked into an inside pocket; in her nightmares Justine had imagined its pages, swollen and blurred by salt water, Evie's image leaching from it into the muddy estuary.

Her car had been found weeks earlier, only days after her disappearance, in the windswept long-stay car park of a ferry terminal in Harwich, locked and empty. They had almost rejoiced then, because it was found at so quintessentially a point of transit, not a final destination, not even, surely, for a suicide. There were no cliffs in Harwich, there was no lovers' leap, only bleak, silvered mud flats, a brown trickle of water at low tide, a slew of identical articulated lorries awaiting embarkation. Justine had found it hard to imagine Evie in such a place, setting off on a rusty ferry full of booze-cruisers for a container-port in Holland or a closed-up, off-season Belgian seaside resort. But perhaps, if what she had wanted was escape, or anonymity, it might have seemed a perfectly symbolic point of departure. That, at any rate, was what Justine persuaded herself at the time.

Those four fraught weeks passed like an extraordinary and disturbing dream, while each of them tried to make sense of Evie's disappearance, imagined her with a new identity, in America, or New Zealand, or Italy, starting her life again somewhere thrilling and foreign. Living with someone else. With a shock Justine noticed bland little paragraphs about Evie in the papers, no more than a sentence or two and buried away at the tail end of the news pages. *Mother's Mystery Disappearance.* They must have been placed by the police press office, because certainly Martin had nothing to do with the newspapers. For a brief moment Evie became 'School Run Mum', and once a paper used an old photograph of her, laughing at a student party fifteen years earlier.

Whenever Justine saw such a piece her stomach would churn, as though Evie had been stolen from them not by a rapist or murderer, but by the reproduction of the grainy image, the smudged newsprint, the inaccurate details of her life. They tracked down an ex-boyfriend – not one Justine remembered – to say she was promiscuous, although he denied it later, and they got Dido's name wrong. One or two journalists appeared in the late summer drizzle outside their terrace in North London, and for a while Martin took Dido to stay with a cousin, to get away. But Evie's disappearance was not big news; she wasn't young or vulnerable enough, and eventually the journalists and their umbrellas evaporated.

Martin was in and out of the police station – more than once Justine had been asked to collect Dido from school because the detective in charge of the case wanted to interview him yet again. He seemed to keep his cool; he always arrived to collect Dido calm and unruffled, only maybe a little tired. Justine had tried to ask him, once, what they said to him; only because she couldn't imagine what it must be like to be confined in a police interview room, interrogated or cajoled, to know that you are suspected and to be helpless. Martin had just shaken his head, just a trace of contempt in his voice.

'They don't know anything,' he'd said simply. 'All that manpower, all that time – they find nothing.'

And Justine had just nodded, wondering whether he had misunderstood her, was deliberately evading her question, or was subtly letting her know that she was intruding.

For a few weeks after Evie's disappearance, as summer turned into autumn and the leaves began to coat the London pavements, Justine and Louisa had phoned each other often, as if they were as close as ever. They skirted around the subject of Evie's disappearance; instead they talked about old times. The three years they'd spent in and out of each other's rooms in that West London mansion block loomed large; they reminisced over every essay crisis, every boy invited back for a barbecue in the communal gardens, every coffee-fuelled late-night soul-searching session. Justine and Louisa, although they never said so, both felt that they could have done without each other better than they could manage without Evie. She was the cata-lyst, the live wire, the exotic; she was fierce, determined, she would do something one day. Without her they would have been nothing: suburban, timid, domestic specimens. That was what they were struggling against now she had disappeared.

Every day of that month Justine had woken with an odd, lost feeling; a small, insistent tug that told her something was hands; she slid them into the Aga, shut the heavy door, clicked on the kettle, dropped her apron in a laundry bin and then, finally, she came around the table to kiss Justine. Justine inhaled her scent, a faint whiff of lily of the valley mingled with vanilla. Louisa sat down, and they both sighed together.

'This is a nice surprise,' said Louisa. 'Is everything OK?'

'Mmm,' Justine nodded, uncertainly. 'Sort of. How about you?'

'Oh, well,' Louisa said. 'It's a worry, isn't it? I can't get it out of my head. Have the police been to see you?' The kettle boiled; she got up and went over to make the tea.

They hadn't. What would Justine have said? 'I didn't notice anything unusual?' She shook her head. 'How about you?'

Louisa frowned. 'Yes. Twice. But we couldn't tell them anything. What does one say?' She seemed distracted suddenly, and looked over at the oven. 'Can you smell burning?' she asked vaguely. Justine couldn't smell anything.

Louisa went on. 'It would just have been guessing, after all, wouldn't it? Martin's a dark horse, perhaps something was up in the marriage? I think that would be irresponsible. Nothing more than gossip. And how do you explain what kind of person Evie was, to some – some – adolescent policeman? I do think they're getting younger. Policemen.' She sighed again.

She had a point. Evie's life wasn't – consistent. Had never been. They would never have predicted, after all, that the Evie they had first known, with her adventurous sex life and romantic, globetrotting past, would have been the first to settle down. And if they had, that she would have stayed put for long, in a North London terrace with a child and a husband, all her passion invested in something so small-scale as family life. Ironically enough, Justine remembered that she, Justine, had been allocated that fate when they were all girls together, talking about the future. Perhaps because she was from a large family herself, they had predicted that she would be the first to produce a child. Justine looked down at her hands against the kitchen table, beginning to show signs of age against the smooth, pale wood. She looked up.

'I wonder where she's gone,' she said, repeating the old, obvious question without thinking. 'She could be anywhere. She could have just run away, couldn't she? That's what's hard to explain, to someone who didn't know her. A policeman. Didn't you always think, however long she'd been settled down, she could still just make a break for it? Being Evie.'

Louisa pursed her lips, just a little. 'Well, I don't think she ever took her responsibilities that seriously, do you? Marriage, children, that kind of thing; you just can't go on living just as you always did. Taking holidays in term time – do you remember when they all went to New York when Dido was five? I mean, New York!'

'Yes, but—' Justine began to protest; she remembered the trip; it had seemed quite natural at the time, the way Evie had described it, the Museum of Modern Art, the Bronx Zoo, the Staten Island Ferry. But she couldn't tell Louisa about the other Evie, not lighthearted at all, clinging to her baby as though to save herself from drowning. Vulnerable and desperate. 'That doesn't mean she was a bad mother.'

Grudgingly Louisa shrugged. 'No, no. I didn't exactly mean that. But she was never quite – domesticated. Was she? And frankly, family life, well, it's not a romantic adventure, is it? Evie always wanted it to be, carried on as if it was. It's hard work. Perhaps she finally realized that. She did seem – I don't know, a bit down. Last year.'

Justine nodded. That much was true; there'd been a while, a matter of months, when Evie had gone quiet, stopped phoning, had refused an invitation to a launch party for one of Justine's authors, at the Chelsea Arts Club, her favourite place. Justine thought back now to the telephone conversation, and the dullness, something like fear in Evie's voice when she'd said, *no. I can't,* leapt at her from out of the past. She felt a coldness in the pit of her stomach; guilt. *Why didn't I hear that, then? Or did I just ignore it?*

Justine bit her lip, and looked up at Louisa. 'But I thought,' she began, anxiously, 'I thought she was coming out of that. It started to seem like just a blip. I mean, she was at your party, the Christmas before, wasn't she?'

'Yes,' mused Louisa, 'without Martin, though. Wasn't she?' Justine felt a tug of sadness somewhere, remembering Evie at that party, drifting out into the frosty garden without even a cardigan, telling Lucien about some plan she had, for a holiday or a trip, to somewhere like India or Zanzibar. She'd been full of plans.

'Besides,' Louisa changed tack, 'the timing would fit. Wouldn't it? Dido's quite grown up now. I mean, if she and Martin were – drifting apart? Is that what they say?' Justine had stared at her, aghast at the implication. Is this how it happened, when marriages broke down? Could no one else tell, could the presence of children, of the child Evie had loved so passionately, matter so little? She thought of Martin, the way his eyes followed Evie around a crowded room, an invisible thread joining them, and she couldn't imagine him allowing Evie to drift away, casually. He'd never let her go. Slowly she shook her head.

'I can't see it,' she said bluntly. 'And I can't see her leaving

Dido, either.' And then Louisa had turned away, and sighed, not in reproof, this time, but something more like hopelessness, a note so uncharacteristic of Louisa that Justine listened.

'Oh, Justine,' she had said, 'I'm sorry to say this, but you really don't know, until you've had children, what you are capable of. Good or bad. You lose control. That kind of love – can be too much. Sometimes you just want things to be simple again.' Then Louisa had fallen abruptly silent, as if she'd given away too much.

Justine had finished her tea without saying anything, setting the empty cup down in the sink. 'Sorry, Louisa,' she said. 'I shouldn't have just turned up. Thanks for the tea.' Louisa nodded. 'Lovely to see you,' she said, vaguely, her mind somewhere else.

In the lemon-painted hall, full of the smell of late roses, Justine paused, her hand on the door, and turned to say goodbye. It was very quiet, she realized, no sound of Tom bashing away upstairs as usual, still unable to believe his word processor wasn't the old manual typewriter that had always required force. She opened her mouth to make some light-hearted remark about it, but something in Louisa's expression dissuaded her, a warning look.

'Bye, then,' Justine said. 'Bye.'

All the way back on the tube Justine had tried to put the pieces together, but they refused to fit; Evie wanted freedom, but she loved her family. They had wanted Evie to be starting a new life, in New Zealand or Spain or Morocco, drinking mint tea in a blue-tiled hammam, but there in the stuffy, neon-lit underground train such a picture seemed ridiculously naïve. With a chill of foresight she understood that Evie's life belonged to the dull-witted, adolescent policemen now, to their files and notes and mugshots. What had happened to Evie might have been horribly random, might have had nothing to do with her character, her longings and dreams; she'd become a crime statistic; a newspaper report. Missing.

There had been a post-mortem, of course, and an inquest. Justine had gone alone, Louisa had come with Tom, who appeared red-faced and blurry with drink and unhappiness. Evie had drowned; her lungs had been full of seawater. There were some areas of bruising, but nothing definitively indicating foul play, no marks of strangulation or restraint. The coroner had questioned Martin quite closely about Evie's state of mind, making very little allowance for his own unhappiness, Justine thought. She had wanted to explain to the coroner that Martin was not good at showing his emotions, that it was clearly an agony to him to be standing there discussing Evie with a coroner's court full of strangers. There'd been an implication that she might have been neurotic; Martin had said, stiffly, that he didn't believe that his wife was suicidal.

There was a fuzzy image from the closed-circuit cameras in the ferry terminal. It was a lonely-looking place, grey and draughty at the tail end of August in the North Sea wind; the passengers were not for the most part dressed up for glamorous travel as they might have been in the bright, warm cocoon of an airport departure lounge. The terminal was not considered a major terrorist target, and their security measures were basic, the cameras a long way from cutting-edge technology. The still the police had showed Justine, when they came to interview her, had shown Evie standing at the ticket desk, filmed from above, her face a pale indistinct oval, her body foreshortened and blurred. To Justine she had looked fearful, and uncharacteristically hesitant, but perhaps that was just hindsight.

If Evie had been boarding an aircraft perhaps more information might have been available about her intentions; someone would have looked into her face and asked about her luggage, whether she had packed it herself, whether she wanted to check something in. There might have been others in the queue to remember her. But no one seemed to travel by ferry any more and the place was half empty. There was no proof that she had even embarked on the crossing for which she had bought a ticket; one or two passengers on the boat thought they might have seen her, standing alone at the rusted metal rail, but they couldn't be certain. She might have fallen, she might have been pushed; she might have walked into the sea or jumped silently from the town pier; a coastguard gave evidence that any of these could have been consistent with the location of her body.

So the indistinct black-and-white image was all that remained of Evie, a shoulder bag on her arm that might have been big enough to contain spare clothes, a toothbrush, to indicate that she was on her way somewhere, that she would be going to bed that night. But the shoulder bag had never been found, perhaps its contents were lying half-buried on a sand bar or a mudflat, the bag itself disintegrated to nothing more than a buckle and a zip. The inquest returned an open verdict. It was extraordinary to Justine that so momentous a thing could happen and yet leave so little trace.

Chapter Twelve

Justine came out of the dark of the steep, narrow stone staircase that led to the viewing platform and blinked in the brilliant sunlight. She was – they were all, now, as she was the last one up – perched on the very top of the stupendous, logic-defying dome that dominated every view of Florence. She stood with her back to the platform's central pillar and looked out over the sprawling city as it shimmered in the mild September sun; the view was breathtaking. Up here, so far above the dark, narrow streets of the medieval city, the sky seemed suddenly vast and perfectly blue, just streaked here and there with wisps of cloud. Justine could see domes of terracotta and verdigris punctuating the red-tiled roofs and the grid of the city's streets all seeming to converge on the huge cathedral, she could see beyond the city to the hills and the suburbs. At the airport, beside the green river winding out to the west, a distant aircraft was coming in to land and she could almost, or so she imagined, see where the soft blue air met the sea at the western horizon.

missing, that there was a puzzle needed solving. She couldn't talk to Lucien about Evie; whenever Justine began, to wonder aloud in his presence what Evie might have been thinking, he grew oddly impatient, didn't want to know. Lucien had never been one for introspection; perhaps he thought it self-indulgent, feminine. One early evening after work, on impulse Justine had taken the tube out to Hammersmith instead of her usual bus back to Lucien in Notting Hill, to see Louisa and Tom.

Louisa was there, of course, having given up full-time work once she'd had the children. Tom let Justine in; he seemed distracted, and Justine thought perhaps she'd disturbed him in the middle of writing a piece. He gestured vaguely towards the kitchen before heading back upstairs, slowly.

Louisa was baking muffins in the kitchen for the children's lunchboxes the next day; just looking at her made Justine, coming through the door after a day at work and an hour on the underground, feel weak. She sank on to a chair, and waited for Louisa to finish.

Although the two were poles apart, Justine liked sitting in Louisa's kitchen as much as she liked sitting in Evie's; perhaps the only kitchen she never felt quite comfortable in, she reflected as she sat there, was her own. Or rather, Lucien's. Where Evie's was all creative chaos, Louisa's represented order, and absolute control; there was no mess, no clutter; not even a dusting of flour despite the baking going on. It was all pale wood and slate, with an Aga, a butcher's block and a butler sink, secret drawers and carousels all tucked away behind handmade cupboards, all researched, chosen and saved for by Louisa.

Louisa smiled over at her, the muffins in her oven-gloved

A little below them and perhaps a hundred metres away was the pink and green candy-stick of the bell tower where other tourists, tiny as dolls, were standing pressed against the wrought-iron grilles with their cameras. To the south, dark-green hills spiked with cypresses rose out of the crowded city, here and there on their slopes façades of marble and gold glittered like buried treasure among the trees. Breathless after the climb – 463 steps to the top – and half-stunned by the volume of humanity on the streets below after the silence of the forest, Justine stood still for a long moment or two, grateful for the cool solidity of the stone at her back and the distance between her and the crowded streets.

The plan to come to Florence had been made over breakfast, and to everyone's surprise had been suggested by Martin.

'I'd like to see the Medici library,' he stated abruptly, standing by the door with his cup of coffee. 'Evie – Evie often talked about it, the Michelangelo staircase. She said you had to see it. Among other things.'

Startled, no one could think of a reason to disagree straight off; after all, it was no more than an hour away, the treasure-house of European art. And Martin seemed determined.

'I didn't know Evie knew Florence,' said Justine.

'Ah, yes,' said Martin. 'In her year off before university she spent a couple of months here, some art history course or other. Staying with a family.'

They looked at him expectantly.

'Anyway,' he went on, sounding reluctant, 'there's an exhibition of Da Vinci's machines, I think. At the library.'

Dido made a face. 'Oh, Dad,' she said, 'machines?'

The ghost of a smile appeared on Martin's face. 'You don't have to come, if you don't want to,' he said.

Louisa had an idea. 'Why don't Justine and I take Dido shopping?' she said. 'We could do something together in the morning, then split up. We could meet back up at the restaurant in the evening?'

Tom looked at her with weary indulgence. 'Very selfless,' he said. 'Whatever happened to culture? I suppose I get the boys, then?' At this Sam and Angus, for whom the prospect of a library visit or a shopping trip had generated no enthusiasm, cheered and jumped, pulling at his arm.

'Don't look like that,' said Louisa. 'You could take the boys to the park, or something. I'm sure there's a good park in Florence, isn't there? The Tivoli? Boboli?'

'Yeah, Dad, a park,' said Sam. 'That'd be OK. And maybe they have arcades there, you know, games arcades? Even in the bar yesterday they had Grand Theft Auto.'

Tom sighed. 'Oh, God,' he said, in mock despair, and the others, even Martin, had laughed. Even as Justine laughed with him, though, she thought Tom looked tired, his eyes rimmed with pink; it was as if there was something inside draining him, syphoning off the avid, robust vitality she had always thought of as Tom's defining characteristic.

Justine looked at Tom now; flushed with the exertion of their climb he looked exhilarated as he knelt against the rail with his arm around Sam and pointed across at the hills and the domes that punctuated the city skyline. There was something about being so high that Justine felt too, the giddy, euphoric sensation that came with danger and the dramatic change of perspective. Whatever it was, Louisa seemed immune to it though; she was standing, stiffly holding Angus's hand with white knuckles, trying not to look down. The boys had climbed all the way up on their own, even the last, steep, claustrophobic steps up inside the curved skin of the dome with only a flimsy handrail for support where Lucien, who did not like enclosed spaces, had become rather tetchy.

Angus and Sam had particularly enjoyed the gallery that led half-way around the inside of the dome, high above the nave, because it afforded them point-blank views of the garish visions of hell painted on the ceiling. They had had to be shushed to stop their giggling at the devils impaled on pokers, and writhing naked bodies, as they were in danger of offending the faithful below. It was here, not right on the top in the open air, that Justine had felt the vertiginous lure of the drop, the urge to lean too far over the handrail and free-fall down, just to see what it felt like.

She felt a weakness in her legs at the thought, and into her mind's eye flashed a picture of Evie at the flaking rail of a cross-channel ferry, looking down at the white flare of its wake, considering how cold the water might be, how far down there was to fall. Justine held on tight as she edged around the gallery; below her it was a sheer drop two hundred feet down to the cold gleam of the apse's marble floor where worshippers knelt, tiny as ants below them, and the tourists shuffled in herds from one side-chapel to another.

Once out of the trapdoor at the top, Justine felt nothing but exhilaration in the bright day, the glorious panorama wheeling around them. Beside her she heard Lucien sigh, and she turned to look at him.

'God,' he said, 'it's a bore, isn't it, this tourist trail? The place is heaving.'

He looked around the viewing platform which, although not empty, was far from heaving. Justine said nothing, not wanting to disagree with him straight away.

Lucien went on. 'I don't know why we decided to come here, really. It's so over-rated. Did you see all those groups? Following their guides just like sheep.'

Mildly, Justine protested. 'We walked through some beautiful bits. I bet if you wander about on your own this afternoon you'll find some undiscovered part of Florence. You're good at that.'

Lucien didn't answer, but he stepped forward a little and looked out over the city, considering.

'Maybe,' he said reluctantly. He looked across at Louisa, who was pulling at Tom's sleeve in an attempt to persuade him to go back down. She looked anxious, one eye on the boys as they pressed against the apparently insubstantial, waist-high rail. Dido appeared beside her, coming around the rail from the far side of the platform with Martin's hand resting protectively on her shoulder.

'Do you really want to go shopping with those two?' he said. 'A girls' outing?' He sounded disgruntled. 'They're just designer con-merchants, those shops, Prada, Gucci, it's all rubbish produced in the third world, you know. It's an international conspiracy.'

'Uh-huh,' said Justine, which constituted a refusal to comment. She diverted him. 'I think it would be nice for Dido,' she said. 'We're not going to be buying designer handbags, you needn't worry. And I quite like shopping, once in a while.'

There was defiance in her voice, because Lucien had always maintained to their friends, without always asking her opinion first, that she was above all that. She stood alongside him in the fight against global capitalism. If left to herself she would probably agree with him, but there was something about being press-ganged into it that she resisted. And although Lucien was very inventive and thoughtful in his gift-giving – coming up with vintage scarves, hand-woven rugs, bits of salvaged marble sculpture – sometimes she longed for the vulgar thrill of a shiny handbag, a high-heeled shoe or a tissue-wrapped frock. And she did like shopping, once in a while. She thought of Evie. Dido was looking across at them, and Justine smiled at her.

'I'm going back down,' said Lucien shortly. And he turned and walked towards the exit.

Paolo stirred at the sound of the cars passing, but only a little; he drifted in and out of sleep and the tail-end of a dream of surgery. He dreamed he was in theatre, masked and gowned, trying to repair a child's complicated fracture subcutaneously, looking at the luminous splinters of bone on an X-ray screen, but every time he slotted them together they sprang apart. He struggled awake. The bed was warm, outside the sky was an electric blue where the points of a few stars were still visible.

I need to get back to the hospital, he thought, wearily. Back to work. He knew he had to make a decision.

Anna had seen the English cars go past, in a hurry, off to the main road. Too early for just a shopping trip, she thought, and besides, they were all going this time, so perhaps it was a day trip somewhere. I hope they know to get back before it's too late, she thought to herself; I wouldn't like to be bumping down that road in the pitch darkness.

There was a cool edge to the air this morning, Anna thought, as she stepped out on to the stone flags of her shaded terrace, but it wasn't unwelcome. The older she got the more Anna grew to appreciate the autumn; it took age and experience, she understood now, to stop longing always for the summer to come. And, after all, autumn was the most delicious season; the little vans from the vineyards loaded with round golden muscatel grapes as sweet as nectar would turn up in the market square, announcements of the arrival of truffles were chalked up outside grocers' shops and porcini in wooden crates appeared on every corner in Siena. There was a great deal to be appreciated, even so late in the year.

Upstairs she could hear Paolo moving about, up early today. She wondered what had got into him; he was quite unlike himself. He had something on his mind, but at least it wasn't Livia any more.

Anna had never liked Livia, and that was the truth, and she couldn't see what Paolo saw in her. She was pretty, Anna admitted grudgingly, and she could see that perhaps a mother was not the right person to analyse her son's love life. Paolo had been too romantic, perhaps; he had believed her to be what she was not. There had always been something about Livia that had seemed wrong to Anna; she didn't want children, she didn't cook; she enjoyed her work in the hospital labs, certainly, but she was paid good money for it too. She made no sacrifice for anyone else; she wasn't interested in home-making. Still, Anna thought uneasily, they might have said that about her, too, as a young woman; living away from home, independent, and selfish; at the time it had not seemed that she had any choice; it hadn't seemed as simple as that.

Of course when Anna herself had fallen in love it had not been as simple as that either; her lover had had a wife of his own to provide for him. When for the first time Anna had tried her hand at home-making, laid the table for them in her attic flat, he had stood and stared at the rolled napkins and the water glasses, frowning as though aware for the first time that he was doing something wrong.

167

Anna took a cloth and wiped the dew from the table on her terrace, and quickly, with a briskness born of long practice, she pushed the memory away. In a week or two the table would have to be put away for the winter, she reflected. Not quite yet. She heard Paolo in the kitchen and she went back in to the warm dark room. He still had that dazed look about him, dark circles under his eyes, face a little crumpled with sleep, and she heard him sigh as he filled the espresso pot.

He looked around at the sound and smiled when he saw her. 'Mamma,' he said.

She reached for the coffee pot.

'I'll do it,' he said. 'Sit down.'

Obediently, for once, even feeling a kind of relief at being told what to do Anna sat at the kitchen table and watched Paolo spoon the coffee into a pyramid in the metal filter then carefully screw on the lid, his big hands surprisingly deft. He took even the smallest task seriously, she realized; he never did anything carelessly. Perhaps that had seemed dull to Livia.

'What shall we do today then?' he asked, sounding cheerful, to her surprise.

'I haven't thought,' she said. 'Is there something you want to do?'

Paolo paused, considering something. 'I'd like to look for mushrooms,' he said, surprising her again. 'On my walk yesterday I thought I saw some of those yellow ones you like, down by the river. Perhaps we could go down there again.'

His expression had changed; no longer distracted, Paolo was looking at her a little warily, and for some reason Anna was reminded of her son as a small boy trying to pull a fast one. The throaty burble of the little aluminium coffee pot indicated

168

the arrival of the coffee, and Paolo turned from her to take it off the flame before it burned.

Anna considered his back. All that way down there?' she said, reluctantly 'What, you mean near Il Vignacce?'

He shrugged, pouring the coffee, his back still turned. 'Yes, that way. Is it too far for you?'

Anna wondered why Paolo wanted to go there, after all this time. To see the foreigners? She looked at him, her head on one side. If he wants to go, she thought, taking a deep breath. 'No, not at all. I think the walk would do me good.'

He turned to face her and smiled, but before he could say anything she went on.

'But I think it might be better tomorrow; then we could call in on those people at Il Vignacce. They won't be there today, because I saw them going off in their cars first thing this morning. They must be off on a day trip. Did I mention I met them yesterday?'

'Oh, yes?' said Paolo, and she could tell straight away from his tone that it was, as she had suspected, the English at Il Vignacce he wanted to get a closer look at, not the yellow mushrooms. 'When was that?'

'In town, of course,' Anna said. 'When you were on your walk. Well, that's to say, I met some of them. Montale introduced us. We're their neighbours, if you think about it, even if they are seven kilometres away. I expect they'd like visitors, stuck down there, don't you think?'

Paolo shrugged. 'Maybe,' he said. 'Were they friendly?'

'Yes, for English people. You know, polite. I don't know if I met all of them; I think perhaps there was one missing, who stayed behind. But the children were lovely, two boys, and an older girl but she kept very quiet. I said you might be able to tell them a thing or two about hiding places in the forest.' She looked up guilelessly at him from the table, and saw him smile.

'OK, OK, Mamma. Tomorrow we'll go for a walk, and maybe we'll go down there and look for the mushrooms. So what about today?'

Chapter Thirteen

'Do you think I need to, you know, change my – the way I look?' At the plaintive note in Louisa's voice Justine looked up from the two-day old newspaper, and frowned.

Louisa was scrutinizing her image in a huge, up-lit mirror. It covered the back wall of the gleaming wood and steel interior where they were waiting for Dido to emerge from a changing room. Down a cobbled street somewhere behind the cathedral, the shop was intimidatingly fashionable, and, if it hadn't been for their desire to please Dido, the women would probably not have gone inside.

Silver speakers hung from the ceiling, as gleaming and curvaceous as flying saucers and vibrating with bass noise; the music might have been from Mars, too, for all the common culture Justine found in it. A willowy, dark-haired salesgirl, beautiful enough to be a model, was folding sweaters on a glass table in the centre of the long showroom, her movements so decorous and soothing that she might have been observing a sacred rite. Beside the mirror, where Louisa was standing, was a row of velvet-curtained cubicles into which Dido had recently disappeared with an armful of low-slung jeans and shrunken-looking sweatshirts.

'Why?' asked Justine. She was not used to hearing Louisa express self-doubt. Perhaps, she thought with alarm, it was a sign of age.

'Oh,' sighed Louisa, 'I don't know.' She sounded bewildered. 'Tom's – he's not himself. He drinks all the time.' She turned to Justine. 'He doesn't eat. I wondered if it might be me.' She turned away again and looked at herself, perplexed.

Justine followed Louisa's gaze; framed by the mirror, dressed in a version of her neat, pastel uniform which today consisted of a pale-blue sweatshirt and cropped cotton trousers, Louisa looked, as she always did, small, trim and pretty. Ever since Justine could remember Louisa had been the same, never doubting her own taste, decisive, practical and unruffled by fashion or her mother's criticism. Louisa's appearance, like so much else in her life, seemed to Justine to be a matter of discipline.

She had been very determined, for example, to regain her figure after the boys' births – Justine remembered Louisa saying at the time that she didn't want anyone to be able to guess that she'd had children – and she had succeeded.

Justine had found this unaccountably depressing, perhaps for what it said about her own idealized view of motherhood, or about men's, or Louisa's inexorable transformation into her own mother, who had taken a cocktail dress into the maternity ward with her and managed to fit into it three hours after giving birth. While admitting to a grudging admiration for Louisa's iron will – all those salads without dressing, grilled chicken breasts with the skin carefully removed – Justine had thought even then, though she hadn't voiced it, that if she had a baby she would not care if it was written all over her body, she would be so triumphant. And it was unsettling to think that now, despite all the time and effort Louisa had spent to look the way she did, the sit-ups, the squash, the waxing and ironing and bleaching, she should suddenly be unhappy with herself; it seemed as though she had lost faith. Justine wondered what was going on.

Justine looked up at her friend from the hard, modern sofa, the newspaper on her lap, and waited for her answer. Louisa was turning slightly away from the mirror, looking back at her body and frowning as though she didn't recognize it, the small waist, flat stomach, sharp, elegant brown ankles.

'Oh, hell,' she said, helpless and impatient. 'I don't know. It's just – you know, you go along thinking you're doing things the right way, more or less, ended up with the right person, doing the right job, or whatever, then something happens and you're not so sure any more. It's like that.'

Not Louisa, thought Justine. 'You're not sure if you're with the right person?' she said. 'Tom?'

'No,' said Louisa. 'That's not exactly—' she broke off. 'I meant him. I always thought I was what Tom wanted, that he liked me as I was, but—' At the sound of her rising voice the salesgirl looked up from her reverie and Louisa fell silent; Justine glanced at the curtain below which Dido's ankles were visible.

Louisa went on, more quietly. 'You've got your job, you've got something to show for yourself. I know I've got the kids, and, I mean, I love them, you know I do ...' She paused, sounding almost anguished. 'But they grow up, don't they?

173

They're not really mine, not in the long term. They'll get girlfriends who hate the mother-in-law and before you know it, you don't see them any more.'

Justine laughed with disbelief at the sight of Louisa's thirty-five years of defiant self-belief going up in smoke. One by one they seemed to be giving in to age and disappointment, even Louisa, and reluctantly Justine found herself wondering if what Lucien had said might have been true after all. About Tom and Evie. She pushed the thought away, and concentrated instead on what Louisa had just said, which was easier to deny.

'Come on, Louisa,' she said. 'Don't be ridiculous. They're hardly about to get married, they're only what, six and nine? And they're not going to stop seeing you, they love you. They'll probably want to marry a girl just like you.'

Louisa grimaced at the thought and turned her back on the mirror. She looked down at her hands, something sheepish in her stance. She sighed. 'But – oh, all right, all right,' she said. 'Do you think it's an early menopause, then?'

'What, you, or Tom?' Justine asked. But she had a nagging feeling that they had missed the point somehow; that Louisa had been about to confide in her and Justine had headed her off. What was it, exactly, that she didn't want to know about her friends' marriage? But despite herself, Louisa laughed, and as though her laughter was a signal, at that moment the swagged velvet of the end cubicle was drawn back and Dido appeared. She was wearing a tight, plum-coloured T-shirt and dark denim jeans above which gleamed a flat, pale strip of midriff. She flushed a little, one arm bent across her body in a shy gesture, but she looked radiant and was smiling at them.

'What do you think?' she said, and Justine and Louisa both smiled back at her with relief, at the interruption, at Dido's happiness, even at the thought that they were no longer girls on a shopping spree, but the older generation looking at the younger.

'Lovely,' they said together.

'*Bella*,' said the salesgirl, smiling and nodding her head like a geisha.

They had divided up on the crowded steps at the front of the cathedral, Tom with the boys, the three women together, Martin and Lucien each alone.

The agreement was that they would make separate arrangements for lunch but would meet back up at seven at a bar with tables in the Piazza della Signoria. The bar, called Rivoire, was elegant, overpriced, in Tom's estimation, but very easy to find, and from there they could go to the restaurant together.

The women had stood, irresolute, on the cathedral steps, and watched as the men traced their separate paths between the backpackers sitting in the sun, through the queue for entry to the cathedral that snaked right around its great green and white marble bulk and back on itself, around the horsedrawn carriages waiting in the sun for tourist custom. Justine had watched Martin walking north towards the old market and the Medici library, a tall, purposeful figure; she tried to imagine how he would spend his day, and failed. When she turned back she could see Tom as he headed purposefully towards the south, the boys trailing behind him, bickering and pushing, but Lucien had already disappeared.

Now, as the women stood waiting to pay for Dido's purchases in a narrow street on the far side of the city, Lucien was walking through the elegant cream and grey *pietra serena* porticoes of the Uffizi. Without a sideways glance that might betray interest in their efforts he strolled past the street artists propped against every pillar, each one cajoling passers by into having a caricature drawn, or buying a watercolour of the Ponte Vecchio. There was a long queue waiting under the colonnade to get inside the museum, clustered here and there into patient groups being lectured by their tour guides on what they would see once they gained entry. Lucien by-passed the queue and slipped in through a side door, but no more than twenty minutes later he was back out again, holding a small, postcard-sized paper bag with the museum's logo printed on it with an air of satisfaction.

Lucien tucked the small paper package into his pocket and crossed the long, rectangular flagstoned courtyard, an airy refined space filled with jostling sightseers, balloon sellers and cheap reproductions stacked for sale in plastic folders. At one end stood the heavy stone battlements of the Palazzo Vecchio, at the other an arcaded view across the river, but Lucien ignored both, slipping between the tall buildings and down an alley lined with the bright windows of expensive artisan boutiques.

By the time Lucien reached the end of the street he had bought some gloves made of very soft dark-red pigskin, a heavy silk shirt and a set of handsome gold cufflinks modelled on an Etruscan design. He spent some time in each shop, discussing the methods of production and source of materials; he didn't like to buy anything that was not produced locally, and using traditional techniques, and he prided himself on making human contact, on treating people as though they were equals. When he bought the last item, in a shop like a jewel-box, lined with velvet and inlaid wood and smelling of mahogany, Lucien had lightly pointed out to the saleswoman that the Etruscans

176

had not worn cuffs, let alone cufflinks. He asked her the Italian for cufflinks. She had laughed, prettily, and he had asked her if she could recommend somewhere for lunch.

She was called Silvia. 'Do you know anywhere good?' he had asked, confidentially, smiling at her. 'Not a tourist place.'

Tentatively Silvia had suggested a little winebar just across the river, where the tourists, she said with a shrug, generally were thinner on the ground. Lucien thanked her thoughtfully. At this point Silvia did, she admitted to herself later, once the door had closed behind the Englishman, expect him to ask her to join him; it would not have been the first time that an overture had been made by such a customer, although naturally she would not always accept. This one, though, was well dressed, handsome, confident; the kind of man who would not be turned down. But he didn't ask her to lunch, not even for an aperitif; she had the feeling, however, that the possibility hovered between them and he took some pleasure in refusing it. Even the shop's manager, who had observed the exchange from the small back room where he had been sorting stock, had waited with one ear cocked for the invitation to come. As the doorbell swung into silence behind their last customer of the morning and no invitation had been issued, not even a single word of flirtation, he leaned back and looked through into the shop, observing his pretty assistant's tiny frown of discontent. Well, well, he thought. Not that sort of man, after all.

It was in the bar that Silvia had recommended that Lucien now sat, drinking a large glass of expensive Chianti and contemplating a steaming dish of risotto with shaved truffle, at a marble-topped table with a good view of the passers-by. Lucien seemed pleased with the choice; it wasn't cheap, but it was an attractive place, wood-panelled and bright with polished glass and silver, and quiet. Besides, it wasn't that Lucien disliked spending money, more that he disliked waste, buying expensive dinners or unnecessary gifts for those who didn't appreciate them, paying for someone's compromised taste. He looked around at the delicate wall-sconces, the refined carving of the cornices, with some satisfaction as he ate. Along one wall were long glazed doors that had been opened to offer a view out into a quiet, stone-paved side-street, and it was while he was enjoying the air and the view this afforded that Lucien saw Martin.

Martin wasn't alone. He was walking slowly down the centre of the street, his arm around a red-haired woman. She was about his age, freckled and white-skinned, and in fact it was she Lucien had first seen, being on his side of Martin and very beautiful. She was tall, with a long, high-cheekboned face, dark, tawny hazel eyes, and she was unnaturally pale, as though she'd had a great shock. There was something intense about the pairing; neither of the two was speaking and it looked to Lucien as though the woman might be crying. He watched, frowning, as slowly they walked to the end of the street and around a corner. For a moment it looked as though Lucien was considering paying up and following them, but instead he sat back in his chair. He ordered an espresso, and slowly, thoughtfully, as though his mind was elsewhere, he began to look through his purchases.

The women were enjoying themselves. They'd been to a smart bar for lunch, and found themselves herded to the marble counter with a crowd of elegant Florentine women, all of them dripping with emeralds and eating tiny bowls of pasta standing up, leaning against the gleaming counter and talking

178

fast. They'd watched to see how it was done by the locals, then imitated their orders. Justine ended up with linguine with clams, Louisa rigatoni with spinach, Dido a risotto sticky with cheese. Giving up on conversation in the cheerful din, they ate hungrily, staring around at their exotic surroundings; a stern barman polishing champagne flutes, a gigantic Murano chandelier hanging low in the centre of the tea room, baroque murals, glittering silver.

It was hot even in the shade as, replete, the three women wandered through the streets. Now that it was long past midday, approaching three, the tall buildings kept all the direct light out of the narrow alleys, but it was deliriously warm, a steady, dry heat that could never have been replicated at home. They had found their way down closer to the river, where every street seemed to have a tempting bright vista at the end, and tiny shops were set in the bottom of every tall building. After the quiet of the long lunch hour the streets seemed to be filling up. There were mothers and their daughters, dressed identically, sleek hair back, dark glasses and cardigans draped over their shoulders, deep in conversation; tourists and handsome couples arm in arm, looking in the shop windows as their owners came out to open their shutters.

'Aren't you going to get anything?' Dido asked, hugging her expensive bags to her chest and smiling with unselfconscious delight. Her cheeks were pink with sun. 'Go on,' she said. 'Mum used to love going shopping.' And her face seemed to lose a little of its radiance.

'Oh, maybe,' said Justine, partly to please her, to bring the glow of happiness back. Oh, Evie, she thought, despairing suddenly; it was one of the things that made it hard to believe she no longer existed; she had made such clear choices about everything: what she wore, what she liked to eat, where to go on holiday. Where did all that go? All that information, all that hard-wiring, disposable after all.

She smiled at Dido. Never mind Lucien, she thought, defiantly. It's none of his business. If I see something I want, I'll buy it. The problem was, Justine wasn't like Evie; she wasn't ever that sure abut anything.

So they wandered on, with hours to kill before the appointed time, past shops full of marbled paper, tortoise-shell obelisks, gilded mirrors. They paused at a tiny jeweller's, tucked in profanely under the massive, sombre wing of a church, and looked in at the display, full of baroque coral and gold and pearls; pendants, bangles, rough-cut diamond daisies for earrings. There were plenty of expensive, gleaming boutiques, plate glass and artful displays, but nothing that tempted Justine in. It didn't seem to matter; holidays should be like this, she thought, just wandering the warm streets, plenty of time. Then a woman passed them walking the other way, about their age, wearing a flowered dress wrapped and tied at the hip, crimson and pale pink, long, fluted sleeves, little red sandals. They all stopped to look at her, unable to help themselves; she seemed oblivious, pausing a little way on to look in at a display of shoes, ribboned satin and punched leather, thoughtfully stroking her chin.

'That's nice,' said Dido, with enthusiasm. 'You'd look lovely in that, Justine.'

'Mmm,' said Justine, wistfully. 'It's pretty.' The woman seemed to exist in a different universe, somewhere brighter, more optimistic, where there were places and occasions to dress up for.

'Ask her where she got it,' said Dido, nudging. 'Go on.'

'No!' said Justine, laughing at Dido in surprise; suddenly

it struck her how like Evie she was, the way she thought everything was possible. Had once thought. Dido had that same natural sweetness.

Dido rolled her eyes; something about her expression tugged at Justine's memory.

'Well, I will if you won't,' Dido said, smiling, and as Justine and Louisa watched in startled admiration Dido crossed the narrow street and politely stood near the pretty woman in her flowered dress. After a moment she seemed to notice the girl standing attentive at her elbow, turned away from the shop window and addressed herself, a little bemused, to Dido's bright face. With gestures and sign language and a bit of her year's Italian thrown in, Dido managed to communicate her question. She looked back at them across the street, smiling and happy, sure everything would be fine. Like her mother.

Louisa and Justine looked at each other, the same thought in their heads, almost tearful as they recognized the scene played out in front of them. Evie had done the very same thing, on Bond Street of all places, when they were all still students. She had seized a haughty, well-heeled woman by the elbow because she liked her coat and managed to charm her into giving away its origins. Evie had not betrayed a moment's dismay when she discovered it came from the most dauntingly expensive shop on the street, and had just thanked the woman seriously and begun to plan where she might find a decent copy.

Triumphant, Dido came back to them with her prize: information. 'Down there,' she said, pointing towards the river. The pretty woman stood and watched them go from behind dark glasses, smiling and shaking her head.

It was a tiny, bright window between a grocer's and a shop selling engravings of the city; in the window stood a mannequin in a suit of dark-blue silk, narrow-waisted, pearl buttoned, with deep cuffs. It looked expensive; handmade. Inside double rows of hanging identical dresses and waisted shirts, one above the other, of silk, linen, flowered, geometric-patterned, pink and red, cornflower blue and chocolate brown crowded against each other in the narrow space.

A bell pinged as they entered, and at the far end of the shop a curtain was pushed back to reveal a heavy-duty sewing machine and rolls of cloth. A young, serious-looking woman came out from behind the sewing machine, untying an apron. She approached them with a tentative smile; perhaps it was clear that they were not Italian, and they soon realized that she had no other language.

'Wow,' said Dido.

'It's a dressmaker's,' said Louisa, reverently. 'A real dressmaker's.'

Once Justine had explained to the assistant what she was looking for, half-embarrassed still at her own persistence, the dress was located quickly, and smilingly, with nods and gestures, the seamstress encouraged her into a tiny curtained corner of the shop. Telling herself that it would certainly not fit, and if it fitted would not look the same, Justine put it on.

It felt perfect. The fastenings were clever, a button and a tie at the waist, it fitted closely without being tight, it crossed over just low enough at the front not to be demure and the narrow sleeves turned back in a little cuff, halfway along her forearm. Justine couldn't see herself, but suddenly she felt as though she had a waist, a bosom, a long neck, slim wrists. She felt like a different person. Reluctantly, lest she be disappointed, she came out of the cubicle to look in the mirror, and when she saw herself she flushed with relief. She turned a little in front of her reflection, seeing someone confident, independent. Stupid, she thought. It's just a dress. But Louisa hugged her.

'You look beautiful,' she said.

'Gorgeous,' said Dido. 'Go on.'

Defiantly Justine bought two; one flowered, one in scarlet linen, feeling the unfamiliar glow of a secret pleasure as she handed over the bundle of bright foreign money. Together they burst out of the shop, talking and laughing with excitement, holding their bags like trophies, ridiculously happy.

'Your turn now,' said Justine to Louisa, laughing, as she caught her surreptitiously sneaking a backward look into the window of a shoe shop as they passed.

'Well,' said Louisa, shamefacedly, 'perhaps just a look.' And before they could voice their agreement she had slipped into the shop.

Left outside, Justine and Dido sat down on a stone bench that ran along the foot of the building opposite Louisa's shop. Dido put an arm through Justine's. 'This is nice,' she said.

'Yes,' said Justine, waiting. There was a pause.

Dido sighed. 'Mum used to take me shopping,' she said, hesitantly. 'She – she'd just started taking me to the places she bought her own stuff. I think she was fed up with me pinching it.' She looked up at Justine. 'When – when they found her, I went up to her room, I got a jersey out of her drawer and – I put my face in it. It smelled of her, you see. It was a red one, mohair. I always wanted it.' She looked up at Justine, her eyes liquid.

Justine felt some memory tug at her. She nodded, thinking of the smell of her father's top drawer, peppermints and tobacco, and pulled Dido a bit closer. 'It'll get better,' she said, stroking her hair. 'Eventually.'

They both fell silent for a while, leaning against the cool, rough stone of the wall and looking at the passers-by; the narrow street was busy now. At the far end of their bench two elderly ladies, elegant in navy blue and dark glasses, had found a spot in the sun and were enjoying a leisurely conversation.

Then Dido spoke. 'When you said – Mum was unhappy. Must have been unhappy. You're right. She stopped – she stopped enjoying things. Shopping, painting, you know. But I thought she was getting better When she – when she went. She'd been fine for ages.'

'Mmm,' said Justine, thinking. It was true, that last time, that summer evening, she really had seemed fine. Listened carefully, as she always did, to what was happening in Justine's life. Justine nodded. 'Was there anything in particular? That made *you* think things were improving?'

Dido shrugged a little, looking down at her hands in her lap, and Justine couldn't see her expression. 'She bought a dress,' she said, slowly. 'A summer dress, and some shoes to match it, red suede sandals, with high heels.'

'The kind of thing you might buy for a holiday,' Justine mused, half to herself. 'A summer holiday?'

Dido didn't raise her head. 'Except we didn't go away anywhere. I never saw her wear it, after she brought it home, that first time. It wasn't in the stuff we – we gave away. After.' She looked away, up the street, her face still averted.

'I just wish – you can't help wanting to know, but Dad goes over it and over it in his head, I know he does. He wants to know why. Whose fault it was. But she's not coming back, what good's it going to do him? I just want it to be over.'

'Yes,' said Justine. 'I can see that.' She was looking ahead, at the plate-glass window, glittering with shoes, but not focusing

184

on them, nor on Louisa, emerging from the door with a bag. She was thinking of how it must be for the two of them, Dido and Martin, alone in that house.

'Does he think it was his fault?' she asked, carefully.

Dido looked puzzled. 'Why would you think that?' she said, slowly. 'I – no. I don't think so. Maybe sometimes . . .' her voice tailed off, and she bit her lip. 'He never – he never did anything to hurt Mum.'

Justine felt sorry, sure she'd upset her, now. 'No – it's nothing,' she said quickly. 'It was a stupid thing to say.' She paused, looking at Dido's small, downcast face.

'I think we all want it to be over, not just you.' she said. 'It will be. Sooner or later.'

'How long are you staying then, *caro*?' Anna asked carefully. They stood at the bar at Il Cinghiale, waiting for their espresso, on their way home for lunch. At their feet were a couple of bags of shopping; four fat slices of *sbricciolona* from Giovannino's cabinet in greaseproof wrapping, half a dozen eggs, some apples, flour, meat. A handsome bunch of grapes sweet enough for Anna to smell them through their damp paper wrapping, a head of garlic, some big red tomatoes, soft and splitting with ripeness at the end of their season.

It was nice, Anna thought in a moment of uncharacteristic weakness as she waited for her son's reply, to have him here. It was much easier to have someone to stand shoulder to shoulder with her when Giovannino gave her that look. Paolo had not said, in fact, when he planned to return to Rome and she had not wanted to raise it with him for fear of sounding clinging.

'Oh, at least until the weekend,' said Paolo, slowly. 'Maybe Sunday morning? Depending on the weather, of course. It seemed a long time since I was last here for more than a night, I just thought ...' He was thinking of his empty flat, the pile of crumpled shirts on the ironing board, the cold stove. The longer he stayed away, the less he wanted to return.

Anna laughed. 'I'm not complaining,' she said. 'Stay forever, if you want.' He looked at her.

'Well,' he said, and there was something in his tone that caused Anna to glance up at him sharply.

'What?' she said.

'I'm thinking of leaving the hospital,' Paolo said quickly. 'Maybe trying for another position closer to you, like Siena perhaps.'

'Why on earth ...?' Anna was incredulous. She knew how hard he had worked to get to his position in the hospital hierarchy, how many years of obsequy to his superiors he had endured, how many night shifts on casualty.

Paolo sighed. 'Mama, I worry about you out here on your own. I don't see enough of you, and you're all I've got, after all.'

Anna sighed, and raised her eyes to heaven. 'Not that, again,' she said. 'Paolo, I'm perfectly capable of looking after myself. And as for being all you've got, I know what you're trying to say.' She looked down the bar at Giovannino, who was polishing glasses and pretending not to listen. She didn't attempt to lower her voice. 'I didn't set out to deprive you of a father, you know. That's just the way things worked out, and I've never lied to you about him, not once.'

Paolo made an exasperated noise. 'Not lying is one thing,' he said, turning his back so that he didn't have to watch Giovannino craning his neck, and facing his mother. 'And not telling the whole truth is another. If you tell me he's dead, then I believe you. But – I don't think you understand what it's like, not knowing anything, nothing at all. Whether he was dark or fair, tall or short or fat – nothing. A good man, or – or not.' He saw her frown, as though she hadn't thought about it this way before, and he marvelled that he hadn't dared say it, either.

'I don't mean right this minute,' Paolo said, as he saw her catch the barman's eye over his shoulder, warning him off. 'But – sometime. We're both getting old now, you know, me as well as you, and one way or another, soon it will be too late.' He looked as if what he was saying caused him pain.

Anna looked at her son sadly, because she knew he was right about that, at least.

'I don't know,' she said. 'Let me think about it' She looked about her with agitation, as if she was feeling herself somehow trapped, there in the warm dark bar, smelling of roast meat and herbs and grinding coffee, filled with her own countrymen, most of whom she had known since she was born, or they were born. Paolo looked at her with resignation, aware that she had not answered him, once again. To some it might have seemed odd that Paolo had asked this question so many times, phrased differently, over so many years, and still he had not received an answer; not, however, to those who knew his mother.

Anna looked back at Paolo. 'Don't give up your job, *caro*. It wouldn't be good for you to move out here, not now. You know what I mean, don't you? Your wife leaves, and you just go home to mother.' Paolo looked uncomfortable. She went on. 'You won't find happiness that way, you know. And I'm not just changing the subject, either.'

Paolo smiled, despite himself. 'You could be right, mama,' he said. 'You usually are. OK, I won't move back in. Not yet, anyway.' He tried a joke, admitting defeat. 'But there are some mothers who would give their right arm for the offer, you know.'

Anna gave him a sardonic look. 'Are there indeed?' she said. 'Sorry to disappoint you.'

Shaking his head, Paolo laughed, and they walked out into the autumn sunshine, arm in arm.

Chapter Fourteen

The terrace at Rivoire was almost full when they arrived in the Piazza della Signoria, breathless and weighed down with carrier bags. The piazza itself was humming with life, and at first they couldn't see any of the others at the yellow-clothed tables. The clientele was about half and half foreigners and Italians, but they all seemed well heeled. The Italians, it seemed to Justine, stood out a mile; men in linen and dark glasses, honey-skinned women with gold jewellery, obedient children with white collars and shiny hair drinking milk. The foreigners were more of a mixed bag, indecorous, garish, with their designer shorts and pink faces, in front of them extravagant ice-cream concoctions with flags and wafers or litre jugs of beer.

A couple of beautifully dressed, deeply tanned Italian women drinking mineral water on a front table looked the three of them up and down as they stood scanning the bar's terrace. From their discreetly logo-ed sunglasses to their manicured feet in high-heeled sandals, the women were finished in every detail, and the look they gave the English group was not so much hostile as disbelieving, as though they were wondering what kind of people would want to come to the smartest bar in Florence looking as they did. Justine had to remind herself of her purchases sitting, folded in tissue, at the bottom of the shiny bags; she could feel the first creeping approach of regret already, in anticipation of what Lucien might say. She closed her eyes for a second, imagining herself again as that different person she had seen in the tiny shop. And, after all, she surprised herself by thinking, it's my money.

Justine looked up again and suddenly she saw Lucien, sitting on the far side of the terrace. At least she recognized his shoulder, because he was turned away from them and engaged in conversation with someone on the next table. He was good at that kind of thing, casual intimacy had always come easily to Lucien, chatting to strangers, as long as he liked the look of them. She called out to him, his head turned towards the sound of her voice and for a fleeting moment she saw a curious expression flicker across his face, a kind of blankness, as though he didn't recognize her. But then he smiled and waved, and with a curious sensation of relief Justine waved back. She saw heads turning towards Lucien, and she remembered how people looked at him, and she felt she had been uncharitable. She was lucky to have him, after all.

'Come on,' she said to the others, 'there's Lucien.'

'God, I'm gasping for a drink,' said Louisa, as they made their way between the crowded tables. 'I wonder where Tom is?'

'And Dad,' said Dido, looking around. 'But it's not even seven yet.'

Lucien had a martini glass in front of him, and a small dish of olives and canapés. 'You won't believe the prices,' he said, as they sat down. 'Talk about a tourist trap. I'd stick to coffee and mineral water, if I were you.'

'Certainly not,' said Louisa indignantly, and Justine, who had been prepared to give in and have a mineral water, felt her spirits lift. 'I think I'll have what you had, thanks, Lucien,' Louisa went on. And she lifted a hand high in the air to summon a waiter.

'What have you got there?' Lucien said to Justine, peering down at her bags. He sounded querulous. 'Oh,' she said, blushing, 'just a couple of things. Not expensive, really.'

'It's crazy,' he said, sighing. 'Just because you're on holiday, you're suckered into thinking you have to buy stuff.'

Justine opened her mouth to remonstrate with him, to point out the bags that Lucien had stacked beside his own chair, but the words evaporated unspoken in the soft evening air and the gentle murmur of conversation around them. She found she couldn't be bothered.

'There's Tom,' said Dido, and pointed. He was wading towards them through the crowded square, even more dishevelled than usual and with an ice-cream-smeared boy clinging to each arm. He looked tired and pale.

'Oh, God,' said Lucien, 'they'll never let them sit down looking like that.' He looked uneasily round at the waiter approaching them.

'Oh, shut up, Lucien,' said Dido suddenly, and stood up and waved. Tom! Over here!' And sat down again, grinning. 'Can I have some wine?' she asked.

Louisa looked dubious.

'Go on,' Dido said. 'Dad lets me.'

Louisa sighed. 'Half a glass,' she said. 'With water in it.'

Tom and the boys arrived while they were ordering from the waiter who, although he appeared slightly taken aback by their number and appearance did not, as Lucien had predicted, order them off the premises.

'A martini, yes, please,' said Tom, his spirits seeming to lift as he sat down heavily in the wicker chair. Lucien, looking disapproving, asked for a mineral water.

'I'm paying,' said Tom, looking across at Lucien a little sharply and although Lucien did not change his order in receipt of this information he did look put out. The boys clamoured for Coke, and Lucien pursed his lips.

The waiter, a small, business-like professional with a damask napkin over his forearm and a deep tan, took their order and departed, and the group sat back and looked out over the busy piazza. Tom sighed, and Justine looked at him. If a little weary, he seemed contented enough now; perhaps it was the pleasurable anticipation of the first drink of the evening, and in such a beautiful place.

And it was beautiful, suddenly; the ceaseless human traffic they had battled against all day now seemed a happy sight, so many motivated people in close proximity, all with some- where to go and someone to talk to. Opposite the bar's terrace on the far side of the piazza loomed the honeyed stone and tall, crenellated tower of the Palazzo Vecchio, asserting the power of government. Massive and benign in the dusk, the battlements were warmed and softly lit by the last rays of the sun as it set and the tiny, shadowy shapes of bats were begin- ning to dance around the tower in the fading light. Looking up over the many heads at the ranked clover-leaf windows and bright flags inset in the great façade the palace seemed to Justine to mute the noise of the crowd into an agreeable hum, dwarfing them into insignificance in its shadow.

The terrace was a pleasant place to be; it caught the last of the sun as it sank behind the pale arcades of the Uffizi and seemed at the centre of all the evening life of the city. Under the table Justine could feel the crisp, reassuring shape of her purchases, expensive carrier bag, the tablecloth was clean and ironed, at the next table a honeymoon couple in their Sunday best were drinking champagne, and all around them was the happy murmur of relaxation and the clink of glasses.

Dido was sitting beside Justine, hands across her stomach, looking happy. Her face, flushed after a day walking in and out of the sun was, Justine realized, just like Evie's when Justine had first met her, her cheekbones prominent but still softened by youth and a suggestion of plumpness. Only her thick, dark eyebrows were like Martin's, and a certain serious-ness in her look, although that was something she had gained from her experience of life rather than either parent. Just now, however, everything about Dido seemed more relaxed than she had been since they arrived, and Justine suddenly felt optimistic that the holiday might, after all, turn out to have the desired effect.

The drinks arrived, and suddenly their little tablecloth dis-appeared under frosted glasses viscous with alcohol and spiked with olives, and dishes of canapés, tiny sandwiches, *salatini*, cashews. In their excitement at the sight of so much Coke the boys rushed the table, overturned a bowl of crisps and were banished to play in the piazza.

'They'll be all right,' said Tom wearily, and Louisa, who

had been about to protest, closed her mouth again. As one, they reached for their drinks in the moment of blissful calm that followed.

Dido tentatively took a sip of her wine and water and grimaced. 'I wonder where Dad is?' she said, frowning, as carefully she replaced the glass on the table.

Tom blinked. 'Oh,' he said slowly, remembering. 'Sorry, he called me.' He pulled out a battered mobile, and looked at it as if it might remind him of what Martin had said. 'He wanted the address of the restaurant, he's run into someone, and he wanted to meet us there, later.' Justine saw Lucien look up, and for a moment she felt an involuntary twinge of dislike for the expression she saw there, something like superiority, and avid curiosity carefully but not quite perfectly concealed. It was as though he knew something he didn't intend to share.

'Martin's got your mobile number?' said Louisa.

'He asked for it before we left England,' said Tom. 'In case one of us got lost en route, breakdowns, that kind of thing. You know Martin, he's organized.'

Louisa nodded absent-mindedly, but it was obvious to Justine that in fact none of them knew Martin very well at all. And now that they were all here, in something approaching sociable congregation, and he was not, Martin's difference from the rest of them seemed even more pronounced; a dark horse. Certainly Justine had not known he had friends in Florence, and by the puzzled look on Dido's face she hadn't either; she wondered who it might be. It seemed quite improbable to Justine that one might just happen across an acquaintance on holiday, on the one day they happened to choose to venture out of the woods. But just as she was speculating on the odds against such an encounter, something remarkable happened.

'Lucien Elliott! God, is it you? What on earth are you doing here?' A woman's voice, piercing and unmistakably English, was raised over the hum of conversation on the terrace and several heads turned at once.

Just on the other side of the waist-high hedge of bay that divided the terrace from the passers-by, a small blonde woman had raised her arm and was fluttering her hand at them. Justine glanced across at Lucien, who was looking startled, and just a little evasive, she thought, although perhaps that was Justine's imagination.

At first Justine had no idea who the woman was although as she looked a tiny chime of recognition began to sound. Bobbing eagerly towards the break in the hedge that would allow her on to the terrace, the newcomer was tiny, with sleek blonde hair to her chin, and wearing tight, sumptuous clothes, some kind of short, dark-red beaded T-shirt and minuscule velvet jeans that revealed the flat stomach of a twelve-year old. The surprise was her face; half concealed by the shining wings of streaked hair, it was, if not quite haggard, certainly a generation older than her body. Close behind the woman was a stocky, tanned man in an expensive linen jacket; on his face as he followed her was an expression of stolid resignation.

'Friends of yours?' murmured Tom to Lucien as he stood.

'Ah, yes, sort of,' said Lucien vaguely, turning away from Tom and smiling half-heartedly at the woman and her companion, who were now almost upon them.

'Darling,' said the woman, and over Justine's head she enfolded Lucien in a professional embrace, pressing first one

195

cheek and then another against his. Justine could smell her scent, as it enveloped her in an expensive musky cloud. 'Isn't it extraordinary,' said the woman, 'do you know, I'm always recognizing people in this bar. I think everyone who's anyone must come here, sooner or later.'

'Penny,' said Lucien, each of them holding the other by the forearms now in a kind of stand-off. 'How lovely.' He broke away and turned to introduce her.

'This is Penny Montgomery and – or are you Penny someone else, now?' he said, turning his smile on Penny Montgomery's companion, who looked back at him without any change of expression. He too looked faintly familiar, although Justine could not place him exactly.

'Oh, yes, didn't you know? I was sure we invited you to the wedding . . .' said Penny, momentarily vague. 'This is my husband, John Truman, so I'm Truman now. Montgomery still at work though.' She grimaced apologetically. 'Have to keep up the corporate identity.'

'Penny runs a PR firm,' said Lucien.

Then Justine remembered her; she'd run some newspaper awards ceremony, and Lucien had gone on being sent an invitation, Mr Lucien Elliott and Guest, for years after he'd stopped writing his column. Penny Montgomery must have had a soft spot for Lucien; it wouldn't have been unusual. Women found Lucien attractive. Justine was surprised Tom hadn't recognized Penny, as he'd always been invited to her receptions too, naturally enough. And Penny had always been there in person, power-suited and shiny-haired, greeting her guests as they arrived and liaising conspicuously with speakers and sound technicians.

'This is, er, my wife, Justine,' said Lucien, and Justine saw a barely perceptible lift of the eyebrows as Penny looked her over. She was used to this reaction, which she interpreted, by now, as a mixture of surprise that Lucien should be married at all (their wedding had been a quiet affair, Lucien didn't want a big, vulgar splash) and resentment that he should be married to her.

Penny turned away to bestow the same perfumed embrace on Tom; it was obvious that he knew perfectly well who she was, too. But certainly she had changed, Justine thought; to start with her body seemed to have shrunk to half its previous size, with the exception of her breasts which seemed to have gained independence and stood unnaturally high and round. She had a different image too; no longer brisk and suited, she seemed preternaturally teenaged, even down to the navel ring that winked above her velvet jeans. Perhaps this was how PR queens were supposed to look these days, and she had to keep up, or it could be the influence of her new husband. Justine could see Louisa leaning forward eagerly towards the glamorous presence, and even she had to admit the evening had been given new life by the diversion.

'Sit down,' said Tom, pulling an extra chair in to the table. 'Here, have my seat, I've got to go and get the boys, anyway' As he stood to go after them Tom seemed to think of something, paused and put a hand on Lucien's forearm. Lucien looked uneasy.

'Lucien,' he said, and although Tom may have intended his communication as an aside it was certainly audible to all of them, 'invite Penny and – John? – invite them along this evening, why don't you?' He smiled broadly at Lucien's discomfiture, then he turned on his heel and left in search of the boys.

'How lovely,' said Penny, seizing Tom's chair then simultaneously lighting a Silk Cut and wafting a hand in the waiter's direction. Her husband sat down beside her with an audible sigh.

'So,' she said, 'what are you all doing here?'

Chapter Fifteen

Anna was taking some washing in from the line strung between the almond trees beside the house; the sun was almost down and the dew was beginning to form in the crystalline evening air. The hills were blue in the dusk and the beauty of it struck her suddenly with a melancholy force, perhaps because such a view should be shared and she so rarely had anyone to share it with. It was not like Anna to think like this.

Luca – she had not permitted herself to think of Luca for almost forty years, but now, it seemed, she was going to have to – Luca had never been here, to her mother's house in the hills. Of course, he could never have come. She had told him about it, at his prompting; reluctantly, though, worried that he would be disappointed. It was where she came from, the place that appeared in her dreams, the kind of thing one shares with a lover, although Anna didn't know that then, she could only think of his elegant wife, and how she might compare.

She looked back at the terrace, where Paolo was sitting in

the last of the sun, reading a book at the table with the concentrated attention that was, like his smile, only now beginning to remind her of his father. They had known each other for so short a time, she and Luca, barely six months, and had been lovers for only half of that, that Anna found it strange that she should suddenly be able to recall him with such clarity. She had sealed the memory up against the light and buried it for all those years and at last it was to be opened, it contents musty and outdated but perfectly preserved, the faces undimmed by the passage of time.

Anna felt a stirring of dread. What could she say to Paolo that would satisfy him after what she now admitted must have been so many years of imagining, and yearning? Was his father dark or fair, fat or thin, good – or not? Paolo had inherited his father's dark skin and his beautiful smile, but like the Violas he was strongly built, had always been a sturdy child, not tall, with a broad face and hands, a strong Roman nose. Luca had been narrower, with an almost ascetic look, and deep-set, dark eyes. She thought of Luca as she had first seen him at Cinecitta, shouting from a stack of pallets in the woodyard to a taciturn audience of carpenters and metalworkers. She hadn't given him much thought then, hadn't exchanged a word nor even a look with him, but his face had reappeared in her dreams for days afterwards.

They hadn't had long together, but it had felt as though Anna had known him for all of her life. There was plenty that was known about him; everyone knew where he was from, how he was formed, politically; there were other things only she ever found out. He had been the son of *contadini*, like her, but from a village to the south of Rome instead of the north, and from the plains, not the hills, his family had been devastated by the war. His father had died in Russia, conscripted into fighting for the Germans on the eastern front, his mother had died of pneumonia brought on by starvation and only he and his two sisters survived, although they were never the same, so he said. Luca had not said what had happened to his sisters during the war but she had not needed to be told; the stories were too familiar, too dully terrible to be exaggerations, the starvation, rape, mutilation, torture that had become commonplace treatment of women as the Allies advanced and the fighting intensified. Luca had needed to set those things right, or at least to be moving in the right direction, against the tide. A good man, until she came along, anyway.

How could a mother explain that to a child, that he had been the cause of so much unhappiness? That if he had not been born his father might still be alive? How could she begin? She smiled at Paolo as she passed, disguising her thoughts; her arms full of washing that smelled of bracken and birch; of autumn in the air. In the spring it would smell of almond blossom, foaming pink and sweet.

Perhaps she could begin by telling him where they had met, she and Luca. Paolo knew that, at least, or thought he did; he had guessed it from the first time she had taken him to Cinecitta. The inescapable sense that his family was there, somehow, by the way he was recognized and touched like a talisman by the extras, the workers in the canteen, his downy head stroked with affection from the first day she brought him to work with her. He didn't know that was because of her, not of Luca, that none of them, as far as she knew, knew who his father had been any more than he did. Or not for sure, anyway.

At one time she had thought that Paolo would want to

work at Cinecitta, he loved it so much, but then the times had changed, the old studios had become moribund and the atmosphere, although not entirely gone, was not the same either. Almost to her relief her son had seemed to become jaded with the place; as he grew, and the film studios declined, he seemed to realize the foolishness of looking for his father there, among the great actors lording it on the back lots.

'Come inside, *caro*,' she said. 'It's getting cold.' Paolo looked up from his book, something about Italy and her dissidents, some history, with a look of faint, wary surprise and Anna wondered whether he knew, already, and was just testing her. She transferred the washing to one arm and rested her free hand on his shoulder.

'In a minute, mamma,' he said, and carefully he placed a marker in his book.

Down at the far end of the long restaurant table, Justine looked across the debris of their first course – a green pool of olive oil on a plate, transparent slivers of ham and some bruschetta still uneaten, a crushed cigarette packet, half-empty bottles and ranks of smeared glasses – at Lucien. She couldn't hear what he was saying, but she didn't need to; with Lucien it was quite enough to watch and besides, she could probably guess. His shirt-sleeves were rolled up to the elbow and his finely shaped brown forearms rested on the table; between his hands he was fiddling with the silver paper from a cigarette packet as he talked easily to Louisa, occasionally looking up at her with his heartbreaking half-smile. He seemed to be in a good mood again. To give him credit, although he obviously hadn't wanted Penny Montgomery and her husband to come to dinner, once it had become inevitable he had been very gracious about it, making polite conversation with them about the charms of Il Vignacce and undiscovered Tuscany.

'Miles from anywhere,' he said, 'absolutely unspoilt.' Waxing lyrical, overlooking the inconvenience of the unmade road and the leaky fridges; he was good at that. From time to time, like this, quite unexpectedly Justine would be reminded of how she had fallen in love with him.

The night of Tom and Louisa's Christmas party had been bitterly cold, the pavements glittering with frost outside the long, uncurtained windows of their drawing room. The party, by the time Justine arrived, was already on the wane, the room was half empty and the few conversations still going on were desultory, petering languidly out as people began to yawn and drift home. Lucien had seemed to want to keep Justine to himself, to stop her from leaving, and together they had stood in a warm corner by the fire that smelled of the eucalyptus and pine that Louisa had used to decorate the mantelpiece. Lucien had begun to talk to her about his garden. He had mentioned a pleached lime hedge he was planting, going into detail over the pruning, the colours of the leaves in spring against the sky, the scent of lime blossom and the bourbon roses with which he planned to underplant the trees. He seemed so committed, so absorbed.

Justine had never been accustomed to masculine attention; not blonde, not tall, not beautiful, she thought of herself as the opposite of eye-catching, and that had suited her well enough. She had always worked alongside the few men employed at the publishing house, their professional relationship undisrupted by any unprofessional advances on either side. She told herself that this was a good thing; it made for a harmonious and uncomplicated working day, but around then, around the time of that party at the tail-end of another year of office celebrations and pairings-off, it had begun to fret at the edges of her consciousness, the sense of having been left out.

But as Justine had stood there in Tom and Louisa's drawing room with her glass of flat champagne, looking down at the dying fire and listening to Lucien, she felt as though she had entered a parallel universe in which she was quite a different kind of woman. She felt the warm glow of Lucien's attention, his passionate need to describe his garden to her as though she, uniquely, would be able to understand its beauty, to sympathize with his choices and the obstacles he had had to overcome to create it. What drew her, what mesmerized her, was not just that Lucien's subject, so appealing, so sensual, was quite unlike the usual, bored conversation, about work or gossip or television, that people made at parties. It was the sense Justine had that she had been chosen by him; at one stroke she was no longer superfluous, she had become desirable.

Lucien had had other girlfriends. People – not well disposed – had pointed them out to Justine, at the beginning; a tall, supercilious society blonde called Juliet Fleming, a sculptor who managed a house full of artists in Hoxton; Claudie Richler, who worked in the city as a currency dealer, and had a little cocaine habit. Lucien was still on good terms with all of them, which was a good sign, Justine thought; sometimes he went out for a drink with one or the other of them, and Claudie Richler had asked him to design her roof garden.

Justine had even been introduced to one or two at parties, and she had never known whether to be pleased or dismayed that none of them were anything like her. They invariably treated Lucien with amused fondness, not quite seriously, and Justine was only very occasionally made to worry, by something someone said or a look that passed between them, that there were things about Lucien she didn't know, things he had experienced with other women that they didn't share. Lucien hadn't married any of them though, as he pointed out to her on occasion. She looked across the table at him now and felt a wave of longing, or perhaps it was insecurity; the need to reach over and touch his smooth brown forearm, to claim him.

In Florence the restaurant Tom had chosen was in the brick-vaulted *cantina* of a huge, dark palazzo in the Santa Croce area of the city, where the streets were even narrower and more tortuous, it had seemed to Justine as they had made their way there, than those they had negotiated in the day. Down below street level, however, the restaurant was warm and bright, already bustling with custom, the air full of the seductive smell and sound of cooking and a long table laid along one wall, waiting for them; when they arrived Martin was already there, sitting at one end of the table, alone and so preoccupied he barely seemed to notice they were there. Then he seemed to pull himself together, shook the Trumans' hands and they had all shuffled around the table, jockeying for position at the table miraculously relaid to accommodate the unexpected additions.

Tom had orchestrated the seating with gusto; he seemed to be enjoying himself. The food was served promptly, which was just as well; the alcohol seemed to have sharpened everyone's appetite. They had drunk more than enough, between them; Tom and Penny in particular had been drinking steadily since they sat down at Rivoire and showed no sign of slowing now. Although neither was obviously drunk, there was an air of recklessness about Tom in particular.

Justine was between Martin and Penny's husband, John Truman, with Penny herself opposite; Lucien had ended up as far from her as he could be, with Louisa on one side of him and Dido on the other. Behind Louisa, as she listened to Lucien talking (about cooking, Justine decided, as she watched him dip his forefinger in the puddle of olive oil and hold it up to Louisa), Angus was snaking his small arms around her neck, pulling her back towards him while she tried to pry his fingers off her throat, smiling and listening all the while.

Justine watched them together, mother and son entwined, and she thought Tom had been right about how alike they were, although most observers might have disagreed. Louisa was so decorous and fair and calm where Angus was dark and stubborn and wild, but Justine knew that beneath her carefully maintained poise Louisa was as obstinate and irrational and determined as her younger son. It occurred to Justine that perhaps, when you had children, your secrets all were spilt, your childhood tantrums and foibles recalled. Looking at Lucien, wondering what he had been like as a child, Justine supposed that exposure might suit some parents better than others.

Beside Justine Martin was eating with quiet concentration. Only when he had finished the last crumb of his bruschetta did he look up, wiping oil from his chin with a napkin. He smiled at her apologetically.

'You met a friend,' said Justine, smiling back, 'so Tom said. I did wonder what the odds would be against meeting someone, just like that, out of the blue. And then these two turned up, too.' She inclined her head very slightly across the table at Penny, hoping not to draw attention to the gesture.

Martin looked at her oddly.

'Well,' he said, 'the odds, well, that depends. Probability.' Justine remembered that Martin's undergraduate degree had been in mathematics, and wondered whether she was about to get a lecture, whether in fact, this was the kind of thing that interested Martin. 'I don't know,' he said. 'It's a good subject, actually.' And he leaned back, and looked at her. 'Things aren't as random as we often think. Birthdays, for example – they aren't randomly spaced throughout the year, certain dates are more common than others, for a number of reasons.'

Justine nodded, thinking of Valentine's Day, power cuts, evenings drawing in. All the reasons for conception on one day and not another. And Evie disappearing, she thought, but did not say. We all thought that was out of the blue, didn't we? Out of nowhere.

Martin went on. 'Throwing a dice, there you can estimate probability; that's a random event. But when you calculate some odds, there are factors, why one horse is the favourite and not another. We just can't see them, not if we don't know anything about racing, anyway. Holidays, for example.'

He paused, looking down the table. 'What are the chances of a holiday with old friends turning into a disaster? You don't like to think about all the stresses involved, working towards chaos. But they're there.' He smiled at her, not unkindly, but there was calculation in his eyes too.

Justine, of course, knew immediately what he meant, but she didn't want to follow him down that path. She changed the subject. 'So your friend,' she said, 'the one you bumped into here. That wasn't just coincidence?'

'No,' said Martin, 'not really. I knew she would be here.' He stopped. It had not occurred to Justine that the person with whom Martin had spent the afternoon might be a woman. She wondered suddenly whether he would marry again; she had assumed that he would not, somehow, perhaps because she thought of Evie as quite irreplaceable.

Martin went on. 'Rossella – that's her name – she lives here. She's – she was a friend of Evie's.' He turned his fork on his plate.

Justine sat back. 'You arranged to see her? Before we came?'

Martin nodded, something intent and inward about his expression, as though he was going over something in his mind as he spoke. 'I always planned – well, – she was Evie's friend, not mine, I'm not as good as she was at keeping up with people. I couldn't face finding all their numbers, telling them all what had happened, so I left it, mostly. I thought they'd find out – the papers, you know, bad news travels fast.'

'So' – Justine didn't understand – 'Did she know, about Evie? You mean she didn't know? You came to tell her?'

Martin shrugged. 'I just thought, being here – Evie and Rossella, you see, they were very close for a while. Evie lived with her family for a couple of months, on her year off. Went on writing to her, oh, for years.'

Justine nodded. She had known Evie loved Italy – the house had been full of prints of Renaissance frescoes and engravings; perhaps, it occurred to her, that was why Dido had chosen to learn Italian. Justine remembered a medieval map of Florence – Fiorenza – that had hung in the Elliotts' hall. She had not known about Rossella but then, Evie's life had always been full of secret compartments. There just turned out to be more of them than she had thought.

Martin went on. 'I couldn't have told her on the telephone, but I thought if I was here, in Florence and I didn't go and see her, tell her, that would have been inexcusable. But you can see – you can see why she didn't want to come to dinner. After that.' There was a kind of stiffness in his voice. Justine nodded.

'I'm sure you did the right thing,' she said, but Martin

208

still frowned, as though he was concentrating. Then he looked up.

'Sorry?' he said. 'Yes. I think I did the right thing.' He looked at her, weighing something up, and Justine thought he was about to ask her a question but they were interrupted by the noisy arrival of more food. A long platter of gleaming buttery pasta, glass bowls of salad then another half dozen bottles of red wine, white wine, water. When she looked back at him across the clatter and the waiters the question was gone from Martin's eyes, and they turned to their food.

Opposite Justine, Penny was holding her hands palms up towards the food, refusing the pasta because of her wheat intolerance. And a diet that prohibited any combination of protein and carbohydrate.

'So bloating, gluten,' she said, patting her flat stomach and lighting up another Silk Cut. Almost toxic, actually, if you ask my allergist.' She pushed her plate away a little, as if its mere proximity might bring on a reaction, and resumed the animated, if one-sided conversation she had been having with Tom.

'It used to belong to the count of something or other,' she said, waving the smoke away imperiously. 'They'd let it go to rack and ruin, of course, garden full of rabbits, overrun with weeds and the cypresses all seem diseased. But there's a sweet little man from the village who's seeing to that for us. We've bought a little all-terrain vehicle to keep out here, we just get a taxi from the airport. And we've got a charming architect on board. Rather dishy, actually.'

Across the table her husband snorted. Justine knew who he was now; not personally, but from newspaper reports of the money he had made from floating his internet company just before the bubble burst. Penny was still talking.

209

'The roads are no good, unfortunately, so it does take a while to get anywhere.' She made a little face. 'But we've got some lovely neighbours. All English, I think it's these cheap flights, but rather well-known, some of them. I'm sure there's a Lord something on the next hill. And did you know,' she leaned forward, 'Sting's got a place down the road. Apparently he's in our local trattoria all the time.' She sat back with an air of satisfaction, and inhaled deeply.

'How nice,' said Tom, absently. He had hardly touched his food, although he had a bottle of wine at his elbow that was almost empty. He was looking down the table at Louisa and Lucien as he spoke. 'Is property a good investment out here, do you think?'

'Of course, it wasn't cheap,' Penny shrugged, as if to indicate that if it had been, she would not have been interested.

'You can say that again,' grunted John Truman, forking pasta into his mouth. His expression was of absolute boredom with the conversation. Justine thought perhaps she should be making more of an effort; he was, after all, her neighbour at table and she had not attempted a word so far.

'Was it difficult?' she asked, tentatively. 'I mean, you hear how complicated it is buying property here. All sorts of people to pay'

Truman looked at her briefly, then returned to his food. Justine was wondering whether perhaps that was how he had made so much money, by not wasting his time on polite conversation, when, with more than a hint of impatience, he replied.

'Had nothing to do with all that. Paid an agent, paid the *notaio* chap, he sorted it all out. Now we'll pay the architect, I suppose. Bunch of criminals, the lot of them. Food's good though.' He laughed sourly.

'Does it have a swimming pool?' Sam asked, excitedly. Truman frowned, and Justine guessed that he did not like children. Miserable sod, she thought, and then wondered whether it was quite healthy or fair to be judging everyone according to their desire to reproduce.

'It's got one. Not big enough, though,' said Truman. 'Silly little circular thing, no good for lengths.' Savagely he sawed at his bread. 'What do they put in this stuff? It's hard as a rock.'

'Can we go and see them, Mum,' Angus said, pulling at Louisa's sleeve.

She grimaced apologetically at Penny. 'No, darling,' she said, shaking her head at Angus. 'I'm sure Penny and – John – they're busy. And you've got your own river to swim in, you haven't even bothered to find it yet.'

'Oh, by all means ...' said Penny, vaguely, as if she was thinking of something else, and Justine wondered how drunk she was. She was looking at Martin with uninhibited curiosity.

'You're not – are you Martin Law?' She leaned heavily towards him, her elbow slipping on the table.

Martin looked at her, something not quite benign glittering in his dark eyes. He smiled politely. Poor Martin, thought Justine thinking of all the coverage of Evie's death, knowing that people would still be judging him by what they had read in the papers, inferring his guilt over their breakfasts. Down the table to her left out of the corner of her eye she saw Dido turn her head in their direction.

'I am, yes.' He sounded resigned, but the smile stayed on. Penny's face composed itself into a mask of sympathy.

'I'm so sorry,' she said. Her voice was lowered almost to a whisper, 'How – how are you? And your daughter?' Along the line of heads Justine saw Dido's draw back sharply.

211

'Well,' said Martin, stiffly, 'well, fine, actually. Thank you.' His tone was final, but Penny persisted.

'It must be so difficult to feel – closure. Not knowing.' Justine saw a muscle twitch in Martin's cheek, and wondered how long he would allow Penny to go on. He said nothing. A waitress was moving swiftly around them, clearing plates, and Martin leaned back to allow her past.

'Is there – did they find anything more out about why she—'

Martin interrupted her. 'No. Nothing.' he said. 'Look,' his voice was even, but there was an edge to it, 'do you mind if we don't talk about it? It upsets my daughter.'

Penny nodded tipsily. 'Ah ... oh yes, of course.' She looked down the table at Dido.

'Pretty girl,' she said, after a moment. 'Isn't she? But then your wife was. I suppose it can be a burden, beauty. Attracts the wrong sort of person.'

Martin looked at her sharply, although to Justine she appeared merely to be rambling. He opened his mouth, perhaps to put an end, finally and definitively, to the conversation, but it was at that point that Tom started up, and whatever Martin might have said was lost.

In retrospect, the evening was almost guaranteed to end badly. They had all drunk too much, they were all tired by a long day and they should never have invited Penny and John Truman. Justine wondered, later, what had possessed Tom to insist they came, too; it could only have been to annoy Lucien. Why did they dislike each other so intensely now, when once – at Tom's parties, Penny's launches – they'd seemed to get along perfectly well? Getting away from it all, she concluded, didn't always bring out the best in people. Or perhaps they hadn't got away from anything.

Restaurant dinners on holiday were often bad-tempered, in Justine's experience; you went because no one wanted to cook any more, the children would fidget and their mothers would snap and there was always a row over the bill. But the suddenness with which the fight flared up could not, she thought, have been predicted. It came out of nowhere, or so it seemed, and later Justine found herself wondering what Martin made of this particular random event, because at no point did it seem to take him, at least, by surprise.

The conversation with Penny had been interrupted by Tom calling, too loudly, down the table to Lucien. His tone was boisterous and aggressive, cutting through the pleasant murmur of the other diners around them. One or two heads turned in his direction. He *is* drunk, thought Justine, and wondered who would be driving home. She could see Louisa's face as she looked at her husband, impatience giving way to mortification and beside her Lucien, his lips compressed with anger, waiting.

'What do you think, Lucien?' he called. 'With your famously refined tastebuds? What shall I say in my piece?'

'Leave him alone, Tom,' said Louisa, looking at her husband sharply. 'He doesn't have to sing for his supper.'

'No,' said Tom, 'I'd like to know. After all, I'm sure Lucien thinks he could do my job.'

Lucien snorted. 'It's hardly surprising you can't taste the food any more, Tom,' he said, openly hostile now. 'Just give up, why don't you? You're pathetic.'

'Hold on,' protested Louisa. 'I think that's a bit—' She was interrupted by the sound of Tom's chair as he stood and it was pushed back. The restaurant fell silent, and some of the diners looked down at their food, although still more looked across to see what the matter was.

Now even the boys were beginning to look uncomfortable, Angus holding tight on to his mother's arm and Sam sitting stiffly upright in his chair, his face pale and anxious. Dido was looking down, her hair screening her face from view, but her shoulders were hunched.

'Darling,' Louisa turned to look up at Tom, pleading with him silently, but he didn't even look at her. Beside Justine John Truman raised his eyes to heaven, his look of impassive boredom barely dented, but opposite them Penny was looking eagerly down the table, a spectator waiting for the next move.

'It's pathetic to support your family, is it?' Tom asked, savagely, his face ruddy with anger. 'We can't all indulge our higher selves, can we? We can't all rely on women to keep us. Some of us have to work for a living.'

Lucien made a movement in his chair as if to leap across the table, and Justine knew that if this went on their holiday would be over, there and then. But into the silence Martin spoke, and his calm voice held a warning.

'Sit down, Tom,' he said. 'Stop it, you're upsetting the children.'

Tom looked at Martin, frowning, then at his sons, and with a defeated look he sat back down in his seat. He pushed away the untouched plate of congealing pasta that sat in front of him and put his head between his hands.

Martin held up a hand and beckoned the waiter. He asked for strong coffee, and the bill, fixing the man with a determined smile until, uncertainly, he nodded and turned away.

'I'm going to get the car,' said Lucien, shoving his chair back abruptly and standing up. 'I'll be outside in ten minutes.' And without looking at Justine he left. Tom grunted as if to say something, but Louisa shook her head at him fiercely. The waiter returned with a trayful of coffee cups and *cantuccini*, and then Tom seemed to gather himself, reaching decisively for the bill and thanking the man with scrupulous politeness.

Martin drained his coffee, and stood up; almost immediately Dido, looking pale, sprang up too. 'Have some more coffee, before you go,' he said to Tom, not an invitation but an instruction. 'We'll see you back at the house. Let us know what we owe, won't you?'

He had barely got out of the door before Penny leaned across the table towards Justine, almost knocking over a glass. Justine could smell her perfume, the wine and cigarettes on her breath as the other woman stifled a hiccup.

'Well,' she breathed, excitedly, 'quite sexy, isn't he. In a scary sort of way.'

Next to Justine John Truman made an exasperated noise.

'Get your coat, Penny,' he said. She did not move, still leaning on her elbows across the table.

'Are you talking about Martin?' Justine frowned at her. She did not flatter herself she was confided in for any other reason than she was the only one left within range.

'Mmm,' said Penny, slurring a fraction. 'You can see why she married him. Although of course Lucien's gorgeous, too, always had a thing for him. But the husband, well. You know what they say, though, don't you? They all say he did it.'

Justine recoiled. Beside her John Truman was standing now. 'Did what?' she said, although she knew.

'Pushed her. Off that boat.'

Justine heard a sharp intake of breath from Louisa. Tom was staring into his glass.

Penny Truman went on. 'You know, did she fall, or was she ... And who wouldn't? She must have driven him mad, the

215

way she behaved. With men, I mean. All right, all right, I'm coming,' she said, swaying a little as she stood, shaking off her husband's arm on her shoulder. And when she had gone, none of them left at the wreckage of the table felt like saying a word.

The journey home in the dark seemed much longer than it had that morning, in the other direction. In the car Justine was silent all the way along the superstrada, brightly lit and still busy, the cars flashing silently past in the night. Lucien seemed distracted. On their way past Siena they got caught up in a great tangle of by-passes and ring-roads, bridges and filter lanes. The thought of all this superstructure constructed around the pristine little city left Justine faintly depressed, all of it there to deal with people like them. Tourists.

Lucien was tense, she could see his hands clenched on the steering wheel and heard him snort angrily when another car cut him up at a particularly indecipherable conjunction of lanes. Then suddenly they were out of it, on a narrow, fast minor road, unlit, pitch black and absolutely foreign. A truck stop flashed by, and then nothing, just the black hills rising up on either side and a line of tail-lights in front of them. The evening air through the open window was warm and it seemed as though, at last, it was just them, anonymous in the darkness, going home.

'Wouldn't it be lovely,' she said, turning to Lucien, 'if we could stay here, just us? Get away from – from it all?' She was thinking of the restaurant table, the litter of food and crockery, the raised voices, ragged with anger long suppressed, the history between them all. Evie. Perhaps it was each other they needed to get away from; the circle of friends.

Lucien said nothing, his eyes on the road, and for a moment

she wondered whether he had heard. But then he shook his head a little. 'I don't think that would work,' he said wearily, as if he didn't know what she meant at all. And Justine said nothing after that.

Paolo heard the cars go past, down the hill to Il Vignacce, still awake although it must have been after midnight. He was sitting as he had been for an hour or more, since his mother had gone to bed, and watching the fire burn down in the stove, listening to the dying sound of the cicadas in the umbrella pines on the ridge. On the table by his side his book lay open.

At the crunch of tyres outside he thought, they are driving too fast, and wondered, briefly, where they'd been. He wondered whether the woman he'd seen swimming was in one of the cars, driving perhaps, or just sitting in the dark, beside a husband, or a lover, or between her children, if she had them, in the back, one asleep with his head on her knee. They'll be gone soon, he thought, this week, next week.

Paolo felt weariness settle on him like a blanket, and not just because of the late hour. It was the thought of staying there, deep in the woods, sitting every evening beside the fire and listening to the sounds of the world going on without him, the insects, the animals, the passers-by.

He had been reading too long, he thought; his book was a history of political activity following the war, a story of struggle and idealism that had left him feeling weary and inadequate, ready to abdicate all responsibility to his fellow man. What difference could he make in the world, after all, patching up drunks and teenagers night after night? He closed his eyes and thought of the forest, the trees standing silently around the house, empty and peaceful. It would be so easy, here, going back to his family's home. He didn't need to prove himself to a father he'd never known.

'A good man,' had been her last words before she climbed the stairs. 'He was a good man. Like you.'

As silence fell again in the woods and only the faintest reverberation of the cars' passage hung in the air up here on the ridge, Paolo turned out the lights and went up to bed, in the room beside his mother's, in the house that had been his grandmother's. But it was a long time before he slept.

At Il Vignacce the cars were parked up under the trees, the children put to bed, the boys grumbling as they were carried sleepily upstairs. One by one the lights went out; kitchen, bathroom, bedroom, the shutters closed but two men sat out in the dark; Martin and Tom, looking up at the stars.

'Tomorrow,' Martin was saying, 'you'll have to do it tomorrow. Look, just go and see the place first. You don't know until you've got there. Do it as a favour to me, OK? At the very least, it's a good enough excuse to get away.'

Tom sighed. 'All right,' he said dully. He turned his face up and looked at Martin wearily. And then?'

'Then you can go to Florence and talk to her.' Martin stood up, his hands in his pockets, restless. 'If you don't believe me – and I can see why' – and he laughed, a little bitterly – 'just talk to her.' He leaned down and looked into Tom's face in the dark. 'It's the only way.'

Chapter Sixteen

Looking back on that morning later, it seemed to Justine that she should have known that everything was about to change; it was in the air. Even as she lay cocooned in sleep, far off to the west the great swirl of an autumn depression was beginning to gather over central France. Mists were settling in the deep valleys of Provence and Liguria and further up a soft light rain had begun to fall on the parched stalks of sunflowers, stubbled fields and the ripening vineyards of the Rhone. In the Maremma an early morning wind blew thistledown across the pasture and in her sleep Justine turned over and pulled the quilt up to her shoulder.

So early that she thought she must have been dreaming, the sky barely silver through the open window, drowsily Justine registered the sound of a car starting up outside. She felt a shifting of weight in the bed as Lucien rolled over and pushed up her T-shirt, his warm hand on her hip in the half-darkness. She closed her eyes, wanting to forget who she was, to be someone else, somewhere else.

When Justine woke again the room was flooded with light and the bed was empty beside her. For a while she lay and looked at the beams above her head, the rough red tiles orderly between them, at the brilliant blue of the sky against the ridge of black trees through the window. For a time everything seemed perfectly clear; the walnut chest of drawers gleaming in the sun, her new red linen dress folded on a chair, even the sound of the birds in the tree outside and the faint acrid smell of woodsmoke in the air, all sharp and perfectly defined. Home seemed like a distant dream to her already; she tried to remember it, as though she'd been bereaved and was trying to reconstruct the face of someone dead. She tried to picture the kitchen, the junkyard elegance of their drawing room, the view she loved through the long French windows into the London street. But she couldn't give it substance. It was here that was real, the grazing cows, the silent, sweet-smelling woods, the beams over her head; the rest of it seemed dark, pointlessly oppressive.

Then from below she heard a wail rising up through the window, and Louisa's voice, sharp with anger. The door opened, and Lucien came in with a cup of tea. Justine turned her head on the pillow; he smiled conspiratorially and rolled his eyes at the sound from downstairs.

'A bit of a domestic, I think,' he said, and as she heard the note of determined cheerfulness in his voice Justine remembered the night before, foreboding settling on her shoulders like a weight. With a sigh she raised herself on the pillows and took the cup from him.

'Oh yes?' Justine said cautiously, hoping against hope that the scene in the restaurant had been forgotten by everyone else, if not by her.

'I think the children are getting on Louisa's nerves,' Lucien went on. 'Tom's gone.' He sat down on the bed beside her and the cup chinked in its saucer, spilling a little.

'What do you mean?' Justine said, more sharply than she intended.

'Didn't you hear the car?' Lucien said. 'This morning?' He looked at her with the ghost of a smile, knowing.

Justine nodded absently, thinking as she raised her tea to her lips. It tasted faintly sour, and she wondered if it was the foreign water, or the milk going off in the ancient fridge.

'So where's he gone? You don't mean he's really gone?'

Lucien looked away from her, out of the window. The voices from below had fallen silent now.

'Gone to Grosseto,' he said. 'To look at a restaurant and an organic farm. That's what Louisa said anyway.' His face was still turned away; she could only see the plane of his cheek gleaming in the sun and his fine straight nose, but she thought he was frowning. Something came back to her from last night, and carefully she set the cup down on the marble of the side table.

'You don't think it's true?' she asked. Lucien turned back towards her, the light from the window behind him putting his face in shadow.

'Oh, I don't know,' he sounded impatient for a moment. 'It's a mess, isn't it?'

'You'd gone,' said Justine slowly, 'hadn't you? When Penny Montgomery said – about Evie—'

Lucien turned towards her, frowning. 'Said what? Jesus, that woman. She didn't know Evie.' His face was dark, and suddenly he sounded furious. Justine felt warmed by his indignation, his defence at last of Evie.

221

'Oh,' said Justine vaguely, suddenly unwilling to repeat the words, 'just, something about – just gossip. Something about Evie and men, the effect she had on men, or something. About making Martin jealous. You don't think – do you think Evie was unfaithful? She never said anything. I always thought they were so happy' She was lost in the thought, wondering how she could have missed all this.

Lucien shrugged, and when he spoke he sounded fed up. 'How could you have known? It's not something people talk about, is it? We hardly saw them.' And with a sudden movement he sat on the bed and put his arms around her, his face against the hollow of her throat. Instinctively she put her arms around him too, feeling the warm weight of his torso against her, the tensed muscles in his back.

'I'm sorry,' he said, 'about last night.' His voice was muffled, and Justine wasn't sure what he meant.

'What are you sorry for?' she said. This was not like Lucien.

'Oh, you know. Letting Tom get to me. Making a scene.'

'Well,' she said reasonably, 'it was hardly your fault.'

Lucien sighed, sitting up and away from her. 'Do you mind?' he asked, his face slightly averted. 'Going out to work? What Tom said about your supporting me. You know if you asked me to, I'd go and find something. I always thought you enjoyed it. But if you thought – that was the right way to – manage our lives, I'd get a job. I could do it tomorrow – well, perhaps not quite tomorrow, but when we get back.' He turned and looked at her, eyes wide open and innocent.

Justine hesitated. This was what she had wanted him to say – for how long? – but there was something about the way it was phrased that made it more complicated than she had thought to accept. She thought of getting back to England

222

suddenly, and her little cubicle, the piles of typescripts, the authors fretting about spelling and sequencing and historical accuracy, the coloured pens and checklists in her neat, careful writing. Of course the prospect did not make her happy or eager as it once had, but it did hot fill her with despair, either, did it? She thought of Lucien in an office, and she knew it wouldn't work.

'Oh, no,' she said, with only a little resignation?'It's fine. I mean, you know it's fine. It's just—'

Lucien looked at her and she saw a tiny flicker of relief, behind his careful smile. Then he said it.

'I know, it's just – the baby thing. Well, maybe we could. You know. Have a baby.' He looked at her cautiously, his eyes narrowed, waiting.

A breeze blew the thin curtains at the window and Justine felt the hairs on her bare arm rise; she hadn't thought it would happen like this. She knew she should take it slowly, but in fact she found she had little desire to jump up and down, to start planning. Is this what I want? The question leapt at her, unbidden, out of the air. She leaned her head against Lucien's shoulder and said, 'Thanks.' *Thanks?* she thought, aghast. 'I mean, if you think it's OK.' And together they leaned back on the pillows and looked out of the window at the late summer sky, still a clear, pale unclouded blue. They didn't look at each other, perhaps for fear of finding out what the other was really thinking, or giving themselves away.

Leaving Lucien in the shower, which drummed and hissed above her as she descended the wooden steps, Justine passed the boys sitting mute and chastened at the breakfast table downstairs, swinging their legs and staring at spilt bowls of

223

cereal. She stood irresolute in the doorway, the sun on her face. Outside on the grass she could see Martin walking to and fro, talking into his mobile, head down.

'Yes,' he was saying, encouraging, 'a long avenue of cypresses, it's at the top. He's waiting for you.' He glimpsed Justine in the doorway out of the corner of his eye, straightened and lifted his hand absently before turning to look across the pasture, his back to her now and his voice indistinct. Justine turned back inside.

She found Louisa in the dim undersea light of the bedroom downstairs, sorting savagely through clothes, a pile of dirty children's things at her feet. Justine felt a qualm, thinking that this was what motherhood seemed mostly to be about; putting clothes in piles, and shouting.

'Are you OK?' she said, unsuspecting, and as though the words had set a fuse Louisa blew. Her hands flew up in the air then down again, she sat down on the bed violently, her jaw set, and brought her hands, clenched now into fists, down to her knees. Then she put her face down between them and her shoulders shook silently.

Justine sat beside her, the sense she had had earlier of a delicate equilibrium established in the house evaporating. It's all falling apart, she thought, helplessly. Every time I try to put it back together. She put an arm around Louisa's narrow shoulders.

'What's happened?' she asked. 'Lucien said Tom's gone to look at an organic farm?'

Louisa looked at her, shaking her head helplessly, her cheeks damp and rough, with crying, or tiredness. Justine hadn't seen her like this before; she was barely recognizable.

'I suppose it might be true,' she said. 'It's what he told me.'

224

Justine frowned. 'Why wouldn't it be true?' she asked.

Louisa gave a long, tired sigh, shuddering a little like a child who has cried herself out.

'Because he's not going to write it up, is he? He's lost the column. They're sacking him.'

'What? Why?' Justine was staggered. Tom was one of the leaders in his profession; he had been, once at least, a trail-blazing journalist. A household name. Even if he was falling off a bit, that name alone had always been worth tens of thousands of readers.

Louisa looked at her, despairing. 'This last year,' she said, 'he's been – something's wrong with him. Drinking, yes, he's always been a drinker. But now he drinks so much he can't taste the food, he's been thrown out of two restaurants, he had a stand-up row, in front of customers, with one chef.' She sighed. 'I knew all this.' She stopped for a moment.

'And?'

'This morning, Tom told me. I don't know why, something to do with last night; he had a heart-to-heart with Martin, after we'd gone to bed. Maybe Martin said – maybe he thought he had to explain why he lost it with Lucien. But he told me that last week, when we were getting ready to come here – I was packing, I suppose I wasn't paying much attention – his editor called.'

Louisa looked lost for a moment, contemplating her culpability. 'Anyway someone – a big name, a chef, phoned the editor, said he watched Tom in the restaurant car park when he'd said he'd get a taxi, paralytic, they watched him get in the car and drive himself home. Of course Tom – when he told me – he said he wasn't that drunk. But if I'm honest, he probably was. I should have seen it coming.'

'Did – did the police—' Justine, horrified, couldn't finish the sentence. Louisa looked at her, hopelessly.

'No. It didn't go that far. But Tom said – there were – threats; you know what people in the restaurant business are like. Well, maybe you don't know.' She sighed. 'The word goes around. Sometimes I wonder if – if there's something else he's not telling me. Something important.'

Louisa stopped and looked down at her hands, her shoulders sagging. 'I wonder if – I wonder if he's not well.' Her voice was dull, hopeless. Justine had never known her like this.

'You said – you said, he'd been like this, since last year?' Justine said slowly, thinking. Louisa looked up.

'Yes,' she said. 'Since – since Evie died.' For the first time, it seemed, Louisa looked at her directly, and Justine could see that there was something Louisa had to tell her.

Up before Anna, Paolo worked in the garden for two hours, clearing rampant weeds from the vegetable patch, the fence and around the olive trees, untangling the olive nets in preparation for their modest harvest. When at ten thirty the sun was high in the pale sky, Paolo had drained his second cup of coffee and walked back inside into the warm kitchen to find that his mother was still not down, he decided to investigate.

He found her upstairs in her bedroom, standing in her dressing gown in front of the heavy country wardrobe, a massive piece of furniture that had since either of them could remember stood in the same place, beside the window in the farmhouse's marital bedroom.

It had been used by his grandmother, and by his great-grandparents before her and it was huge: dark seamed oak inlaid with marquetry stars of elm wood and standing on great balls for feet. He had often wondered, as a boy, how it ever came up the stairs. His grandmother had not had more than three or four pieces of clothing she considered worth hanging up at all, and even they were sober, dark garments. A woollen dress, he remembered, with a white starched collar. For the most part, he thought, she had used it to store the good linen. The cupboard smelled of cedar inside, balls of the rarer wood hanging up along its rail to keep moths away.

Now the wardrobe stood open to reveal the neat ranks of red and dark mossy green and damson and grey, dresses and suits and shirts, wool and silk and cotton all pressed and clean and waiting for their season. But his mother was just standing there, irresolute, frowning as though uncertain of why she was there at all. He was taken aback; this was not like his mother. Anna was decisive in her habits of dressing even more than in any other aspect of her life; she always knew what the right thing was to wear, for every day of every month and for all weathers.

Anna was not vain, she never fussed in front of the mirror, never took things out and put them back, never had the need of a chair on which to throw discarded garments. But clothes were significant to her all the same, and in a particular way. Anna had made every one of her garments herself, to her own exacting specifications; she had selected her materials, cut her patterns, everything lined and fitted and hemmed, as if to say that she, and no one else, made her the woman she was. The one thing she was not, ever, was irresolute, as Paolo now saw her, and what might have been perfectly ordinary hesitation in another woman made his heart sink when he observed it in his mother.

'Mamma?' he asked.

She turned towards him.

'What's the matter?' he said.

Anna sighed. 'I don't know what to wear,' she said, fretfully. She looked at Paolo's worried face, and tried to laugh. 'It's the weather,' she said. 'Perhaps it's the weather.' And she looked through the window at the faint cool hint of grey on the horizon.

Paolo nodded slowly. 'It's getting cooler,' he said.

And we're walking down to Il Vignacce today. To the river,' Anna said, just a little more firmly, trying to reassert herself.

At least it's not her memory going, thought Paolo with relief, and he nodded. His mother looked at him, smiling a little, and he could see animation returning to her expression. He took her arm, and suddenly she was her old self; he could feel her galvanizing herself into decision beneath his hand. She reached into the back of the wardrobe and brought something long and white, it came out slowly, pale and heavy it slithered out between the wool suits and the winter coats. Anna reached up and hung it on the cornice of the wardrobe, where it hung right down as far as the red cotto of the floor. It was a wedding dress.

Chapter Seventeen

They were up at the top at last, out of the valley and in the light. The day was lovely, a late September morning that, in England, would have been like a last glimpse of summer before the grey shutter of winter banged shut on the year, the promise at least of some future spring in the mild, fresh air. Here, in Italy, even after so few days of sultry humidity, horse flies and parched grass, it seemed something more decisive, the point at which summer ended.

To Louisa and Justine, hot and damp with sweat after the exertion of their climb – something like four kilometres of uneven rocky path winding steeply up from the valley floor through the scrub and pine trees – the breeze was a blessing. The two women were sitting side by side on a slab of limestone overhung by some prickly gorse-like plant, their feet in sandals red with the metalliferous dust of the hill-path, and in silence they took turns to drink from a plastic water bottle. Beyond them the track, rutted and just wide enough to accommodate a vehicle, continued its irregular course along a ridge before descending once again on the other side.

They had not talked much on the way up as if by common consent, even though the reason they had left the others behind, left the suddenly stifling confinement of the valley and the pasture and the endlessly, peacefully ruminating cows, had been so that they might talk. Initially, though, the strenuous climb up from the river had not allowed for it and then, as they had walked in silence, they seemed to lose the urge to speak. As they made progress up the steep hill the mental tally of each step, the regular sound to each of the other's breathing became therapeutic, a soothing rhythm that neither of them felt disposed to interrupt.

They had left the boys with Lucien, who had looked at first as though he might have raised an objection if Justine had allowed him an opportunity, but she hadn't. Sam and Angus paid him little attention, anyhow, continuing some obscure game behind the house while their morning was planned for them at the front. When Justine and Louisa walked around to find them the boys were standing with their backs pressed flat against the stone of the house, their hands behind them, sharing an expression of comical complicity, of some activity stifled halfway through. Justine thought of the endless secrets that had to be kept from parents by children, or so they thought; their private games, the speculation about adulthood, their perceptions of their parents. Wearily Louisa told them to be good, and they just nodded in silence, dimpling with suppressed laughter.

There had been no sign of Martin and Dido other than the front door to their side of the farmhouse standing open in the sunlight, but Justine had not gone across to explain. She told herself, by way of excuse, that they would be back soon enough; the truth was, she felt reluctant to explain why she and Louisa needed to be on their own; she didn't know where it might lead. There was something about Martin's sceptical gaze that, she thought, would expose any attempt to disguise what was going on; he would know immediately, she thought, that Tom had gone, that Louisa was near to desperation, and that it had something to do with Evie. And then there was Dido, whom they all wanted to protect; surely it would do her no good to see it all unravel in front of her. If that was what was going to happen.

Besides, Justine told herself robustly, it might be good for the men to work together for once, instead of maintaining the stand-off that had characterized the holiday so far. Briefly Justine wondered why Lucien was like this with other men; never explicitly hostile but ceaselessly, subtly competitive and territorial. Perhaps only she could see it; or perhaps they were all like that; Tom and Martin too, but she could only see it in Lucien.

First Justine and Louisa had gone upriver a little way, away from the bathing pool; this was where the most obvious path up to the ridge had been indicated, Justine decided, on the old map. They had gone through a stile and down a narrow track fenced on either side with rusty barbed wire, and the air had become damp and cool as they approached the gurgle of the water. They had glimpsed the sunlit clearing of another pasture through the trees at one point, and elsewhere heard the sound of cowbells reverberating in the dusty green light that hung between the tree trunks. It had been difficult to tell from the sound whether the animals were behind or in front; the effect was curiously eerie, the hollow sound indicating the invisible presence of another creature, like a foghorn in mist.

They had walked beside a narrow stream through the arched hazel clumps that formed a dark roof over their heads, crossed the river on stepping stones that were warm from the sun and then began to climb. The sound of the cowbells had receded, to their relief; neither of them looked forward to an encounter with a bull, dangerous or otherwise, in the confined space of the valley floor. They climbed with only the rasp of the cicadas for company, and even those sounded fainter now than they had been in previous days as if the insects could feel the approach of autumn and were conserving their strength.

The change of perspective that came as they climbed up out of their valley and away from Il Vignacce was a revelation that cheered them instantly. The first steep climb had taken them scrambling over a path studded with rocks rust-red with iron ore and glinting here and there. Around them in the dense woodland as they climbed they could hear the rustle and snap of forest creatures startled by their approach, and at one point Louisa stopped, with an exclamation of surprise, having come across a handful of tortoiseshell-striped porcupine quills, scattered like spillikins across the path. She gathered them up.

'Dido might like them. Don't you think?' she said to Justine.

Then Justine had rounded a bend just ahead of Louisa, and stopped short, Louisa coming up behind her with a sound of surprise. Suddenly they could see into the next valley, and on a hill on the far side perched the stone houses of a tiny hamlet, much smaller than Montequercio, no more than half a dozen dwellings straggled along a ridge but inhabited. There were washing lines with tiny shirts hanging to dry, the unmistakable shape of an espaliered fig like a splayed hand against a south-facing wall, and some terraces of olive trees.

The knowledge that there was a next valley at all came almost as a revelation to Justine, ridiculous though it made her feel. She had pored over the old map with Lucien, but she had found it quite indecipherable. The map's antiquity, the crabbed copperplate script that described long-extinct farm-steads and houses, the broken lines that should have indicated paths but seemed to lead nowhere, the tightly packed contours that denoted hills and valleys, none of it had made any sense to her. So to have managed to scramble out of the river valley and come upon this view of the outside world was like the cool breeze they now felt on their faces. It dispelled the feeling Justine had begun to have that, apart from yesterday's brief excursion to civilization, which had already begun to seem like a disturbing dream, they were in some lost place dangling in isolation at the end of a long dirt track, just Il Vignacce and the main road and no fellow human beings in between, just the cow bells, the endless trees and the trickling water.

The women trudged on, around another bend and then another, winding forward and back across the unforgiving, pine-clad face of the hill in full sun, working their way on and up. Occasionally a splash of red paint on a tree had encouraged them, just as one or the other was about to spec-ulate on whether their path led anywhere at all. At one point, not far up the hill, they paused for breath, looking around through the ranked trees, and Justine saw that they weren't alone. Some distance away in a clearing she saw a man's back, a tall, broad-shouldered man, his hand resting on an elderly woman's shoulder as she sat next to him. They seemed to be talking. The sight encouraged her; the implication of their presence was that to be out walking was quite natural, not quixotic or hysterical, not something only a foreigner would undertake. And there was something about their attitude, the man's kindly, thoughtful aspect, smiling down and listening, that made her feel comforted, among friendly, civilized people.

She and Louisa passed the ruin of a building, too tall to be a cowshed, stone-built, picturesquely ivy-clad, and half-swallowed up by the forest. The untended, overgrown wreckage of some olive terraces straggled below it, the bent old trees waist high in long, silvery grass and the delicate blown globes of seedheads, and the whole human construction almost completely reverted to wilderness. Both Justine and Louisa stopped together when the ruin came into view; it was a pretty place, and it was hard to see why it might have been abandoned.

Then quite suddenly they were at the top; catching their breath, they looked out at the vista. They could see a series of interlocking valleys, their outlines softened by the vegetation, and the little village they had seen earlier was strung along a ridge in the distance and bleached pale gold by the midday sun. Then they looked back at each other.

Louisa's face had the wiped look that sustained exertion brings. 'So,' said Justine, 'what's been going on? What's this all about?' Up here in the open air, she thought, it would have to all come out.

There was a moment or two of silence, filled by the noise of insects and the distant whir of a chainsaw. They must be near the clearing where the logging was carried on, Justine found herself thinking. Then Louisa sighed. 'I should – I probably should have told you about it a long time ago. Right at the beginning, even. It's just that she said – Tom said she didn't want anyone else to know.'

'To know what?' Justine looked at Louisa, who looked away. 'Was she –? Louisa, was Evie having an affair with Tom?'

'I – I don't know,' said Louisa. 'Not for sure.' She stopped, and Justine suppressed her impatience.

When she saw that Justine was waiting, reluctantly Louisa went on. 'He says – well, when I asked him, outright, oh, about two or three months after she disappeared, he – I've never seen him so angry. Outraged. But I don't know what I was supposed to think. He was so unhappy, it was like he'd been bereaved, properly, as though she meant more to him than anything else, and he just didn't get over it.'

'But he said no? He denied it?' Louisa nodded.

Justine frowned 'But he was—' the question seemed even more intrusive, somehow, to Justine, and she hesitated to ask it. 'He was in love with her, but he didn't actually—'

Unhappily Louisa nodded again. 'He didn't say that exactly, but I suppose that's the only explanation. He just said, he didn't know how I could ask the question. He said I couldn't understand, that he loved her in a way I wouldn't understand. He wanted to help her. To protect her.' She snorted, trying to express contempt, but sounding only unhappy. Her chin cupped in her hands, elbows on her knees, she stared into the distance, across the tree tops.

Justine thought of Tom; it must happen, she supposed. You marry someone, and then you find someone else – the odds made it almost inevitable, the odds against your locating the perfect match, falling in love right away and finding it recipro- cated, keeping it up all through courtship and marriage and work and responsibility and ageing. Is that what happened to me, Justine wondered, so briefly that she barely settled on the thought before turning away from it again, did I find the right person? She supposed that perhaps you never knew until it was too late, and you glimpsed the right person, at a party, on an aeroplane or in the street, over the shoulder of the one you'd settled for. Evie had always been that kind of person; you longed to be like her, to have some of what she had – taste, spontaneity, humour. And what would be the right thing to do, then? What had Tom done?

Slowly, Justine thought back to the words Louisa had first tried to take back. 'So – when you said, she didn't want anyone to know—' Louisa bit her lip, but Justine went on. 'What did you mean?'

Louisa looked at her helplessly. 'He told me not to say anything.'

'About what?'

'On the day Evie disappeared, she came to us first. After she'd dropped Dido at school, she came to our house. I saw her.'

Justine felt as though her face had been frozen; she could barely move her jaw, and the words came out thickly. 'What did she say?'

Louisa sighed and passed a hand across her eyes. 'I don't know. I wasn't there – I was at school, helping in the classroom with Sam. He's been having trouble with – oh, never mind. I was just on my way back, at the end of the street, walking down towards the house, and she – she was leaving. She turned the other way.'

Justine pictured their pristine terrace, pelmeted damask at the windows, white stucco porches and bay trees like lollipops stationed at the doors, and Evie, the last sight of Evie. A back view maybe of her red coat coming down the steps from Louisa's dark green front door, as jaunty and bright as a magpie, a splash of renegade colour in the spotless affluence of the street. She was overwhelmed suddenly by a sense of longing; how she wished she had been there to call Evie back, or even to be the last one to see her, hers the last friendly eyes laid on her. She felt a trickle of sweat running down her back beneath her shirt, cooling instantly in the wind. The wind sighed in the umbrella pines along the ridge behind them, and across the valley the treetops seemed to be glittering beneath the brilliant sun, and she thought how strange it was to be discussing this here; a London street, Evie's last hours on a cold day in England, laid out between them on a foreign hillside.

She started again. 'But – why—' Justine broke off, the realization dawning that this had not come out at the inquest, that this might be seen by some – by the police – as vital information withheld. As incriminating. But then, she thought, Evie was alive when she left their house. So it would not be incriminating, but the opposite. She tried to order her thoughts, to set the facts straight in her mind but they were like the contours on the map; she could not tell which were hills and which valleys. Doggedly, she persisted, concentrating on what she knew to be significant facts.

'Why didn't you tell the police?'

Louisa put her hands to her face and rubbed her eyes as if to clear something from them.

'I asked Tom, when I got in, and he said she hadn't been over, that it must have been someone else. If I'd said, to the police, that I thought I saw her, but I was wrong – well. It would have sounded odd.'

'Could it have been Evie?'

'Well,' said Louisa slowly, 'at first, when he denied it, I

decided I could have been wrong. But – well, you know Evie. It's hard – it was hard to mistake her for anyone else.'

Justine nodded, but she didn't say anything. She waited for Louisa to go on, and after a moment or two she did.

'When we realized she'd disappeared that very day, when Martin rang, I did wonder. Tom had been – odd that day, when I got back. Pale. I asked him again, could she have come to the door and he hadn't heard her ring. Tom said no, and he was working in the drawing room by the window, so he would have seen her even if he hadn't heard her.'

She shrugged, weary. 'And he never said anything, all through the inquest, said nothing. It never occurred to me – Tom's not someone who's good at covering up, in my experience. I mean, just look at him. He's not doing a good job, is he?'

Louisa wiped the sweat from her forehead with the back of her hand and left a smear of dust. Her hair too was dull with it, and dry as straw. She looked as though she had gone beyond caring how she looked.

'So?' Gently Justine prompted her. 'So how did you find out, that it was Evie at your house that day?'

'I asked him again. After – oh, a long time after the inquest. He was still so depressed, and it wouldn't get better. And he admitted it. I think' – she hesitated – 'I think he missed her so much, by then, that he wanted to share it with someone. That he'd been the last one to see her.' Louisa put her face in her hands, and Justine knew what she must be thinking: why me? What did Evie have that I don't have? She would be too proud to say it, though. Gently Justine put a hand on her shoulder.

From somewhere back along the dirt track they could hear the intermittent roar of a heavy vehicle approaching, and distractedly Louisa turned her head towards the sound. Justine sat up straighter, thinking; it seemed to her that something was still missing from Louisa's account.

'So, the thing she didn't want anyone to know – was that she had been to see Tom?' This made no sense to her; and indeed Louisa was shaking her head.

'No.' She sighed. 'I think there were plenty of things she wanted to keep secret, and I don't think Tom told me everything. But he did tell me she told him she hadn't been well, and she was leaving, and not to say anything about her having been there.'

Not been well? Remembering Evie's face, grown thin suddenly, Justine thought furiously; had there been anything at the inquest about Evie's health? Something – there had been something, something small, not life-threatening. Something mentioned in passing. Justine couldn't remember. 'Leaving Martin and Dido?' she asked. 'She was leaving them?'

Louisa nodded. 'I think he just thought she needed a break; that's one of the things that he's blaming himself for, for not making sure. I don't think he knew she was going to – harm herself. Because he would have stopped her. Wouldn't he?'

The roar of the flatbed lorry bumping up the track towards them grew loud in their ears and a cloud of orange dust heralded its imminent arrival. Louisa looked at Justine beseechingly. And Justine put an arm around her friend's shoulders, grateful that the din prevented her from saying anything more.

Chapter Eighteen

The wedding dress had not been made for her marriage to Paolo's father; it was instead of her marriage. Anna felt the absurdity keenly as she tried to explain it to Paolo, that she had begun the dress only after his father was dead. As he looked wonderingly at the waterfall of white silk crêpe, she saw he recognized her work in the tiny buttons down its back, in the handstitching and embroidery. She had taken down the old roll of wedding crêpe given to her when she left the workshop for Cinecitta – a fine joke, they'd thought it then, to give it to her, thirty-five and never been kissed, for all they knew anyway. Or maybe they really had all hoped she would marry; perhaps the girls had been being kind after all, Laetizia with the wall eye, Chiara with her string of boyfriends and the rest of them, twittering and giggling after her; perhaps they had thought that the white crêpe might bring her luck. Whatever their motives, none of it mattered now. Anna, thirty-eight, pregnant, unmarried and a widow all at once, was never going to walk down the aisle.

Anna had made enough of them over the years to be able to construct the perfect wedding gown in her sleep, and that was almost what she did. Through the remaining months of her pregnancy, after work and before exhaustion took over, fumbling her quick fingers and weighing down her eyelids, she made the dress. She laid out the fabric on her cutting table and, with her great shears, crisply she cut a close-fitting bodice, darted front and back for a young girl's narrow ribcage, not a woman six months gone. She shaped and tacked and hemmed a draped neckline, a long train, little puffed shoulders and long, narrow sleeves. She covered forty-eight tiny buttons with silk, four for each sleeve and the rest down the length of her spine, and sewed forty-eight tiny loops to hold them. She finished the dress three days before Paolo was born, when another woman might have been edging baby blankets or smocking a christening gown.

Anna saw Paolo look from the tiny-waisted dress, a dress for a princess in a fairy story, to his mother, small and compact and sensible in her dressing gown, and she saw him try to imagine her in this story. She sighed, and pushed him out of her room.

'Let me get dressed now, there's a good boy,' she said. 'We're going down to get those mushrooms, don't think you're going to get out of it now.' And she smiled to reassure him.

There would be some modern psychological explanation for the wedding dress; displacement activity, no doubt. It soothed her, the tiny stitches, the expanse of blank white silk, soft and cool. After all she could not attend her lover's funeral as a wife, she could never have dressed in black, pulled her hair and wailed in the street, so she had to do her mourning somehow.

She had been there, at the back, along with hundreds of others, people who had never known him at all but were standing shoulder to shoulder with a comrade, shouting slogans as they marched behind his coffin through the pungent summer streets of Rome. From that day Anna's hatred of politics bloomed, a loathing of political demonstrations, speech-making, rabble-rousing; she might have embraced the struggle, for the sake of Luca's memory, but she couldn't; every cell in her body refused. She had felt sick to hear their chanting that day, an aggressive nausea that invaded every cell of her body as she stood there, pressed against the wall by the relentless mass of passing mourners, sweating in the heat. The weight of the unborn Paolo was no greater than a peach but the unnatural solidity of his coiled shape inside her stubbornly growing, pressing outwards, became a part of the impossible physical burden of her grief and her guilt, and turning away from the procession to escape she had fainted dead away in the door of a baker's shop.

That was the first time Anna had admitted to anyone else that she was pregnant. Of course the baker had known straight away, and given her a queer look; fortunately she was some way from home, and he was not her baker, so he must only have guessed – from the lack of a wedding ring on her finger or her dead-white pallor? – at her situation. Perhaps it had been because she was no longer young that he'd looked at her like that; as if she might have known better, at her age. His wife had looked at her in a more kindly way, when called down from the window upstairs, where she'd been watching the cortège pass. She told Anna to get to the hospital, just to be on the safe side, and that was where the work had begun, the struggle to keep him. That was when she had known, under the disapproving scrutiny of the duty sister, that she would not be able to give up, throw herself into the Tiber and have done with it.

*

'I'm going about this from the wrong end,' she said to Paolo, apologetically, as she locked the kitchen door carefully behind them and took a grateful breath of the cool air outside. Tiny buds of olives were swelling on the gnarled silver trees, and the grass had grown long and pale in the little meadow over the road, among it angelica and wild garlic gone to seed. She could smell rain, despite the bright sky, was the thought at the back of her mind, not even a thought, a countrywoman's base, ineradicable instinct. 'I don't seem to be able to start from the beginning.'

The road was silent and empty in the sunlight; the little morning traffic it saw had already been and gone. The forest ranger in a fancy jeep heading down to monitor the pollution levels in the water, the loggers, Montale with his trailer had all disappeared down the hill before Paolo had even come out on to the terrace with his coffee. The two of them, mother and son, crossed over and set off on through the long grass of the clearing opposite the house, making for the path to Il Vignacce.

In the kitchen Paolo had remonstrated with Anna that there was really no need, if she didn't feel up to it, to go on such a long walk; they could just go a kilometre or so to the little lake, or into town. But Anna had shaken her head; she wanted to go down there. She couldn't tell how it was all going to turn out, after all; what Paolo might say, or think; what she was going to say herself. It would be as well to be out and doing something.

Anna had forgotten how delightful it was to walk through the trees on a day like this, the smell of autumn properly in the air, cooling but not cold yet, and bright overhead through the leaves. Even the promise of rain later and the knowledge

243

that Paolo was still waiting for her to explain his existence could not dispel the extravagant private pleasure she felt once they were in the forest, her childhood home. She had not been down this way for some time, not for years, but the path was familiar to her. It began with a little cobbled pavement which in the spring was the course of a stream, now just a mossy groove in the hillside. Then they passed by a cave formed by an ancient rockfall, one slab balancing on another and carpeted inside with rusty brown beech leaves, where Anna had hidden as a child and Paolo after her. As they picked their way carefully through the dry, slippery leaf covering, ahead of them the compact black shape of a young boar, fat on the summer's rich pickings of nuts and fruit, broke cover and hurtled across their path on comically short legs. The rustle and clatter of its hooves on the forest floor was loud in the silence.

Anna took a deep breath. 'I know you always thought he was a film star,' she said, apologetically. 'Or maybe you hoped?' She half-turned towards her son walking beside her.

'Perhaps when I was young,' Paolo said, shaking his head slightly. 'Not now. I think I'd rather he wasn't now.'

She sighed. 'Just as well then. He was a worker, just like me, at least, that's how he started. He was a set-builder, though he'd moved on by the time I met him.'

Paolo said nothing, just took a deep breath of the clean air of the woods, and they walked on in silence. A light wind blew through the trees and the dainty yellow leaves of the birches shivered.

'If you want me to begin at the beginning,' she went on, slowly, 'I met your father's wife first. I met her before I met him.'

To begin at the beginning; Anna had met her lover's wife before she met him. She felt a kind of anguished awkwardness as she said the words to Paolo, as though this was too blunt a way of breaking the adulterous impropriety of their relationship to him, when all she had meant was to be faithful to the truth, the historical truth. It was never easy to talk to one's children about love, perhaps, but this was an agony. In order to explain to her son how he came about she couldn't restrict herself to the bare facts; they would explain almost nothing, she realized, except a sad, familiar old story of weakness and betrayal.

If Anna really wanted him to understand, she would have to remember it all herself, that was the trouble. Then she'd have to shape it into a story for him, a story that had some meaning and didn't leave him thinking of his father as weak, his mother as hard as stone.

It wasn't as though they were a nondescript couple, Luca and his wife, Amalia; they were a beacon of goodness and hope. He was a leader and an idealist, a fierce champion of the people, she the beautiful red-headed daughter of a wealthy philanthropist, kind and clever and good. She had come for a fitting; the irony was, Anna was at the film studios permanently then, she had only been recalled as a special favour. Everyone had wanted to do them a favour, emblems of a better world, the post-war, post-fascist world; people would shake Luca's hand in the street.

'She had a lovely figure,' said Anna, absently, looking at something far away. Down below them on the steep slope the sparse foliage low down on the trees seemed to hover in the green half-light, but nothing moved except the dust of ancient crumbling leaves in the air. It was very quiet.

'Her skin was quite white, like milk, and she was tall. Long white arms, and a twenty-two-inch waist, even after the child.'

You could tell that she was the daughter of wealthy parents from that alone, Anna mused, almost talking to herself, her long straight limbs, her perfect skin, her gleaming red hair. A war spent nourished on good meat and vegetables, no doubt a larder hanging with hams, stacked with flour and eggs and sugar, in her parents' great villa above the heat and dirt of the city It was very near Paolo's hospital, that old villa, although that was something she didn't say to him. It wasn't just her clear skin that showed her happy upbringing; everyone said Amalia had a temper as sweet as that of a lamb reared by hand, sunny and kind and clever and generous. The daughter – their daughter – had been more serious.

'A child?' The ground had flattened out here and Paolo stopped suddenly, putting his hand out, gently but firmly, to stop his mother too. 'A daughter?'

Anna nodded, looking away from him. 'Four or five years old, she was then. I only saw her once.'

The little girl had been like her father in temperament, resembling her mother in appearance, a slight, freckled child standing beside the rolls of cloth and watching closely while Anna had measured Amalia, tall, upright and bare-shouldered in her petticoat, for a dress. Not a ballgown, nothing so frivolous, just a day dress made of dark wool crêpe, but Amalia hadn't been able to give up her taste for beautiful things entirely when she married a poor man, that had been obvious to all of them as they watched her turn slowly in front of the mirror.

It was easy to see why Luca had fallen in love with Amalia; she was Sleeping Beauty waiting to be kissed, the mythical prize for a suitor pure in heart. Not so easy, Anna found as she searched her memory, to explain why he had fallen so far in love with a small, shy, dark-haired seamstress approaching middle age as to pull his life down around his ears.

Chapter Nineteen

The flatbed truck passed them with agonizing slowness, and unwillingly Justine and Louisa stood and walked behind it as it went, lurching alarmingly on the uneven road and braking hard at every bend. It was loaded with what looked at a distance like short, stubby logs but was in fact something lighter: cork. The bark of a hundred trees was stacked in piles like curved terracotta roof tiles, pale coral-red inside, like something still living, dark and calloused on the outside. Three men sat with their legs dangling from the back of the lorry, dusty boots almost touching the ground. Their clothes, their skin, their hair were all blackened to the same uniform seamy griminess and gave them a look of timeless, sinister antiquity, like chimney sweeps or savages from an old colonial engraving. They smoked in silence and stared, expressionless, at the two women through the cloud of reddish dust that rose in their wake.

As they walked Justine compacted the empty plastic water

bottle and put it into the little rucksack of Lucien's that she had snatched up from the kitchen table when they left. She noticed that her forearms were beginning to burn in the midday sun, and reached into the bag for some sunscreen; sunburn encouraged the lack of pigmentation to spread, and usually she was more circumspect. Groping in the bag's nylon depths she drew out not sunscreen, but Lucien's mobile. Thoughtfully she weighed it in her hand; once he'd been bullied into having one, needless to say he had chosen a model from the top of the range. It was so small it could pass for a cigarette lighter – not that anyone had cigarette lighters any more now that they'd all grown up and given up – and rounded like a silver pebble. Lucien was not capable, she thought with a mixture of pride and irritation, of buying anything cheap and ugly.

'Why don't you call Tom?' she said, turning to Louisa, flipping it open. 'You've got to talk to him, haven't you? You have to, Louisa. Even if it means finding out something you don't want to know, you can't go on like this.'

Louisa looked unhappily at her. 'Now?' she said, looking around them at the empty woods, the distance between them and civilization.

There's nowhere to hide up here, thought Justine, slowing her pace to allow the lorry to gain distance ahead. But it wasn't like Louisa to run away from an unpleasant duty, and she felt sorry for her.

'At least up here you're likely to get a signal,' she said, trying to sound matter of fact. 'Martin couldn't get one at all down in the valley the other day.' She nodded across the hill to the radio and phone masts just still visible clustered on the far peak. Resignedly Louisa sighed and reached for the phone.

Justine watched Louisa's face as she listened, the mobile

pressed to her ear. She looked resigned, but alert; there was a readiness in her expression that was encouraging, something like the old Louisa. From the receiver Justine could hear the tinny bleep, sounding on and on, and she wondered where he could be; whether he was ignoring the sound in a bar some-where, or couldn't hear it. Just as they were both about to give up and Louisa was turning towards Justine with a despairing look, there was a click, and a voice answered. Louisa's face lit up, and for a fraction of a second, before she reminded herself of the desperate situation their marriage was in, Justine felt envious. But almost immediately Louisa's face clouded over, and she was trying to explain something.

'No, no, he's not – Justine had his phone. How did you know?' She was frowning into the phone, exasperated at being deflected from her course. 'Stop it, Tom,' she said. 'I'm up at the top, with Justine, there's a signal up here. Lucien's still down at the house. I'm *just using his phone.*'

She spoke through gritted teeth, and Justine sighed despite herself, and turned away. What had Tom got against Lucien? His self-control? His freedom?

'Tom, where are you?' Louisa was trying to get the conver-sation back on course. Justine could hear no response.

'Please, Tom.' She spoke softly, but with determination. 'Please. The children – look, we need you. I know there are other – I know you're very unhappy. Whatever's been going on, we can sort it out. I – I love you. Come back.' Louisa's voice was still quiet, but Justine could see the strain in her face, any trace of freshness and youth rubbed out suddenly. Her hand around the phone was white-knuckled. 'Tom?' Justine held out her hand for the phone and reluctantly Louisa passed it to her.

250

There was background noise wherever he was, voices, tinny music, the clatter of a bar being set up. 'Tom, it's me,' she said. 'Justine.' She heard him sigh, closer.

'The job's nothing, Tom,' she said. 'None of that matters. The boys – we all just want you to come back. Louisa – they'll be so unhappy without you.'

At first she could hear only the noises from the room behind him, but then Tom spoke,

'It's not just the job. There's something I've got to do,' he said. 'Maybe – maybe it's the only way to sort out all this. Look after Louisa.'

'Louisa needs you, Tom,' Justine said, 'not me. You've got to come back and tell us what's going on. You can't deal with this on your own.' She heard him sigh again.

'You don't know, though,' he said. 'You don't want to know. Everything that's happened – you wouldn't say that if you knew'

Somewhere at the back of Justine's mind a tiny warning sounded at the words: if I knew what? 'It's OK,' she said, trying to subdue the urgency she felt. 'None of it matters.' But perhaps her alarm had made itself heard, or she had reached the limits of her ability to reassure, because there was a click and Tom, the bar, the music and the voices were all gone. Ahead of them at a fork in the road the lorry lurched abruptly down to the left and disappeared from view, leaving Justine and Louisa alone.

'I was leaving,' said Anna, continuing hesitantly, knowing that if she stopped now she might never go on with the story. 'Just letting myself out at the street, after the fitting. They were standing there on the pavement, right in my way. I almost knocked them over.'

She looked at Paolo, standing beside her, his head bowed as he listened intently, hands behind his back. 'Go on,' he said.

Anna sighed, but she went on.

It had been a dull day at the beginning of winter; cold, overcast and spitting with rain. Anna had been pulling her headscarf tight under her chin as she left the building, padded out by her second best winter coat, which was a miserable faded black. Amalia, his wife, stood there with her face turned up to her husband, bright in the grey street. Her back was to Anna, and she was wearing a light mackintosh belted tight and smart at the waist; everything about her was carelessly perfect. Anna just looked up over Amalia's shoulder and there he was; she looked into his face and she saw something there, something that was just for her. She looked back down, dazzled.

Then Amalia gave a little jump and turned, suddenly aware of Anna at her shoulder. It may even have been that she saw her husband – Luca – looking past her at something, but she could not, Anna thought, have seen the look itself.

'Anna!' she exclaimed as she saw who it was, and Anna could still feel the arm that fell lightly on to her shoulder, his wife's arm embracing her, her stirring of unease. She had looked down at her boots.

'Luca,' Amalia said, smiling at her husband, perhaps knowing that it would please him that she treated her seamstress as a friend, but her warmth no less genuine for all that. 'Anna's the cleverest woman in Rome. With a needle, at any rate. Where are you off to now, Anna?' she asked.

Bristling a little at Amalia's patronage, suddenly, uncharacteristically emboldened, Anna had looked up again, and pushed her scarf back a little from her face. It was the first – and only – time in her life that she had consciously offered herself to a man for approval; it was such a small gesture, but at the time she had the feeling that she was taking a great risk.

'I just live up there,' she said, pointing up to her front window at the top of the neighbouring building. 'I'm going home for my lunch. Then I go back to Cinecitta. That's where I work, normally.'

'Oh, but Luca's going to Cinecitta this afternoon, too,' said Amalia. 'You must have seen him there? He works with the unions; a union coordinator, do you know?'

'I spend most of my time in wardrobe,' said Anna. 'We're confined there, you know. We don't get out much. But of course, yes, I've heard of – of him.' Then she smiled and made as if to turn away from them.

'Luca – look, Anna,' Amalia said, turning back to look at her husband and taking Anna gently by the elbow to hold her there. 'Come and have lunch with us, then Luca will take you out there, in the car. We have a little car.'

Anna had opened her mouth but found that she could not think of the right response; then he had spoken, for the first time. His voice was deep and hesitant.

'Yes,' he had said, 'good.' And just as she looked up, he had smiled.

Anna stopped, and looked around her in a kind of daze. Neither of them had been paying very much attention to the way they were walking, and they had come to a clearing with the mossy trunks of some huge fallen trees across it. It was light and warm, the carpet of beech leaves soft and dry in the sun. But the sky overhead was not as bright as it had been; a veil of fine, high cloud, not immediately distinguishable from the fading sky, had drifted silently across from the north-west.

253

'Where are we?' said, Anna, frowning. 'I don't recognize this place.'

Paolo stood for a moment, looking around him. The clearing was on a south-facing slope, sheltered, at the blind end of a little valley, blocked by a spur of land, clogged with climbing vegetation run wild and not apparently leading anywhere. Below them stood a crag of bare rock, raw after a recent landslip; a path led above it around the edge of the slope, deeper into the unpopulated dead centre of the reserve, southwards and away from their destination. Logically, Anna knew that somewhere further below them must be the principal track through the forest, but it looked like they had reached a densely overgrown dead end.

'It's all right. I know where we are,' Paolo said.

There was something different about him, Anna thought; perhaps it was because she was suddenly feeling her age, her resilience undermined by the walk and the effort of revelation, but her son no longer seemed, as she had always thought of him, to be dependent on her, but rather the other way around. Perhaps that's how it should be, she thought.

'Sit down, Mamma,' said Paolo gently, spreading his jacket on one of the fallen trees, and she did what he said. He sat beside her, elbows on his knees, face between his hands in concentration.

'So,' he said, 'you went to eat with them.'

Looking off into the distance, Anna nodded slowly. She turned to look at him, he met her gaze and as he watched her remember Paolo could suddenly see what perhaps his father had seen in her; there was something alive and determined about her face. Her eyes were bright, and if you rubbed away the web of lines, the softened jawline, all the small signs of age, her face under the headscarf in that grey Roman street could have been beautiful. What makes a man fall in love, after all? A look, an impression, the feeling that someone else can see what he is thinking, someone understands. Beauty is only a part of it.

'You have to understand,' Anna went on, and Paolo wondered that she could be unaware of how intently he was trying to understand. 'I was thirty-eight. Before – I had never missed something I hadn't had. I saw girls with their boyfriends – but I couldn't behave like that. There was no one to protect me, so I had to protect myself. I kept myself to myself.'

Anna stopped abruptly, and Paolo nodded, aware as he had not been before of his mother's lonely determination for those many years in her little flat, working, sleeping and waking up to work again.

'It was my last chance,' she said.

His mother had been exactly the age he was now, thought Paolo, and he knew what she meant. 'Yes,' he said, and he sighed, a sound infinitely weary.

Anna, who heard in the sigh her son's despair at the thought of her compromised life, was defiant. 'I know she – I know I should have thought of her. His wife. She was – she didn't deserve it. But – she had always had everything, and I had nothing. It didn't seem particularly wrong, that some of it should be mine. It seemed right.'

'It's OK, Mamma,' said Paolo. 'I can hardly blame you, can I? Where would I be if—'

Ruefully Anna shook her head, looking down at her hands, calloused and blue-veined, lying idle now in her lap.

Paolo went on, speaking as gently as he was able. 'But what did you think – what did you think would happen? How long did you think it would go on, without her knowing?'

The distant rumble of a vehicle approaching, some way off through the trees below them, registered only subliminally, a marker for civilization and the proximity of a path out of the forest, a faintly ominous sound, growing louder.

Anna passed a hand across her forehead, and for a moment her face was hidden. 'I don't know,' she said, wearily. 'We didn't get a chance.'

Chapter Twenty

At the tiny click as the line went dead in Justine's hand Louisa had turned away, hugging herself as if she was cold, although in the sheltered pocket of the hillside where they had come to a halt the still air was humid and warm.

Justine looked down at the mobile; in one corner of its stamp-sized screen an icon representing an envelope blinked at her. She frowned, then sighed with exasperation.

'I can never work out how to collect messages on this thing,' she said, crossly, jabbing the call button to see if it might at least tell her where the message had come from. It said, number unknown. She held it out to Louisa, who shook her head distractedly, and turned as if to go. Then Louisa turned back in a panic.

'It might be from Tom,' she said, suddenly breathless.

'It knows Tom's number,' said Justine. 'The phone knows his number.' And Louisa turned away again.

Justine held the phone to her ear again, then she heard it,

the breathless intimacy of Penny Truman's voice. *Just calling to say sorry, darling. Hope I didn't make an exhibition* ... She sounded husky, hungover. 'You know, say anything I shouldn't have. But really ...' Her voice became indistinct for a moment, and Justine could hear a man's voice, impatient in the background. Then the voice was loud again suddenly, clearer than before. *But what are you playing at? You must be mad, coming out here, with them of all people. Talk about playing with fire.* There was a pause, as though she was wondering whether she should say any more, a click, and Penny Truman was gone.

Justine could feel Louisa's eyes on her, and with an effort she thrust Penny Truman and her insinuations out of her mind. 'Let's just get back, then,' she said, quickly. 'Shall we? Lucien can sort out the message when we get down there.'

Louisa said nothing, nor did she move, but just stood there, frowning at the line of electricity pylons that strode across the dark forest canopy into the distance. Justine realized that going back down into the valley would effectively cut them off from Tom. She hesitated, unwilling to express to Louisa her feeling that they had, anyway, reached the point of no return. There was nothing more they could say that would influence him, and Justine was quite certain that his mobile had by now been either switched off or abandoned altogether. They would just have to wait, and hope. She opened her mouth, but before she could say anything Louisa turned towards her sharply.

'It was always going to come to this,' Louisa said, taking her by surprise, so precisely did she express what Justine had been thinking. 'He's got to make up his own mind.'

Justine took a deep breath, and nodded gratefully. 'We'd better get back,' was all she said. 'The boys – we've been away a good two hours now.'

258

On the gentle downward incline the path followed to begin with, right at the fork where the lorry had gone left, it was fast going, and their spirits lifted, despite everything. They rounded a sharp corner and met a breeze coming up the valley, light but persistent, that cooled them. The heat seemed to have gone out of the sun, too, although it was midday. At this rate, Justine thought, it'd take them no time at all to get back home.

They came to the pretty olive grove, the long grass beneath the olive trees, the seedheads; the ruined house. Reluctant to pass on, they looked curiously around the deserted farmstead but there was no more sign of life than there had been earlier. Louisa sat down beside the path, and with a sigh lay back in the long grass, arms above her head. Justine lay down beside her, and together they gazed up through the branches of a small olive tree, hiding among its silver-grey leaves the shiny green fruit.

'I feel better, now,' said Louisa. 'It's funny, but I do. At least I know – well, I know more than I did.'

Justine nodded, the dry grass tickling her cheek. There was a silence, then Louisa spoke again.

'I'm sorry I was a bit of a bitch. That first day – God, it seems months ago, doesn't it? Poking my nose in about you and Lucien, babies and all that. I think I was just feeling – sometimes, being a mother, you want to let people know it's not that easy. Having babies, looking after them. You lash out.'

'You weren't a bitch,' said Justine, touched. Then on impulse, rolling over to look at Louisa she said, 'Lucien's agreed we can have a baby, now. He – he was reluctant before.' As she said the words, something about them didn't sound right, and she frowned.

'He's agreed?' Louisa raised herself on her elbows, frowning.

Uncertainly, Justine nodded. 'Well,' she said, turning the words around in her head, 'I mean, we decided. Both of us.' But they hadn't, of course; for his own reasons, Lucien had given her permission, which wasn't quite the same.

'Yes, of course,' said Louisa, 'That's wonderful! That's just – of course, it is hard work, you know. But it's worth it.' She put an arm around Justine and gave her a squeeze.

'And maybe,' she went on, 'it'll be good for Lucien, too. He seems a bit, I don't know. Out of sorts. Needs something to focus on, maybe?' She smiled at Justine uncertainly.

'Mmm,' said Justine, vaguely, thinking.

'You are happy, though?' said Louisa.

'Yes,' said Justine. 'Yes. It's just – after all this time, it's not quite what I expected.' She lay back down, not quite sure that she would be able to explain herself to Louisa. You are happy? She didn't know.

The next stretch was the steep, rocky slope that led almost straight downhill to the valley floor, where they'd found the porcupine quills.

After less than five minutes Justine's calves ached with the effort of braking her descent on the steep slope; beside her, Louisa was breathless with concentration. They paused for a moment, and in the silence Justine thought she could hear something above them; a murmur of voices speaking softly, insistently among the trees. The women looked at each other, then set off again.

Justine had taken the left-hand side, where the rocks were stepped conveniently, and soon she was ahead of Louisa, who had first had to pick her way across a scree of loose stone before slotting in behind, in Justine's slipstream. Dogged, silent with concentration, Justine felt the rhythm of her descent take over, and although she was aware of Louisa falling behind she could focus only on where she would next place her foot. Here, then there, then here again, the sound of her own breath loud and monotonous in her ears. It wasn't until she reached a kink in the path, almost at the bottom, that she stopped and turned back to share a smile of triumph. Only Louisa wasn't there.

They'd had lunch in Da Giovanni's, the three of them, a small, bustling, whitewashed place off the Piazza dell' Fico, full of workmen eating ham and pizza *bianca*. Amalia had tried to draw her out, but Anna had felt inhibited and had said little. She had only felt on safe ground when asked about home – her childhood home, that is, and she'd found herself talking about the hills and the forest and their little rows of vines before she'd felt their eyes on her and fallen silent, blushing stupidly.

While they said goodbye in the Via della Pace, Luca kissing his wife, Anna had stood obediently silent, pretending interest in something on the other side of the road. She gazed blankly at the headlines pasted on the side of a newspaper kiosk; murder at Ostia. She stole a look, though, just as the barman standing in his doorway and the hardy handful of customers sitting at the tables outside the bar looked, as Amalia lifted a hand to wave and walked away, tall and straight, long red hair twisting down her back. She was magnetic, a golden talisman they all wanted to touch. Anna wondered what could be happening, and she didn't look at Luca when he spoke.

'This way,' he said, nodding to a side-street. 'The car's down here.' He turned away abruptly, and she followed, feeling as though many eyes must be on her.

Alone with him in the small, dusty Fiat bumping through the narrow streets behind the Piazza Navona, Anna had been overtaken by doubt. One look, after all, could be mistaken for something it was not, even if Anna had never made that kind of mistake before, and Luca Magno – well, whatever reputation he had, it was not for womanizing.

Sitting upright in the passenger seat, jolted by the car's erratic progress on thin tyres and holding tight to her bag on her lap, Anna had stared straight ahead, aware of him beside her, all the way out to Cinecitta. He only spoke once, taking his eyes from the road briefly.

'How long have you lived alone, like that?' he said. And suspecting pity, Anna had held her head high and answered as lightly as she could, 'Oh, ten years. A bit less, maybe.'

Still she hadn't looked at him, but out of the corner of her eye she saw him nod gravely. 'You're brave,' he said, not laughing, but softly, and she thought he meant it. Generally people thought there was nothing brave in it; they thought she was a bit odd; soft in the head. They both fell silent, after that; the journey had never seemed so long.

But when they stopped, as he leaned down to take her hand and help her out of the low-slung car, Luca held both her hands and looked at her until she had to raise her eyes from the dusty kerb and look back. She had trembled, after the strain of keeping silent and not looking, and tried to pretend it was the cold. Luca had nodded, put his arms around her and pressed her against him, apparently oblivious to the fact that at any time someone might walk around the corner. She still remembered the exact feeling, although she couldn't express it, the feel of the prickly wool of his jacket against her cheek, his heart beating against her throat, the sweet smell of tobacco and his sweat, before he released her and they stood apart again. Perhaps it might have been nothing to a different woman, but that embrace was the single most significant instant of Anna's life, and she had known it even then.

'And that was that,' said Anna, looking up. 'We met again, the next day; I drank coffee with him at the railway station, on my way to work; we hardly said anything. I don't think we could believe what was happening.' She closed her eyes and thought of the station bar, a hundred bodies jostling for their breakfast, shouting their orders, pushing them towards each other, she and Luca. The barmen calling to each other, the hiss of the coffee machine and the heavy clank of the trains beyond the glass.

When she opened them again Paolo was looking at her, but he expressed neither understanding nor disapproval; he was waiting for what would come next.

Anna sighed. 'Neither of us was the kind of person to take things lightly. Deception. Whenever we saw each other – not often; he came to the flat once a week, perhaps, for six, or seven months – it was a struggle. He wanted to stop, but he couldn't; I knew I should put an end to it, for him, but I couldn't.'

Paolo cleared his throat. 'Did he know? Did my father ever know about me?' At the hoarse sound of his voice, Anna looked up at Paolo, and it was as though she had never seen him before. She could not separate him from his father now, in her mind.

It's easy, she thought, when they're children, to pretend that they need to be older to understand properly, to put it off, but, really, love is easiest to explain to a child. She knew that now. She could have simply said, we loved each other. She remembered Paolo as a little boy, the warm weight of him in her lap, how she used to whisper to him how much she loved him, before he could speak.

The mossy log was damp and hard even through Paolo's waxed jacket, and Anna's back ached; she stood up.

'He died before you were born,' she said. 'You always knew that.'

'But did he know?'

'He knew,' she said slowly. 'I should never have told him, though.'

'Why?' said Paolo. 'Didn't he have a right to know?'

She looked at him oddly, the anger in his voice chiming with his words in her head; suddenly something slotted into place. 'There's something you haven't told me,' she said, slowly. 'Did Livia ever get pregnant, Paolo?'

'Mamma,' he said, looking down, 'I'm sorry. That's – finished. Livia – there were things we didn't agree on. It wasn't for me to change her mind. But this isn't to do with Livia. Please. Tell me, just tell me.'

Anna put out a hand to touch his arm, wanting him to turn back to her. 'I didn't want to tell him, because I didn't want to blackmail him into anything. I wanted it to be because of me. That he left her.'

Anna was surprised to find that she didn't feel ashamed, telling her son these things; shame had been the reason for her silence, she could admit that now. But when she opened her mouth to speak at last she found it had evaporated, along with the guilt and the blame and the ancient passion, all burnt out. She looked back at her younger self and thought; what else could you have done?

They had had a row, she and Luca; their only row, standing facing each other in the flat, the little windows open to the street below and every word they said no doubt avidly received in the neighbouring flats, old Giulia downstairs cocking an ear over the washing-up. She had told him first that he would have to leave Amalia; she made her voice as hard as she could, to make him afraid of what she might do. And then, hearing herself, she found that she could not disguise all the anger she had accumulated, at being condemned to be the other woman, the lesser one. At the injustice of her finding him when it was too late. She wanted him to leave Amalia because he loved her, not because she was pregnant, and that was when she almost broke down, when she saw the look of desperation in his eyes and knew that it would not happen.

Then Anna had taken pity on him; it was, after all, too much to ask. The world did not work that way, giving to those who have not, taking away from those who have. You don't have to leave your family, she said. And only then had she told him, once it was too late and her voice was dull with despair, the only thing he might have left his wife and child for.

'I did tell him. In the end.'

'What did he say?' asked Paolo, his eyes on the ground.

What had he said? 'Really?' he'd said, and he had sighed, a long sigh as though one burden had been lifted only for another to be placed on his shoulders, and he'd raised his head from between his hands to look at her. A look of such stunned confusion as she had never seen.

'He – he was happy. In a way.' Cautiously Anna looked at Paolo.

It wasn't as though she hadn't known what Luca thought about children; it was practically a part of his political manifesto: he believed that one was enough, that they were a luxury the world could not afford. She thought it was part of his determination to deny himself until the world had become a more just place; she had never thought, in her spinsterish naivety, that she would fall pregnant (how could she not have known? she wondered now) and his conviction would be put to the test. But she did, and it was. She thought of the look she had seen in Luca's eyes when realization dawned and wondered how she could describe it to her son. Disbelief, alarm; wonder, longing. It's not as simple as that, she wanted to say to her son; you wait. Perhaps he already did know.

'I don't think he ever got as far as worrying about what would happen once you were born. But I think the idea – that you were there, on the way – I don't think he could help himself. He was happy. Perhaps – after—' She stopped. Perhaps, she wanted to say, after he left me, he began to think of all those other things; but looking at Paolo's averted face she thought, perhaps that's enough. And it was true; when Luca had left her, he'd looked happier than she'd ever seen him.

He'd walked down the greasy, dark, malodorous stairwell as if he was sleepwalking, into the street but then, just as he stepped off the kerb to walk away and she thought, what have I done, he turned and waved back up at her in the window. And that was the last vision she had of him, his face upturned and suddenly smiling, dazed with happiness, saluting her.

'I don't think he could have been more proud of you, Paolo,' she said, knowing it to be true, 'if he'd known you. You're just like him.'

Paolo lifted his eyes at last, but just then, from below them, in the valley, they heard a cry.

Justine hadn't heard a sound, she only knew that Louisa had vanished. She looked back up the hill but could see only the stones of the path, red with dust, and the dense undergrowth on either side. She shouted, and for a moment she thought she heard a weak cry in response, but a bird started up in the hedge at her shout, floundering and flapping in noisy alarm, and she couldn't be sure. Scrambling back up the hill, reaching for the stones with her hands to help her up, she was soon panting with the effort, and although the sky was overcast now her shirt clung to the sweat forming on her back. Justine was in a panic; she'd been careless; she shouldn't have gone on so fast. She should have turned to look back.

Justine had almost retraced her steps to the top of the steep part of the slope where they had set off together and she had last seen Louisa, when she heard something like a sob, only angrier. The path was enclosed here with vegetation, crowding up on either side, and Justine looked wildly about, trying to judge where the sound had come from.

'Louisa?' she called. 'Lou?'

'Here.' There was something confusing about the direction from which the answer came; Louisa's voice was muffled and it almost seemed to be emanating from underneath her.

'Down here. Oh, bloody hell.'

A stunted cork tree, its trunk stripped up to shoulder height, stood at the edge of the path where Justine had stopped. It was surrounded by lesser trees; etiolated saplings, some hazel and clumps of something tough, prickly and aromatic like myrtle, lined the path edge. Justine leaned against the trunk of the cork tree and peered forwards into the undergrowth. It was not what she had expected; the ground, which she had assumed to be level, fell away sharply at the edge of the path, where a landslip must have sheered off the natural slope. Beneath her feet Justine could feel the earth crumbling away, and she took a step back. Standing as close as she dared to the edge she leaned against the tree and cautiously she looked back into the shadows.

'Louisa?' she said again.

'Here.' Louisa's voice was clear now, coming up to her from the foot of the slope.

The flat glare of the overcast midday made it difficult to see anything at first, but gradually her eyes adjusted to the gloom and she could make out Louisa's blonde head in the shadow below. She was hunched over her knees, but when Justine called down to her she tipped her head back and looked up, her small pointed chin giving an impression of defiance although even at this distance everything else about her body language betrayed distress.

'Careful!' she called up sharply to Justine. 'It just drops away there.'

Cautiously Justine turned and lowered herself backwards down the bank; it was about twelve or fifteen feet down, not sheer rock, but hard, dry earth, a lump of stone or a root offering a handhold here and there, but more often crumbling away under her scrabbling fingers. All the same, it took no more than a minute for her to get down, slithering the last few feet and landing with a gasp and a thud next to Louisa.

Louisa looked at her anxiously, still hugging her knees. Justine put an arm around her shoulders.

'Are you hurt?' she asked. 'What have you done?'

Louisa winced as she extended her right leg, and let out an exclamation of frustration and pain mixed."

'Bloody hell. It's so stupid,' she muttered angrily. 'I'd stopped, just for a minute – I thought I saw some more of those porcupine quills. I was just catching up, climbing down behind you. I put out my hand for support, to lean on the tree up there, must have missed it. I didn't see – ow!' She broke off as Justine gingerly pressed a swollen-looking ankle.

268

'That hurt,' she said, crossly. 'No, sorry. It's not your fault.' She looked back up the bank to the filigree of leaves, black against the light, at the top. 'I didn't realize it sloped down like that.'

'So what happened?'

'I wasn't concentrating. I didn't look where I put my hand, I went to support myself on the tree and I went over the edge. It's ridiculous!'

She sounded outraged. Justine looked at the slope, from which roots protruded like coarse hair, exposed by the landslip, gauging the distance Louisa must have fallen.

'I couldn't believe how far down I went,' Louisa said. 'I put out my hand to try to stop myself.'

There was a raw-looking graze on Louisa's forearm and the heel of her hand, and Justine could see twigs in her hair. But she seemed full of angry energy again, which was a welcome change from abject misery.

'It's my ankle, that's the only thing. It got caught in something. As I came down. A tree root, or something.'

'Lucky you didn't break your neck,' Justine murmured absently, following Louisa's gaze up to the light. It seemed a long way back up, and a quick assessment of their situation confirmed her fear that they were going to have trouble getting out of the forest unaided. The mobile had long since lost its signal, she couldn't haul Louisa back up that bank on her own, and even if there was a way out of the undergrowth further down, she'd need guidance to find it. In the background she could hear the fading chug of the logging lorry; surely it couldn't have got far. Quickly she made a decision.

'Look,' she said, seizing Louisa by the arm, 'if I climb up and run back to where we were, where the road forked, maybe

I can catch up with the lorry. They might be able to help get you out. Back to the road.'

Uncertainly Louisa nodded and, unwilling to waste any time, Justine jumped up. 'I'll be as quick as I can.'

Panting up the steep slope, Justine found herself wishing she was fitter; up and down these stones twice in one day at speed and her lungs were burning. She thought of Louisa sitting alone at the foot of that steep slope in the dark, and felt a shiver of claustrophobia. Better get back quick. She climbed on; the logging lorry could never have got down this road. She wondered how long it could have been since this way out of the woods was passable other than on foot; when had Il Vignacce become so cut off? With the little hidden village perched so tantalizingly close on the next ridge, this must once have been the natural way out.

At the fork the going was easier; the road Justine turned on to was almost level, the rust-red gravel fine and dusty. She began to run. The laboured sound of the lorry ahead of her grew louder, it was obviously moving with painful slowness; she could hear her own breathing too, rasping as it burned her throat. She rounded a bend, and there it was, swaying ahead of her. She could no longer run, but she was almost there; she could hear their voices, although she couldn't make out what they were saying. The men looked at her incuriously as she approached, then, at her frantic gesturing, one of them shouted back over his shoulder and the vehicle came to a halt. Within a few steps she was upon them.

There were three men sitting on the back of the truck, another perched perilously on top of the load, standing as the truck stopped. Justine saw the face of the fifth man, the driver, gleaming with sweat as he craned his neck to look back at her from his cab. Justine could not have spoken straight away, even if she had formulated the words, she needed first to catch her breath. As they watched her, one of the three men feeing her removed the stub of a cigarette from between his dark lips and flicked it down into the dust. He said something out of the side of his mouth to another of the men and they all laughed; nothing about the laughter invited her to share in it with them. Then they fell silent, watching her.

Trying to control her breathing, Justine spoke, but the words came out in a rush. She concentrated on slowing her speech down, enunciating in her best Italian, but the men showed no sign of understanding.

'My friend is hurt,' she said again, 'I need help.' But their faces did not change; they looked at her as though she was an animal in a zoo, an inferior species trying to communicate. The fourth man jumped from the top of the log pile to the ground; it was quite a height, some nine or ten feet, but he landed silently. He came along the side of the lorry towards her, and behind him Justine could see the driver climbing down from his cab.

Justine felt her throat tighten in panic; all she could see were their dark, expressionless faces bearing down on her. The driver, whose face she still could not see, said something in a thick, guttural voice and without turning away the man who had spoken earlier replied. Their speech was quite unintelligible to Justine; it was not Italian. It could have been dialect, some North African language, Albanian; something dense and glottal. She made one last brave attempt to communicate, looking from one to the other of the men as she tried to extract a response, any clue that they were willing to help her, but again they laughed. Justine felt her sense of

271

being able to judge the situation slip. No, she thought. She turned and ran.

Paolo and Anna were almost at the road and they paused in their argument as they saw the pale flicker of a figure running along below them. Whoever it was, was partially screened from them by the bracken and the rich striated brown of the umbrella pines' bark; the sound of coarse laughter echoed up from the road below. The impression was of a raucous gathering; suddenly the forest seemed full of life and sound, not an empty place.

Anna sighed. 'You see, it could have been anyone. Just someone out walking, startled by something. Nothing to send us off on a wildgoose chase.' She looked weary, perhaps in anticipation of the effort of beginning her story again. Paolo felt sorry for her, and guilty; he didn't want to force her.

'Come on, Mamma, it sounded like someone in pain. Don't you think?' Paolo said uncertainly, unsure whether the sound they had heard had been an appeal for help.

Anna shook her head a little. 'I don't know how you could tell,' she said, smiling at him. 'Did they teach you that in medical school?'

Despite himself Paolo laughed. 'You learn that one on the job,' he said. 'Still, I don't know how we'd track down whoever it was, not in all this.' He gestured around at the great expanse of trees below them, moving a little in the wind, the leaves of the holm oaks and poplars showing silver as they shivered in the breeze.

'If they're on the path, maybe we'll come across them,' said Anna, in an attempt to console him. Slowly they set off again, climbing down through the ferny groundcover to the path below, the path that would eventually lead them to Il Vignacce. It was quite light up here, where the trees grew sparsely, but looking down the path the foliage seemed to encroach much more and the way seemed dark. Overhead the sky was a pale, uncertain blue, the sun lacking the strength to illuminate.

Once she was out of sight of the lorry, turning around once to be sure no one was following her, Justine's panic slowed, and when she turned off downhill at the fork, she began to feel foolish. And yet, how could she tell? She hadn't been able to make them understand. And even supposing she had physically dragged one of them down to where Louisa lay, how claustrophobic then would that dim ravine feel, just Louisa, Justine and one of them, one of those laughing men, the three of them confined just out of sight of any passer-by? She clambered down across the stones of the path, aware that it was cooler now; aware of cloud closing in overhead; it occurred to her suddenly that it might come on to rain, sooner or later, and she felt a qualm.

She approached the corner where she had left Louisa and was overtaken by anxiety that she would not recognize it, that she had already passed the cork tree overhanging the scree, or that when she got there Louisa would be gone. But there it was and there, when Justine craned her neck, half-afraid still, to peer down the slope, was Louisa.

'Lou?' she heard herself whisper.

'Oh!' Louisa looked up, gasping with relief. 'It's you. I—' She tried to stand, to get closer to Justine, reached out for a hanging branch, but her ankle gave way and she let out a yelp of pain.

'Careful!' called Justine. 'Sorry, I – there's no one. We'll have to manage on our own. Wait there.'

273

'Couldn't I – perhaps, with you up there, I could get up some of the way on one foot, and you could pull me?' Louisa was trying to sound brisk, her old self. Doubtfully Justine shook her head. Louisa was trying to stand again, and to show willing Justine took off her backpack and set it carefully aside. She lay down, her body over the edge of the path, and leaned down towards Louisa's hand, which was fluttering palely at her in the dim light. But there were at least a couple of metres between them, and even though Louisa was hardly a heavy-weight, Justine simply wouldn't be able to pull her up.

'No,' she said, reluctantly, 'it's not going to work. I'm coming down.'

The bank seemed to crumble and give way beneath her fingers even more this time, and a fine shower of dust followed her down. Justine could not imagine hauling Louisa back up without incurring more damage to her ankle, or somewhere else; what if they both fell, and neither could climb out? What if the ankle was broken?

Justine tried to let none of these misgivings show when she reached Louisa; she put an arm around her.

'I think,' she began, 'I think we're going to have to walk out, on our own.'

'All right,' said Louisa, uncertainly, but she wasn't looking at Justine. Justine followed her gaze, up the bank to the path.

A shadow had fallen across the bright space above them, and she heard voices. Someone had stopped up there, just where Louisa had fallen and at once Justine thought of the loggers. Then she remembered the backpack. She'd left the backpack on the path. She subdued her mounting panic, and listened. They were speaking Italian. She took a deep breath, and shouted.

'*Aiuto!* Help.' The voices stopped.

274

Paolo, who had stopped at the sight of the small backpack resting, almost hidden, by the side of the road, turned towards the sound.

'*Ecco!*' he said triumphantly, turning to Anna. She made as if to go to the edge of the path, following the voices. Gently Paolo put out a hand and stopped her.

'No, Mamma, let me have a look first. Just wait here. 'OK?' Reluctantly Anna stopped; seeing that he was right.

'*Arrivo!*' he called back into the undergrowth. 'I'm coming. Stay there.' He elbowed a clump of gorse aside and holding on to the trunk of the cork tree, leaned forward to look down in the direction of the voices.

The sound of a voice offering help in English, even heavily accented English, was somehow infinitely reassuring, and Justine saw Louisa's shoulders sag with relief. Just as well, she thought, even if we do look like idiots. Better able now to see in the half-light, she could see that their rescuer was a tall man, dark and broad-shouldered, and he seemed to be having less trouble than she had making his way down the slope. When he turned to face them at the bottom she felt almost sure it was the man she had seen earlier, talking to the elderly woman. He had an open, rumpled face, and looked concerned, and for some reason in his presence Justine felt herself relax.

'OK, OK,' he said, turning at the bottom, and there was a note in his voice, cheerful, soft and practised, that Justine liked. 'What has happened?'

'I fell,' said Louisa, reluctantly, looking up at him. 'I hurt my ankle.'

'Ankle?' he said, pondering. Louisa extended her leg in front of him in the half-light, wincing again, and he nodded.

'Attention,' he said, 'be careful. The *caviglia*, yes. Ankle.

Anything else?' he asked. 'Your head? Your—' he tapped his back and made an exasperated sound to himself. '*Schena*. Back. Spine?'

Louisa shook her head. 'No, no. Nothing else.'

Justine was silent, watching his careful solicitude and startled herself by the realization that she wished it was her ankle he was turning so gently in his hands. He glanced across at her for a moment in the gloom, and she saw him frown a little, as if trying to remember something. He turned back to Louisa.

'I am Paolo Viola. My mother lives up there.' He jerked his head uphill. 'In fact, I am a doctor,' he said, as though by way of explanation for his line of questioning. '*Ortopedia*. Orthopedic surgeon.' He held out his hand, and despite themselves both women laughed at the formality of his hand held out, and the improbability of a doctor being here just when they needed one. In the gloom Justine saw him smile for the first time, and Louisa shook his hand.

'It's too dark here to see,' said Paolo Viola. 'There is a way down here, I think, that goes back to the path. Where – where have you come from?'

'Il Vignacce,' said Justine, speaking for the first time since his arrival. 'Down there' – she nodded to the path – 'near the river?'

He nodded. 'OK. I know. Perhaps we can get there. I just – my mother. One moment.' He leaned back and called up to the path, where they could see someone standing on the path against the light. 'Mamma!' He spoke rapidly in Italian, and Justine made out only the name of their house: Il Vignacce, and an affirmative response. She took in the measured, rational way he dealt with their situation, his concern for his mother. Paolo turned back to them.

'She will go down there. My mother. Is there someone who speaks Italian?'

Justine grimaced. 'Only me, really,' she said, 'but maybe they'll manage.'

He shrugged philosophically. 'Perhaps.'

They both smiled at once, then Paolo turned back to Louisa, quickly.

'I can carry you,' he said, matter of factly, and before Louisa could protest he had leaned towards her and in a swift motion picked her up, first across his body as you might carry a child, then gently manoeuvring her over his shoulder in a fireman's lift.

'This way,' he said, gesturing with his free arm across the slope in the direction of the river, where the undergrowth seemed to thin out a little and more light filtered between the evenly spaced trunks of trees. Obediently Justine followed him towards the light, Louisa's blonde head resting passively on his shoulder.

As she made her way carefully down the rocky path following Paolo's instruction Anna felt quite breathless with the effort, not just of the walk, which although it required circumspection was not strenuous, but of revelation. It was actually a relief to be alone, she thought, concentrating on stepping from one stone to the next; it gave her a breathing space to think about how to get to the end of her story. Except that she didn't want to get to the end.

The wind was getting up a bit, and Anna looked up at the sky, where, although it was still relatively clear overhead, the cloud was moving smoothly in banks across the horizon. She hurried on down the hill towards the river. She knew this path well, although it was a long time since she'd been down here; not since her departure from the country as a girl had she come down so far. Higher up, she remembered, was the old Neri place, up towards Iesa, the village on the ridge. They'd had olive groves and what had once been a beautiful house – three storeys high with a hay barn and a cowshed and fig trees. It was all overgrown now, no roof on the house any more, so Giovannino said. It had been on the road out once, long ago, out of the woods to civilization, but time, war and neglect had put paid to that.

Now the road stopped at Il Vignacce, unless you were on foot.

Down this way, where she now walked, led to the hazelnut groves that flanked the river; as a child she'd hidden and played house in their deep cool shade, splashing in the little streams that fed the Merse. She recognized the steep red canyon of the path, the last stretch of the way to the river, and it came back to her how easy it had seemed to clamber down from stone to stone then. How little a child is able to predict old age, she thought, still baffled herself by how easily she had slipped from being a girl to being an old woman. And just beyond, just across the river and up through the trees, was Il Vignacce.

The closer she drew to the old farmhouse and recognized, one after another, the secret landmarks of her childhood wanderings, the more Anna wondered at her superstition for all these years. She had avoided coming down here for so long, just as she had avoided thinking about Luca, and now that it was all here in front of her once again it seemed so unexceptional. It had no special power; it hid no secret horror. Suddenly it came to her, and the thought made her feel unaccountably tired, that it didn't matter where her father had died, just as it didn't matter where Luca had died. What mattered was keeping going, after all. She pulled her son's coat closer around her and picked her way down into the gloom of the hazel copse that would lead her directly to the river.

It was just as she remembered it; there was the trickle of brown water, the valley floor thick with leaf mould darkened by the seeping damp of the river. She heard the solemn clang of cowbells somewhere over to her right, between her and Il Vignacce, and stepped lightly across the water towards the sound.

The sun came out again just as Anna walked up from the river, out of the trees and towards the bright open pasture, and the first thing she saw was a long table laid for lunch. It stood beneath a pergola on her side of the house but the scene was unpopulated; Il Vignacce itself, bathed suddenly in light, seemed deserted, although the door stood open. It was silent and there were no deckchairs or children's toys on the sunbleached grass; nothing to indicate the presence of the English visitors except the table and the open door.

Anna looked across the pasture and then she saw them in the distance beneath the trees that ringed it: a tall slender girl, long hair down her back and the hump of a backpack on one shoulder, was walking slowly away, two boys, smaller figures, running ahead of her. As she watched they slipped between the trees on the far edge of the field and with this tiny, marginal activity gone, the scene was empty once again.

Anna approached the fence and stopped at the gate. She was close to the table now; she could even see the finely cut shadows of the leaves on the pergola cast on the white linen of a tablecloth still stiff with creases from the drawer, shifting as the feathered foliage moved in the wind. The table was set for eight with plain, heavy china – Piero Montale's third best dinner service, no doubt, thought Anna, not good enough for their grand new house. A handful of pale pink cyclamen and their mottled, heart-shaped leaves wilted a little in a glass jar at the table's centre as if pining for the shady obscurity of the woodland where they'd been found.

Anna could smell cooking: wine and tomatoes and garlic; a bowl of salad and some bread were already on the table. Feeling her responsibility as a mother she wondered what the time was; she hadn't thought it was so late, not time for lunch already? Surely not, if the children had been allowed down to the river to swim? In the silence, the hiss of a tap turned on inside the house made Anna jump; almost as abruptly it stopped, and she heard a muttered, angry exchange of words she did not understand in the dark interior. A man appeared in the doorway, a water jug in his hand.

Anna had seen him before, of course; Montale had introduced them in the market square. She'd almost forgotten that as she hurried down here, that she'd met them already: the children, the woman and the three men, one dark, one fair, and this one, tall, green-eyed, curly-haired and handsome. He looked different today; almost unrecognizable, in fact, as the open, cheerful type whose hand she had shaken in the square. As he came through the door he was frowning and Anna felt self-conscious, unable to tell if it was because of her, or something that had happened inside the house before he saw her. Then, as they looked at each other, she saw recognition dawn in his eyes, and Anna found herself both relieved and unsettled by the change that came over him. With what seemed like an effort his brow cleared, with deliberate care he set the jug down among the plates, and he smiled politely across the table at her.

Remembering why she was there, Anna approached the gate. 'Permesso?' she asked, waiting for permission to cross the threshold. He nodded and reached for the latch and opened the gate, turning as she entered to glance back at the house. There must be someone else here, she thought, with relief.

'There is – one of your party is injured,' she said in Italian, pointing back towards the river, and he looked blank. She tried again, slowly, frustrated by her inability to speak his language.

'The signora has hurt her leg,' she said, patting her ankle, grimacing to indicate pain, then pointing back into the trees. 'Not serious, I think. Niente di grave. My son is bringing her.' She mimed a carrying motion, and although the man still looked a little uncertain she thought he understood. He motioned to her to sit down, and turned towards the house.

'Martin!' he shouted, something curt and reluctant in his tone. Another man, the dark one, came out of the house, looking, by contrast, quite composed, but Anna could tell, even with her limited experience of men, that she had interrupted something between these two. She took a deep breath, and began again.

Chapter Twenty-One

It took about twenty minutes to get to a place where they could stop, where there was enough light to get a good look at Louisa's injury. Paolo walked ahead of Justine in silence, slowly and steadily so as not to jolt Louisa who lay as still as a child on his shoulder. They had to make their own path through the undergrowth, some of it sticky with burrs, or clinging with tiny, thorny tendrils; unfamiliar climbing plants like vines gone wild and again Justine was glad that she and Louisa were not trying this alone; it was one thing to be on a marked path, quite another to be in the middle of nowhere.

Paolo seemed to be aware of Justine behind him; once he paused and half-turned to make sure they were all still together. It was humid and Justine lifted the back of her hand to her forehead to wipe away the sweat and grimaced at him apologetically; he looked quite cheerful, still, even under his burden, and barely warm. From his shoulder Louisa exchanged a sheepish look with Justine.

'Not far now,' he said. 'You can hear the water.' But Justine could hear nothing. She shrugged, and he shook his head, smiling at her. 'Soon,' he said, and together they walked on.

For something like twenty minutes more they struggled through the undergrowth, Justine's legs aching now from the effort of negotiating the uneven terrain, then suddenly they came to a clearing and it was then that Justine heard the sound of the river. Ahead of her Paolo stopped, and bent to set Louisa down carefully on a broad, flat rock beside the water. Justine looked around them; they were at a narrow stretch of the river, where the water was sluggish and shallow across pebbles between densely overgrown banks, a few large boulders diverting the water's course here and there. It was quite idyllic, in fact, and as she gazed at the dark water and heard the soft liquid sound of the stream for a moment Justine forgot why they were there at all. She found herself wondering where the pool she had swum in, and the cliff that had enclosed it, might be from here. She turned to Paolo, about to ask him, but then she saw that he was busy.

He was kneeling at Louisa's feet; carefully he took her bruised ankle between his hands. The flesh was puffy and swollen around the joint, and beginning to discolour. Louisa flinched when he touched her foot, her face pale and set; at her tiny gasp Paolo automatically murmured something in Italian, intent on his examination. Justine watched as very gently he felt around the joint, running his hand along the awkward conjunction of bone and muscle and cartilage. His hands were not as she would have imagined a surgeon's, his fingers not fine and slender but big, almost clumsy-looking, like a workman's. All the same, she could see Louisa's shoulder sag a little as she relaxed, and he seemed to know what he was doing.

Then Paolo sat back on his heels, and sighed. He looked up at Justine, but he was focusing on something else; the injury, perhaps. His eyes were dark brown, and turned down a little at the corners, giving him a slightly melancholy look. He opened his mouth to speak but then his focus changed, and it was as though he could see her and she had made him forget what he was about to say. He frowned a little, and looked back down at the ankle he held between his hands.

'OK,' he said. 'It is not broken. A—' He made a twisting motion with his hands, and looked at Justine for help.

'A sprain?' she said, tentatively. Nodding, he smiled, and Justine felt something, a kind of fluttering, behind her chest wall, but she held his gaze.

He tapped his forehead. 'My books – when I was studying, some of them are in English. Sprain, I remember.' He turned to Louisa, who was looking at them quizzically. 'So,' Paolo said, smiling. 'Don't worry. Just put your foot in the water for a little, here, where it is cool. The swelling will become less. Then from here,' he gestured along the river, 'it isn't so far to Il Vignacce. Soon we can go on.'

Gingerly Louisa lowered her foot into the water, which, although it looked dark from a distance, was very clear, and let out a little gasp of relief as her ankle dipped below the cool surface.

Paolo laughed abruptly. 'Leave it there,' he said, standing up; Justine found him beside her, and together they looked around in silence. They were surrounded by dense vegetation, willow, bird-cherry, bog-oak and hazel growing unimpeded in the fertile soil of the river valley, branches dipping low over the water and enclosing them. It was very quiet.

'I swam in this river,' said Justine. 'It must be deeper up there?' She pointed towards Il Vignacce.

Paolo nodded. 'It is a beautiful river,' he said. 'Very clean. Very pure. When I was a boy, I would swim here too. Sometimes with my friends, sometimes on my own. But not at Il Vignacce; there was no pool there then, I think.' He stopped, looking down at the water, as if he was thinking of something else. Then he looked up at her again. 'Are you here – for a long time?'

Justine shook her head slowly, looking around at the clearing, the enfolding green of bushes and trees, unwilling to leave it suddenly. 'Not much longer. Until the weekend, perhaps. It depends.'

On whether we can stand each other for that long, she thought but did not say. The future had never seemed less certain; despite the fact that a holiday usually was more definitely circumscribed than most things – flights booked, channel crossings arranged. So significant did that parcel of time seem to be in the planning, no one ever dared imagine a holiday curtailed, the reasons would have to be too serious to contemplate. Death; critical illness; the breakdown of relationships. Irreconcilable differences. But once you were all gathered there, in the healing idyll of your own meticulous planning, close-up the whole structure seemed laughably flimsy. Things flew apart. She heard the echo of something Martin had said – it seemed like years ago, not just the previous evening. Something about stresses working towards disintegration.

Paolo said nothing as all this went through Justine's head; but just went on looking at her.

'But you like it here.' Looking into Paolo's broad open face, Justine nodded. It wasn't a question; it was as though he knew what she was feeling, knew that she didn't want to leave. And something in his expression, so thoughtful and sympathetic, seemed to be telling her that she didn't have to. Suddenly self-conscious she put a hand to her face, pushing her hair back; her sleeve fell down to the elbow of her raised arm.

'Ah,' Paolo said, as if he had understood something and reached for her, touching her forearm, 'vitiligo.'

Justine flinched, and in her throat she felt her breath catch, a sense of having been discovered.

'It is quite common here. In Italy,' he said, mildly.

She could feel his warm fingertips on the soft, vulnerable skin inside her elbow, where it was very white, and suddenly she felt faint, as though he had touched a pressure point, somewhere where nerves clustered. She dropped her arm and turned quickly towards Louisa.

'Better?' she said, lightly.

Louisa looked at her curiously, not fooled. 'Mmm,' she said, slowly, looking from one to the other of them. She looked back at her foot, white against the dark stones on the river bed and lifted it, dripping, from the water. 'Yes,' she said, more firmly, 'I think so.'

For a moment, Justine realized, she had forgotten about Tom, and Evie, and the rest of them. About Lucien, too. Better get back, she thought with resignation; sort all this out.

The sound of bells started up behind Il Vignacce, not the occasional languorous clang they had become accustomed to but a tolling as insistent as an alarm. Then the cows were there in the woods above them, an incongruous sight among the trees but clambering with surprising agility until they reached the road, the real road, out of the wood, where their pace slowed as abruptly as it had quickened. The lead cow, meandering now on the gravel path, let out a bellow, and the others followed, the calves skidding and slithering behind her on the stones as they descended. They drew up in front of the house like a reception committee, or a lynch mob, nuzzling the fence and staring. Your time's nearly up, they seemed to be saying. On the other side of the fence stood Lucien and Martin, staring back.

Anna sat at the table, where they had pulled a chair out for her, and absent-mindedly pulled at the hem of the tablecloth where it was coming down. Heavy, coarse linen, block-printed with a pattern of rust-brown grapes around the border, it smelled of the cupboard. They had brought her a glass of water, too – well, the dark one had; she had felt suddenly quite weary, as though she had come a long way, and found herself among strangers. She didn't know what they were saying, but she could tell they didn't like each other. She looked across at the animals making their way down the road, and wondered what had set them off in such a hurry. A vehicle higher up probably; Montale on his way down in the pick-up, or someone else.

'You just stay here then,' said Martin contemptuously.

Lucien didn't turn towards him at the words, but instead stared straight ahead, eyeing the cattle with dislike.

'No, no,' he said. 'You're making a point, obviously. Even though we probably won't find them, and even if we did find them we wouldn't be any help. And the food—'

'Oh, for Christ's sake,' said Martin, coldly. 'You and your bloody food.'

Lucien shrugged. 'I didn't hear you complaining before,' he said. His face was white. 'I think something's burning.' He turned on his heel and walked into the house.

Martin turned to look at Anna, sitting at the table, and she smiled at him, her face pale in the shadows, before turning to look down towards the river, in the direction from which the others should come.

And as she looked, Justine appeared, framed by the trees; pretty girl, thought Anna, automatically, at the same time unable to suppress a reflexive disapproval of her dusty dress and tangled hair. But there was something about her, as she climbed she seemed full of energy and determination, an antidote to the palpable negativity between the men left behind. Anna stood, and behind Justine she could see her son, with the fair girl in his arms.

It didn't take Justine long to see what Anna had seen between Martin and Lucien as she climbed towards the house; their faces were barely in focus but her heart was already sinking. What's the matter with them now, she thought, fired up with adrenaline and fierce impatience by their trek through the woods, triumphant at the success of their rescue mission. Lucien walked towards her, his face full of concern; Martin walked past her towards Louisa.

'Is she all right?' Lucien asked.

Justine looked at him thoughtfully. 'I think she's fine. Sprained ankle. Would you believe we were rescued by an orthopaedic surgeon? At least I think that's what he is. He's been – very helpful.' She stopped, glancing across at Paolo, who was lowering Louisa on to a chair. 'He happened to be passing.' Lucien raised his eyebrows reflexively, but she wasn't sure he was listening.

'What's been going on here then?' she asked.

Lucien shrugged. 'Nothing much.'

She couldn't tell whether his air of unconcern was affected or not.

'I'm making lunch,' he said. 'I'm hoping the oven doesn't let me down.' He grimaced theatrically. 'It's hardly high tech. The kids have gone down to the river – Dido wanted to take the boys. Said she'd look after them.'

'Right,' said Justine, impatient suddenly with Lucien's gloss on events. 'Have you had a row with Martin?' she said, before she lost her momentum, allowed him to smooth things over.

Lucien raised his eyebrows in mild surprise. 'Why do you say that?'

'Come on,' she said, 'it was like High Noon when I walked up the path. You were glaring at each other.' She looked across the fence at the cows, heads blithely down in the grass now, a big creamy cow nudging her calf affectionately as he butted her flank.

Lucien laughed, but she wasn't convinced. 'We were just a bit anxious, probably. To be quite honest, we weren't quite sure what had happened.' He nodded at Paolo's mother, sitting at the table, her hand on her son's shoulder. 'Your surgeon's mother doesn't speak English.'

Slowly Justine nodded, but she wasn't sure she believed him, that nothing had been going on. She turned to look for Martin. Louisa was sitting on a chair at the table, looking paler than usual but composed, almost cheerful, as the two men knelt at her feet. Paolo, the doctor, was saying something, demonstrating something to do with the working of the joint, using Louisa as his patient exhibit, and Martin was listening intently, absorbed. As though he could tell she was looking at him, the doctor looked up, but did not smile.

'You've made lunch,' she said, 'the table looks lovely. Will there be enough for – everyone? These two – Paolo and

Anna? – they really helped us out back there. It would be nice to be able to invite them.'

'I suppose so,' said Lucien with a shrug, but he didn't look too happy about it. 'I'll put the pasta on.' And he went back into the house.

Chapter Twenty-Two

Paolo had disliked Lucien the moment he saw him. After he'd made sure Anna had recovered from her mercy dash – she'd looked a little pale to begin with, but the colour seemed to be returning to her cheeks – Paolo sat at the table with the other one – Martin? – and talked about the injury – Louisa's sprained ankle. He seemed intelligent and knowledgeable, and Paolo told him what to do; an ice-pack, elevate the ankle, rest it. He had assumed Martin was Louisa's husband to begin with, he took such an interest. But then they had a discussion, over Paolo's head, literally, about when someone called Tom would be back, whether it would be in time for lunch, and it became obvious that Tom was her husband. All this Paolo absorbed without really listening, while he watched Justine and Lucien, standing between the table and the door of Il Vignacce, talking.

Were they married? From where he sat Justine's left hand was not visible; he could see her hair coming down from a

291

knot, heavy and dark and slippery, the nape of her neck and the smooth pale curve of her bare calves. It was obvious that they were together, though, from the way they had separated themselves off from the rest, from the angle of their bodies towards each other. There must be a critical proximity that denotes intimacy; the point at which you can detect the other's body heat, perhaps. But in their case it wasn't, he thought, a relaxed intimacy; something seemed to be wrong. Paolo wondered what it could be.

What are we doing here? Paolo asked himself, not for the first time. He felt as though his life had been overturned. After all his careful preparations, his imagining, his waiting and coaxing, his mother had told him the truth. His father was Luca Magno, a man he had heard of, and had read about; a minor figure perhaps, a historical footnote, but a man whose death had been the subject of speculation and public mourning. And now he was here, among foreigners whose lives should be of no interest to him; he should bid them a polite farewell, he and his mother should walk back up the hill, but he found himself curiously reluctant to do any such thing. And so he just sat in the humid shade, watching the girl. He smiled when he was addressed and accepted their invitation to stay and eat; Anna, he thought, could do with the rest.

He couldn't remember seeing a ring on Justine's finger, when they were alone down there by the river, but then he hadn't looked. He'd been looking at her hair, her mouth, the pale soft skin on the inside of her elbow, her profile as she gazed along the river.

Paolo didn't trust Lucien but grudgingly had to admit that he could cook. He had almost laughed at his mother's look of alarm when they'd been invited to lunch; she didn't believe for one moment that a scruffy group of English holidaymakers would be able to prepare anything palatable. They sat beneath the tree; the day was overcast, the air hanging warm and heavy with moisture in the clearing. There was no wind now to dispel it down in the valley where they sat, cocooned by the forest, the trees around them absorbing any breeze. Paolo looked down the table, and for a moment he thought Justine was looking back. But then she turned away quickly, and he couldn't be sure.

Justine stared down at her plate, where a swirl of red peppers still lay in their puddle of oil, electric orange and spicy. She reached for her glass, cold, yellow white wine, and drank to cover her confusion.

It was quiet without the children, and from a distance the table of holidaymakers and locals beneath the tree must have looked festive; the kind of scene adorning an expensive travel guide, or an account of idyllic, harmonious expatriate life. Martin sat at the centre of the table like a dark, serious paterfamilias, radiating authority. The food was delicious, and Lucien had presented it beautifully, as usual; the salad as pretty as a bouquet with red and green chicory, peppers slippery and bright with oil, a rich, dark glaze on the meat.

As was becoming the rule at their communal meals the drink was being consumed more enthusiastically than the food, and for once Lucien appeared to be drinking as much as anyone else, filling his glass steadily. Down the centre of the table a surprising number of wine bottles were ranged, some empty, plenty still to be drunk, threading their way like a procession in and out of the dishes and the smeared glasses.

Louisa, well mannered as ever, was having a friendly, if halting, three-way conversation with Paolo and his mother, involving considerable good-natured translation and some lengthy pauses. Justine listened, sitting back in her chair so as not to attract attention. It drew her in, Anna's story; Justine found herself piecing it together from the snippets translated by Paolo; it sounded romantic told in this way. She wondered what the war could have been like here, in such isolation, and what it must have been like to move from here to Rome. She wondered how Anna's father had died; she hadn't said.

'So you work in Rome?' Louisa was asking Paolo.

'Yes,' he said. 'A specialist orthopaedic hospital.'

He sounded weary, suddenly, and serious. Grown-up, thought Justine.

'Should we save some food for the boys?' asked Martin, suddenly, interrupting.

Justine looked up.

'I thought I'd make them a sandwich,' Louisa said, wearily. She looked pale. 'They don't really – they probably wouldn't eat this stuff. What about Dido?'

Martin's brow clouded slightly. 'Perhaps I should – but she likes to look after herself. And she hardly eats anything, anyway.'

Louisa bit her lip, but passed no comment. 'How long have they been down there?' she asked instead, smiling brightly. It looked to Justine as though she was trying not to seem a fretful mother. 'I'm losing all track of time.'

'They went just before you got back,' said Martin. An hour and a half, maybe two?'

Louisa nodded, apparently unconcerned. There was a silence; over their heads the tree moved a little as a breath of wind sighed down from the hills around them, and the faint shadow of its leaves shifted on the tablecloth.

Anna said something to Paolo, who turned to Louisa, smiling. 'Your husband is visiting Grosseto, for business? As a restaurant critic?'

Louisa hesitated; before she could say anything, Lucien spoke.

'He'd had enough of us,' he said, cheerfully drunk. 'He wanted to be alone. Going through a difficult time.'

Justine saw Paolo look at Lucien, frowning, and felt uncomfortable. She wondered how much Lucien had had.

Louisa spoke.

'He's fine,' she said, her voice shaking slightly, looking hard at Lucien before turning to Paolo. 'He's gone to look at an organic farm in Grosseto,' she said firmly. 'A vineyard and a restaurant. Maremman cattle.'

Lucien went on. 'Things haven't been too easy for Tom lately. Have they? Terrible shame.' He gave Louisa an attempt at a sympathetic smile and sipped his wine.

To Justine's surprise, it was not Louisa who responded this time, but Martin.

'I wouldn't worry about Tom, if I were you, Lucien,' he said, smiling.

Lucien raised his eyebrows, looking around the table for support.

Martin went on. 'I had a long chat with him last night. It sounds like a beautiful place – the vineyard he's gone to see; I encouraged him. It's for sale.'

Across the table Justine saw Louisa frown as if she might be about to say something, but she didn't.

Lucien, however, sat up in his seat. 'For sale? Tom wants to buy it?'

He sounded sober now, and incredulous, almost angry; it

was exactly the kind of thing he'd like to be doing himself, thought Justine, he's angry because someone's on his territory. It was as if, today, she saw Lucien through someone else's eyes; someone who was not all that well disposed towards him.

'Or I might,' said Martin, casually. 'We talked about Tom managing it. Maybe it's just one of those things – a fantasy. But I thought it could be interesting. Might cheer him up.' And Martin looked at Lucien, head on one side, as if daring him to argue with the idea that Tom might need cheering up.

'Long way to go for a fantasy,' was all Lucien said, looking around at the table with a rather forced smile. Justine didn't feel like smiling back at him.

'Well,' said Martin, 'I don't think he saw it that way. And anyway, there's something else – an errand he's running for me on the way back. Picking something up.' And he leaned for his glass, putting an end to the conversation.

Well, thought Justine. Well, well.

Lucien opened his mouth, then closed it again. Far beyond them, on the edge of the pasture, the cows looked up as two tiny figures appeared from out of the trees, running towards the house.

Chapter Twenty-Three

Down by the river the flat sunlight was leaving the bathing place as the shadow of the great cliff lengthened. The water was black in the shade, and beside it, on the dusty ground, sat Dido, her knees drawn up to her chin, hunched over the little rucksack in her lap. Now that she was alone she was thinking of her father, and Lucien, the sound of their voices echoing around the valley in the scalding, humid air and the name hanging in the air between them. Dido rested her cheek carefully against her knees, trying not to make any sudden movement that would disturb the delicate equilibrium inside her head, and she thought of her mother. Not Evie, Mum. Leaning down to say good night.

Dido's eyes felt hot and dry, but she didn't blink and she didn't cry; it seemed to her that it was all about to end. She felt sick. The river was a wavering silver line across her vision, and she was finding it difficult to focus. The air seemed thick around her suddenly, alive with dust and tiny insects, the heavy mineral scent of the river and the woods' slow decay. Slowly she got to her feet, still holding her head as though it might break, and unsteadily she walked into the water.

The boys were out of breath by the time they reached the adults, but they were laughing. Justine was struck by how brown they'd become, already, their skin startlingly dark against hair bleached almost white. Leaves and twigs stuck to their bare legs, damp still from the river; they looked like wild children, nurtured by wolves in the forest, returning to civilization. The heavy silence that still hung over the table underlined even further the division between adults and young, and for a moment or two each looked at the other with something like incomprehension.

The boys shuffled, bumping against each other and giggling, awkward with all eyes on them. Anna said something to Paolo, smiling and gesturing towards the boys; it sounded soft, like an endearment. Justine thought, how un-English a response it was to the presence of children.

Then Louisa sprang up, and hurried around the table towards her sons as though they might escape if she didn't pin them down.

'Are you hungry?' she asked, brushing leaves from Sam's shoulders then putting her arm around him and pulling him against her with awkward tenderness. 'Where's Dido?'

'Starving,' said Sam, looking up at her. 'What is there?' He eyed the food on the table suspiciously.

'She sent us back,' Angus said. 'She said she wanted to sunbathe.' He rolled his eyes and took a piece of bread from the table.

Martin was frowning. 'Perhaps I should go and get her?' He looked at Louisa, appealing for advice.

Louisa hesitated, considering Martin. Justine felt sorry for Dido, consigned either to over-protective adults or small boys for company.

'No – no,' said Louisa finally. 'Leave her alone, for a bit longer anyway. Don't you think?'

Slowly Martin nodded. Then Louisa turned her attention to the boys, taking each of them firmly by the shoulders and sandwiching them between her place and Paolo's at the table. Paolo looked down at them kindly.

'It's good, the meat,' he said, smiling and pulling the plate towards them. They looked first at the dark remains of slow-roasted pork with juniper and then at Paolo with transparent distrust and he laughed.

'Do you like this river?' he asked, pointing across the pasture. 'When I was a boy, like you, this is where I came, with my friends. Of course this' – he gestured at the house – 'it was *rovinato*. Ruined. With ghosts.' He pulled a face and then they laughed; behind him Anna shook her head at his imitation of a ghostly howl.

Martin spoke. 'You must know all this very well,' he said, gesturing at the silent hills around them. Outnumbered, thought Justine, gazing at the acres of undulating, uninhabited forest and thinking how it might look from above, their tiny group around the table, and all those trees.

Paolo nodded his head a little from side to side, equivocal. 'Quite well,' he said. 'Not as well as when I was a boy. But yes. There is another bathing place, further down there,' He indicated to the left, upstream. 'A waterfall, where you can dive. Not far.'

299

At this the boys, who had been industriously refuelling on meat and bread, both looked up at once.

'Cool,' said Sam, cautiously. 'A waterfall? Will you show us where it is?'

He made as if to set off straight away, one foot already planted on the ground, but firmly Louisa pulled him back into his seat.

'Eat first,' she said.

Paolo smiled. 'Of course,' he said. 'If you want. If your mother thinks it will be all right?' He looked at Louisa. 'My mother and I can take them, after they've eaten? And you can rest the ankle.'

Helpless, Louisa capitulated, but Justine could see that she was grateful. Although it did occur to Justine, a fleeting qualm she tried to ignore, that it was only the presence of the Italian visitors that was keeping the atmosphere between the rest of them even superficially civilized.

Lucien, perhaps to speed things up, stood and offered coffee to Paolo and Anna. '*Caffè?*' he pronounced, carefully, smiling as he offered up his Italian accent for criticism, but Justine was weary of his charm, and just shook her head. She saw Paolo look at Lucien, considering him in silence; it was like seeing a couple of strange dogs eyeing each other up.

'Thank you,' Paolo said, eventually.

The coffee was drunk in contemplative silence, the heavy warmth of the afternoon slowing their movements. Overhead a light aeroplane aimlessly described circles in the hazy sky, its thin high engine sound rising over the silence. With a sigh Justine rose to clear away the remains of their lunch; Martin sprang up to help. Lucien didn't do washing-up; he cooked, and he stayed at the table, sitting with a kind of immovable satisfaction, working his way through the remaining wine.

Anna Viola stood, a little stiffly, and gestured her readiness to help, but her son, with a sound of mild exasperation, remonstrated with her in Italian before offering himself in her stead.

'No,' said Justine, 'thank you.' Suddenly she felt uncomfortable that Paolo and his mother were here, with Lucien like this, sitting like a great sulky child at the table. She nodded at Louisa, on whom the day seemed to have taken its toll. Installed close to the house in a reclining chair with her ankle elevated, she looked browbeaten and weary as Sam and Angus both pulled at her elbow, asking if there was ice cream. 'Could you really show the boys your waterfall?' Justine went on. 'I think they'd love it.'

Paolo nodded. 'Of course, I will.' He paused for a moment. 'Will you come too?'

The invitation was stiffly correct, but he looked directly at her, appealing to her to accept. She liked him, Justine decided suddenly, reckless with wine. And she liked his mother.

But she sighed. 'I don't think I can,' she said, feeling that life, and holidays, were more complicated and burdensome than was tolerable, sometimes. Why shouldn't she just go? 'Maybe I'll follow later.'

Paolo nodded, 'Hey,' he called to Sam and Angus, 'the waterfall?'

They abandoned Louisa without a backward glance, ice cream forgotten, and were at his side. Anna and Justine, in spontaneous unison, laughed at their eagerness.

Once they'd gone, only Lucien and Justine remained at the table; Justine looked across at Louisa, sleeping peacefully in her armchair beside the house, and decided not to disturb her.

She looked like a child asleep, all the lines of age and anxiety softened, and Justine thought, poor Louisa. Poor Tom.

Lucien was silent, brooding over something. His skin had darkened already, Justine noticed, and the faded blue of his shirt made it look even darker.

'Thanks for lunch, Lucien,' she ventured. 'It was great. I think even the Italians were impressed.'

Lucien shrugged slightly; looking out across the pasture.

'I'll just go and help Martin with the washing-up,' she said, impatient suddenly and trying not to sound it, pushing back her chair. 'Then I might walk down and get Dido with him. I'd like a swim.' She wasn't prepared for Lucien's response.

'Can't he do it on his own?' he exclaimed with sudden savagery, standing up and turning away from her. 'I've hardly seen you on this holiday. I'm packed off to the supermarket, or you'd like a walk with Louisa. Or having a heart to heart with Martin, your new best friend.' He didn't look at her.

Justine was taken aback. 'It's only the washing-up,' she said. 'Come and talk to me while I'm doing it, if you want.' Although even as she said it she realized with a faint sinking sensation that he was right; she had hardly seen him so far this holiday. And that she didn't really want him to follow her inside now.

At home, it was clear to her suddenly, they hardly saw anyone else, she was Lucien's exclusively – pampered and fed by him like a favoured pet; the two of them cocooned in a state of perpetual cosy intimacy. Out here in the wilderness, the shock of realizing what had been going on outside their relationship all this time, all the turmoil in their friends' lives to which she had been oblivious, her life with Lucien seemed myopic and suffocating. And, she suddenly suspected, he didn't like her talking to other people, and she wondered why.

302

So when Lucien responded to her suggestion by turning away from her in refusal, wordlessly angry, she was relieved. All the same, automatically she tried to placate him, her hand on his shoulder.

'Maybe we could all go down to the river,' she said. 'Later.'

Lucien sighed. 'It's all right,' he said grudgingly, turning back towards her. He was frowning; something was still bothering him, Justine could see.

'He wasn't the perfect husband, you know,' he said, abruptly. 'Martin. He wanted her under his thumb. Would you like that? He frightened her, with all that brooding intensity of his, that's what I think.'

'What do you mean?' said Justine. 'How do you know?'

Lucien shrugged. 'Never mind,' he said. 'You weren't the only one she talked to, that's all.'

Justine frowned, but Lucien just shook his head. 'Go on then, if you're going,' he said, and there was no warmth in his voice. Standing close to his smooth, handsome face, which she knew almost as well as she knew her own, Justine couldn't tell what he was thinking any more. If she'd ever known. And as she turned away she had a sense of foreboding, as if something cataclysmic was about to happen between them and she was powerless to prevent it.

Inside everything was cool and neat; a rug was folded on a chair, the washing-up that had been the bone of contention already dried and stacked. She could look right through the house and out of the low window at the back, framing a view of slender tree trunks stippled and soft with lichen. They stood motionless for as far as she could see, in a green haze, poised and waiting.

She almost tripped over Martin in the gloom; he was

303

leaning back on the sofa and staring at the ceiling. When her eyes adjusted to the dim light she could see that he was smiling.

She sat down beside him. 'I want to talk to you,' she said.

Montequercio was almost asleep in the dull, warm afternoon. It was the time of the siesta, almost every window was shuttered against the flat light and lizards flickered undisturbed up the soft pink brick of the walls, a little disorientated, perhaps, by the signs of change in the weather. Inside mothers and grandmothers, their duties temporarily suspended, the kitchen floor clean and the dishes put away, would be sitting with their feet up in the dim light still in the floral aprons they used for cooking lunch. They would close their eyes just for a moment, while their husbands or sons were already snoring beside them in a favourite armchair, a copy of the sports paper open and unread on their sagging knees.

One or two restless souls, of course, would be found out even on such an afternoon; the kind of woman who never stopped scrubbing, for example, her knuckles red and raw from housework that was never done. She might be hanging her dishcloths to dry or nipping to the grey dumpsters on the main road with her rubbish tied neatly in plastic bags, looking up at her neighbours' closed shutters and wondering how they found the time. Lonely widowers, or the kind of man – or woman – for whom an afternoon watching a spouse's breast rise and fall in sleep, mouth dropped unflatteringly ajar, was an uncomfortable reminder of how little life resembled the future he had imagined for himself.

So, to accommodate these, and the occasional thirsty tourist in transit, both the Cinghiale and the Bellavista stayed open in the afternoons. At one o'clock sharp the few shops closed;

the Co-op, the newspaper stand, the *pasticceria* all pulled down their blinds and their proprietors retired for a long lunch. The little oval piazza would empty out quite suddenly, bleached white and dusty as a desert ghost town. But for Carlo and Giovannino, the barkeepers, the long, dead afternoon stretched ahead of them, a time to wipe down counters, clean out the icecream cabinet and re-order the stock room. Across the empty piazza they would eye each other, these two, to gauge which of them was losing most money in these stifling, lifeless hours.

This afternoon, however, Giovannino had three customers in the dim interior of the Cinghiale, even though one of them hardly counted, being his own brother, Piero. As both a man incapable of idleness and one for whom the company of his wife was not unalloyed pleasure, Piero abstained from taking a siesta on both counts. Generally he spent the time riding from one part of his land to another on his tractor, talking to his cows down in the valley or roaring about in his pick-up, checking the olives and keeping the *Albanesi* who cut cork for him up to the mark.

Today Piero had dropped in to the bar because his wife's cooking had reached a new low. He didn't understand it, when he thought of the magnificent kitchen he'd built for her, with a wood-burning griddle for meat, a big range, fitted cupboards and everything she could possibly want. But she was obsessed with the microwave she'd made him install; she scoured the supermarket for ready meals although they were still a rarity in Montequercio, marvelling over the convenience. So here he was, on a stool at the bar, ruminatively chewing his way through a fat fistful of fragrant meat and herbs and proper Tuscan bread, his mood slowly improving.

'Will you be shutting up, down at Il Vignacce, after this week?' asked Giovannino, who was taking down all his bottles of *aperitivi* and *liquori* – crème de menthe, Averna, scotch, the lot – and carefully wiping them off. 'It's been booked up all summer, am I right?'

Piero grunted, barely looking up from his sandwich. Giovannino went on, contemplatively.

'Amazing. A full five months rent. You have to admit,' said Giovannino, shaking his head disbelievingly, 'you'd never have said you'd have ended up renting the old place to people like that. People with money to burn. Tourists, eh?'

Piero raised his head at this, eyes narrowing suspiciously. 'Do you think I should be asking more for it?'

Giovannino shrugged. 'Could be. But don't you see my point? It was an albatross, that place, a millstone round our necks. Bad luck, ever since the war. And now look.'

Piero went on eating. 'Suppose so,' he said, eventually. 'Early days yet, though, so don't come asking for your share of the profits quite yet, eh?'

Giovannino raised his eyes good-naturedly to the ceiling. 'None of my business, Pierone. I'm not after your money. I certainly don't want the hassle of slogging down there every five minutes collecting foreigners' rubbish. Unblocking their sinks.' He replaced the last of the bottles on the shelf behind the bar, clean and sparkling now, each one polished off with a dry cloth, and came around the bar to stand in his doorway. He looked up at the sky for a moment, then turned back to his brother,

'And I don't want to be having to drag them all out behind the tractor, when it comes on to rain and they want to go home.' Giovannino nodded outside. 'Because the rain's coming, that's for sure. Tomorrow, maybe tonight. Better hope most of it falls on Siena.'

Piero grunted again, refusing to rise to his brother's bait. He took a long draught of his beer, draining it. He set it down on the marble counter with a chink, but his brother the barman paid no attention.

'No wonder you don't make any money in this place,' said Piero.

In the dim recesses of the bar Giovannino's other two customers were eating slowly, without obvious enjoyment. Tom and his companion seemed to have other, more serious matters on their minds than the excellence of the *porchetta*, to judge by their faces and the silence between them. Tom cleared his throat.

'This must be difficult for you,' he said. 'Coming to meet us all like this. Perhaps you're nervous?'

Opposite him sat a pale, red-haired woman; a woman Lucien had seen crying in a Florentine backstreet the previous day with Martin's arm around her. Rossella. She took a sip of water, considering his words. Slowly she shook her head. 'I feel as though I know them – you – already, I think.'

'And will you tell them?' Tom asked. 'Everything?'

Rossella spread her hands in a gesture of helplessness. 'I feel I have an obligation. To Evie. And they have to know, don't you think?'

Tom pushed his plate away, the sandwich half eaten. 'Yes,' he said, with a sigh. 'Of course.'

They both fell silent for a moment, looking through the gloomy interior to the bright rectangle of the door and the marketplace beyond. But neither of them seemed ready to leave quite yet.

mop and do the floors. Piero seemed to recognize them. He shook the man's hand and as Giovannino went into the back room for his mop he heard his brother ask them politely how everything was going. But when he returned they'd gone, left him a tip on the bar and brought their plates back to save him a trip to their table.

'He's one of them, one of my lot,' said Piero. 'The English down at Il Vignacce. Looks like he's found himself an Italian girlfriend.'

After contemplating the bottom of his empty glass thoughtfully for a moment or two, with a reluctant sigh Piero replaced it on the bar and went to the door, where his brother joined him, mop in hand. In the piazza the Englishman and his companion were climbing into a dusty old Volvo with English plates. An odd couple, thought Giovannino, in passing. In silence the brothers looked up at the threatening sky, where far overhead the black outline of a tiny plane was visible against the grey, the high-pitched stutter of its engine fading in and out on the breeze. A drop of rain fell at Giovannino's feet on the stone pavement.

Chapter Twenty-Four

They sat side by side on the sofa, looking out of the window out to the back of the house, overheard only by the trees. A sweetish smell, of the decaying plums perhaps, drifted in from outside. The front door was a bright rectangle, light falling through it on to the soft red brick of the floor.

As Justine's eyes adjusted to the half light she could make out the outlines of the walnut sideboard, the gleam of the long kitchen table, through a door the worn marble of Louisa and Tom's bathroom, the pile of clothes Louisa had been folding that morning still sitting on the bed. In the silence all was peaceful; she didn't want to leave this place, Justine thought again. She turned to Martin, at last; he was looking at her thoughtfully.

'Did you mean it,' she said, 'about Tom? Buying the place in Grosseto? It looked like it was news to Louisa.'

Martin leaned his head back and laughed. 'Yes, poor Louisa. I think she'd had enough surprises for one day. I'm sorry about that.' He paused, frowning. 'The truth is, I hadn't planned it, no. It was a spur of the moment thing, when Tom and I were talking last night. But I think it's a good idea, actually. Don't you?'

'Well,' said Justine slowly, thinking of Louisa's creamy white London drawing room, her silver frames and gardenias, her French-polished tables, and how it might compare with something like this room, this farmhouse, isolated, at the mercy of the climate, gloomy perhaps in the winter. Louisa's mother. Could Louisa live without all that? Perhaps that was what Louisa needed, to get away from all that; Tom struggling to keep his head above water, her mother's querulous, needling presence. She tried to picture Louisa on a parched Mediterranean hillside, with unpredictable plumbing and hectares of grapes to harvest.

'Actually,' she said, pondering, leaning her own head back against the sofa cushions and turning it on its side to look at Martin, 'you're probably right. Louisa could do it, even if Tom couldn't.' Martin laughed, and she felt herself liking him, despite Lucien. 'But it's a bit of a risk, isn't it? And have you got the money? And you and Tom – how would you get on? I mean—'

'Well,' said Martin, considering, 'risk. Everything's relative. As for the money, I haven't done badly.' He sat up then, elbows on his knees, being practical.

As he said it Justine realized she had never had any idea whether they had been rich or poor, he and Evie. But now, after even so few days with Martin, she realized, he could quite plausibly be a millionaire. He gave off that kind of calm certainty, about everything except his daughter, anyway. You could imagine him unruffled, making quick, clever decisions, day in, day out.

'Good,' she said, meaning it; thinking, they probably need it.

Martin went on. 'And Evie 's life was insured, we were both insured.'

For some reason Justine found this information faintly disturbing. Martin looked at her.

'So I wanted to spend that money, the money they paid me after she died, on something—' He hesitated, looking for the right way to explain. 'On something for her.'

'And Tom?' Justine looked at him.

'Tom?' said Martin, mildly. 'You mean, could I work with him, knowing he was in love with Evie?'

Justine stared at him.

'It isn't news to me, Justine,' he said, turning to look at her. She could see his face clearly now, an open face, unafraid. 'Not Tom.'

There was a sound from the doorway, a feather-light sound, but they both heard it, and turned towards the door. In the hot, flat light that fell through the door a tiny lizard, curved into an S-shape, stood briefly immobile on the warm brick before flickering back outside, making minuscule displacements in the dust.

Martin turned back to Justine. 'He's not good at hiding what he's feeling. I'm surprised you didn't see it, but you're a romantic, aren't you?'

I suppose I am, thought Justine, if that means wanting everything to turn out right.

'Maybe it seems strange to you,' Martin said slowly. 'I can see it does. But Tom was never going to – it wasn't *an affair*.' He pronounced the word with a kind of contempt.

Martin went on, talking almost to himself now. 'It was

312

an idealized relationship they had. Platonic. It wouldn't have worked any other way, the practical stuff would have killed it. Tom's not practical, is he? You said it yourself, Louisa deals with all that.'

About time someone else did it for her, Justine found herself thinking, as she thought of Louisa outside in the chair, worn down by her responsibilities.

He went on, quietly, as if he too was thinking of Louisa just outside the door. And now Evie's – now she's dead—' Martin looked away from her, as though he didn't want her to see what was in his face. 'Tom and I – in a way we've got her in common, now. He reminds me of her.' Martin closed his eyes for a moment, and Justine tentatively put out a hand.

'She loved you, you know,' he said, turning at her touch on his arm, and his tone was odd, stifled. 'She wouldn't have wanted you hurt.'

Justine stared at him, torn between longing and confusion, wanting to know, suddenly, what Evie had been thinking. 'What do you mean?'

She thought of the last conversation she'd had with Evie, when she'd sounded almost as Martin did now, trying to communicate something obscure, asking whether she and Lucien were happy. She thought of Lucien's photograph of Evie smiling, with Dido at her shoulder. Had that smile been trying to tell them something?

'Evie never meant to hurt anyone,' he said again. 'But she had a blind spot. Like we all do, I suppose; sometimes she couldn't see, didn't want to see, that what she was doing would have consequences.'

'Do you mean Evie killed herself?' said Justine. 'That's how she hurt us?'

Martin shook his head. 'Not exactly,' he said. He gazed out through the door, unseeing.

Justine stared at him, turning over what Louisa had said. 'Was she ill? Louisa—' Then she stopped, not wanting to give Tom and Louisa away, wondering whether Martin had a right to know. She took a deep breath.

'Louisa said Evie came to see them, that morning. Told them she was going away, she was ill and she needed to get away.' Justine waited to see what he would say; somehow she expected him to grab hold of her, interrogate her. But Martin wasn't like that, she realized; he just nodded.

'She had a mild but progressive illness,' he said with an odd formality, as though he was a doctor. He named a disease of the nervous system Justine had heard of; common enough, it came in different forms, some severe, some less so. She thought, of Evie getting that news and suddenly she could see her haunted face all those years ago, in a cold kitchen with a baby in her arms. 'What if I couldn't move? Couldn't go to her?' Justine closed her eyes, cold with the shame. *She never said.*

'It wouldn't have killed her,' Martin said, sounding sincerely puzzled. 'Her mother had it too; the more severe form. It did kill her.'

In the silence that followed, they both heard a distant whine, the sound of a vehicle far away, but getting louder, but neither of them could focus on what it might mean.

'What?' said Justine slowly, opening her eyes, trying to process what she had just heard. She shook her head. 'No. Her parents died in a car crash. In Spain. It was one of the first things she ever told me.'

Martin sighed. 'No,' he said, 'she made that up.' He put his head in his hands, moving it from side to side as if to ease

314

some pressure. 'That's what I mean,' he said, but Justine didn't understand.

'But you don't think she killed herself – because she was ill? It makes it more likely, doesn't it?'

When Martin spoke his voice was muffled by his hands. 'We'd talked about it, I made sure we talked about it. Her illness.' Justine thought of Lucien's sneering comment on Martin's – what had he called it? – his *brooding intensity*.

Martin went on, paying her no attention, talking to himself. 'She wasn't on her own – she would never—' He raised his head. 'There are things – what happened to her parents for example – things she didn't tell everyone. And other people – know things about her I don't know. Didn't know.' He stopped abruptly. 'But I think I know what happened now. Just wait – wait until Tom gets back. Until we're all here.'

Justine nodded, unwillingly; there was something in Martin's voice that made her uneasy. He sounded nervous, as though he was asking her to sit down before delivering bad news. 'Just one thing,' she said, 'before – while it's just us. You and Lucien – is this to do with Lucien? You were arguing. You don't like him, do you?'

'Justine,' said Martin, shaking his head, 'you've never seen Lucien as he really is. He only thinks about himself.'

Justine sighed. 'I know him better than you do,' she said, but even as she spoke she wondered. 'He looks after me.'

'Looks after you!' Martin was angrily contemptuous. 'He uses you. Without you he'd be – pathetic. He'd go on living in a house someone else paid for, pleasing himself, freeloading. Letting other people buy his drinks. You've got to see that.' He stood up.

Justine felt queasy. She was tired of it, all of a sudden, worn

Giovannino glanced down the room at his customers, but they didn't summon him, so he went on with his ruminations. 'Just think what old Anna Viola could get for that little *podere*, if she felt like letting it out,' he said, turning to his brother. 'A lovely place, that is, a view all the way down to Grosseto on a good day, a bit of land.' He sounded pensive, thinking of the time he'd spent there as a boy, fooling about in the woods with the others, Paolo and the rest. Paolo's grandmother had made very good *schiaccata all'uva*, flat bread with the first sweet black grapes baked into it, and chestnut pudding, though she hadn't often wasted it on her grandson's friends. His stomach rumbled at the memory, and he realized he hadn't eaten yet.

Piero wiped off his mouth with a handful of napkins, his chin shiny with aromatic grease, and this time fixed Giovannino with a reproving stare.

'She's got more sense, that Anna Viola,' he said. 'Nice woman, too.' He was thinking of the wave she gave him every time he headed on down to the woods, and of the stories his parents had whispered to him about her. Anna's father shot by the Germans as a partisan down in the valley, at Il Vignacce itself; the father of her child dead before Paolo was born. Not that she'd ever said a word, not Anna; they'd heard it from her mother, who couldn't help defending her daughter against the women of the village and their rumour mill.

Giovannino smiled, glad to have provoked his brother into saying something at last. He nodded. 'Yes,' he said, chewing it over. 'Nice woman.'

At that they both fell silent, and the other two customers walked up to the bar to pay. Giovannino had almost forgotten they were there, tucked away behind the jukebox with their water and their sandwiches; he'd been about to get out the out with puzzling over it, with dealing with their bickering. She looked away, towards the front door and the outside. The sun was fading; the sharp edges of the light cast into the room were blurred and indistinct now. As she looked, Lucien appeared in the doorway.

'Someone's coming,' he said, shortly, and turned back outside. They got to their feet.

Justine and Martin stood in the doorway and looked; beside them Louisa was stirring in her deckchair. High up on the hill Justine could hear the sound of a car, still invisible beneath the forest's dark canopy; the roar of an engine, intermittent as it bounced and dipped with the road, but getting closer.

'What – what's happening?' asked Louisa, dazedly, sitting up in her chair. No one said anything; they were all looking the same way.

They were looking past the cowshed, following the zigzag path of the road which was just visible through the screen of the trees. They looked up across the face of the hill to where a cloud of dust marked the arrival of the car she had heard earlier. From where they stood they could only see that it was a long, low vehicle, its colour obscured by dust, and it was moving painfully slowly, crunching around the bends, its passage marked by the flapping of birds in the leaf canopy. Only at the final bend, when the screen of trees had thinned to the last remaining few birches, did it reveal itself as Tom's Volvo, and it wasn't until the car emerged from the trees and had got almost as far as the cowshed that Justine could see that Tom had a passenger.

Anna and Paolo let the boys run on ahead of them down the steep, uneven path to the waterfall. Anna felt strangely relaxed

316

now, after all the commotion, the encounters with foreigners, the effort of trying to work out what was going on between them at lunch.

Quite unable to translate what the English visitors had been saying, it had all the same seemed to Anna that there was very little in the way of human warmth to bind their group together. And where among Italians the very act of eating at the same table would have softened some of their differences and brought them just a little closer, in this case it seemed to have had the opposite effect. Do the English simply not like each other, she wondered, or do these people have a particular reason for fighting over everything? She gave a mental shrug, and looked sidelong at Paolo, grateful for his good nature and his transparency, to her at least. They walked on, side by side, after the boys.

'I haven't been down here since I was a child,' said Anna slowly, breaking the silence. 'I dreamed about it often enough.'

Paolo looked at her with surprise. 'Why didn't you come?'

'I left it too long. I began to be afraid.' She looked away, as though searching for something among the massed ranks of silent trees.

'Afraid of what?' Paolo's voice was puzzled.

She sighed, feeling foolish. 'I don't know,' she said. 'Ghosts. My father—'

'They brought him down here?'

'It might have been,' she said. 'Somewhere near, anyway. I always had it in my mind that they brought him to Il Vignacce, it was abandoned then, soon after the Germans arrived. We – we children thought there were ghosts here, just as you did, even before – before he was taken from us.'

Soberly Paolo nodded. 'I can see,' was all he said.

But it did seem other worldly, even to him: the uncertain green light in which dust motes and shreds of gossamer hung suspended, turning slowly; and the tiny noises, the creeping, rustling, ticking sounds that might be one thing or might be another. Paolo and Anna were at a bend, the house now just out of sight and below them hung the damp, cool, misty air that drifted up from the river. Anna stopped for a moment, her face thoughtful.

'If you leave things,' she said, 'if you don't go back and look again at the things you are afraid of, they change, your mind works on them and works on them, when you aren't looking.' She looked at her son for a moment, wondering whether he understood, before she went on, 'At first I used to dream of rescuing my father, and I could see him as clearly as ever, his face that I loved. But then I began to be afraid, I thought of him dead, coming back from the dead. Do you see? The more you bury your head under the pillow, the bigger the monster grows.'

'Yes,' said Paolo. He thought of his own father, changing shape in a child's starved imagination.

Below them the boys had stopped, crouching over something on the path; as Paolo and Anna approached they turned their small brown faces up towards them, bright with excitement.

'Dinosaurs,' Sam breathed in awe. Anna frowned, and bent to look; it was a small bone, clean and white. She smiled at them, and shook her head. 'Too small,' she said in Italian, gesturing with her hands as though measuring a fish.

'We can bury it,' said Paolo in English, and enthusiastically the boys agreed, already shovelling with their hands in the leaves and ivy. Solemnly they placed the bone in the hollow they had made and covered over the spot with elaborate care. Anna and Paolo stood over the boys and their tiny ritual, and looked at each other.

'Are we nearly there?' asked Sam, when he'd finished smoothing over the earth. Paolo nodded. 'Nearly. Can you smell the river?' He held up a finger and sniffed the air, and, looking at him curiously, the boys did the same, down to holding their own fingers in the air.

'I can smell something,' said Angus, uncertainly, wrinkling his nose. 'Something cold.'

'That's it,' said Paolo. 'Come on. Let's go.' And the two boys set off again, galloping and skidding on the stories. 'Careful!' called Paolo after them, shaking his head and laughing despite himself.

'You see,' said Anna, 'children, they're good for you. They keep you young.' It was as close as she could come to a reproof, to coming back to the subject of Livia, and children.

'So you're glad you had me then,' said Paolo, smiling, knowing where she was going and deflecting her.

'Don't even joke about it,' said Anna. 'How easily I could not have had you, it makes my blood run cold.'

Both of them fell silent then, their thoughts returning to the moment at which she might have been able to choose, the terrifying randomness of life brought into being, or denied.

The path had become flattened and narrow, densely overgrown on both sides, the rampant growth held back only by rusty barbed wire. They had reached the valley floor itself. Paolo took his mother's arm.

'How did he die, Mamma?'

She sighed, and turned to look at him. His death – Luca Magno's death – had been a public event. Not a famous man,

319

not a household name, but a man who had significance in many others' lives. There had been speculation when he died that it had been an assassination, and she knew that Paolo would be aware of that, now that he knew his father's name; a Mafia killing, someone high up in the film business sick of Luca's troublemaking, jealous of his power. It was a part of history, all that speculation, but she knew that was not what had happened. She hadn't been there, but she knew.

'There were witnesses, of course,' she said slowly.

Anna had pored over every written word about Luca's death, stored the papers until they grew yellow, then thrown them away one day, suddenly afraid of the questions Paolo might ask. There had been a street trader who swore he'd seen someone give Luca a push, just at the last moment, just as the tram loomed behind him. Luca had reached the Largo dell' Torre Argentina, where the great steel and glass monsters shot past each other thick and fast, their wheels shrieking against the tracks, gliding unstoppably towards their destinations. It was less than ten minutes after he had left her.

Then, the witness said, no doubt clutching his tray of sweets in case someone stole it while he was talking to a reporter, the mysterious assailant had vanished, quite vanished. Just like an assassin, they're taught to disappear into thin air once the deed is done, he'd announced with an air of certainty Another witness, a pale, nervous young woman out on an errand for her mother, had fainted dead away at the sight. When she was revived, sitting in a nearby bar with a glass of warm water and brandy, she said she'd seen him, positively seen Luca Magno walk in front of the tram. He'd turned, looked up at it and then stepped out in front of it quite deliberately. This was the report that haunted Anna, but she knew it was not true, because she'd seen the look in Luca's eye when he had left her no more than ten minutes earlier. Could her memory so deceive her? It was true that in her misery, in the agony of self-examination and reproach that followed his death, she had doubted everything, but she knew now, remembering how it had been, that he would not have killed himself with what she had told him fresh in his mind. It was too new, too astounding; he would have needed more time to turn it into despair.

Ahead of them came a whoop of pure excitement. The boys had come to the waterfall, and Anna and Paolo quickened their pace. They passed through a stile that kept the cattle from the waterfall and its precipitous drop, and there were the boys, hopping from leg to leg as they stripped off their shorts, giggling as they fell over each other in their haste. The path ended in a narrow beach of mossy stones, the dark water of the river narrowing towards two giant, squared-off rocks, flat on the top. On this side of the waterfall the river was deep and dark and narrow, forced between the rocks; beyond, on the other side, Paolo could hear but not see, as the water gushed out white and thundered into a pool below.

Paolo went on ahead to make sure that there was enough water for them to jump into, clambering on to the great flat rocks, which were still warm with the day's heat. Below him the pool was ice-green, foaming with the falling water and deep; he'd never been able to understand why here the water was so pale, a fairy colour, while upriver it was so dark.

'All right,' he said, smiling at the boys, 'you can jump.' And as they shot past him, gasping with excitement on the brink, Sam, the older one, glanced back at him for reassurance, and then they were gone. He turned back to Anna.

Looking at her son, Anna hesitated. What could she tell him?

There was only one out of all the stories that had rung true. An account lacking in drama, perhaps but that did not necessarily make it false. A middle-aged woman on her way home from the market, clutching a string bag containing some onions, a stick of celery and a piece of beef skirt, her coat buttoned up to the chin and her face sagging with the memory of what she had seen.

'Tell me, please,' Anna had said, begging her, once she'd tracked the woman down to her little one-room apartment above the roaring traffic on the Viale Aventino. 'Tell me.'

He'd had the oddest look on his face, the woman said, as if he was dreaming. She'd been struck by it, a half-smile as if remembering something sweet. He'd been walking along the pavement towards her, he'd had a hat on, pushed back from his forehead and she remembered thinking him handsome. She hadn't noticed the tram, either, she'd been looking at this young man – well, youngish – and something about him had made her think of her own husband, when they'd just met and he'd arrived to collect her from her father's house so that they could walk out together. A dreaming look, looking forward to some sweet thing.

'He's dead now, my husband,' the woman had said, apologizing for Anna didn't know what, for being a widow, for being a sad case, for not being able to tell the story straight. The room smelled stale, of laundry not aired, leftover food, and loneliness.

'It was an accident,' Anna said to Paolo, and hearing the words she knew that she believed it, finally. No one had been to blame, not Anna, not the unborn Paolo, not Amalia and her daughter, not the tram driver.

It happened as if she'd been in a dream herself, the woman

322

had said, looking down into her lap, her hands working nervously. Or as though the whole scene had been slowed down, the women in their coats pushing past, the man selling lottery tickets, the grumbling queues waiting for the trams on the periphery of her vision; she'd watched it happen. The man – Luca Magno – he kept coming towards her, one foot in front of another, his hat jaunty on his head, not looking at anything but something playing behind his eyes. Then just as the tram came past, looming up behind him, he seemed to lurch as though he'd missed a step, and he tilted sideways. She saw a look of disbelief on his face, puzzlement. He fell the wrong way. And after that all she could remember was the noise, the terrible raucous shriek of brakes, and someone screaming.

'He fell in front of a tram,' Anna said, and she could hear herself apologising. It was such a small thing, such a quick, stupid thing. A joke; an accident. Just like the way she heard the news, a girl at work the next morning, mouth open, eyes wide, as she related the story of Luca Magno, killed by a tram. It should have come by some other means; she should have known. Anna had felt something draining out of her, and her whole body turned cold. She had thought she might be sick, but she had had to go on looking down at her work – a boned, brocaded corset that she had been finding rough against her hands. She had to look away and pretend Luca Magno was no more to her than to anyone else.

She looked at Paolo. 'He – Luca wasn't looking. There was no mystery to it, not really. I'm sorry – you had to wait so long to hear it. But, you see, I hardly knew him, that's how it seems to me now. You – you were the important thing.'

Paolo made as if to speak, but she shook her head. 'There were all sorts of suggestions, of course. I mean, about Luca's

323

death. People like to make up stories about something like that, they can't believe there could be just no reason. But I know. I do know'

Paolo turned away, for a moment, dazed, but he felt as though something had fallen away and left him free. He breathed deep, and let the breath out. Over the stones appeared the two small wet heads of the boys, like seals, but he barely saw them. Sam was first up, Angus scrambling after him. They skipped towards him across the slab of warm stone, his own younger self reincarnated. Whooping with excitement they grabbed Paolo, butting their heads against his chest, a damp patch spreading on his shirt, reaching for his hands to pull him with them. 'Come on!' they said. 'Come on, you too.' Without looking down, automatically Paolo let his hand drop on to Sam's head, and rested it there. He stroked the damp hair, and the boys fell silent.

'OK, Mamma,' he said. 'Now I know, too.'

Chapter Twenty-Five

Wordlessly Lucien had gone over and hauled the rickety double gates open to allow the car in. Justine watched; Lucien narrowed his eyes against the dust that rose in the car's wake, and looked down at Tom's passenger. Louisa was standing beside Justine, leaning against her for support. She was looking at Tom, scanning his face.

The woman was the first to climb out of the car, stiff perhaps after a long journey to judge by her grimace as she straightened up. She was a tall woman, not Italian to look at, not at all, freckled and fair-skinned, with long, wiry hair, the colour of red gold, tied back at the nape of her neck. She looked around the group, her reception committee, and nodded very slightly. There was something like calculation in her clear grey eyes, Justine thought, as though she was looking to see who was there and who was missing. Justine wondered what she had been led to expect.

'Rossella,' said Martin, holding her lightly by both arms,

and greeting her with a kiss: 'I wasn't sure – thank you for coming'

'It's fine,' said Rossella, her voice accented and surprisingly deep, and she smiled. Her pale face was illuminated by the smile; she looked beautiful, quite suddenly, and something about her, some warmth, or radiance, made Justine think of Evie. This is her friend, Justine thought wonderingly, and then she knew why Rossella was there. She's going to tell us.

Tom had put his arms around Louisa, and Justine could see her shoulders trembling with relief, and the effort of not crying. He was murmuring in her ear, something gentle, and stroking her hair. Then he looked up from Louisa's shoulder.

'Where are the boys? And Dido?'

'Oh,' said Louisa faintly, her face softened by whatever it was he had said to her, 'they're at the river. I mean – I sprained my ankle, and – it's a little bit complicated. But they should be back soon.'

Tom helped her into a chair and knelt to examine the ankle. To Justine's eyes the swelling seemed much less now. As Louisa allowed Tom to minister to her she seemed to soften, to grow content.

'Shall we go inside?' said Martin, looking up at the sky. 'It's not quite raining yet.' Rossella pulled out a chair and sat down. 'Better outside,' she said. 'There's still a little summer left, I think.'

They sat down, the five of them, beneath the small tree; a light, persistent wind had got up, over their heads the leaves of the little oak were moving restlessly. Around the pasture the wind moved like a wave through the trees, flattening the leaves and turning them silver.

Lucien brought out a small aluminium pot of coffee, a crumpled bag of biscuits and some tiny cups; he'd even found a half-full bottle of grappa somewhere. It appeared to Justine that all this fussing about with glasses and trays was a kind of diversionary tactic; perhaps it always had been. He put the tray down and held out his hand to Rossella, smiling his easy smile.

'Lucien Elliott,' he said.

Rossella looked at him gravely for a moment, before shaking his hand. 'Rossella Bandini,' she said. She continued to study him, but said nothing.

'Rossella was a friend of Evie's,' said Martin, and Lucien glanced at him quickly, then looked away. Was it the first time Evie's name had been out in the open among them all, Justine wondered? Lucien seemed to shy away from the sound.

'Yes,' he said, indistinctly, not quite looking at Rossella. 'From Florence?'

'How did you know?' asked Martin.

'I – didn't you say? I think it must be the accent,' said Lucien.

'Actually, from Rome originally,' said Rossella. 'But I have lived in Florence since I was a small girl.'

Justine looked at their guest; she could picture Rossella framed in one of those Florentine windows with their great pointed stone arches, or sitting reading in an apartment with a garden, cool and green, everything in its place. Then she thought of their lives in London: taking the tube or the bus to reach each other through the dirt and the noise, trying to talk in each other's crowded kitchens without being inter-rupted by children, or lodgers, or husbands. Or overheard. No wonder Evie had kept hold of Rossella, kept her secret; Justine found herself longing for such a friend, one who might

327

sit and read her letters in the ancient, narrow streets of a distant city, consider her private joy or grief, find the solution to her dilemmas.

'I wanted to meet you all,' said Rossella in her slow, careful English, looking around the table. 'I have heard about you, from Evie, of course.' A single drop of rain fell, warm and heavy, darkening the linen of the tablecloth; for a moment they were all silent, waiting.

By the waterfall, Paolo, Anna and the two boys were walking in the hazel grove that ran alongside the river. It was still warm. Anna thought that perhaps by tomorrow it would have turned; that was usually how it went when autumn finally arrived. There was a last day of reprieve.

The boys didn't seem worried; they were running in and out of the copse, whose roof of interlocking branches seemed, so far, quite weatherproof and which provided a dry, musty shelter. Paolo had taken off his jacket and the jersey he'd slung around his neck and each child was now draped in an oversized garment, empty sleeves flapping and whirling as they dodged and ran. Anna liked listening to the noise they made; she felt as though she could stay here until it grew dark, thinking things over. Somehow she felt that once they left this place she would have to pack it all away again and get on with her life.

She looked up at Paolo, handsome in his shirtsleeves beside her. 'What do you think of the English, then?' she said, smiling.

'Funny lot,' he said abruptly. 'They don't seem to be getting on very well.'

'Yes,' mused Anna, 'it can't be what they expected, Il

Vignacce. Maybe they're getting on each other's nerves.' She paused. 'Pretty girl, though, don't you think?'

Paolo shrugged, and looked away from her, bending a little to look out at the rain. 'Which one?'

Anna laughed. 'You know which one. The one who didn't sprain her ankle. The dark one. I'm not blind, you know.'

Paolo smiled. 'Yes,' he said, shrugging his shoulders again. 'She's nice. She's – beautiful.' He paused. 'But she's married, and they're going home at the weekend.'

'Well,' said Anna, 'the way she was looking at you ...' She tailed off. 'And I didn't think too much of her husband, did you?'

'Good cook,' said Paolo.

'That's not everything,' said Anna, and Paolo laughed.

'Mamma,' he said, 'I just looked at her, that's all, and she looked at me. We're not engaged.'

'Well,' said Anna again, her head on one side, 'a look – that's how it usually starts, isn't it? A look can do it.' She looked wistful.

'OK,' said Paolo, laughing. 'That's enough.'

It was as dark as a cave now inside the trees; overhead Anna could hear rain beginning to patter softly on the leaves. Out through a hazel arch she could see it falling silently into the river, spotting the surface of the dark water. It smelled clean, wet leaves not yet turned slimy, the sweet smell of damp wood. She wondered how long it would go on; idly she thought, soon we should go back.

'We should go back soon,' said Paolo, leaning against a stand of hazel, his head brushing the roof, and looking down at her. Anna smiled at his echo of her thought, but neither of them made a move.

'Let them play a little more,' she said. 'It's not cold, not yet. You used to come down here on your own, do you remember?' she asked. 'When we came to visit Nonna?'

Paolo nodded, watching her. Anna was looking at something far away; the boys brushed past her, the smaller one clung to her shoulder as if she was home in a game of chase, but she didn't seem to notice.

'I'm sorry,' said Anna, 'that I didn't bring you home to Nonna before. Sorry for you, and sorry for her. But I was afraid. At first I thought it would be easier – if it was just you and me.'

'It must have been very hard,' said Paolo. 'Don't worry.' He put an arm around her.

These days, of course, not so many hospitals were run by nuns, but then – it was hard to find one that wasn't. At the Bambino Gesu, the maternity hospital, they rustled down the corridors like flocks of pale grey birds; now you'd be hard pushed to find a nun in a habit, even in Rome. Something about the band of white around their faces made them look – what? Pure, sweet, wise; at first anyway. Until you were pregnant, and unmarried, and frightened.

Anna had bought herself a ring so cheap it left a sooty mark around her finger, and she wore it when she went again to the doctor, after that first time. When she went into labour she put it on, just before she left the apartment with her little bag packed, a clean nightdress, baby things, napkins, soap. The ring was loose on her finger – she'd managed to grow thinner during pregnancy, with the sickness and misery – and she felt sure it stood out a mile that she had no right to wear it.

The Bambino Gesu was a long building that took up one side of a little piazza, elegant shuttered buildings around a crumbling fountain, near the river. The hospital itself was a beautiful, austere building of grey stone and white stucco, its frontage arcaded above three steps down to the square, and above each arch was a plaster plaque in blue and white of the holy child. Anna had told them that she was a widow when they asked where her husband was, standing with her bag in the gloomy marble hall, its floor dark red and green marble. The sister just nodded and wrote something in a ledger, a deep frownline etched between her brows. Anna carried it off better than a young girl might have, but since the occupation how many husbands managed to impregnate their wives then die before the child was delivered? Although in this case, it was nearly true. Only half a lie.

Anna followed the sister down a corridor, she could not now remember her name, called after a saint, Ignatius or Aquinas, a man's name. Pausing once to lean against the wall as a contraction stopped her in her tracks, through the narrow slit of a window she caught a glimpse of green, an arcaded stone cloister around some grass, and she felt a tremendous longing to escape, to feel the air on her face. In the corridor a sallow young woman was pushing a bit of rag listlessly up and down with a broom. She wore a dirty apron tied twice around her thick waist, and Anna had wondered for a second whether she had come in here to have a baby and had never got out again.

They walked on past a series of looming statues: the Virgin and child, Mary Magdalene at the foot of the cross, the figures gazing down sternly with their sightless marble eyes. The room at which the sister finally stopped was whitewashed, a band of pale blue painted at waist height, and it contained four narrow wooden beds, none of them occupied. It was unnaturally silent. Even if the mothers could be made to keep silent, surely the babies cried?

A doctor was brought to her after a while; a pale, seedy man in a white coat who looked as though he didn't get out in the fresh air, a dusting of grey stubble on his chin. He didn't ask about her husband or anything else, and looked at her with very little interest, just pulling up the thin, backless gown they had given her. He put his hands on her belly and pushed his clean, cold fingers hard into her lower abdomen to feel for the position of the head; Anna was shocked into silence by the abrupt, emotionless force of the examination. He nodded in her direction, not quite meeting her eye, and affected a smile.

'Hurts now, eh?' he said, still smiling. Then he turned and said something to the sister that she did not hear, before leaving the room. She didn't see him again.

When Anna was in labour, she thought she might die; that was the thought that circled monotonously in her head as the pain rose and fell, but by then she hardly minded. The sisters came and went angrily, slapping things down on an iron trolley in the corner of the room, and after an hour or so she decided to ignore them. It was as though her vision had narrowed to a small spot ahead of her on the pale cracked plaster of the wall, and her life depended on her keeping it in her sights. Then there was a nun there all the time, standing beside her, as though they knew something she didn't.

Anna remembered looking up at the sister at her bedside, a woman in late middle-age, her blue eyes the only distinguishing feature in the otherwise uniform grey of her appearance, like the window on an outside world that was no longer accessible. Anna looked up at her as if to ask what it was that

332

they knew, but she found she couldn't speak. Then the pain changed and it was as though something was turning and expanding inside her, there was nothing she could do to act against it. Then there was a great surge, and there he was: a thin, bleating cry, and an unfamiliar presence in the room that sent shock waves through the air. For a fraction of a second as Anna looked down between her knees he seemed to her no more human than a puppy: eyes creased shut but a red mouth wide open in silent rebellion, his arms flung out wide, his tiny fingers curling inwards.

'*Un maschio*. Male,' the sister said, disapproving of him already.

Then something moved into place in Anna's mind, something she had not been able to locate until now.

'A baby,' she'd murmured, hardly aware of what she was saying.

The sister made a contemptuous sound. 'What did you think it would be, Signora?'

They knew, all right.

'You might as well take that off,' the sister had said, briskly, tugging at the ring, after Anna had been washed and they'd taken him away somewhere. She wanted to know where, but they wouldn't tell her, not to begin with.

'No,' she had said, grateful for once that she was not a girl, but a grown woman. 'Get him back.' There was a room in the convent, in every convent, where unwanted babies could be left anonymously, to be treated as orphans.

'I want him,' she said again. And eventually they had brought him back. Perhaps they thought it was punishment enough, that she should have to live with the evidence. Even now Anna marvelled that she had made them do it, the freakish luck that she had found the determination at the exact moment she would need it.

Anna had sewn just one little smocked nightgown; made of wool she had lined it with cotton so as not to scratch, and embroidered it with lilies. She had worked almost in her sleep, unable to think what she was doing it for, finishing it in a hurry before she was overtaken by superstition. She marvelled when she took it out to dress him, trying to manoeuvre his arms into the sleeves, at how little she had imagined this. A baby. He had lain there, silent on the pale blue hospital blanket, staring up at her with a dazed look.

Anna left the Bambino Gesu before Paolo was six hours old. Barely able to walk herself, she held him folded tightly against her as she walked back down the endless corridor, past the statues standing guard and out into the mild spring air, and she didn't stop until she was back in her own home. Their home.

'I took you home, before they could make me change my mind,' Anna said to Paolo, the rain falling heavy now over their heads, looking at him. He put his arm around her.

'It wasn't easy, of course, you're right,' she went on slowly, pulling back as she remembered the questions, the struggle to find the money for everything. 'But it's not as if I was the only one. In those days – it happened. The difference was, I was older; Nonna couldn't have passed you off as her own, she was nearly seventy. I thought – well, I thought it might be better to wait. Before I told her.' Anna sighed, admitting that she had thought this more than once, and had been wrong each time.

'I got along all right, at work. No one said anything to me; they wanted to help.' A blanket shyly presented, baby clothes, a home-made cot outgrown. The girls at work, pressing Paolo to their faces as though they wanted to eat him. 'I managed. So I didn't go home; I didn't tell her. Nonna.'

'When did you come back, in the end? Come back here, I mean.' Paolo put a hand to the corner of his eye, rubbed something away.

'When my grandmother died. I had to, then. Not just for the funeral; I had to tell Nonna, she had a grandson.'

Paolo was silent. Then he looked up, and nodded. 'Mama,' he said, 'you did the right thing. What else could you do?'

And she closed her eyes. 'That's it, then,' she said. 'There's nothing more to tell.'

'The sister?' said Paolo. 'His wife, and her daughter?'

Anna sighed reluctantly. 'I don't know,' she said. 'They left Rome, after Luca died.' She frowned, as though she was remembering something long forgotten.

Paolo watched her face, and after a moment Anna went on, slowly, reconstructing an invisible scene from fragments of buried memory.

'She came to see me – to see you, after you were born. Amalia.' She spoke hesitantly, with reluctance. 'I hardly knew she was there, really. I didn't want to think about who she was. She brought a present – what was it? Something for you to wear. She brought the little girl with her. She'd grown; taller and thinner, I remember that. Amalia said they were leaving Rome, going north. That was the last time I saw either of them. Of course—' Anna stopped, looked down.

'She had no idea.' She shook her head, still frowning at her hands, held out in front of her, and for a moment Paolo wondered about her just as he had that morning when she couldn't think what to wear. 'None.' She looked up at him then. 'I'm sorry,' she said. Paolo took her hand. 'No,' he said, 'I'm sorry.'

335

Just then, both boys, Sam and Angus, rushed at them from the far end of the grove, hollering as they came like savages, holding something up they had found in the water. They tugged at Paolo's sleeve; when he didn't move, the younger, Angus, ran across to Anna and flung his arms around her legs, pulling at her. She pushed him away, laughing despite herself.

'We've got to go back,' Angus said, urgently. 'Look, the rain's getting worse.' They turned to look, and they saw that he was right.

For a moment or two they sat, irresolute, at the table, as the silent rain fell, soft and warm, on their cheeks, on their shoulders, and the dark spots on the tablecloth merged. Then Justine got to her feet, gathered up the tablecloth and the little jar of cyclamen, and suddenly they were all standing up, bumping into each other in their haste to get in out of the rain. Louisa hobbled inside with Tom supporting her gently.

Il Vignacce seemed almost cosy with the lights on, the sound of the rain on the roof and all of them sitting around the dining table. The door was standing open but it was still warm, and one after the other they all sat around the table: Rossella, Martin, Tom and Louisa side by side, Lucien. Justine set down her bundle of damp linen and the flowers Lucien had picked. Wild flowers; thoughtless, really, although no doubt he had intended to charm them with the gesture. She sat down, directly opposite Rossella; the last at the table.

'You met Evie – when?' she said.

Rossella sighed, as though this was what she had been waiting for. 'My stepfather had known Evie's father. They studied together in London; after the war, at the London School of Economics. Perhaps you know it?' Rossella looked around the table, feeling awkward suddenly about what she had to say. Justine smiled at her.

'Yes,' she said, 'we know it.'

Rossella went on. 'Her mother died, when she was very young. Twelve, or thirteen. A terrible age, I think.' The image of Dido, standing waist-high in the river and frowning, came to Justine. A terrible age, not grown up, not a child. Impossible to comfort. She said nothing.

'But—' Louisa began to say, frowning, but Justine looked across at her and shook her head, very slightly.

'Evie's mother had a chronic disease; she had it all the time Evie was growing up, and Evie's father took care of her. Evie too, sometimes. My father would talk about it to my mother; they corresponded, you see, he and Ted. It must have been very difficult. I listened; I was – I am a little older than Evie. Three years.' Rossella stopped for a moment, her eyes clouded.

They looked at her expectantly.

'I began to write to Evie, then. Pen pals, you know.' Rossella smiled a little awkwardly. 'She was so – alive, in all that' – Rossella made a sound of frustration, trying to find the right word – 'all the sickness – like living in a hospital. She needed to escape from her life. From her home. So she wrote to me. When her mother died, she told me that she was relieved that it was all over. Then four years later her father killed himself. Perhaps he was waiting as long as he could, until she was almost grown. And then Evie was alone.'

Justine thought of the silence Evie had kept with all of them, for all of those years; the alternative history she had constructed for herself to obscure this one, while all the time she smiled and listened, laughed and partied. Across the table Justine could see Louisa's eyes, wide with shock, and Tom, his arm around her, steadying her. She looked at Lucien then, but she couldn't tell what he was thinking.

Beside Rossella sat Martin, his hand on her forearm, watchful. Waiting.

Outside the rain fell relentlessly, slanting grey across the rectangle of light framed by the door. And Justine thought, they'll be sheltering somewhere; let them stay away, just while we hear this. The whole story.

Tom spoke, his voice rusty after a long silence. 'So Evie' – his voice faltered over her name – 'she came to you, then?'

Rossella nodded. 'She lived with us for one year. In Florence. I think we helped her; she became happier, certainly. We are a small family – but not quite a regular family, you know?' She was looking at Justine, who shook her head slightly, not understanding.

'I mean – my real father had died, too, when I was very young, and perhaps that helped. With Evie, to know she was not the only one. It was just my half-brother and me, my mother, my stepfather, a small apartment in the city. Very crowded, with a little terrace, not even a garden, you know. An ordinary place. But,' she sighed again, wistfully, 'we loved her very much – my mother, always tried to cook something nice for Evie, to make her eat. My brother adored her. You know how Evie is. Was. You fall in love with her.' She shrugged helplessly.

Justine saw Louisa nodding, saw her mouth turn down at the corners and she realized that, despite Louisa's briskness, her impatience with Evie's unorthodox life, she had loved her as much as anyone.

'Then she was offered a place at university in England. In London. She was so surprised; so happy. She had thought she would not be successful when she made her application, you see; there were – gaps. In her education.'

Great glaring holes, thought Justine, Evie's life was full of them. She found herself shaking her head.

'And we never saw her again.' Rossella put a hand to her forehead and slowly rubbed at her temple; she was not melodramatic, not the over-emotional foreigner they might have expected. She was dignified, composed, but there was grief in every crease and plane of her pale, freckled face.

'Never?' ventured Louisa. 'She never came back?' They looked at each other, she and Justine, thinking, *We got her, instead.* Landing on that checkerboard tiled porch in Evelyn Gardens with her busted suitcase. *But we didn't hang on to her, did we?*

Rossella shook her head. 'No. She continued to write to me. Right up until – the end; I kept all her letters. All of them. But she never came back.'

Martin cleared his throat and spoke. 'She never wanted to come back to Italy,' he said. 'Whenever I suggested it.' He looked lost, suddenly. 'I couldn't understand why; she never made anything of it, just always had a reason for suggesting somewhere else.'

Rosella put her hand over his on the table. 'I think – now, I think perhaps that it was because she had decided to begin her life again. Perhaps the new story – the one she told you, Tom told me this – seemed less tragic; just an accident. A car crash – no one would look at her and wonder—'

'If she would go the same way?' Justine finished the sentence for her.

Rossella nodded.

'And did she?'

339

'What do you mean?' said Rossella slowly, although it was clear she knew already.

Justine felt everyone's eyes on her as she spoke. 'Did she go the same way? Did she kill herself, just like her father? Did she throw herself off that ferry because she had the same illness, the one that killed her mother? Did she write and tell you what she was going to do?' Justine felt out of breath, suddenly, and she stopped.

No one moved, not one hand shifted position on the table and the only sound was the softly whispering rain. They waited for Rossella to speak.

'No,' said Rossella sadly. 'There was someone else.'

The pasture was empty now; silently the cows had moved on to more sheltered grazing further down and the soft, ceaseless rain fell only on the coarse grass. The woods along the river looked darker now, and the gurgle of the water below was louder, more insistent as it rose. The rain fell on and on, but no one appeared in the gap between the trees that led down to the bathing place; despite the weather, it seemed that Dido was reluctant to leave her seclusion and return to the farm.

Downstream, Anna and Paolo were toiling slowly up the hill from the waterfall, while the two boys ran ahead, hiding behind trees and in scratchy clumps of gorse, apparently oblivious to the rain. The forest dripped around them in the silence, but they were largely sheltered here. Il Vignacce's red roof appeared, then the stone façade of the farmhouse rose on the brow of the hill. The shutters had not been closed and electric light spilled out of the open door, but no one was to be seen, only one more car was parked there. Anna paused, to catch her breath.

'We might need to beg a lift back, in this,' she said, looking across at the distant dirt road and an erratic, milky stream of rainwater running down, gathering dust from the surface, to form a swelling puddle by the gate. Paolo nodded.

'Yes,' he said. They stood all together in the shelter of the trees, contemplating the house and the stretch of grass wet with rain that they must cross to get there.

Chapter Twenty-Six

They stared at Rossella, at her pale face downlit by the lamp that hung over the table.

'Someone else?' said Louisa faintly.

Justine looked across at Martin; at Rossella's words his head had dropped, and he was looking down at his hands on the table. She wondered if he was prepared for this.

Rossella nodded. 'She wanted to escape; she wanted a new life. Again. She met someone. Fell in love with someone.'

Martin's head was still bowed; Justine saw a movement in his throat. Dido, she thought suddenly, and looked around in panic, out of the window at the fading light. Where's Dido? She could hear something, over the rain, behind the pattering on the roof and the sighing of the wind. They're coming back, she thought, calm down, but she felt distracted, unsettled; unwilling suddenly to turn back to Rossella and go on listening. She was talking now, in her soft, deliberate English.

'She described him to me, not just once, but in many letters she wrote. She couldn't see him very often – he was married. Is married.' Rossella hesitated. 'She said—' She put a hand out to Martin, touched his arm. 'Martin?' she said. 'Do you really—?'

'Yes,' he said, his voice oddly stifled. 'Go on.'

Rossella nodded calmly. Justine looked at her serious, open face, the repository of Evie's secrets, and she could see why Evie told her everything.

'She wanted to be young, again, to feel – light. When she became ill. *Allegra* – you know, light-hearted. She always said that Martin was so close to her – so intense. She could never hide anything from him.'

At this Martin made an involuntary sound, and Justine reached out her hand across the table to him, but stopped halfway. She could feel Lucien's eyes on her, and she wondered what he was making of all this.

'So,' said Rossella, with a sigh as though it was more difficult than she had thought to explain all this, 'she needed someone else. Someone who took things – more lightly. He was beautiful to look at, she said.' Rossella shrugged a little, as if to say, how could Evie help herself?

'He made no demands on her; he ignored her illness, or at least perhaps he allowed her to pretend it didn't exist. A creative man, clever. With – charisma. And I think – I think she actually fell in love with him. With Evie, I think, love was everything, at the end, anyway. She thought love would make it all all right.' She looked anguished; it was as though she was trying to defend Evie to them, and it did ring true. She had been a romantic.

Justine dared a brief look across the table at Louisa; she was frowning a little, biting her lower lip, and Justine knew what she was thinking. Tom. She's talking about Tom. She was reproaching herself for having ceased to think of him like this; not creative, not sensitive, for allowing Evie to appreciate him. Poor Louisa, she thought. Tom himself, though, sitting at her side, seemed completely composed and at the same time intent, as if had been waiting for this. Outside Justine could hear the sound of the boys' approach quite clearly; shouting at each other to run.

Rossella went on. 'She had made a decision. In her last letter, the very last one, she said that she had planned everything. She was going to leave. With him.'

'Leave her family?' asked Louisa, slowly. 'Leave Dido?'

Helplessly, Rossella spread her hands. 'She thought she had to do it. Can you see? She thought it would be better for Dido, not to have a sick mother, and for herself, she thought it was her last chance at life. She said – she knew Dido would understand. She – she was going to write. I think she wrote to tell me because she couldn't make herself tell them. Martin and Dido. She couldn't face it.'

'She never wrote to tell you,' said Justine, looking at Martin; it wasn't quite a question, she knew Evie hadn't written because if she had, Martin would have told the police and there would have been no mystery. At least until the body was found. But somehow Justine couldn't believe that Evie would leave without saying goodbye, at least to Dido. Something stirred in the recesses of her memory, but she couldn't reclaim it, whatever it was, not yet. She turned back to Rossella.

'Where was she going to go? They. Where were they going to go?' Who could he have been, this man? Justine tried to imagine Evie meeting a married man in a wine bar, making secret phone calls, excuses. A new life. She couldn't summon up such a picture. What kind of man could it possibly be, to be good enough for her?

'They had planned everything. Or perhaps – perhaps it was Evie who did the planning.' Rossella hesitated. 'They were going to travel in Europe, a boat to Spain, Bilbao then Seville, drive to Provence, Venice.' She pronounced each name in the Italian way, and the destinations sounded alluring, exotic. A grand tour, late in the season. 'They were going to come to Florence.' And then she stopped, her grey eyes focusing on something far away.

'But they never arrived,' Justine finished for her, bluntly.

Rossella shook her head. 'No.'

Justine sat very still, dizzied for a moment by the new information whirling in her head, waiting for it to settle. Then she saw Evie, that fuzzy outline on the security camera in the windswept foyer of a ferry terminal. A slender, indecisive figure standing there alone, looking out for someone; waiting for her last chance at life. Poor Evie.

The boys were in the doorway behind her now; Justine could hear their ragged breath, but she didn't turn her head. She looked straight at Rossella, holding her gaze, and she could feel the others' eyes on them.

'You know who he was, don't you,' she said, almost in a whisper, and very slowly Rossella nodded. Justine felt Louisa's eyes following her, and she met them.

'Yes,' said Rossella, and beside her Justine felt Lucien shifting his position, the tiniest movement. Justine held Louisa's gaze, as though they had a pact.

'Lucien,' said Rossella, looking at Justine, her eyes full of anguish. 'It was Lucien. It was your husband.'

Chapter Twenty-Seven

Justine continued to look at Louisa, as Rossella's whispered words hung in the air between them; she couldn't move. It was in Louisa's face that Justine read the truth; she could see relief that it wasn't Tom's name hanging in the air between them, and shock. But also, in that fraction of a second, she could see Louisa believed it, and Louisa wasn't good at deceiving herself. Justine felt sick.

'This is outrageous,' she heard Lucien bluster by her side, but still Justine didn't turn to look at him.

And then everything began to unfold in front of her as though in slow motion. Numbly Justine looked around the table at their faces, at all the faces except one, and they might as well have been strangers; they pitied her, and the thought filled her with horror. She stood up, and heard herself make a sound, an inarticulate cry that fell on her ears as though from somewhere far away.

'Sweetheart,' Lucien said, standing too, taking her arm. She stood there, the endearment ringing utterly false in her ears, the warmth of his fingers like a brand on her arm, and with what seemed like a terrible, paralysing slowness the implications of what Rossella had said unfolded inside her head. She forced herself to turn towards him, although all she wanted to do was run for the door and take a great gulp of fresh air.

'You were in Wales,' she said, slowly, thinking of those forty-eight hours after Evie's disappearance when she'd tried to get hold of Lucien. 'On that course. Weren't you? Did you—' She stopped, thinking frantically. 'Were you with her all the time? Did you meet her? Did you—' And she stopped, unable to articulate the thought that had just occurred to her, and focused on Lucien's face, at last. He was looking fixedly into her eyes, as though trying to stop her looking away at the others; his face was pale beneath the tan, and there was no trace of his cheerful smile.

'No!' he said, urgently. 'No – I never – you've got to believe me. I had nothing to do with – nothing – I was in Wales, all the time. I can prove it.' But she had turned away; her stomach churned at the sound of his voice.

Justine didn't know where she was going, but she had to get out. At the door the boys were crowding in, oblivious to the turmoil unfolding inside, and they pulled back to let her out. As she passed she registered their little golden-brown faces, crowned with fringes bleached platinum by the sun, looking up at her curiously.

Justine stood in the doorway, not knowing where to go. The heat fell on her like a stifling blanket; she passed a hand across her face and closed her eyes briefly, willing the images behind them to disappear. She could hear his voice down the fractured line from Wales, cheerful, then sympathetic, soothing her. *It'll be all right, she'll turn up.* Sickened, she wrenched her thoughts away. Think of something else. Someone else. Where's Dido? At the gate beneath the trees, twenty yards away, she could see two figures: Paolo, tall and broad-shouldered, and a smaller figure: Anna. No Dido.

Paolo and Anna were approaching, no more than a couple of yards away now, and she could see concern in their faces. Paolo was looking at her, and she found herself looking back at him. There was something in his expression, a kind of gentleness, and for a moment she had the impression that this almost-stranger could somehow help her out of all this; briefly she experienced the urge to fling herself at him, beg him to make everything go away. *Stupid*, she thought, hopelessly. And she looked away again, past him at the empty, rain-sodden pasture. Behind her in the house she could hear the sound of voices raised, fierce argument across the table, and she couldn't stand to listen for a moment longer. She ran out into the rain.

By the time she reached the barbed wire that ran alongside the woods, Justine was soaked to the skin. As she left the pasture and went into the trees any remaining brightness was leached out of the air and a filmy luminescence remained. It smelled musty down here, as though the warm rain was activating the decaying process of the forest floor, bringing the spores of some ancient fungus back to life. It was very quiet, and every tiny movement, every leaf disturbed by the rain, seemed to make itself heard.

She skirted the shadowy hazel grove, its arcaded gloom cavernous and sinister as the light faded. Dido, she murmured to herself, poor Dido. We'll be in this together. Once through the gate she made her way between the shoulder-high hemlock and teazels shedding seed as fine as dust in the damp air;

almost there. The great lichen-blistered cliff loomed on the far side of the dark water, but there was no Dido. Panic ballooned in her chest.

The dusty beach of mulch and bark was empty; not even a sweet wrapper to show they'd been here. Its surface was scuffed here and there by feet, and Justine could see a depression where someone had been lying; in the shadow of the cliff the dark surface of the pool, where Justine half expected to see Dido's dark head pop up like a seal's, was undisturbed. The river glided on, regardless, and Justine thought of the weight of all that water, moving, never stopping. She could feel her heart pounding, and breathed slowly to fill her lungs again.

'Dido?' she called, turning back to the river. 'Dido!' She was shouting now, but no one appeared. Justine waded into the water.

Upstream, the river was quite empty, it flowed down towards her between the trees and not a movement or a sound interrupted the softly falling rain. The water around her ankles was cold, as though it had come from a long way up; between her toes the texture of the river bottom was elusive; sandy, gritty, slimy. The shining wet green of the bushes on the bank as far as she could see offered no clue to Dido's disappearance, no movement other than the minute bounce of raindrops on the leaves.

Rossella, thought Anna as she looked through the door and saw the gleam of red hair, a pale profile barely illuminated by the weak light from the door, and for a moment she had the curious sensation that she was seeing something from a great distance. 'Rossella,' she murmured under her breath but Paolo still heard her.

'What, Mamma?' Inside the room the tall, beautiful red-haired woman got to her feet and turned towards them, mother and son, as they stood, dripping, on the threshold, neither in nor out.

Something's been going on here, thought Paolo. There was an atmosphere inside the house, thick as fog, the echo of voices raised in anger still hung in the air. He turned back to look across the drenched pasture; what must have happened to make her rush off like that, into the rain? Justine. Someone should go after her, he thought, and just as he decided it should be him the husband, Lucien, pushed past him and headed for the gate. Paolo frowned as he watched the man go, hunched under the downpour.

'It's her daughter. Amalia's daughter. Luca's—' Anna broke off, and she looked about her distractedly. Then she pulled back from the door and sat down, weak suddenly, an old lady, on the stone bench against the house, barely sheltered from the rain.

'What?' said Paolo, astounded. 'Luca's daughter? No, mamma. No. How – how could you possibly tell?' But Anna nodded sadly.

'It's her. She looks – just like her mother. She's the right age, isn't she?' She shrugged helplessly. 'I can't explain it. But it's her.' Shaking his head in astonishment, Paolo turned back to look inside, and there she was, at the door, coming out to meet them.

Rossella smiled apologetically. 'How do you do,' she said. 'Rossella Bandini.' She held out her hand. Speechless, Paolo took it. 'Paolo Viola,' he said. 'This is my mother, Anna.' Anna sat on the bench, hardly sheltered by the overhanging eaves, looking down at her hands.

'A pleasure. There's a lot going on in here,' said Rossella, apologetically. A lot of confusion.' A man appeared at her shoulder from out of the gloom; a tall, fair-haired Englishman Paolo hadn't seen before, rather weary-looking. His hand was offered.

'Tom,' he said, 'thank you for looking after my boys.' He seemed to take in their bedraggled appearance, then. 'Look,' he said, 'you can't sit out here; shall we go into the house next door? You can dry out a bit. Rossella—?' he appealed to her wordlessly.

At the sound of the name Anna's head dipped even further, and Rossella took her by the arm. 'Shall we go next door?' she said, concern in her voice, and helped Anna up.

Inside the house Louisa watched Rossella go to the door with something like relief; the burden of hospitality to Paolo and Anna was, under the circumstances, too much for her. Martin stood, silent, in the shadows at the back of the house, looking out into the darkening green of the woods that seemed closer now, somehow Sam and Angus were on either side of her on the sofa and gratefully she held them against her for a moment, damp and warm. 'Where's Dido?' Louisa asked, feeling a little dazed. 'Did you see her – at the waterfall? On the way?'

'No,' said Sam.

'But we found her thingummy,' said Angus. 'Her scarf thing.'

'Her bandanna,' Sam pronounced confidently. 'It was in the water.' He thrust his hand into his soaking pocket and held it up, a squeezed pink rag.

Louisa frowned and reached out her hand for the scarf, trying to fit this small piece of information in with everything else. She sighed, her head hot and aching with the effort of understanding what had been going on. 'Upstairs,' she said, trying to gather her thoughts, trying to sound firm. 'Get some dry things on.' When they didn't move she pushed them a little. 'Now,' she said, 'go on.' And reluctantly they shifted.

Once they were upstairs, their footsteps audible as they ran from room to room in some new game now they had been released from adult supervision, Martin turned towards her. 'Do you think I did the right thing?' he said, an uncertainty in his voice Louisa had never heard before. Again she sighed.

'Well, of course – I'm relieved, actually. Of course I am. That it had nothing to do with Tom.' And she looked away, at the door where Tom had left with Rossella.

'But you always knew that, didn't you?' said Martin robustly, his old self again briefly. 'I did. Tom couldn't have done it to you. Or to Dido and me. He couldn't have left the boys. And even if it had been Tom – I think they'd be here now. He wouldn't have let Evie down. He'd have done whatever she asked, they'd have gone on their world tour, he'd have pushed her round Venice in a wheelchair. Only – she wasn't going to die, that's what I can't stand. She'd have come back, in the end, if she hadn't – if she'd never met Lucien.'

Louisa shivered; she felt a little feverish, and her cramped legs ached. Cautiously she stretched out her swollen ankle on the sofa. 'Do you think—' She felt light-headed suddenly, and she wasn't sure how to proceed. 'Do you think – could it have been all in Evie's mind? You know—' she searched desperately for an explanation that would allow them to restore the status quo. 'She might have gone a bit mad, with all the stress. Started fantasizing.'

Slowly Martin shook his head. 'Do you think that's possible?'

'I don't know,' said Louisa helplessly. 'I can't believe – do you think he went with her on that boat? Do you think he – had anything to do with – with—'

'With Evie's death?' Martin finished for her. 'Lucien? Can you imagine it? I don't know if I can.'

'Surely the police – if he'd been there, they'd have seen him. On the close-circuit television or – or something. The way they found Evie.' Louisa's eyes were dark, horrified at the picture their speculation was conjuring up. She looked about, desperately, and there Tom was, in the doorway, and he looked at them.

'Only Lucien knows,' he said, his voice rough with emotion. 'Evie's dead, so only Lucien knows.'

'Poor Justine,' said Louisa. 'Poor Justine.'

Chapter Twenty-Eight

Justine closed the gate behind her. She was soaked through now and her throat was hoarse with shouting. In the rain she blinked back tears of desperation. What a mess, she thought, what a mess. All of it: Evie, Lucien, Dido. Me. She thought of Evie and Lucien, talking in the garden at Tom's house, thought of Dido, looking up at her from the river, asking if she knew why Evie had gone. Why didn't I see? How did I allow this to happen?

Justine forced herself to slow down, brought the nauseating whirl of speculation in her head to a stop. Evie and Lucien. She thought of Lucien, sleeping sound and unworried beside her every night, and of Evie's haunted face, Evie at the doctor's, Evie staring at Dido, until she thought she'd go mad. As though she was someone else she watched and saw how it could happen, how Evie, desperate and afraid, seeing her life slipping away from her, might want someone like Lucien – unthinking, irresistibly self-absorbed, amoral, whose even breaths would get her to sleep at night. And it wasn't as though Justine didn't know what Lucien was like. She had no claim on him, he'd made sure of that: no bank account, no children, no property in common. It was all quite clear to her suddenly, and curiously, she didn't feel sick any more, or angry, just a kind of numbness.

Overhead the glare was gone from the sky; and it was getting dark. Dido. The thought of the girl in the forest at dusk came back to Justine and with it the sickening realization of the mess they had got her into. Trying to subdue her panic, she wondered what time it could be. Five, six? She could feel fear, creeping around the edges of her rational mind, looking for a way in; her breathing felt shallow and rushed. *I've got to get help before it gets dark.* She turned to walk back to Il Vignacce.

It was quiet at first, the forest dripped around her, but as the gloom intensified Justine seemed to hear more and more; rustling, crawling sounds, the snap of a branch. At one point she heard the unmistakable trampling of something large blundering through the undergrowth, shadowing her, and she stopped. 'Dido?' She meant to shout, but it sounded more like a frightened whisper when it came out, and there was no reply.

She turned back, forced her trembling legs on over the uneven ground, the rocks and branches, boggy bits that might have been mud underfoot, a patch of fading light appeared above her. Gratefully she focused on the opening between the trees, stumbling on up the slope as quickly as she could. Then, from out of the shadows, something came at her, something dark and solid, breathing heavily. She screamed, or thought she did; the sound that emerged was a hoarse whisper.

For a moment she thought she was going to faint; her legs felt as boneless as rubber and she felt nausea rising inside her.

She swayed, and would have fallen if Lucien hadn't taken hold of her arm. Close to like this she felt no familiarity; it was as though a stranger had come up to her out of the shadows. He even smelled different; there was something sour, sweat and foul breath, coming off him in the dark.

'Lucien,' she forced herself to say, 'let go.' He dropped her arm.

Neither of them moved; Lucien said nothing. Justine looked past him, up at the fading watery light in the pasture. 'Were you having an affair with Evie, Lucien?' she asked, feeling that horrible calm descend on her once again.

'I – no,' he said, 'I mean, it wasn't – you have to let me explain.' He sounded as though he was trying to hold his voice steady, give it the old casual confidence.

'You were,' said Justine. She knew it for absolutely certain now.

'But it wasn't – I didn't start it,' he said, defensively. 'You know what Evie was like. It was hard to say no to her, sometimes.'

'You're not a child, Lucien,' Justine said, and as she spoke she realized that that was exactly what he was. A spoilt child. She pushed him away.

'It was – it was like a game,' he said. 'Just a bit of fun. Not like you and me. I can't lose you.' He sounded almost outraged. 'You're – you're everything to me, Justine. I need you. Evie had this – fantasy. That we'd travel the world together.'

'And you went along with it,' said Justine, as cold as ice. 'You booked that week in Wales. You let her think you were going to go with her.'

'She wouldn't listen,' he said, flatly, sulkily. 'I tried.'

'You mean you were too much of a coward to say anything.'

356

She heard Lucien sigh, as though she was the child, refusing to understand. 'It didn't mean anything. She got the wrong end of the stick. It was just supposed to be a bit of – light relief, you know.'

From me? thought Justine, feeling ill, suddenly, really ill, her head spinning but Lucien went on, unaware of the effect his words had had.

'But no, it had to be some great tragic romance, for Evie.' He sounded impatient, and Justine realized he expected her to sympathize with him, but she felt nothing but disgust. Standing there in the gloom she was overcome by a terrible flat, empty feeling, confronted by the evidence of her failure, of her misjudgement, and suddenly all she wanted was to be rid of him, never to have to listen to him again.

'I don't want to hear it, Lucien,' she said, shortly. 'Listen to me. Dido's gone. She's disappeared. We've got to look for her.'

'God, kids,' said Lucien. 'She'll just be waiting under a tree. I bet this is what she wants, everyone running around looking for her. God, you should have seen the fuss she made, this afternoon, just because Martin and I were—' He stopped. Justine heard an echo of his old bravado, and was suddenly, furiously, irrationally enraged.

'Were what?' she shouted, her face close to his. 'Did you have a row with Martin? Did he ask you about Evie? And she heard it all? No wonder she doesn't want to come back.'

'She couldn't have – well, how was I to know she was listening? She's not my responsibility.' He sounded quite cold now, and she could feel him shutting down against her, giving her up. She became steely in response.

'Just listen, Lucien. Don't you think you've done enough damage here?' She felt him turn away from her sullenly at the reprimand. 'Go back, tell the others we need to look for her. Get – get Paolo – the Italian, the doctor. Get him to call the police, or the forest patrol or the farmer – anyone. Tell them – I'll follow the river. I'll go upstream, that's the most likely way she'd have gone.'

For a moment they both stood there, immobile. Justine felt as though her entire body was humming, galvanized with anger and exhilaration. Then, with an angry sound Lucien turned and went; she could hear his quick, agile movements as he climbed the slope, leaving her. It was only then, alone in the dark, that Justine realized what she'd done.

Chapter Twenty-Nine

There had been a small pile of dry wood in the fireplace where the three of them, Paolo, Anna and Rossella, were now confined by the rain, and more logs were stacked beneath the pergola outside. The fire was burning strongly now and the light flickered around the rough whitewashed walls; Anna sat on a small brick seat built in beside the fire but she couldn't seem to get warm. Paolo was pacing up and down in the dim light, and she knew what was bothering him; Rossella, who didn't, was looking from one of them to the other with increasing concern. Then Anna took a deep breath and she spoke.

'Bandini?' she said, faintly, looking at Rossella. 'That's your surname? Or your husband's name?' In Italy married women, as a rule, keep the name they were born with; Paolo looked at his mother, and she shook her head at him.

Rossella frowned a little, puzzled. 'I'm not married,' she said. 'But – well, once I was something else.' She paused. 'My father died when I was very young; I didn't really know him at all. I took my stepfather's name. My birth father was called Magno.'

'Ah,' said Anna, and she exhaled slowly, a long sighing breath, 'yes.'

'You knew him?' Rossella smiled, interested and quite unconcerned. Anna thought, she can't remember him. Luca. I mustn't cry, she thought, not after all this time. Poor Luca.

'Yes,' she said, 'and your mother too. Amalia. Is she—'

'She passed away,' said Rossella. 'Five years ago. She had cancer.'

'I'm sorry,' said Anna. 'She was kind to me – a long time ago.' She paused, and felt that perhaps more explanation was due. 'In Rome. You used to live in Rome. I was a seamstress, and your mother came to me for a fitting. You came to my workshop once, too. When you were a very small girl.' Anna felt a fluttering in her throat, thinking of that small, serious, red-haired child, as though she wanted to say more but she didn't know how.

Then a tiny frown appeared, a faint crease between Rossella's eyebrows, and almost imperceptibly she nodded.

'Yes,' she said, slowly, 'I know who you are.'

Paolo stopped, halfway across the room, hearing something in Rossella's voice, and turned to look at her. Her pale cheek turning rosy in the firelight she looked up at him, and smiled faintly. He had the impression that she was about to say something but then a sound of voices raised next door intervened and they all turned to look in the direction from which the voices came.

'What do you mean, she's gone?' Martin's face was white. Tom put out a hand to steady him, or perhaps to stop him from

360

hitting Lucien. Their faces – Martin's and Lucien's – were very close, and Martin's fists were clenched at his sides.

Lucien shrugged. 'That's all she said. Gone.' With a nonchalance that was not quite convincing, Lucien nodded towards Paolo, who had come to the door and was looking in, with a slightly dazed expression.

'Perhaps we should get the locals to help look for her,' said Lucien. 'That's what Justine said; and she'll set off upstream after her. But the kid's probably just gone off in a strop, don't you think? She'll turn up soon enough.' For a moment Martin stared at Lucien, and Tom tightened his grip on Martin's arm. But then he turned away, as though Lucien had not spoken.

'Tom,' he said, 'would you – talk to – him. To Viola? Tell him to phone the – I don't know, the police? Perhaps there's someone else, the forestry people?'

Tom nodded. Lucien stood there defiantly for a moment or two then, ignored, turned on his heel and went inside. Neither Tom nor Martin looked after him.

'I've got to go,' said Martin, desperately. 'Now. Please, Tom? This is my fault. If she's lost – it's my fault.' His certainty seemed all gone now; he looked stunned.

'Don't be stupid,' said Tom. 'Go on. I'll sort it out. But Martin—' Martin looked up. 'If Justine's going upstream, you go down. OK? Don't leave the river – and if you see Justine, tell her the same. Or they'll be looking for three of you, not one.'

Justine was no more than five hundred yards upstream from the little beach where Dido had last been seen when she heard Martin's voice calling after her, ragged with desperation in the near darkness. She turned back; it took her no more than five minutes to reach him. He was standing on the bank where Dido had been sunbathing; in the clearing there was only the faintest residual twilight now, but at least the rain seemed to be easing.

'OK, OK, Martin,' she said, quietly. 'We'll find her.' She could barely see his face but his agitation was palpable.

'It's my fault,' he said, almost moaning. 'We had a row. Lucien and I. She must have heard us – oh, God – I wasn't thinking—' She saw his head move, from this side to that, as though he was in pain. 'I told Lucien he'd killed her; he said she couldn't stand us any more. I didn't know, God, I didn't know.'

'None of us did,' said Justine. 'It doesn't matter now.'

Martin made an anguished sound. 'How long – when did the boys come back? She could have been gone for a couple of hours. You don't think – she could have been taken by someone?'

Justine resisted his panic. 'No – no,' she said slowly, 'There's no one else here.' But she felt that they couldn't possibly know, surrounded by this vast darkness. She tried to sound convincing. 'I think you were right before. She was upset, she didn't want to come back, and now it's dark, she's just staying put. Waiting for us to come and find her.'

It seemed likely enough to her; Justine could remember the feeling clearly enough from her own childhood. They'll be sorry, she would think, hiding in the tangle of brambles that obscured the garden fence, they'll be sorry they didn't think of me, but often enough no one ever even noticed she'd gone.

'The important thing is, to get moving,' she said. 'You go downstream, I'll go up. OK?'

Justine couldn't see, but she thought he nodded; certainly he turned away from her where they stood in the lee of the great cliff and set off towards the distant muted roar of the waterfall downstream. It was as though he hadn't been real; even the shadowy indistinct shape of him, a patch of darker darkness, was swallowed up in the night.

Now, thought Justine, I'm really alone, and then it hit her. It was over; there was no Lucien, she had no husband, she had no home, nowhere to go back to. She was alone in the dark. Justine waited for the panic to overwhelm her, bring her to her knees in the stream, but it didn't happen. Instead she felt an exhilaration that expanded her lungs; she wanted to shout. She took a breath, to calm herself.

'Dido!' she called. 'Dido!' The rain was easing; from behind a cloud the thin gleam of the moon briefly showed her the river's path ahead of her, sliding down towards her stippled with drops, and reluctantly she began to walk upstream.

Justine was wearing her sandals in the water and the leather soon turned slimy underfoot, but it made it easier to walk on the uneven riverbed. There were large stones, slippery with some kind of vegetable growth, and smaller, sharper ones, but she was glad she was here, in the open, not fighting through undergrowth in the dark. As she walked Justine continued to call out, trying to make it a cheerful sound, not angry, not desperate. It was slow going; after about half an hour the moon came out, casting its cold silver light on the pitch-black rippling river. Justine shivered, and for the first time the thought occurred to her that they might not find Dido.

Despite the exertion Justine was beginning to feel cold; the water felt icy now, her thin, damp linen dress was worse than useless, and she felt the first creeping insinuations of doubt.

Surely, she thought, this is where she'll be; Dido wouldn't have left the river's path; she's got common sense. Has she, though? Justine felt a stirring of guilt at how little attention they'd paid to Dido, acting as though her mother's disappearance was a puzzle to be solved, very little to do with her. But perhaps – if Evie'd been having an affair, perhaps Dido knew more than any of them. The thought struck her with a force that stopped her in her tracks. Had Dido known, all along?

Justine looked around her; she had reached a narrow stretch of the river, the banks stretched up steep and dark and mysterious on both sides, and she felt suffocated, suddenly.

'Dido!' she called, and now she could hear the fear in her voice, of what Dido might have done. 'Dido, darling. I'm sorry. Can you hear me?' She listened, holding her breath, but she could hear nothing, only the ceaseless gurgle of the water. She let her breath out in a sigh, about to walk on – but there was something, something that gave her pause. A low sound, not verbal, a mumbling as though someone was talking in his sleep. She felt the hairs rise on the back of her neck and she stood very still and listened. It came again, and slowly Justine raised one foot then another in the water, trying not to splash as she advanced towards the sound.

A little way ahead a large flat slab of limestone, perhaps six feet square, lay half in the water half on the bank; it looked smooth, by day perhaps an invitation to lie down there in the sun. Where the great plane of rock met the land one end was shrouded in shadow, surrounded by dense, bushy growth. Justine reached it, leaned down and placed her hands on its flat surface that gleamed white in the moonshine, and peered into the dark. Before her eyes had adjusted, before she could see anything in there, she heard the sound again, very close;

a whispered, incoherent exclamation in a soft, high voice, a shocking, involuntary sound like something raving,

Justine pulled at the vegetation, ripping it aside to get a better view. As the moonlight shone past her and illuminated the whole surface now of the rock and the rough scree of a bank beyond it, she saw something curled up there. Someone. It was Dido, her head resting against her backpack, knees tucked up against her chest as though she was trying to keep warm. Her face was very pale, one cheek exposed to the moonlight, and her eyes were closed.

'Dido?' said Justine, reaching out to touch her. 'Dido?' She tugged harder now, almost shaking the girl in an effort to rouse her. She leaned down and looked into her face, their noses almost touching, but still Dido didn't wake up; she wasn't making a sound now. She was very cold.

Chapter Thirty

The rain was all but stopped now, and Il Vignacce stood in the dark, its shutters closed against the night. The fire in the smaller half of the farmhouse had burned low; there was no one left to tend it, Anna, Paolo and Rossella having gone with Tom back up the hill for help. Upstairs, in Lucien and Justine's bedroom, the room where they had begun to talk about having a child together some twelve hours earlier, a suitcase lay open on the bed. Lucien was packing.

At the foot of the stone staircase Louisa paused in the flickering firelight, and leaned on the banister. Her ankle was still painful, but the swelling had gone right down, and after a moment she took another cautious step up, and another.

Lucien wasn't aware of her presence at first; she watched him from the door, observed the care with which he folded his soft denim shirts, his gamekeeper's trousers, arranging them in the old leather suitcase. As she looked on he packed a cedarwood shaving bowl, a leather sponge bag, some tissue-wrapped purchases. On the marble-topped chest of drawers stood some of Justine's things; a bottle of scent, a scarf, the tube of sun-screen, factor 60, and in the open wardrobe her clothes still hung, untouched. Louisa could see the carrier bags, too, from their afternoon's shopping in Florence, standing by a chair, the red linen dress unfolded on top. Could it only have been yesterday?

She must have sighed, because suddenly Lucien turned. For a moment she thought he was going to give her the old famil-iar smile, but it faded before it had begun, and the expression that replaced it was barely recognizable; there was a kind of surliness in his face that she'd never seen before.

'Boys in bed?' he asked over his shoulder, as he turned to go on with his packing.

'You'd better be quick,' Louisa said shortly, as if he hadn't spoken. 'If you want to get out of here before they get back.' She felt unlike herself, looking in at Lucien from the outside; cool, dry, angry.

Lucien snorted, but didn't turn round. 'Come off it, Louisa,' he said. 'No one wants my help.'

'Very convenient for you,' said Louisa, looking at his back. 'If you had any decency, you'd try to help anyway, whatever any of us thought. Dido's out there on her own. And Justine. You're a coward, Lucien.' She sounded bitter, incredulous; she had thought Lucien was better than this.

'I don't believe in making things any more painful than they have to be,' said Lucien over his shoulder. 'For me or for anyone else. That's a lot of sentimental crap.' He closed the lid of the suitcase and turned to face Louisa. His eyes were flat and cold, his beautiful green eyes; he looked at Louisa as though she was a stranger.

367

'Did you kill her, Lucien?' she heard herself asking, and looking at the man before her, the man she had invited to countless parties and had known for more than a decade, she sincerely had no idea any more whether he was capable of it. Of murder. 'Were you there with her?' She could hear the sound of an engine somewhere far away, the beat of a helicopter's rotors.

'Don't be stupid, Louisa,' he said curtly. 'Evie killed herself. Sooner or later they'll prove it, I'm not worried. This is a – a witch-hunt, and you're a lot of bloody primitive puritans. Besides, I've got an alibi. Fifteen guys on that yurt-building course in Wales. Oh, and one woman, in case you think fifteen guys would lie for a man they barely knew.'

Louisa nodded, but she continued to look at him.

'We had an affair,' he said. 'People do. It's not a crime. Do you really want to sleep with the same man for the rest of your life? With Tom? Or are you just jealous?'

She shook her head a little, as though she was brushing him away. 'So when it got serious,' she said slowly, a bitter queasiness turning over and over inside her, 'when she needed you, needed you badly, you just dumped her? Did you give her any explanation at all, or did you just leave her there, waiting for you? While she was planning to run away with you, you were booking yourself a fortnight on the other side of the country?'

He turned away again, and pulled the suitcase off the bed. 'Come on, Louisa,' he said impatiently. 'Just because you and Tom have to cling pathetically to each other for the rest of your lives, doesn't mean we all have to. Marriage isn't what it once was, you know. Life's for living.'

Louisa remembered something then, something Justine had said. Lucien saying they could have a child, at last.

'If you have children ...' she said, slowly, 'if you have children, it's different, isn't it? Or is that pathetic, too, looking after a child? Yes, I suppose you wouldn't have wanted to be landed with the nappies and the childcare, would you? That kind of stuff is for women who can't think of anything better to do, like me.'

Lucien shrugged, and came towards her, the suitcase in his hand, suede jacket over his arm. 'I never planned on being a househusband, no. If that's what you mean. Not my thing.'

Louisa went on. 'What were you going to do, let Justine have your child, then leave her when you'd sorted out someone else to look after you?'

'She's the one that wants a child,' Lucien said. 'Let her manage it on her own.' And he pushed past her, leaving her looking in to the empty room, the rumpled bed, the wardrobe half emptied.

He half-turned on the stairs and looked back up at Louisa on the landing. 'Evie knew I wasn't coming, really,' he said, quite coldly. 'She was kidding herself; she was a fantasist, you know. It was the best way; the only way to convince her it was over.' And he turned away and went on down the stair.

Louisa stood at the top of the stairway in the shadow until she heard the sound of the car starting up outside, the creak of the gate and a bang as it closed behind Lucien. Only then did she start the slow descent on her throbbing ankle, one painful step at a time. When she reached the ground floor she sat, unable to go any further, beside the dying fire and waited.

High up on the ridge Tom and Paolo were on their way back from the village, Tom in front in the battered old Volvo, Paolo behind him in his own car. They rounded a bend, the

Volvo braked and swerved suddenly and the next thing Paolo knew he was almost off the road. All he could see was the glare of headlights on full beam coming towards them, then the jaunty little hire car accelerated past, and was gone.

Chapter Thirty-One

As she heard the whup of the helicopter approaching Justine clambered out of the undergrowth and into the stream. She stood in the icy water and waved her hands uselessly over her head in the pitch darkness, her shouts feeble against the colossal noise of the rotors. A searchlight swung below the machine, a cylindrical beam of white light trailing over the trees; Justine stood in the river and waited for it to reach her, but the helicopter swung away too soon, veering and pitching in the wind. Unable to believe it would not immediately return, Justine stood there a moment; but when the noise receded, she sank down on the rock and put her head in her hands. Think. Dido. Had she had taken something? Drugs. An overdose. She climbed back over the rock and took hold of her, pulling at her unresponsive weight. She eased out a narrow wrist and felt for a pulse; after an awful, long moment of scrabbling fear she found one. She was unable to time it, but it felt slow, an age to wait for each tiny throb. She didn't know what to do. Gently she eased the backpack from beneath the girl's head, and unzipped it. She pulled out a zip-up cardigan, a book, some keys, identifying each by touch in the darkness. No pills, no blisterpack or bottle. At the bottom of the backpack she felt the shape of the photograph in its leather frame, Evie smiling up at Lucien over her shoulder. She didn't look at it.

Justine held the keys in her hand; on the fob was a tiny torch, a kind she knew; she twisted the end to turn it on and a feeble yellow light shone on her hand; she turned it in the light, registered the patch of paler skin, a pool of white over the bones and tendons strung inside her wrist, but she felt nothing. It occurred to her like a revelation that, however robustly her conscious mind might deny it, she'd always secretly been afraid that if she hadn't got Lucien, no one else would accept her, like this, disfigured. But now it seemed so small a thing, barely noticeable, no worse than a freckle or a birthmark.

Steeling herself against the dark Justine turned the torch off again, to conserve what was left of the battery. Then she took the cardigan and tried to push Dido's arms into it, to warm her up; her limbs felt lifeless and clammy, like rubber. The girl made a sound again, and Justine pressed her face to her cold cheek. 'Dido?' she whispered.

'Mmm-mm,' said Dido. 'Mm-mum?' There was a dreamy longing in her voice.

'It's me,' she said, urgently. 'It's Justine. Wake up, Dido.' She took the girl's shoulders and shook her gently, and she could feel some resistance at last, some sluggish life returning to her muscles. Justine grabbed the torch and shone it into the girl's eyes; Dido flinched and made a sound, a low moan. Justine knew she should look at the pupils – she recollected something about dilated, fixed and dilated. Dido's eyes were bleary, unfocused, but she caught the pupils as they contracted in the light. Not fixed, then.

'Wha – wha?' Dido's voice was slurred and Justine could feel the girl's body heavy in her arms, longing to fall back to earth, into unconsciousness. 'My head – my head—' she said, her eyes squeezed shut now.

'Dido,' she said, did you take anything? Drugs? Pills?'

'Nnnnn—' said Dido, but her head was lolling; she was trying to shake it. 'No pills. Dad doesn't – doesn't – like—'

'OK, OK,' said Justine, desperate. 'Stay awake, Dido. Someone'll come – soon. Someone's going to come and get us.' She looked about helplessly, but there was no one.

'Jus' cold,' said Dido, slipping back out of Justine's hands. 'Cold.' Justine couldn't hold her; she slumped on to the ground again, and curled herself back in to the foetal position in which Justine had found her.

Justine worked herself around in the darkness, the hard, prickly undergrowth clawing at her, until she was behind Dido. She hauled the girl on to her lap and put her arms around her. She was freezing herself; she thought longingly of blankets, tea. Can I carry her back? Justine wasn't sure. Keep her awake, she thought.

'Why did you come here, Dido?' she asked. 'Why didn't you want to come home?' She felt the girl stiffen in her arms.

'No,' said Dido, 'I don't want – no.' She turned her face and buried it in Justine's shoulder.

'Did you know about it all along?' Justine said softly. 'About Lucien? It's OK, I know too. It's all over now.' She felt a sob rise inside Dido's ribcage, she could feel each one of the bones through the girl's T-shirt.

'I didn't want – didn't want Dad to know,' she said, her face still hidden.

'But you knew?' Justine felt a small movement, the head went up and down once.

'I was sick,' she said. There was a silence, then a sigh, as if speaking was an effort. 'Had a stomach bug at school last year.' Again she came to a halt, fighting the will to sleep. 'I came home early, and they were there. Upstairs, talking. Mum looked happy. I knew something was – was wrong.' Justine could feel the warm wet of tears on her neck, and she knew that Dido was crying because in her mind's eye she could see Evie's radiant face again. All Justine could feel was the same longing, for Evie to be back. Lucien – Lucien was irrelevant, somehow. She could hardly remember what he looked like.

'And did she tell you – she was going away?' Again the small head moved up and down.

'She lef' a letter.' The voice was slipping again, blurred. 'But I knew, when she bought the dress, something was happening. Planning something. It's just I didn't think – I never thought she wouldn't come back. Not ever come back.'

She let out a long, shuddering sigh, like a small child who has sobbed herself into exhaustion. Justine couldn't think of anything else to say that didn't seem like inflicting pain. She rocked Dido against her a little, feeling an odd kind of happiness. A delicious quiet fell over them like a blanket; with only half an ear now Justine listened for the helicopter. Soon, she thought, as she felt the cold settle into her bones, I'll have to get up and start walking. I'll have to try to carry her. Soon.

*

374

Stiff and cold, on the edge of exhaustion Anna turned the key in the lock of her front door, her own front door at last. She looked back at Rossella, behind her on the path.

'Really, there was no need, signora,' Anna said, with a sigh. 'You are kind, but I'm fine now. Really. It's just my son; he worries.'

Anna turned on the light; the house was warm inside, having been shuttered up all day. It smelled familiar, of coffee and furniture wax and woodsmoke; it smelled of home. Anna sank gratefully on to her old divan; this *is* home, after all, she thought. And the past, her life in Rome, falling in love, the apartment where she had hidden from the world like a snail in its shell, seemed like a troublesome dream from which she was, at last, waking up.

Rossella smiled. 'Call me Rossella, please,' she said. 'Besides, I've never been a signora, I told you. And I'm too old to be a signorina now. Anyway, I'm here now. Nowhere else to go.'

She's nice, thought Anna. Perhaps that's what I needed all along, not a grandchild, not the daughter-in-law like Livia, but a daughter. Someone to look after me in my old age; someone to talk to. Ridiculous, she told herself; what a fantasy, but she smiled, despite herself.

'Then you have to call me Anna,' she said, and for a moment they stood there.

'You said,' Anna began, hesitantly, 'you said you knew who I was? Your mother told you about me?' She wondered how that conversation could have gone, and looked down at her old, pale, cold hands.

Rossella nodded. 'She told me about someone called Anna she – she and my father – had known in Rome. A friend, a seamstress, with a son called Paolo. There was a dress she showed me, you made it for her. Beautiful—'

Anna nodded. 'I know,' she said, 'dark-blue silk, gathered on the hip; you were at the fitting.' She sat down; she felt curiously unafraid. Had Amalia known, all along? What could it matter now, after all?

'Shall I make some coffee? Or perhaps tea, at this hour,' she said, but she made no move, only looking up at Rossella from the divan.

'Let me,' said Rossella; she looked about her for the kitchen, and suddenly Anna could see the little girl again, thoughtful, serious, hiding behind bales of cloth in an attic in Rome.

'Over there.' Anna nodded towards the door, and sank back on to the cushions, listening to the comforting clatter of pans, a tap turned on, a spoon tinkling in a cup.

They sat side by side on the divan, each with their hands warming around one of Anna's big white cups full of sweet black tea.

'Your father was a good man, you know,' said Anna. 'And your mother – well, I didn't know her so well. But she was always very kind to me.'

Rossella nodded. 'She told me, when she was dying. You know, I wasn't sure what she meant. Whether she was rambling; it was quite close to the end, and what she said didn't always make sense. It might have been a kind of dream.' She stopped, focused on something far away for a moment. Then she turned and looked directly at Anna. 'She said she always thought my father had a son, too, another child, born after he died. She said she came to see you.'

Anna nodded, and sipped her tea. She felt the warm steamy air on her cheek, and felt quite calm. 'Amalia did come,' she said slowly, with a kind of awe. 'Luca had been dead five months. It didn't occur to me she'd think – I just thought she was being her usual self. Considerate; kind. She brought me some clothes, baby things you'd had, I think. She didn't want to throw them away, she said, but she'd never have another. I – I was in an odd sort of state then. It's like that, when you've had a child. I just took the baby clothes – I've still got them now. Have you got any children?'

Rossella shook her head, still smiling. 'She said he looked like my father,' she said.

Anna gave a little half-laugh. 'Perhaps he did; all I could see was my baby, my Paolo, just himself, I didn't see Luca in him, not then.' They fell silent.

'I'm sorry,' said Anna, but Rossella just shook her head and gently took Anna's cup from her hands.

'Don't be silly,' she said. 'It was all a long time ago. Where shall I sleep?'

Justine hadn't even known she was asleep until the sound woke her. A soft splashing of footsteps, coming nearer, and when she opened her eyes she could see a point of light, moving upstream towards them. Justine tried to sit up, immediately aware of the dead weight of Dido barely warm in her arms, pinning her down. She thought perhaps she should call out, but her every instinct was to stay as still as she could. The sound became louder, more distinct, then it stopped, and she heard a voice.

It was deep, and foreign, but it was trying to speak her language. She opened her mouth, but still nothing came out.

'Hello? Signora?' It was his voice.

'Here,' Justine tried to call, but it came out in a hoarse

whisper. 'Over here.' She scrabbled for the torch and turned it on; the footsteps approached. She shone the torch up at him, a dark figure standing over them, and the weak light illuminated Paolo Viola's face. When Justine saw the broad plane of his cheeks, his wide, soft, serious mouth, she felt herself sway, suddenly, under the burden of Dido's body. She realized that she couldn't feel her legs, which were folded under her and had gone quite dead.

'She – she—' Justine's lips felt numb, and she could hardly enunciate the words. But it seemed there was no need; Paolo was shining his torch into Dido's face, feeling for her pulse.

'What's the matter with her?' said Justine. He leaned down and picked Dido bodily from Justine's lap. 'She said her head hurt – but she seems so weak. Do you think she's taken something?' He shook his head.

'I don't think so,' he said, 'a little hypothermia, I think. We have to warm her.' He took off a jersey, and his waxed coat, and pulled them over Dido's shoulders.

'You too, if you aren't careful,' Paolo said, looking across at her with a look she couldn't quite identify as he rubbed vigorously at Dido's arms.

'Are you all right?' he asked, softening, and she nodded slowly. The truth was, she didn't know, and to her surprise she felt a hot tear trickling down one cheek. Paolo reached out a hand and wiped it away with a quick movement.

'You did well,' he said. 'You did the right thing; probably you saved her life.' Justine nodded and tried to smile. Another tear slid down. She rubbed her cheek against her shoulder hastily.

'Come on,' Paolo said. 'Up now.' Justine unfolded her stiff, numb legs and rubbed them; shakily, she stood up.

'Let's go,' she said.

It took them a long time to get back. Dido, slipping in and out of consciousness, was a dead weight to carry in the dark, and they didn't risk looking for a path among the bushes. They heard the clang of the cow bells at one bend in the river, a gentle, melancholy accompaniment to their trudging footsteps. Nothing stopped them; nothing slowed them down. Justine felt dead tired; she was walking with her eyes shut by the time they reached the cliff, and the beach, and turned away from the river at last.

For the last stretch, climbing up through the trees, they could hear the sound of the helicopter ahead of them, although it never materialized in the sky, not even a trace of its sweeping searchlight. When they came out of the trees into the pasture, they could see why. It was sitting in the middle of the field, its rotors slowly gyrating, going nowhere, its searchlight illuminating only the empty expanse of flattened grass and thistle around it. As they approached Justine could see Martin's back, Tom's arm on his shoulder; they were talking to the pilot. She opened her mouth to call, to tell Martin they'd found her, but only a hoarse croak emerged. When they were almost there, Martin must have heard something, because he turned to look at them, and she could see him almost buckle at the knees at the sight of Dido's limp body slung in Paolo's arms.

'It's OK,' she whispered. 'She's all right.'

Justine left them there, the men standing at the helicopter, too weary to ask what was going to happen next. She turned and walked to the house, where she could see Louisa's small, upright figure silhouetted in the door; it seemed a long way to walk after she had already come so far.

Justine stopped in front of Louisa.

'He's gone,' said Louisa. 'Lucien's gone.'

She looked at Justine anxiously, her face pale beneath the porch light. Justine looked past her at the warm interior of the house, and she felt nothing but relief.

'Yes,' she said.

Chapter Thirty-Two

When Justine woke the next morning the sky was a clear, pale blue and the air was cool. She knew immediately, without looking, that she was alone in the bed; in fact, the whole house was quiet on this side. In the thin early light the room was hers; her clothes in the wardrobe, her brush on the marble cabinet; she saw the vacuum that had been occupied by Lucien and she was only relieved.

She remembered the feeling she'd had, like a premonition, on waking the previous morning, when she'd seen this room full of light and colour, signifying something she couldn't yet understand. Justine thought of Lucien, the weight of him, the space he used to occupy, sleeping beside her unencumbered by conscience or responsibility; not solid, like a prop, but heavy, like a burden. He was gone; she was free, and she felt – triumphant. Even the thought that there was nowhere for her to go back to, the thought of exile from the long windows and pre-Raphaelite glass of Notting Hill, of her possessions in black binbags, of divorce lawyers and bedsits, couldn't spoil it.

As Justine lay there, quite still, looking at the blue sky, she thought of Evie. Setting off without Lucien, probably without even a word from him, for a new life. Perhaps there comes a time, thought Justine, when even someone like Evie loses hope. She imagined that Evie's first instinct, when the realization that Lucien wasn't coming, had never intended to come, would be to go alone. She begins by telling herself it's a new adventure but sooner or later it hits her, standing in line in the ferry's canteen, catching a glimpse of a honeymoon couple, or a happy family on a day trip. She's no longer young, or strong, or hopeful, and it's then, at that moment of weakness, that a different future presents itself. It wouldn't take more than a moment of despair. Justine turned her head to the side, and gazed at the rough texture of the wall. It's over, she thought; Evie made her decision, it wasn't my fault. She's gone.

Outside she heard voices; Tom and Louisa, businesslike, moving to and fro. The squeak and slam of a car door; the boys' excited chatter. Justine couldn't remember what day it was; Thursday? Friday? The tight schedule of the holiday had been overturned. Slowly Justine got up from the bed, went to the window and looked down.

The first thing she noticed was that Lucien had taken the hire car; after all the traffic in and out the previous night there remained only the red Volvo. It stood on the close cropped grass, all its doors open, like a brightly coloured insect prepared for flight. Tom and Louisa were ferrying suitcases and straw baskets, rugs and sleeping bags from the house; the boys sat cross-legged on the grass, sorting through the contents of their little backpacks. They were leaving.

Louisa, clean, shiny blonde and scrubbed in pale blue, was moving around the car. She walked a little gingerly on her bandaged ankle but in spite of that, absorbed in her stacking and sorting she seemed restored, full of energy. On her way back to the house she looked up and saw Justine in the window. She stopped, uneasy.

'Hello,' she said, hands on her hips, looking up. 'Did you sleep OK?'

Justine nodded, and smiled. 'Have you heard from Martin? Is Dido all right?'

Louisa nodded. 'She's fine; they just kept her in for observation. They're letting her out this morning.' There was a pause, and Louisa shifted uncomfortably, looking away into the house.

'Are you leaving?' asked Justine. 'Already?'

Tom came out from behind the car and stood next to Louisa, an arm around her shoulders. 'Sorry,' he said, 'I think it's the best thing to do. There's – so much to sort out back home. This – this holiday was always a bit of a delaying tactic. And there's school – the boys—' he shrugged, helplessly.

'It's OK,' said Justine, smiling at them. 'Really.' Then she remembered something. 'What about the organic vineyard? Or was it just a diversion of Martin's?'

Tom shrugged and smiled his tired, warm smile. 'Maybe. I'll have to talk to him about it, when we get back. Sort things out over there first.' He squeezed Louisa against him. She looked older, thought Justine, but softer, as she smiled back up at her husband.

'I'll be down soon,' said Justine and, released, Tom and Louisa turned away, back to their packing.

Justine stood under the feeble shower for at least half an

hour, until her hair was clean and the pervasive scent of river water and decaying leaves that had haunted her since she woke was washed away. She rubbed in creams and lotions until she smelled instead of a glorious, artificial confusion of rose, gardenia and lily of the valley; then she stood in the bedroom doorway, wrapped in a towel. She wondered what to wear; suddenly it seemed an important decision; everything she could see seemed limp and creased and part of her old life. Slowly she picked up the carrier bags, their contents still pristine in white tissue, and pulled out the flowered dress she'd bought in Florence.

When Justine came down they were all standing beside the car, clean and dressed; Sam and Angus, clutching their backpacks, looked unnaturally tame in socks and sandals. To her surprise they flung their arms around her waist to say goodbye, and it was only then that she felt a sudden weakness, a burning behind her eyes. But Justine smiled, returning their hugs, turned to Louisa and Tom, and the weakness passed.

'See you — some time,' she said. 'I'll call.' And they all nodded.

Justine sat on the stone bench and watched the car bump slowly uphill under the forest canopy, and soon a faint smudge of dust in the dark trees was the only sign that there had ever been anyone but Justine at Il Vignacce.

She went inside; the house was cool and dim. Here and there evidence of Martin and Dido's brief occupancy was scattered about, grey, featureless shapes in the poor light. A paperback book lay open face down on the table, its spine cracked; Martin's jacket hung from one of the kitchen chairs, a sweatshirt curled like a cat on the low, hard sofa. Slowly Justine began to move about the room, gathering things up in her arms. She came to a stop in the kitchen, where the window looking out into the woods at the back of the house stood open, allowing the filmy light to drift inside.

The kitchen had hardly been used; the chipped porcelain sink was clean, the draining board bare of washing-up save one upturned glass. Here Justine had stood last night, looking out into the black, dripping forest as she drank, before she went to bed. Here, where she'd left it, dangling by one strap from a kitchen chair, was Dido's small red backpack; crushed, dirty, streaked with mud and dusted with leaf mould. Justine lifted it off the chair.

When Paolo got back from the hospital, tired and unshaven, Rossella was drinking coffee in the kitchen with his mother as though she'd lived there all her life. Wearily, he looked from one to the other of them until they laughed at his expression of bewilderment.

'Is there – what—' He stopped, began again. 'How are you feeling, mamma? Did you sleep all right?' She smiled at him and he turned to Rossella.

'Thank you, for keeping an eye on her,' he said, uncertainly. 'Rossella?'

Rossella smiled. 'It was a pleasure. We – found plenty to talk about.' She went and stood by the door that led on to the terrace. The air that blew in was cool and fresh after the night's rain. 'It's beautiful here,' she said, looking out over the trees. 'It's a shame I have to go back to Florence now'

Paolo watched as Rossella stood there, and he felt a stirring of amazement, that she should exist, in real life, not just in Anna's memory. He wondered whether they looked alike; oddly, she was beginning not to look like a stranger. With a sigh Rossella turned back inside. 'But perhaps – another time. Your mother – Anna – has asked me to come back and visit.' Somehow she made it sound likely.

Anna looked from Paolo to Rossella and seemed about to embark on an explanation, but thought better of it. She turned away, and took the coffee things to the sink.

'So they're sure she's all right?' she asked, over her shoulder. 'The little girl?' Paolo had called from the hospital on his mobile; he knew his mother would worry. She had reproached herself, for some reason, with the fact that she had seen the girl going down to the river, as she had arrived at Il Vignacce. That perhaps she might have done something to dissuade her if she'd been earlier, or had spoken better English.

He nodded, rubbing his eyes. 'She's fine, mamma. Her father's with her.' He turned to Rossella. 'Do you want me to take you to the bus station?' he asked. 'I got a little sleep – they found me a sunlounger, you know, the ones they give the patients' relatives.' He stretched his neck, twisting it this way and that as though to untangle a knot, and winced at the memory.

Anna snorted. 'I'll take her,' she said. 'You take a shower and go to bed.' And although Paolo opened his mouth to argue, he was prevented from saying anything by a yawn.

The long shutters in his room closed against the light, Paolo laid his head on a clean, lavender-scented pillow, heard the click of the door as his mother left, heard the ignition of the car, then the liquid sound of birds and nothing more. He didn't dream of surgery this time, as the sun rose in the sky outside the shutters, but of a woman's pale body floating in dark water, traced with lines and contours like the map of a mysterious, unexplored delta.

*

The cows came lumbering back up from the river, from whatever secret haven had sheltered them during the wild night, just as Justine came out of the house with the backpack in her hands. They looked so peaceful, unperturbed by rain, storm, or human disaster, so much at home as they emerged into the sun. She sat down on the stone bench and watched them spread out across the pasture, then slowly she unzipped the backpack. She pulled out the photograph.

It was Dido she looked at first. When was the photograph taken? No more than eighteen months before, a sunny day in Kew, a spring picnic in the long grass and daffodils. Lucien had made a complicated terrine, the product of days of fraught preparation, and sourdough bread; the memory of being the audience to Lucien's fussing in the kitchen was like a lingering, oppressive dream; she wanted to blink and shake her head, shake it out. Justine could hardly believe she didn't have to go back to all that; once again she felt a surge of euphoria at the thought of her freedom and looked up at the pale sun, closing her eyes against it, a brilliant silver coin in the sky. The light glowed red-gold through her eyelids, warmed her cheeks, and once again London seemed a long way away. She opened her eyes again, held the photograph up; Dido looked so young. It seemed she'd been a child still, only eighteen months ago: her smooth round cheek squeezed against her mother's, a gap between her teeth that had since closed up.

Then, reluctantly, Justine transferred her gaze from Dido to Evie; to the faded blue eyes squeezed a little at the corners by her smile, her hands holding Dido's wrists below her delicately pointed chin.

Should I hate her? Justine thought, and she searched for anything resembling hate in all the things she was feeling; she didn't even hate Lucien. Justine felt only a kind of burning shame when she thought of him, that she had spent so long defending him, believing in him. She had given him her seal of approval and that may even have been why Evie had placed her trust in him, had fallen for that myth of sensitivity and discretion, the perfect man they had heard Rossella describe. In Evie's eyes now, all she could see was a look that focused on some further point, on something the other side of Lucien, an image of perfection with which she might overlay reality. Justine felt only a tug of grief, that Evie's life was over, she was gone, at last, and hadn't been able to say goodbye.

Justine could feel the wadded paper behind the photograph in its leather frame; she knew what else there was in there, behind the picture. She pulled it out.

A single sheet of heavy paper once cream that had, by the look of it, been unfolded and folded back up fifty times since it was written. Its corners were fuzzed and dirty, it was wearing thin along the creases, a corner turned back. Justine raised it to her cheek, and smelled leather, and the faintest ghost of Evie's scent; she could see a fragment of a word in Evie's big, looped handwriting. Dearest.

Justine heard the car up on the ridge, but she didn't move, sitting with her back against the warm rough stone of the wall, holding the letter in her lap, unopened. She turned the picture frame back over and looked again at Dido, and it seemed to Justine that Dido, at least, was looking back at her. Carefully she slid it back into its hiding place, zipped up the backpack, and waited. *Hers*, she thought. *Not mine.*

She could tell straight away that they were going to leave too; something about the apologetic set of Martin's shoulders as he approached her from the car. Behind him Dido's little oval face peered at Justine anxiously, pale as a ghost in the sun and somehow smaller; for a brief moment Justine remembered the surprising weight of the girl's lifeless body against her in the dark. She smiled, holding out the rucksack, and tentatively Dido reached for it. In response to a look of rising disquiet in Dido's eyes, she shook her head a fraction; did you think I'd read it? And then Dido smiled, and put her arms around Justine.

'Thanks,' she said hesitantly. 'Dad said you came to look for me. Found me.' For a moment Justine didn't feel like saying anything; she just held on tight to Dido's narrow shoulders.

'That's OK,' she said, at last. 'Any time. But – I mean – don't do it again, will you?'

Martin was watching them; he looked tired, something of his certainty gone, but the tension seemed to have evaporated with it. 'I – I think we'll get going,' he said, looking at Justine uncertainly. 'I thought you might want a lift. I mean—' he gestured around at the vast emptiness around them. 'You can't – you haven't even got a car. Since—' He ran out of words. Justine shook her head, relaxing her hold on Dido at last; the girl stood upright, shouldering her rucksack. 'Thanks,' said Justine, 'but I might stay on for a bit. If that's all right.'

Chapter Thirty-Three

Although Justine knew she had only a bit more than a week left, the time expanded, bloomed, until she began to wonder whether she would ever leave at all. In part it was being alone, and in part the delicious monotony that descended on her life in the valley now she was without any means of transport; the insects, the passage of the cows, the daily, dawn mutter of the invisible tractor coming down to pump water.

She swam in the river, floating like a waterlily in the shadow of the cliff. Late in the afternoon a couple with a small child in a grubby T-shirt walked around the corner from somewhere downstream; they smiled and nodded at her standing startled in the waist-high water. After they'd swum for a while, the child between them, in Justine's pool, they got dressed and walked on. Watching them go Justine felt as though she was embedding herself here, unable to move far or fast, she was settling into the landscape like a pebble on the road. The thought that she would ever leave became increasingly implausible; London, her two bus rides to work, the sandwich at her desk, the winebar at five-thirty on a Friday evening, seemed like a far-off, outlandish, society in which she had no place.

After a day or two alone Justine began to feel quite different, as though she had been in a cocoon and some kind of transformation had been effected. She felt strong, calm and bold, all the things she had never been; she wondered whether this was a product of her isolation, or something permanent. She walked a little way up towards the ridge, to get a signal on her mobile, and phoned Lucien.

She heard the tinny, distant ring sounding in the dark drawing room in a far-off place, the Bakelite phone hidden among the animal skulls and pebbles, the furniture Lucien had found in skips. He was at home, of course. Where else would he be? His voice sounded breezy, eager; she imagined the week's trauma sliding off him like water, erased from his memory, and his conscience; she remembered his old girlfriends and that particular look they had that always so annoyed her; pity, superiority, impatience.

'Hello, Lucien,' she said.

There was a barely perceptible intake of breath, the fraction of a second's hesitation.

'Justine.' He sounded solemn. 'Darling—'

'You got back all right then,' she said, drily.

'Yes – I'm sorry,' he said, faintly alarmed now. 'I didn't want to prolong the whole thing. You know—'

'It's all right—' Justine cut him off. 'That's not why I'm phoning. I want you to pack up my things, if you don't mind. Put them in storage, until I know where I'm going to be.'

'Justine,' Lucien said again, and she didn't like the sound

of her name on his lips; that's not me, she thought. He spoke softly. 'It doesn't have to be like this. It isn't as if I – it's you I love.'

'Oh, Lucien,' she said. 'Don't be silly.'

There was a silence. 'Silly?' he said, sounding incredulous.

'We were just playing at it,' said Justine, and suddenly she didn't feel like shouting at him; it seemed like a waste of her energy. 'Not doing the things people who really love each other do, like work hard, have children, help each other out of trouble. Like Tom and Louisa.' She stopped. 'It's not all your fault,' she went on, slowly. 'I was lazy. And scared no one else would have me. That's not the same thing as loving someone.'

There was a silence, a whole, slow minute of it. Justine waited.

'Well,' said Lucien, 'I suppose that's it then.' He sounded crestfallen, and a little sulky.

'Yes,' she said. 'That's it.'

When she ran out of food, Justine studied the old map on the wall of her bedroom and found what looked like a track to the little village on the ridge she and Louisa had seen from a distance. The track, when she found it, led through olive terraces and fig trees, then some ramshackle outbuildings stacked with logs. She felt like a shipwrecked sailor, coming upon the first evidence of civilization; in the village there was a bar with a little grocery store attached. Greedily she filled her backpack with chocolate, fresh milk, bread and cheese, sat at a little tin table under some mulberry trees, their leaves beginning to curl and colour, and drank a cup of coffee, bitter underneath and creamy on top, that seemed the most delicious she had ever tasted.

As Justine sat there in the balmy air, just a fresh, damp hint of autumn on the breeze, a little battered car drew up in the square. Idly she watched; the windscreen was opaque in the sun and she couldn't see who was inside, but when he got out she wasn't surprised, somehow. Carefully Paolo locked up the car, thrust the key in his pocket and straightened up, then he saw her. He stood there a moment, just smiling with delight as though he wasn't sure she was really there, then scratched his head and walked over.

He stood, tall, beside her, and Justine looked up. 'What are you doing here?' she said, putting out a hand to him instinctively. Paolo took it and looked down at it, considering it carefully as he had Louisa's ankle.

He frowned as if for a moment he'd forgotten where he was and why. 'My mother sent me. The supermarket in Monticiano is closed for the rest of the day, and she wanted some shopping. And I like this bar, for a change; no gossiping about me here, they don't really know me, or my mother.' He sat down, elbows on the table, and looked at her.

'And you?' he said.

Justine shrugged, smiling. 'We've got Il Vignacce for – a bit longer,' she said, reluctant to consider a departure date. 'I didn't want to go.' He nodded. 'Have lunch with me,' he said, abruptly. 'Can you? There's a nice place, down below the village, not far.'

Justine nodded, feeling her smile widen as she looked at him. 'Yes,' she said. 'Why not?'

They ate at a small farmhouse with a handmade sign and five tables on a dusty terrace. The other tables were laid, but it was clear that their season was almost over and no other guests expected. From the terrace you could see into the next valley, and they sat beneath a huge, fragrant fig, heavy with soft green fruit.

No menu was produced, but the food, and a jug of dark, warm wine arrived without any specific request being made. Paolo carefully explained what the dishes were; *panzanella*, bread soaked in tomatoes and oil and herbs; pasta with meat sauce, veal cutlets.

'And your – your friends? Their daughter – she's recovered?'

'Yes,' said Justine. 'Thank you – for helping us, I don't know what might have happened if you hadn't been there.' She stopped, and Paolo shook his head just a little. Justine sat back in her chair and looked across at the blue hills, feeling a bubble of exhilaration rise in her. 'They've gone home. All of them. It's just me.' He looked at her then, put down his knife and fork.

'And your husband?'

'Oh,' said Justine vaguely. 'He's not – that's all over. He's gone home too. Without me.' The insufficiency of the explanation sounded laughable to her, but she couldn't think of anything else to say, and Paolo just nodded.

'I'm not going back,' she said then.

'No,' said Paolo. 'Good.' And then he smiled at her. 'Will you be all right, down there?' he said. 'All alone? I have to go back to Rome tonight.' He looked perplexed.

'I'm fine,' she said, thinking of the sound of the water at night-time down below Il Vignacce, the cows coming to greet her every morning.

Paolo nodded. 'Up above you, beyond the cowshed, there should be *porcini* there soon, now it has rained,' he said, ruminatively. 'Mushrooms. You know how to recognize them? Underneath the cap, they are like a sponge, not with the—' And he made a sound of exasperation at not knowing the word.

'Gills?' suggested Justine. Paolo shrugged, laughing. 'Could be,' he said. 'Don't eat anything with gills. Just in case. You mustn't get sick.' He was smiling. Coffee came, and some small hard biscuits.

'You're going back to work?' Justine asked, carefully.

'Yes,' said Paolo, and Justine could hear a little weariness in his voice. She loved the sound of it, somehow, the sound of his labour, his commitment, responsibility shouldered.

'But you'll come back? To see your mother?'

'Of course,' said Paolo. 'You should visit her, you know She'd like the company.'

After they had eaten they walked further down, to a stretch of the river just below the houses that she hadn't seen before. It was shallow here, but the water was cold and clean. They walked in the stream a little way, their shoes in their hands, and at one point Justine lost her footing and Paolo took hold of her hand and kept it. His hand felt dry and warm.

On the way back up to the car Paolo carried Justine's bag, with the water and biscuits and milk and cheese she'd bought at the bar, and held her hand lightly in his.

'I'll take you back down,' he said.

'I'll walk back,' she said smiling. 'I like the walk.' Paolo nodded, not put out. She put her arms around him, not tight but close enough so that she could smell the warm cloth of his shirt.

'See you,' Justine said, pressing her cheek against his. She picked up her bag, and turned to wave back at him, standing there by his car. She didn't hear him start his engine until

395

she had turned the corner and headed down to the path back home, out of sight among the fig trees.

The next morning Justine walked the long way out of the woods, up to Paolo's mother's house, where she found Anna laying out nets under her olive trees in the dewy morning. Anna made her a cup of coffee, and they sat together on the terrace. The vine leaves were all a brilliant scarlet now, and the colours of the trees around the house were beginning to turn.

'You're brave,' was all Anna said, with an odd, distant look in her eye, when she heard Justine was down at Il Vignacce all on her own, Then she refocused, and seemed to be examining Justine, weighing her up. 'Come and see me again, won't you? You could always stop here a night, if you didn't want to walk back.' And she gave Justine a bag of food, bread, pasta, homemade sauce, to carry back down the hill.

'Paolo'll be back soon,' she called after her, looking a little worried, as Justine set off down the road to the valley. Justine just nodded. She wasn't thinking about Paolo, not at all; he drifted on the edge of her thoughts but she didn't wonder what he was doing or when he might be back. She barely thought about anything but what to do next, where to buy milk, when to go for her swim.

The weather remained mostly fine, although it grew noticeably cooler, and Justine was glad she'd brought one jersey with her. There was a brief, unexpected shower one afternoon, and Justine sat inside and read; the others had left her a stack of paperbacks, for which she was grateful. The rain stopped as suddenly as it had begun and the sky was iridescent with blue and pink in its aftermath. To celebrate Justine showered,

put on her red linen dress and went outside to sit in the last of the sun.

It was almost twilight by the time he came walking down the hill, a clean white shirt luminous in the dusk as he approached through the trees. The soft melodious scraping of the insects had started up in the cool evening air, and Justine could see the hazy flicker of bats over the pasture from where she sat on the fanned brick threshold, leaning back against the doorframe. Paolo lifted his hand in a wave as he came to the gate, but she had known it was him already. Against the white of his shirt his skin was dark; he looked very foreign suddenly.

They sat together side by side against the house until it grew quite dark, and Justine could feel the warmth of his solid shoulder against hers, through his shirt. Paolo told her about his childhood visits from Rome to the forest, the places he'd liked to visit as a boy. He told her about his mother, and his work in the hospital, and Justine began to tell him about hers, about the little cubicle where she sat, the piles of typescripts, about London, but she found herself running into the ground, unable to make it sound real.

They ate what there was in the fridge – pecorino cheese, tomatoes, and some cold white wine – on the grass outside, leaning against the wall.

Paolo took the plates, the bottle, the glasses inside; as Justine lay on the grass she listened to him at the sink, washing, then putting things away. She wondered whether you could judge someone by how they moved about a strange kitchen. Paolo came back outside, and Justine got to her feet. Standing in front of her in the light that fell through the open door he put his hands on her waist, defined by the new dress; she felt new all over.

'I'd better go,' he said. 'It's a long walk, and I have to go back to Rome again in the morning.'

Justine put her face against his shirt; she could smell the clean linen and his warm skin through it: dark, foreign, new.

'No,' she said. 'Stay.'

Chapter Thirty-Four

Justine took a bus to Siena. For a city on a hill, it seemed curiously basin-like, scooped like a crater out of the hilltop; she walked for miles down a straight, empty, red-brick street hung with heraldic insignia; dragons and tortoises and flames. It was just after midday, and the clatter of pans and cooking smells were drifting down from every first floor window she passed; everywhere she heard women calling children and grandchildren to eat, and their cries enfolded her in the effortless embrace of an extended family. Justine found a restaurant, and sat down to eat yellow courgette flowers crispy in translucent batter, and something called *pici*, which turned out to be thick, hand-rolled spaghetti swimming in a hot scarlet sauce. When she paid, using her credit card, she did wonder what she was going to do for money, when what she had ran out.

Walking off her lunch up and down the quiet, flag-hung streets, Justine passed an estate agency, then another. Idly she stopped to look in the second window, filled with handwritten cards describing properties for sale or rent. They looked surprisingly reasonable, at least compared with London, and the Italian descriptions were seductive, with their coffered ceilings, terraces and kitchen corners; Justine felt the lure of a place of her own, of domesticity. She went inside, and gathered a sheaf of property descriptions and telephone numbers; when she went on with her walk she looked up and through the open windows of the tall, red-brick palazzi that lined the streets with a newly proprietorial eye. She saw exquisitely faded shutters and frescoes, window boxes, deep eaves and views of the city's striped cathedral, and she began to wonder whether this might not, after all, be possible, if she wanted it badly enough.

On her way back to the bus station by a roundabout, backstreet route, she passed the sign for a little language school with a ridiculously grandiose name; the Oxford Academy of English Language and Literature, or something like it. On impulse she went in, and asked whether they had vacancies for native tongue teachers; she left her name, and her English mobile number. And then, while she was waiting for her ride back to Montequercio beneath an exotic tree that overhung the bus stop, she made up her mind. She really wasn't going back. To her surprise, the thought of all the explanations and apologies that would involve did not fill her with dread; rather, she felt lighter already, ready to begin.

The bus stopped halfway between Monticiano and the road down to Il Vignacce; Justine got off, thanked the driver, and walked until she came to a clearing just before the road plunged down into the woods, still a little way from Anna's house. There was a view of the village where she had had lunch with Paolo, glittering on the ridge far away. She took out her mobile.

Work first, she thought, dialling the familiar number, feeling no sense of it being anything to do with her, any more, the little office space, the rolodex filled with authors' details.

'Roberta?' she said, to her shared personal assistant, looking down at her dusty feet on the path. 'Hello,' said Roberta, without much enthusiasm. Are you back? Did you have a wonderful time? This is a very bad line.' Down the line Justine could hear, in the background, the languid chatter of the terminally bored at the end of the working day; she could almost see the blinking strip-lighting overhead.

'No,' she said, 'I'm still here. In Italy.'

'Oh, really?' said Roberta, still sounding bored. 'You'll be in on Monday, though? Well, Kate Butler called, she wants to go over her last chapter with you as soon as you're back. She's still—'

'No,' said Justine again, 'I – Roberta, you'd better let me have Kate Butler's number. I don't think – I won't be coming back.' She felt her resolve stiffen. 'I'm handing in my resignation, it'll be in the post tomorrow. I just thought I'd better let you know first. For when – when it all hits the fan.'

'Ooh,' said Roberta with horrified delight, giving Justine her full attention for the first time, 'but you can't do that. Can you?'

Justine laughed. 'I can,' she said, and it dawned on her that she really could. 'Now, maybe you should give me that number. I'd better call her next. I'll get a computer and an email address, I'm not in the outback. I'm sure there are plenty of things I can finish off from here, and for the rest, I'll come back and tie things up.' She made an effort to sound as though she'd thought it all through, and even as she spoke she knew none of this was going to stop her. It might take a little while, but none of it was important enough to stop her.

'I'll let you know as soon as I've got somewhere permanent, you can send stuff on, if you have to.' Roberta took down the number, her voice politely neutral now, but Justine could tell she couldn't wait to put the phone down and broadcast Justine Elliott's mid-life crisis, or holiday fling, or marriage breakdown, across the whole open-plan floor. Justine dialled her boss's number.

'Now, Justine,' David said, all fatherly, 'aren't you rushing this a bit? Is it – a personal thing? Just have a bit more time off, I'm sure we can manage that.' Justine turned as businesslike as she could manage, and laid out a rough plan for dealing with her authors for him. David stopped sounding paternal and became angry, then tried desperation.

'Look, you'll really be leaving us in the lurch,' he said. Because it wasn't a matter of money Justine said nothing, but she did wonder why she'd been paid so little for so many years if she was so indispensable.

'I am sorry, David,' was all she said. 'I'll make sure all the loose ends are tied up. If any of the authors really object to my leaving after that – and I can't see that they will – I can always work with them as a freelance. From out here.'

That did it; David obviously didn't want to negotiate freelance rates with her on top of everything else.

'Yes, well,' he said, 'let me think about that. Send me that letter, then.' He hung up. Without hesitation Justine dialled Kate Butler's number. *Then that's it*, she thought as she heard it ring. That'll do for now. She had to try very hard to keep the euphoria from her voice as she told her most difficult author the news.

Montale came by to collect the rubbish; he frowned in puzzlement as he lifted one solitary plastic carrier from the little metal cage; hardly worth the trip. He nodded to Justine, who was reading in a deckchair. 'Not much longer, eh?' he said. 'Out by ten, Saturday?' She nodded, and smiled, then went back to her book.

But by the time Paolo did return, the yellowing headlights of his little car bumping down the track straight from the hospital late on Friday night, Justine's life was in order. A taxi in the morning, an attic studio in a Sienese backstreet she could move into whenever she wanted, the promise of two days a week teaching from October. So she didn't need Paolo, strictly speaking, but when he got out of the car, pushing one of the cows aside to open the gate, she found herself so glad to see him that she couldn't speak. And when he asked her if she'd come back to Rome with him, she didn't need to think about how to answer him. Siena could wait, for a week or so.

Anna waved them off from her terrace on Sunday evening, a hand shading her eyes from the sinking sun. She stood there for some time after Paolo's little car had disappeared into the trees, long enough for the trees to grow dark around her and for the bright doorway into her kitchen to become the only point of light in all the wide forest. Then Anna turned and went inside.

Rose Fell's friends think she's taking a big risk
when she leaves the security of home and career
to move to the beautiful but isolated village of
Grosso, near Genoa. But after a year of emotional
turmoil Rose no longer has any ties back home,
and she relishes the challenges of a new start.

Making a home, however, in the ravishing, haunted
landscape of Italy's Riviera coast turns out to be
lonelier than Rose had anticipated. And it is only when
she is asked to write a profile on one of her reclusive
neighbours, the once-glamorous film star Elvira Vitale,
that Rose feels her new life is really beginning.

But when a young girl's body is found on the local
beach, and the following day Elvira's hard-working
cleaner, Ania, goes missing, Rose finds herself
embroiled in a murder investigation that threatens
the idyll she has worked so hard to establish.

'In the far distance, the great terracotta dome
of the cathedral appeared, like a mirage
shimmering in the heat haze ...'

Gina Donovan arrives in Florence on a beautiful spring
morning to stay with an old friend. She is hoping
for nothing more than a break from her demanding
young family, but as she soon finds out, this most
ancient and beautiful of cities has its dark side.

Within hours of her arrival, Gina meets the elegant
Frances Richardson, who invites her to her birthday
party. As Gina learns, Frances' party is the highlight
of the expatriate calendar. This year it is to be held
in the gardens beneath the city's medieval wall.

However, as Gina's week in Florence unfolds and the
party draws near, a terrible discovery is made. And no
one in this close-knit community is free of suspicion ...